*An
Answer
in the
Tide*

An Answer in the Tide

Elisabeth Ogilvie

When all else fails, we find an answer in the tide.
We hear the rote resounding softly from the shores of
    the island of the heart;
In every body cell a compass points us home,
And we become again the creatures that we were,
    sovereign and apart.

The Islanders—E. OGILVIE

McGraw-Hill Book Company
New York   St. Louis   San Francisco
Toronto   Düsseldorf   Mexico

Book design by Kathy Peck.

123456789BPBP78321098

Library of Congress Cataloging in Publication Data
Ogilvie, Elisabeth, date–
An answer in the tide.
   I. Title.
PZ3.0348An   [PS3529.G39]   813'.5'2   77-26012
ISBN 0-07-047664-0

When all else fails, we find an answer in the tide.
We hear the rote resounding softly from the shores of
the island of the heart;
In every body cell a compass points us home,
And we become again the creatures that we were,
sovereign and apart.

1

In the late afternoon the boats were coming home. The sea was dark blue, streaked with broad bands of marbled green and white, and stippled with cold silver under the northwest wind. It hadn't been strong enough to keep throwing freezing spray over the boats, but each had a thin rime of ice along her water line.

Joanna could watch the harbor while she peeled potatoes at the kitchen sink, and she saw Nils coming in past the breakwater with a load of wet traps on the stern. She washed her hands and left the potatoes in cold water. Shedding her apron and shoes, getting her boots from the mat in the sun parlor, was like shedding one body for another. She could still almost taste the moment when the child Joanna burst from the Homestead like a gull from a cage, and started for the harbor, on the run. Occasionally she had to go back and open and shut the door ten times, which was something gulls never had to do, but the delay made the headlong rush down the hill all the more glorious. With flapping arms and passionate striving leaps she felt ecstatically close to flight.

"If I went whooping and rampsing down to the wharf like that now, I'd be the sensation of the year," she said to the collie who stood watching her put on her old loden coat. "I *knew* then that I looked like a gull. Nowadays the neighbors would probably think of some old black hen running for corn, and damn it, I'd think so too!" She laughed. Rory waved his tail with dignified enthusiasm, and she stroked his head. He wasn't a show collie, his head was too wide between the ears, his nose too broad, his eyes too big. Calm, their amber unclouded by age, they looked luminously into Joanna's eyes while the tail kept in gentle motion. "You stay home this time," she said to him. "It's too cold for you to lie around outside. We don't want you to get rheumaticky. You're a good man, my Rory. I don't know what we'd do without you."

She went across the dooryard and through the open gate at the end of the spruce windbreak. She was tall, as straight and almost as limber as she had ever been. There was an occasional sparkle of white through her black hair.

The sun had cast a powerful heat in the middle of the day, when she'd gone to the Eastern End and back, but now as the earth turned toward evening and the spruce woods threw their dark violet shadow over half the village, the cold deepened, drying to the nose and throat, penetrating boots and gloves.

The houses, wharves, and workshops across the harbor still glowed in sunshine as if they gave off their own heat and light. The village was quiet except for occasional voices from the Bennett wharf where Charles and his son were unloading traps. A gull's call echoed across the sky, answered in chorus from ledges and ridgepoles.

Trap-building went on in the Sorensen fishhouse, the rhythm of the hammer distinct and unmistakable.

There were no children around. All those old enough to navigate on blades went across the island to Hillside after school everyday to skate on the ice pond. At least the children had acquired something unforgettable from a winter of exceptional cold and wind. The hauling days had been few and far between, but the children would always remember these times as the winter when the ice had come early and held up, and they had skated day after day in a long, effortless, enchanting journey from Christmas to spring.

She passed between the Binnacle on her left, and her brother Philip's house on the right, crossed the old deeply

rutted road, and walked on beach pebbles between the Sorensen and Fleming fishhouses out to the Sorensen wharf.

Nils's brother David and his son-in-law were the trap-
builders. They didn't see her pass by, they were working at
the bench on the sunny western side. The unique odor of
fishhouse smoke, a blend of lath ends, dried paint sticks, and
old rope, scented the cold air. Joanna wondered what Dave
and Freddy could possibly find to talk about while they
worked, or if they talked at all. When he was alone in there,
Freddy had his radio-rock turned up to full volume, but
neither Nils nor Dave allowed it when they were in the fishhouse.

Nobody was in the Fleming fishhouse. Rosa ran only about
a hundred traps, and had come in and gone home some time
ago. *Sea Star* lay on her mooring with an almost consciously
contented air, as if she'd been lovingly put to bed for the
night.

Over by the big wharf in the lee of Western Harbor Point
Joanna S. lay across the front of the lobster car, and Nils in
yellow oilclothes stood by her getting his pipe going, while
Mark wrote out the slip. Terence Campion's *Girl Kate* lay
across one end, Terence doing his day's clean-up while he
waited to sell. Out in the harbor Ralph Percy was putting his
boat on her mooring. He was overweight and looked almost
square in his oilclothes, but he ran nimbly from the bow
along the narrow washboard, and took to his skiff without
even rocking her.

The two Fennells were coming in now past the breakwater.
Like Charles and Hugo, these two went partners in the winter,
in the father's boat. It was an arrangement that would never
work for Jamie and Nils, because each liked his solitude, and
Jamie would never tolerate someone else as captain, even a
parent as soft-spoken as Nils.

The rocks of Eastern Harbor Point were turning hot orange
in the westering sun. It was breezing on as the tide reached
its height; catspaws scuttered across the harbor, water splashed
around the spilings. *Joanna S.* left the car and headed home-

wards, seemingly her own guide past the ledges and into the slot between the Sorensen and Fleming wharves. Joanna went to the head of the ladder, and Nils looked out around the canopy and smiled at her.

"What's that song Owen sings about a wee wifie waiting?"

She grinned. "With her work gloves on, too, ready to unload traps."

"They're all wet and cold and dirty."

"And I'm so dainty. Come on!"

"Wait a minute, I'll give Jamie another call first."

"Why?"

But he'd gone back under the canopy, and she heard him speaking into the microphone. "Calling *Valkyrie*. Calling *Valkyrie*. Come in, Jim."

There was no answer, just an undecipherable jumble of voices both near and far. Nils left the set on and went aft. He slid the first trap along the washboard, and Joanna reached for the bridle. "What do you want him for that can't wait?" she asked.

"His engine stopped on him once today, out on Cree Ridge. I just happened to see him drifting. Not that he'd ever give a shout."

"Not unless he was into the breakers," Joanna agreed.

"I went alongside. By then he'd got her going again, but I told him he'd better go in while he could." His upward glance was ironic. "Big mistake." His eyes were blue under eyebrows lighter than his skin, his hair showed silver-blond around the dark blue watchcap.

The trap was odorous with sea bottom, slimy enough with a growth of weed to slide easily over the edge of the wharf. Joanna hauled it out of the way and came back for another. She pulled that one up, and over, and then said quietly, "What do you think?" There was a fine edge of invisible wires in her hands and legs. "Are you worried?"

"No." Another trap. "But the last time I saw him he must have been going for that sweet spot of his halfway between

the Rock and Pirate. If he's broken down again, I want to
fetch him in before I go home and take my boots off."

He didn't have to add, *And it's breezing on and coming
night.* Two Stonehaven men had the local air now, rambling
foolishly on with secret jokes. "Call him again," said Joanna,
"if you can break up that vaudeville team." She yanked a trap
up with a burst of nervous strength.

"In a minute."

"Hey, Jo!" Dave came out of the fishhouse. "Don't touch
that nasty trap!" He took it away from her, twitching the big
water-soaked four-header around and up on end as if it had
been bone-dry and unballasted.

He was younger than Nils but looked older, with deep lines
from nose to mouth. The heavy dark frames of his glasses
hid his blond eyebrows, and his eyes were a more faded blue
than Nils's, reddened as if with eyestrain. Nils was neatly
spare-fleshed, but David was so thin he seemed to be caving
in on himself.

"Hey, I'll help!" Freddy erupted from the fishhouse, boot
tops and hair flopping, blare of radio sound like a comet's tail
behind him.

"I thought I left you lathing over ends!" Dave shouted over
the cacophony.

"I figgered you could use me out here." Freddy beamed
impartially on all. He had a dimple in each cheek, and looked
like a pretty ten-year-old who had mysteriously shot up to
nearly six feet and started to shave.

"When we need your help," said Dave, "you'll be the first
to know. You get back to your hammer if you expect to keep
drawing your twenty percent."

"*Gee-zuss.*" Sad, but not insolent. The boots were notice-
ably heavier on the way back to the workbench.

"And turn down that goddam radio!"

Freddy flapped a dispirited hand and shut the door behind
him. "Kid'll be deefer'n a haddock before he's thirty," said
Dave, standing another trap on end in the line.

"Willing little cuss, though," said Nils charitably.

"Ayuh. Any excuse to leave off his work and go fandangoing around town. In everybody's mess and nobody's watch, that one."

"He puts me in mind of one of those big puppies," said Nils. "All feet and ears."

"There's some hope of a pup growing up to be a dog. He's going on twenty-three, and I haven't seen anything yet that gives me any hope."

"He could be a late bloomer, Dave," Joanna suggested.

"Late is right." He stopped with a trap hanging over the edge of the wharf. "If I ever called him in the morning without him saying, 'Gee-*zuss*, it's *early!*' I'd likely pass out."

"Do you have to keep him on, Dave?" she asked. "Wasn't he working when they—" She hesitated and he gave her a grim smile, and jerked the trap upright.

"When they shacked up? Yep. If you call it work. He made enough money out of his traps to keep his car filled with gas, and himself and her and their gang filled with pizzas and beer. He traded his car every other week for another wreck because the rear end fell out or he burned out the transmission." He yanked up another trap. "His boat sank at her mooring, outboard and all, because of the leaks, and he didn't bother to raise her. His kid brother finally salvaged and rebuilt her. Anyway—" savagely he slammed the trap into line—"if I have to feed those two, he's going to earn it."

"I'd rather subsidize them at a distance and save my nerves," said Joanna. Why didn't Nils call Jamie again? Then she answered herself; because he isn't worried, that's why. And if he wasn't worried, there was nothing to worry about.

Dave was saying, "It'll be a hell of a lot easier when Alice gets here, and that'll be as soon as she gets somebody broken in to take over her job."

"Oh, good!" Joanna said, as if she believed it would really happen. She was again aware of secret wires telegraphing panic. All but one of the traps were up by now, and how long had those two fools been prattling on the air? Oh, they'd

AN ANSWER IN THE TIDE

break for a Mayday, so no Mayday had been called. But what if it wasn't possible to call? *Riding turn;* it meant a warp looped around a leg or wrist, the boat speeding one way and the trap sinking in the wake, hauling a man inexorably out over the stern, and no knife within reach. Jamie always carried a knife, didn't he? If at the moment of ultimate horror he would be able to fumble with numbed hands through oil-clothes and jackets for a knife. No, they should keep the knife strapped in the stern, so they could grab it on the way, but what if it wasn't there?

"Can we go now?" The words jumped from her mouth, and she heard them with surprise, and saw it on David's face.

"Go where?"

Nils said, unhurried, "I thought I'd take a look around for Jamie before I put her back on the mooring. It'll be a pretty cold night to lay out in, even if his anchor holds." He went in under the canopy and spoke; the Stonehaven men fell silent. Jamie still didn't answer, and Nils came out again. Joanna stepped down onto the washboard, moving carefully because of the slippery mess from the traps.

"I saw you and him out on Cree Ridge," Dave said to Nils. "Having trouble, was he? But he got going again."

Nils didn't answer. He started the engine, and Dave said, "I guess I'll go too." He stepped across to the bow and cast off the line.

"You got enough on?" Nils asked him.

"My oilclothes are aboard the boat." Standing up there, balancing easily as *Joanna S.* backed out and around, he turned young again, and almost happy. "I'm just going for the hell of it," he called. "The boy's all right. He's no fool, not that solid mixture of Sorensen and Bennett."

"Did you ever try to make an impression on that solid mixture?" Joanna asked.

"Listen, he was born with common sense, that kid."

Nils brought his boat up beside *Phoebe Ann*, and Dave crossed from one gently heaving bow to the other. Charles Bennett's voice boomed exuberantly from the speaker.

"Where you fellers off to? Looks like you suddenly said 'To hell with it!' and decided to leave home."

"I guess that's what Jamie's done," said Nils. "We thought we'd go take a look. He might've left a note in a bottle for us."

"Oh." Charles's voice changed. "We'll stand by."

"Thanks. I'm going to the east'ard, and I'm sending Dave out around Sou'west Point. He might be coming home that way."

"Then why isn't he calling?" Joanna said angrily. "Or answering?" Nils gave her arm a hard squeeze above the elbow.

"Don't wait too long to sing out," Charles said. "Hugo's right on deck now."

"You hold your horses, Hugo," Nils said. "He could be lying snug in the lee somewhere, saving his battery. I'll give you a shout if I need you."

He hung up the microphone but left the set on. Dave, now in his oilclothes, started up his engine and cast off his mooring. *Joanna S.* moved toward the harbor mouth across the deepening chop, picking up speed and throwing a little spray that flashed in the sun like showers of diamonds. Joanna put her hand in the cold pocket of Nils's oil jacket and he put his hand in over it, and their fingers laced tightly together. She wondered if he was remembering the Stonehaven boat some Brigport men found out in the bay this winter, running by herself. The missing man's friends had hauled all his traps but one, and God alone knew where that one was. If he had died the way they guessed, the lost buoy was held far below the surface because the warp had been shortened by its loops around his leg, and he was down there somewhere between trap and buoy, swinging in the tide like kelp, in the awful peace of the drowned.

No! She didn't say it aloud, but her fingers squeezed savagely on Nils's, and he said mildly, "Ouch."

"I'm scared," she blurted. "I have to admit it or burst."

"How many times have you been scared in your life?" They were going out around Eastern Harbor Point, rolling in the tide rip. "About somebody not coming home on time, that is?"

He was so easy about it, his voice was like a tranquilizing hand. "Oh, roughly a few thousand times, if I start back when I was five. That's when the first time happened for me. The end of innocence, you could call it, because after that I knew how to worry."

"What happened?"

"Uncle Nate was overdue, and Father went out and I don't know who else. No radio then, not that it's doing us much good now." She looked accusingly at the speaker.

"I remember," Nils said. "My father went, and Uncle Eric. Your uncle was lying off the Rock with a broken connecting rod. Fishing while he waited. He did good too. We had fried cod for supper that night."

Her stomach rejected the mere mention of food. "I'd like to think Jamie was fishing," she said, "but I doubt it, at this time of year."

They were going by Long Cove. The following seas hurried them along, cresting on either side and always boiling up just off the stern. The sunshine was still strong. The woods between Long Cove and the Eastern End shimmered in waves of reflected light, and ahead Pudding Island and then Shag Ledge stood up from the sea as rufous crags.

Now they passed Eastern End Cove. Her brother Steve's boat lay at her mooring, his skiff was hauled up and overturned on the brow of the beach. The fishhouse was shut up for the night. In the field above the shore his house looked low and snug against the hard glassy blue of the sky, with smoke fluttering away from one chimney in lilac-colored wisps. A child and a dog ran across the field, and the comparison between the ignorant innocence of the scene and her own dread made her feel that in another moment she'd have to vomit.

Outside the Head, the sea roiled in dazzling deceitful motion to the horizon. It looked as if there were no limits, as if it went tossing and glittering all the way to infinity, as it had for Joanna when she'd first comprehended the earth's roundness. It had become very clear to the child that the sea curved over the horizon, and that if Father didn't stay in sight of the island all the time, he might glide over that curve and plunge help-lessly into the appalling horror of space. It was safe enough for him to haul toward the north and west, where the watery glide to doom was fenced off by land. She thought that a flat earth would be a lot safer than a round one; all the nations could join together and build a great wall around the edge.

"Here, take her a minute," Nils said. She took the wheel and was surprised to see that her hand wasn't trembling, at least not outwardly. Nils went into the cabin and came back with his binoculars. He leaned out past the opposite side of the canopy and scanned the distance ahead. After a few minutes he gave up.

"Can't see a thing in this chop and sunglare." He sounded annoyed, rubbing hard at his forehead. He's worried, she thought in despair. *When Nils worries, it's time to worry*, was a family byword. "I wish he hadn't given up that red jigger sail," he said.

"Let me try," she said. But all she could see with any cer-tainty was Pirate Island itself, a long, high ridge of rock burn-ing coppery-pink in the late sun, with surf flying up along its base. From some areas the blinding flash of ice struck back at her blurring eyes. The island was as brutally indifferent as the sea, because it too was empty. From far away you couldn't see the vacant camps huddled around the narrow scrap of beach.

She looked out past its southwestern tip toward the hori-zon, then silently handed the glasses back to Nils and he looked again, but it was a useless compulsion. They both knew that. Finally he took the wheel and she held the binoculars but wouldn't allow herself to look through them. Coldly she dis-missed her earlier terror about a riding turn. Jamie would never be so careless. Since he was old enough to walk, he'd been trained by his father.

They began watching for pot buoys and finally saw the first green-and-white one, marking Jamie's string in what he called his sweet spot because he always did so well out of it. Their eyes strained for another one and eventually they found all twenty. The radio had been strangely quiet, as if everyone else were waiting too, but Joanna knew it was probably because most of the talkers had arrived in their home harbors by now. Out of the silence Dave's voice startled them.

"No news is good news! Neither hide nor hair of him out here. I've looked in the lee of all the ledges. Now I'm jogging toward the Rock, and I'll work back the way he went."

"Good enough," said Nils. "We're going to take a look around the back side of Pirate. If he's not there, we'll call the Rock. They can see a lot farther than we can."

"Finest kind." They were so unhurried they might have been discussing the springtime moving of gear. Nils put his arm around Joanna. She looked into his face and saw that his calm had become both hard and transparent, like glass.

"Call the Rock now," she said.

"When I'm ready. There's plenty of light yet."

"Besides," she said, "if they're listening, they'd have already told us if they saw anything. That's what you're thinking, isn't it?" She didn't raise her voice. There was a sensation of weakness and looseness in her throat and jaw that made even ordinary speech an effort.

"*Joanna S.* calling *Valkyrie*," Nils said into the microphone. "Come in, Jamie." No answer. They rounded into the lee of Pirate. This side of the high ridge was washed with clear dark blue shadow over its rockfall slopes, and at the foot the water was quiet enough to hold reflections of moonscape shoreline and enamel-bright sky. Black ducks fed in the shallow cove where Joanna as a girl had fished for flounder. The peace was absolute, but even with the birds it was like the peace of a dead planet.

She tried to discipline herself. For over half her lifetime she had lived with the security that Nils knew what he was doing, and this was no time to start doubting. Maybe she'd even imagined that he was frightened now, maybe she'd seen only her own fear reflected. But when he called *Valkyrie* again she wanted to knock the microphone out of his hand and cry, "It's no use! You know he won't answer!"

"How do you spell that name, Cap'n?" The strange voice had a soft drawl. Nils began to spell, and the caller said, "She's in Brigport harbor. Young blond feller."

"That's the one," said Nils. Blissfully weak, Joanna leaned against him and shut her eyes. "Thank you," Nils was saying, moderate as always. "I'm much obliged. Who is this?"

"Dragger *Gemini*, Bristol. We're just leaving Brigport now."

"This is *Joanna S.*, Bennett's Island. Nils Sorensen. I thank you kindly, Cap'n."

"You're welcome. Glad I could give you the good word. *Gemini* out." He was gone.

"You hear that, Dave?" Nils asked.

"Loud and clear!"

"Charles?"

"Ay-up! We all did. Well, glad to get the news. *Mateel* out."

"I'm sorry you were dragged out for nothing, Dave," Nils said.

"Hell, *I'm* not! I hate to go home! I haven't been alone aboard this boat for so long, it's a real pleasure cruise. If I had enough grub and water along I'd put to sea right now and stay there forever like the Flying Dutchman . . . Dunno but I might go anyway. What the hell!—*Phoebe Ann* out."

Laughing at him as if he were the world's greatest comedian, Nils and Joanna came together in a long hard embrace. It passed through her mind that if they'd found Jamie's boat empty they would also have embraced, but in a passion of despair. Finally she said, wiping her eyes, "I've felt like this a couple of thousand times too. It's the kind of relief that's like nothing else in the world. Now I'm starved. Let's go home and eat."

"We'll go to Brigport first," Nils said. "Considering how uncomfortable we've been for the past hour, I'd like to make him a dite uncomfortable too."

2

Nils did the day's cleaning up while Joanna steered, and half-an-hour later they entered Brigport harbor. The breakwater beacon flashed on as they passed it. They moved slowly, looking for *Valkyrie* and watching out for men rowing in from their moorings. This was a long harbor, much bigger than Bennett's, with three times as many lobster boats, besides a few transient shrimpers and small draggers like *Gemini*. In the sunset light it looked crowded and busy. Two outboard dories run by young boys were recklessly chasing each other among the big boats. When they shot across the bow of a small skiff being sculled by a man standing in the stern, he was almost thrown overboard. The second dory slowed abruptly and circled back. The conversation wasn't audible past the sound of engines, but its subject was obvious. The dory went off again, decorously, and the man resumed his sculling toward his wharf.

Tim Merrill's lobster car lay at the end of the old Merrill wharf, which stood a beach away from the big stone dock where on boat days the mailboat landed freight, passengers, and the mail. Randy Fowler's car was anchored in the broad bight between the stone dock and the breakwater, and a float holding bait bins lay close to it. *Valkyrie* was at one end of the car, and Bruce Mackenzie's *Hannah Mac* at the other end. The two boys were lifting a full crate from Bruce's boat to the scales; Jamie's cap was off and his fair head shone almost white.

"So there's the beamish boy," Joanna said. "If he broke

down and Bruce picked him up, why tow him all the way up here instead of home, for heaven's sake?"

"Maybe he wants Josh to work on her," Nils said. He slowed the boat down even more when he headed her toward the car. Someone was adjusting the weights on the scales; not Randy Fowler, who was close to Nils and Joanna in age, but a slight figure with thick curly brown hair flowing out from under a tasseled knit cap, and a bright orange foul-weather jacket over a Norwegian fisherman sweater; it wore tight jeans and short deck boots.

"My, how Randy's changed since I saw him last week," said Joanna. "He's turned into Peter Pan. Or whose boy is being trusted to buy lobsters on the Fowler Company's car?"

"That boy is a girl. Mark was telling me today." *Joanna S.* moved toward the car with a soft shushing of water along her sides, the throb of the engine barely audible because of the racing outboards. "I never got a chance to tell you. She's Noll Jenkins's granddaughter, and she took over yesterday."

"And today by a strange coincidence our son forgets where he left his head. I can't wait to get a look at her. What's Randy doing? Tending store?"

"He's going back to lobstering, and he's happy as a kid with his first boat . . . Hey, remember Noll coming out, back when he didn't have a big company and all the hired help?"

"Captain Oliver Cromwell Jenkins, of the smack *Edith and Maude*," Joanna said. "He was my idea of a corsair, with that mustache. All he needed was a knife in his teeth and rings in his ears. I was a little afraid of him. But Ferris, now," she said dreamily. "His son Ferris. You remember *him*, don't you? Brown plush hair and glasses. He could play the harmonica something fierce. He'd sit on the forward hatch on a hot summer noon and play 'Red River Valley.' We were about eight and that was our song. At least I thought of it as our song, but he probably didn't. Now that I think of it, I did all the talking."

"I remember Ferris," said Nils, "because he was younger than me but his father let him sit on a high stool and steer. And he was on the smack all summer with his father till Labor Day. I hated his guts."

"I didn't know you ever hated anyone, except maybe your grandfather."

"The older I grow the more I can appreciate Grampa's low opinion of the rest of us." He laughed, but she knew he was annoyed with Jamie. So was she, apart from the rapture of relief.

The boat slipped almost silently alongside the front of the car. The three around the scales looked up. Jamie's face showed nothing. Bruce grinned. "Hello, Mr. Sorensen, and Missis."

"Oh golly!" the girl said. "Another new customer?"

"No," Jamie said. He nodded aloofly at his parents and turned away to open one of the car doors.

"Hi anyway." She gave them a quick smile. She had a thick fluff of bangs, a round face with dimples in each cheek. Her nose was pink with cold. "How are your folks, Bruce?" Joanna asked.

"Oh, finest kind. They're gone to Ohio to visit Jeannie for a couple of weeks. Hell of a time to go visiting, but you can't pry Ma off this island by the time the first dandelion greens show up."

The girl took a lobster measure off a hook beside the door of the shed, and Jamie went across the car to his boat and got his measure. Bruce swung around. "Hey, what are you doing?"

"Mr. Fowler told me to check every lobster personally," the girl said, "so nobody can sneak in any shorts or a punched female."

"You think I'd pull that on you?" Bruce sounded shocked.

"You might. I've only known you since yesterday. And I'm a woman," she said amiably, "therefore a legitimate victim."

"My God, you've only known *him* since he showed up here this afternoon, and now you've got him helping you. I think I'm insulted."

She chuckled. "Don't be. I measured his lobsters too."

"But you wouldn't trust me anyway. It's because my eyes aren't blue."

"Oh, your eyes are *lovely*." She was almost as fast as Jamie, expertly holding a cold green lobster in one hand and fitting the brass measure over the carapace, making sure it was snug; looking for the notched tail of the egg-bearing female. Then each lobster was released into the dark water of the car.

"I can see you'll be some busy," said Bruce, "personally measuring a few thousand lobsters everyday. Unless you're hiring Jamie for that."

"Oh, I'll know after a while who I can trust and who I can't. *Whom*. I'll never get a teaching job if the wrong ears hear that. Hey, Jamie, if you don't know these people, Bruce does."

Jamie bestirred himself. "This is Bronwen Jenkins. My mother and father."

"Hello, Bronwen," Joanna said. "I thought for a minute he was going to treat us as a couple of distant relations." Bronwen laughed, rocking back on her heels; her eyes, slightly oblique above windburnt cheekbones, almost disappeared behind her lashes.

"We knew your grandfather," Nils said. "That smack of his was known in every gunkhole and at every island along this part of the coast from way back in the days of twelve-cent lobsters."

"Which he now refers to as the good old days," said Bronwen.

"Well, they were," said Joanna, "because he was young then, and he lived on the water. Maybe he's a rich man now, but I'll bet nothing in his life today can compare with being young, on the way up, and master of his own vessel."

"To travel hopefully is better than to arrive, you mean? Who knows, maybe I'll be on a nostalgia kick of my own someday, and I'll remember this." Sitting on her heels she tipped her head back to look at the dulling fire-opal sky above the blowing tops of spruces on Powderhorn Hill. The first

lights were sparkling like fireflies around the harbor. The outboards had stopped, leaving behind a crystalline silence. "And
I'll say, 'Those were the days,' " said Bron as if she were laughing at herself, straight-faced. "And they *are*. So far." She
knocked on the wood of the car.

"Enjoy them," Nils said.

"I intend to. I even like the smell of good fresh bait." She
picked up a lobster. All the while Jamie had gone on measuring the doubtfuls and finding no illegal ones. He never lifted
his head, and Joanna, considering his nape, remembered how
it had looked when he was two years old and squatting down
to share a cracker with a mallard drake. It still looked vulner-
able, and how outraged he would be to know what she was
thinking. She wasn't being sentimental. If anything, she was
amused because Jamie was uncomfortable. *And so you should
be, my boy*, she told the back of his head.

The last lobster slid into the water. Jamie lowered the door
and Bronwen padlocked it. She gave Bruce his slip and
counted out bills into his hand. "See, I told you I was honest,"
he gibed. He tucked the money into his billfold.

"I humbly apologize ... I wish I could have come to this
job incognito."

"How could you've got the job, then? Randy'd never put
a woman on the car if he could help it."

"I really wanted the school, when I heard the teacher was
leaving at Christmas. I'm qualified, and my being Noll Jenkins's
granddaughter wouldn't have amounted to Hannah Cook.
But I was too late hearing about it." She hunched her shoulders
in irritation. "All *right!* So Mr. Fowler wouldn't have given
me this job if he didn't buy for the company and if Noll
hadn't asked him to give me a try. Sure, I'll admit that!" She
gazed at the Sorensens with a candid intensity. "But he won't
be the loser. He's going back to lobstering and he's happy.
And I've already got him some new customers." She glanced
across the harbor at the Merrill wharf, where there were two
boats at the lighted car. "Of course I may have lost him a
few," she said doubtfully.

"Like all the real honest-to-god male chauvinists," said Bruce.

Her round chin went up. "I hope I can hold this job on my own merits, nothing to do with sex."

"I do, too, Bronwen," Joanna said. "It's a job I'd have loved. Next to being a lobsterman, I mean. If I'd been born twenty-five years later I could be hauling my own traps these days."

"Anytime you want me to fit you out with a string of traps," said Nils, "just say the word."

"Can I have an outboard?"

"You'll start out with a peapod the way your husband and son and daughter did."

"Gosh, all the other kids have outboards," she whined. Bronwen and Bruce laughed. Jamie, who seemed to be searching the sky for wild geese, said unexpectedly, "Want us to get the peapod down from overhead in the barn? You could start getting her ready for spring."

"It kills me to have to refuse such a handsome offer," said Joanna. Nils started the engine. "It's been nice meeting you, Bronwen. Is Ferris your father?"

"It's nice to meet you too, and Ferris is."

"Did he ever learn to play anything else on his harmonica besides 'Red River Valley'?"

"I didn't know he ever played a harmonica! I can't imagine it!" She was overjoyed. "You wait till I see him again!"

"Maybe he doesn't want to be reminded of his wild oats," said Nils. Bronwen leaned on the scales, laughing so hard that Joanna wondered what Ferris was like these days. Plump and pompous? Jamie came across the car to the boat.

"I'm staying over for hockey tonight."

"I don't know how good our team'll do," said Bruce. "Darrell's gone to the main. He may be one of the Quiet Robeys on land or sea, but he's a ringtail peeler on ice. I hear he's got a girl over there. Old Darrell! She must've had to do all the chasing."

"Maybe he's a ringtail peeler with the women too," Joanna said. "Once he gets the idea."

"Sometimes we like these quiet bashful ones," said Bronwen demurely. Nils switched on the sidelights and the boat backed away in a murmurous rush of foam. Through the goodbyes Jamie said, "See you tomorrow," and lifted one hand.

This time they headed down the harbor toward the Gut between the big island and the small narrow one, Marriott, which made the harbor. Where the passage began, they passed an anchored boat strange to Joanna; the cabin was illuminated, with someone moving around behind the portholes. She was at least a forty-footer, broad-beamed and high-bowed, with radar as well as the whips for both radio-telephone and CB. A skiff tailed off astern.

"Who's that?" she asked Nils, looking back and trying to read the name.

"Ivor Riddell. I hear he's going to start fishing Pirate Island himself this spring. Tired of the business end, wants to get back on the water."

"Like Randy Fowler," she said. "The sap must be rising. And speaking of that—" She decided to stop. There was no need to discuss a fact as obvious as the difference between day and dark. Because they hadn't mentioned Jamie's lapse to him didn't mean that he wouldn't hear about it tomorrow, and he knew it.

She moved close to Nils so their shoulders touched. She was hardly ever conscious of having passed fifty until something like this happened; meeting a girl with all time in her hands to play with as she chose, with or without a grandfather's help.

Once they were outside the Gut, Tenpound was a low black hill ahead and then falling off to their left, rounded solidly against the first stars in the eastern sky, with a ghostly dance of surf at its feet. Though they stood well off they felt the power of the surge that was never absent. The lights of Bennett's began to show; first from the house at the Eastern End; then, after the long black stretch of woods, Owen's windows at Hillside showing past the loom of the barn. From the sea beyond the fields, the Rock light swept the sky. Ahead, the breakwater beacon was a steady spark. The *Joanna S.* rode on a bubbling luminescence.

When she entered the harbor, there were the lights all around the shore, and a row of ruddy windows in the Bennett Homestead back on the rise. Other lights seemed to flicker like candle flames behind moving spruce boughs. Home, and she was ready for it, ready to drop where she stood. Who wouldn't feel limp as a shirt on a handspike? she thought. It's one of the privileges of having a child old enough to go out and drown himself.

While Nils was up on the bow making the mooring fast, Charles's boat came out, passing close enough for Hugo to hail them and be answered. *Mateel* went on in her green-white wreath of phosphorescence.

Nils came back to the cockpit with the skiff painter, and Joanna said, "I don't know how much chance Jamie'll stand when Hugo shows up."

"Hugo's only thinking of hockey. Those French-Canadians have it in their blood."

"Don't forget he's half-Bennett, and they have women in their blood."

They got into the skiff, and the breeze helped to hurry them toward land. The oars stirred and scattered light. "I had a hard time keeping my face straight," Nils said. "He was some worried I'd say something in front of Snow White."

"I suppose when you consider the lack of girls around here, we shouldn't be too hard on him, if he was in such a hurry to get a look that he forgot something."

"He's twenty-five years old," Nils said, "and he's gone out enough times himself to look for somebody to realize a new duck is no excuse."

"Nothing is, if your radio's working and you can reach it. But it's a bright, cute little duck, isn't it? And she must be at least twenty-one. Teenagers bore him, thank heavens, and I hope he's too smart to get involved with a married woman."

"As far as I can tell," said Nils, "all the good-looking wives over there are virtuous."

"Thank you, dear, I rely on your expert judgment since Owen reformed." She leaned forward suddenly and grabbed the oar handles. "Hey, what makes you so expert?"

"I listen a lot," he said placidly. She laughed; happy, revived. Rowing ashore in the biting cold and dark of a February night they were, for this moment, as contented and carefree as if they walked in a summer meadow. "I wonder what will happen when Hugo shows up over there," she said. "He's got quite a line, while Jamie stands around looking like a snow-covered Alp against the sky."

"You know why men climb mountains. Maybe some women feel the same way about snow-covered Alps."

"You never did tell me how many women like that you met while you were sailing the seven seas." He laughed, and she said, "That's no answer. Or maybe it's too much of an answer. Nils Sorensen," she hissed dramatically at him, "were you an absolutely different personality when you were in the Merchant Marine? Were you one of these bold sea-rover types with a girl in every port?"

"Don't you think we could leave my secrets buried after all these years?" he asked.

"But somehow I never thought of you as a Viking. I'm looking at you with new eyes."

"Get up that ladder before I toss you over my shoulder and lug you up."

"And drown us both." She went up and he came behind her with the skiff painter. He gave her a pat on the rear and she said, "Sir!"

"Hi." Rosa Fleming called from her fishhouse doorway. "The way you two were carrying on I didn't know if I should interrupt. Then I thought I ought to."

"We're past the stage when an interruption could break us up," said Nils.

"You two," she said. Her voice was husky tonight, and slow, as if she were half-asleep, or depressed. There was lantern-light in the fishhouse behind her, and the smell of a wood fire. "So Jamie's all right," she said, all at once hearty.

Nils went to the end of the wharf to put the skiff out on the haul-off. "Except for mislaying half his brain."

"The new lobster buyer must be a real siren. Freddy and Phoebe filled me in while I was working in here and waiting for the news."

"It must have been pretty interesting, coming from them," Joanna said.

"Fabulous. I can hardly wait to see a real live nymphomaniac."

"Well, we all need something to look forward to on the tag end of winter," said Nils. Rosa went in and blew out her lantern, then walked with them up between Philip's and the Binnacle. Lights flowed out from windows on both sides of the path.

"Those cussed generators sound as if the island was warming up to go to Cash's," Joanna muttered. "Come on home with us and have supper, Rosa."

"No, thanks, mine's on the back of the stove, and then I'm going over to the Percys'. Ralph and I are going to make music." She turned off where the path branched past the well to cross the field. "Goodnight."

3

In the morning, Joanna walked to the shore with Nils and waited while he rowed out to the boat. The sunrise was the color of ripe peaches, and there was no wind. Grass and roofs were whitened with frost that furred the wharf planks. Philip's and Owen's boats were leaving side by side, Owen's helper shifting empty crates around in the cockpit, getting squared away for his work. Terence Campion and Barry Barton were going out to the moorings, Barry kneeling on the middle seat and pushing on the oars, Terence sculling his skiff. Charles and Hugo were putting bait aboard, Hugo talking hockey. If Jamie had enough bait with him he wouldn't come home before he went to haul. He'd probably be glad to put off the hour.

Ralph Percy was on his way to the shore; Joanna could hear him whistling "The White Cockade." It must have been a good session last night. Rosa was expert on the guitar and was learning the banjo, and Ralph fiddled as well as he whistled. Joanna's first husband had been a fiddler too. When he died, she had given the violin to his sister, who first said, "Keep it. Maybe the baby will have its father's gift." But she was sure that she couldn't have endured another fiddler in the house who wasn't Alec, even if it should be their own child. For a long time she couldn't tolerate the sound of jigs and reels; their merriment was like hilarity on the edge of an open grave.

Sometimes, like now, with Ralph's tune piercing the frosty air, she was surprised by emotions that had never lost their edges, even though she had moved into another life. At other times, to remember herself at nineteen was like contemplating a third daughter; time went out of focus with Linnea going on nineteen, and Ellen, the baby unborn when her father drowned, past thirty and mother of two children. Her father had not lived to be that old. He was forever a boy, left behind in a country whose frontiers had been permanently sealed.

For a long time after his death Joanna had fought against leaving him behind. Yet here she stood now, a grandmother with gray coming in her black hair, listening to Ralph's whistle bounce nearer and nearer, watching Nils row out to the boat and thinking they had been long enough together to have grown into an indissoluble "we."

Mostly, except for these surprising stabs, she thought of Alec with a profound sadness because he had been so hideously cheated out of his life and his child.

Nils was aboard the boat now, and she waited until he cast off the mooring and was back in the cockpit. Most of the men were sure-footed as cats, but even a cat could skid on unexpected ice. Steam billowed in gray-blue clouds from exhaust pipes, the sound of engines echoed from the rocks, gulls circled the harbor skies like skaters. Ralph shouted at her from his wharf.

"Top of the mornin' to ye!"

"And the same to you," she answered.

"It's some pretty. Feels airish, though. Probably breeze up southerly. We're about due for a good one." He was cheerful about it.

Nils waved from under the canopy, she waved back, and left the wharf without watching him out of the harbor. She met Rob Dinsmore hurrying away from the Binnacle with the small shaggy red terrier importantly attending him. "Morning, Jo."

"Hi, Rob," she said. "Hi, Tiger." Tiger barked.

"I think so too," she said. "But you'd better talk to Rory about it." She went on. Dave was coming with his long loose nervous stride, head down, lunchbox swinging. He gave her

a nod and an ambiguous growl; Freddy came clumping behind
him holding a doughnut between his teeth while trying to get
into an oil jacket and still hang onto his lunchbox. He rolled
his eyes desperately at her and then at Dave's back disappear-
ing past the fishhouse.

"Here, give me that." She took the lunchbox, Freddy made
a sound around the doughnut, and got himself properly into
the jacket. Then he removed the doughnut and said, "Thanks,
Aunt Jo."

"You're welcome, Freddy." She gave him the lunchbox
and he went running after Dave. Phoebe would be in bed
until midmorning, or she'd be washing her hair, which took
a lot of her time. She was sixteen and at fifteen she had run
away with Freddy, who was twenty-one. They had moved
into a friend's trailer and defied the world. After a couple
of weeks of going in circles Dave and Alice had decided it
would be easier to let her marry him than to try to keep
her in line and in school.

The sun was up over the spruces now, and the woods and
roofs were beginning to steam. Crows shouted above the
treetops. Rory was ready to go out on morning rounds, which
began with following Nils's tracks to the shore. Joanna got
a fresh cup of coffee and sat down at the dining room table
to write to her daughters.

Ellen was easy to write to; she had been an easy child.
Linnie was a different matter. Not that she had ever been
difficult, though she was certainly noisier than either her
sister or brother, but in the last few weeks Joanna had the
strong feeling that her letters crossed strange territory to reach
Linnie, like messages from home delivered by caravan in
the Sahara.

Linnie still wrote a letter a week. She had always been a
very open child, and her letters were full of detail about her
college life. But it was what she left out of them these days
that both intrigued and badgered Joanna. During her Christmas holidays she had talked constantly about one boy. She
thought she had him artfully camouflaged among all the other

names she scattered, but his had kept pushing up above the greenery like a sunflower among marigolds.

She had gone back to school planning to be home again for a few days after her midyear exams; she had always rushed back to the island whenever she could. But Owen's Joss had come home without her. Linnie had stayed behind to work on her skiing, which she explained fully in a letter to her parents. Too fully. Roger Forrester was an expert, and Linnie's technical dissertation sounded as if she were going into training for the Olympic team.

Nils had laid the letter aside without comment, used to Linnie's fervors. "I'd like to get a look at this guy," Jamie said. "Sounds like he's expert at more than skis."

"Oh, don't be so suspicious," Joanna said. "The way you suspect other men, anybody would think you were one of the worst scoundrels in the bay."

"You don't have to be a whoremaster to recognize one."

In her day she'd put up with the suspicions of three older brothers. "You've never laid eyes on him. There are some men who are as crazy about skiing down mountains as you are about chasing herring, and if one of *their* sisters kept wanting to go with you—"

"I wouldn't allow any women aboard when I'm seining." He scowled at her, but they ended up by laughing. It hadn't been mentioned again. Neither had Linnie mentioned Roger or skiing since the midyear break. In his absence Roger was even more noticeable than before, and there was the premise with which Joanna sometimes woke in the morning, and couldn't accommodate; what if Jamie were right?

Once when Linnie was seventeen and they were talking about couples living together, she had said earnestly, "But sometimes it's the *only* way to do!"

"All right." Joanna was reasonable. "What if I were a widow, or divorced from your father, and I fell in love with a man but didn't want to marry him. Or he didn't want to marry *me*. So he moved in with us anyway. What about that kind of living together?"

"In the same house with your *children?*" Linnie was appalled. "You *couldn't!*" Joanna had said nothing, and Linnie laughed uneasily. "You wouldn't anyway, so what are we arguing about?" She hadn't been in a hurry to open any new discussions.

"Hello, Aunt Jo!" Phoebe sang out from the sun parlor.

"Damn!" Joanna whispered. She put her writing materials into Nils's desk. Phoebe came through the kitchen, taking off her down parka. She had a small face, wide across the cheekbones, and a kitten-eyed prettiness that would probably always give an illusion of innocence. Her dark hair, shiny from all the washing and brushing, was knotted on top of her head today, loosened in little curly wisps around her forehead and ears. Joanna was so used to thinking of Phoebe with irritation that the girl's good looks always took her by surprise, and she would enjoy the surprise for about a half-minute.

"We thought we'd come over and see you," Phoebe said winsomely. She patted the front of her pink smock. "Dracula and I."

"That's a terrible name to give an innocent baby."

Phoebe giggled. "Freddy started it. He says it's going to be a bloodsucker and drain away our lives."

"The poor little thing's going to get a great welcome." The half-minute was up.

"Oh, Freddy likes puppies so he'll probably like it once it's here." She flopped into a chair and stretched her arms over her head and yawned. "Daddy was so mad with Freddy because he went back to sleep again this morning. I thought he'd go without him, but no such luck. So of course *I* didn't get any more sleep either." She frowned in a childish parody of wifely concern. "I don't know how long Freddy can stand this. He's just not used to it."

"To lobstering, or to work?"

"You know what I mean! Slaving from daylight till it's too dark to see. Daddy'd have him building traps every night by lantern light, except Freddy'd make such a mess of it," she added complacently.

"Tell me something, Phoebe," Joanna said. "If this is so hard on Freddy—"

"And on me too, remember! I wasn't brought up to live on a place like this, Aunt Jo. You *know* that."

"Yes, I know how you were brought up." Don't we all. "So why are you out here?"

Phoebe pouted, and twisted around in petulant little movements. "We *had* to, after Freddy's boat sank. I mean, we *had* to turn to Daddy because we didn't have a thing in the *world* except a lot of payments for the car and the motorbike, and Dinny didn't want us in the trailer anymore because he wanted to move his *own* girl in. So then we didn't even have a *roof* over our heads." Her eyes filled with tears, which she could manage very easily and fetchingly. "And then I got pregnant, so I couldn't get a job."

Joanna managed to sound merely interested and curious. "But if you could go around with Freddy for so long and not get pregnant, why couldn't you keep up the good work?"

"I *wanted* a baby! My goodness, Aunt Jo, can't you understand that? My sisters have babies, so why shouldn't I? And I promised Daddy that he and Mama can borrow it as often as they want. I won't be selfish and possessive, I *promised* them."

"They must have appreciated that."

"It'll be their *favorite* grandchild." The sun sparkled through the raindrops. "Over all the others."

"I'm sure of that," Joanna said dryly. At least for Dave. "But it seems to me you could have stayed ashore. There's good money in clamming. Why couldn't Freddy do that? Then you could be with your car and motorbike."

"And Freddy misses his engines like *mad*. Whenever we go to Brigport and he sees those kids with their bikes he's so sad it's kind of cute. He thinks maybe he'll get a trail bike and go racing all over the island here."

"The first motorbike that comes onto this island," said Joanna, looking her in the eye, "I'm going to kill dead. I'll get it with one shot right in the fuel tank, fast and merciful. It won't feel a thing."

"Oh, Aunt Jo!" Chimes of laughter.

"I mean it, and I'm not the only one. So pass the word to Freddy. Tell me why he isn't inshore making a fortune from the clamflats."

"He tried it once, but it just about ruined his back. Besides, he was always missing low tide, sleeping past it or being uptown or something. His father's scalloping, but he hates that too." She sighed. "So Daddy just *had* to take us over because of the baby and everything. And so he couldn't fish at Port George anymore because the grounds are too crowded for him to put out a lot of extra gear. But wow, it's Dullsville out here," she rambled on. "When I think what a ball we had at Christmas, and then have to come back to Alcatraz! As soon as it's spring I'm going to tell Daddy we have to have every weekend off just like office people, and we can fly in and have some fun with our friends. We *deserve* it," she said self-righteously.

"But you're not office people. Lobstermen don't have forty-hour weeks, and you know that, Phoebe. Especially when a man has to drive as hard as your father does, because he has to guarantee his helper a living."

"*I* think Freddy should get more than twenty percent, because he's not just an ordinary helper, he's part of the family."

"Your father has all the expenses—"

Phoebe picked up a magazine and began looking through it. Joanna watched her. Twenty years ago in a similar situation she'd have told the girl plainly what she thought of the whole thing, and she wouldn't have cared who got mad; there were a few reticent Bennetts, but not many. Nowadays she could stop to think that Phoebe was the creation of her parents in all respects. They hadn't been forced to bow down to this child. Certainly she hadn't been born expecting it, anymore than her sisters had, even if by now she took it as her natural right. But you couldn't help feeling sorry for David and Alice. Pain was pain, whether or not it was self-inflicted.

Alice had begun the struggle to free herself. She thought

the move to the island was foolishness; she said that if no one rushed to provide for them they wouldn't simply sit down by the side of the road and starve. It was David who would never cease to feel responsible for his heart's darling if he lived to be ninety, which was a doubtful prospect considering the way he looked right now.

Phoebe glanced up from the magazine with a convincing start of radiant surprise. "I'm *sorry*, Aunt Jo! What were you saying?"

"That I've got to get to work." Joanna stood up.

"I thought maybe we could have a cup of coffee."

"I just had one," Joanna said unfeelingly. Phoebe got up with an unnecessary show of heaviness. She followed Joanna out to the kitchen.

"Jamie didn't come home last night, did he?"

"He played hockey and stayed with Bruce." Joanna handed her the parka.

"The new lobster buyer has her own place, that apartment over the Fowlers' workshop."

"It's a nice spot." Joanna rattled dishes in the sink.

"You can tell what kind she is," Phoebe said. "I mean, any woman that wants a job like *that*."

"She's a woman after my own heart. I'd have loved a chance like that, unless I could have had my own boat and traps, like Rosa."

"Oh, Rosie! It's different with her. She doesn't like *men*, if you know what I mean." Insulting delicacy for elderly and unsophisticated aunt. "Bron Jenkins is just the other way. Freddy knows all about her. She'd put out for *anybody*, he says. She's run through everything on the mainland, so she's trying lobstermen now."

"Then you'd better keep an eye on Freddy," said Joanna.

"Not for a while yet! Not till she gets good and tired of Jamie!" With a triumphant laugh she slammed the sun parlor door behind her.

4

*J*oanna thanked Phoebe for one thing; her visit had knocked away any nonsense about Linnie, who now appeared as a monument of common sense and intelligence. But she didn't feel like letter-writing now, and the mail wouldn't go again until Monday anyway.

She started the Saturday beans baking, and then went out to the barn to let the chickens into the sun and scatter cracked corn for them. There were a few elderly hens who were past laying but who came to the sound of their names, or seemed to. The yard between barn, woods, and house was a basin of warmth, and the fowl made busy sociable noises. Rory stood kindly watching them, now and then exchanging an indulgent glance with Joanna.

He heard Jamie coming before she did, and was there to meet him when he came around the corner of the house past the apple trees. He had his heavy jacket slung over his shoulder, and had taken off his watchcap. "Hello," he said, roughing up the dog's back.

"Are you speaking to him or to me?" asked Joanna. "It's hard to tell."

He straightened up, unsmiling. "Good morning, Mother," he said formally. "That suit ye? Or do you want a deep bow? or should I approach on my knees?"

"No, it's getting muddy out here—I thought you were off on the *Ripper* or somewhere. Have you got real trouble with the boat?"

"She stopped once yesterday and she was all right afterward, but I'm not taking any chances. I left her with Josh for a checkup, and Bruce dropped me off at the Eastern End." His eyes were bright blue in a face immobile to the point of stolidity. She looked back at him, waiting.

Finally he said, "Hugo carted it to me last night until I felt like braining him with his hockey stick. I'll apologize to Uncle Charles and Uncle Dave and the old man when they come in tonight. Do you want an apology too?"

"Please don't call your father the old man. And yes, I certainly do want an apology, after imagining you falling off the earth like a leaf sliding off an apple."

That cracked the mask. "*What?*"

"It's what I used to think was the worst thing that could happen, after I found out the world was round. Now that I'm grown up and have one husband, one son, five brothers, two brothers-in-law, and various nephews in the business, I know a lot about other things that can happen. Like riding turns."

"I'm sorry," he said gruffly. "Don't tell me I should've called in, or stopped on the way to Brigport, because I know it. I just didn't think of it, that's all." He didn't shift his eyes, or even move uneasily a hand or foot. "I don't know why, so there's no sense asking."

"All right, all right! Don't be so aggressive. After you've made the rounds that'll be the end of it, but you're not likely to forget again. If you're having a mug-up, why don't you put the kettle on while I gather my eggs?"

"Ayuh. Hello, Aphrodite," he said to the ancient red hen pecking at his moccasin-lace. "Hard to think you were ever small enough to fit in an egg."

"I could say the same about you," said his mother. She went into the henhouse with her basket. When she came into the house the teakettle was boiling and Jamie was putting some doughnuts to warm in the oven. He looked up solemnly at her.

"Phoebe ambushed me when I came up by. She wanted a pail of water, and when I carried it in, know what she told me? She said I was sexy, and she offered me brownies."

"Did you take one?"

"I said 'No, thanks,' and backed out. Fast."

"How's it feel to be a sex object?" she asked.

"Well, considering she thinks Freddy's sexy too, her opinions don't impress me much. If she was a dite older, and sophisticated, I'd be going around with a silly grin by now." They laughed. "Instant coffee'll do me, Marm. Never mind the pot. You having some?" He measured it into two mugs, anyway.

"How was the hockey game?" she asked.

"Fair. Darrell's on the mainland, and the other side drew Hugo, so a tie was the best we could do." They played a highly personal variety of hockey, not having enough men to make two full-sized teams, and the sides shifted membership from week to week.

"Did Bronwen go to the game?" She took out the pieplate of doughnuts and put it on a trivet by his mug.

"Oh, sure. She's taking in everything there is, from church on down. Says in a small place you have to squeeze every drop out of the orange." He gave Rory a hunk of doughnut. "There. Now stop looking down my throat... After the game we went around to the Gibsons', and the guys got up some music. If you've never been shut up in a small room with drums and a couple of electric guitars amplified enough to shatter glass, and the whole thing vibrating through clouds of whacky tobaccy, don't think you've been deprived of a meaningful experience."

"Do *all* those kids smoke pot?"

"No, just a few, and not all the time either. They were showing off last night for Bron. Trying to impress her." He tossed more doughnut to Rory.

"*Was* she impressed? And don't give that dog anymore doughnuts. If it was up to you he'd look like a barrel by now, if fat hadn't killed him off already."

"You hear that, Rory? Nope, Bron wasn't impressed, not the way they wanted her to be." He smiled, looking very much like his father. "She was polite enough, but she was some glad to get out of there before she got stone-deaf and stoned on the fumes. By that time nobody even saw us go. So—" He became very matter-of-fact, as if the whole occasion had been so ordinary it was almost too boring to talk about. "We walked all over the place. It was midnight, and some quiet. She said that's what she expected to find, that kind of silence at night, and a chance to see the stars from one horizon to the other. She knows most of them. We sat on the cemetery wall a while. Didn't talk much." He got up and made fresh coffee for himself.

Didn't talk much, Joanna thought, but you're talking now. Do you know how much you're telling?

"I liked her," she said. "I hope she can make a go of it."

"She sure intends to." He came back to the table, and went on without looking directly at his mother. "She's got to prove something to Randy and to her folks and to herself, though she won't admit that. But I can tell." His indirection was familiar; whenever he couldn't keep an enthusiasm or an emotion to himself, he still couldn't handle it openly, eye to eye, unless it was potent enough to sweep him out of himself. So far this wasn't, but it was enough to give him more than the silly grin he'd mentioned earlier.

"She was disappointed in the music," he said suddenly. "She was expecting some good fiddling. She said that must have gone out with her gramp's good old days. But I told her we didn't have everything electrified to hell and gone over here. I'll bring her over sometime when I think Ralph's all winged out." He pushed back his chair. "Well, I'm going down and bag up, and then work on gear. When it comes off like this you think you'll be shifting traps next week."

"Today's one of February's big jokes," Joanna said. "Next week, a blizzard."

"Well, I'm willing to go along with the gag today." When he had gone, she baked cookies for the crock and for the sewing meeting that afternoon at the Homestead. Jamie came back to the house for lunch, but took his sandwich and a thermos of coffee back with him to have it while he worked. "With any luck I'll have a good stint done before Freddy's

back. I can't work under the same roof with that flea! If Uncle
Dave's planning to stay out here, he ought to have his own
fishhouse. I don't know how the old man—" he corrected
himself, cocking his eyebrow at her—"how Father can stand
it."

"I don't think Dave's planning anything," said Joanna. "I
think he's just going from day to day. He says he expects
Alice by spring, but she never liked it here under the best
conditions, which these aren't."

"Well, I can always rent space from Rosa."

"Dave's got enough on his mind without thinking he's
driven you out."

"Don't worry, I won't slat and slam out of there like Uncle
Owen in the old days before he mellered down."

Rory went back to the shore with him.

The sewing meeting brought the women together once a
week. Phoebe sometimes attended, if the storage battery for
the portable television needed charging so she couldn't watch
anything, or if she felt the need of coddling. She could always
get this from some of the women, and Joanna suspected that
she craved it oftener than she wanted anyone to know. After
all, she was only sixteen, and there must have been times when
she was not quite so arrogantly self-assured as she seemed; she
must surely be a little awed and frightened by what lay ahead
of her.

Joanna gave herself a ten-minute limit. When Phoebe didn't
show up within it, she went out the back door and through
the woods behind the barn to the Bennett meadow. The afternoon was soft, dulling with warm-looking clouds, brightening
to new blue. The wind had sprung up southwest, carrying the
sound of the rote on the outer shores and the clang of the bell
at the Breaker. Gulls rode the air currents, and kinglets and
chickadees moved in the slightly swaying spruce tops, nuthatches along the trunks. Ice snapped in the alder swamp. The
children were skating again today over on the ice pond, but a
week of thaw would finish off that and the hockey games at
Brigport.

Joanna walked slowly on yellow-brown grasses pressed flat and sodden. Her resistance to an afternoon spent indoors was dragging at her like a sea anchor. She could remember it thus when she was ten and even younger, and it had never grown any weaker. She wanted to play hookey now, taking the track across to Goose Cove and going by the shore all the way to Sou'west Point. She stood for a little while at the junction of the paths, listening to the swash and smelling the fresh rockweed flung up onto the stony beach.

Tomorrow I'll go and stay all day, she thought. But it wouldn't be the same; she wanted to go *now*. "Duty calls," she said aloud, sarcastically. Duty was once school, and now it was the quilts to be auctioned off this summer for the Island Medical Center at Stonehaven. She took the path up to the Homestead.

It was a good afternoon, as they usually were. She stayed to help Mateel with the dishes, and had another cup of tea with Charles when he came up from the harbor. When she got back home, Nils and Dave and Jamie were having coffee and some of the new cookies. She invited Dave to stay for baked beans, but he said that Phoebe had something special planned. "Whatever it is, it'll be drowned in pizza sauce," he added morosely. "Sets me on fire just to contemplate it. But she's trying, so I'll make a valiant attempt."

"Kid'll be born a pizza addict," said Jamie.

Dave gave his head a good-natured cuff. "When are you going to beget some little Sorensens for us?"

"No hurry," said Jamie.

"Sigurd's boy's in no hurry either. What ails you fellers?" He leaned back and said half-sadly, half-smiling, "Ah well, maybe you're right. The very best life that ever was led, always to court and never to wed. Eh, Jim? I'd like to be twenty-five again."

"Seeing as you can't," said Nils, "how about drowning your sorrows?"

"Nope, no more coffee. I'll go on over home and be back later. We're playing a little pool tonight," he said to Joanna.

When he had gone, Jamie said, "I was watching Freddy today, and I know why he's got such a springy step. His pants are so tight he can't put his heels down. Keeps him bouncing. When he takes them off at night he probably collapses from exhaustion."

He went into the bathroom to clean up. A few years ago some of the islanders had combined to hire a well-driller; not the massive oilwell type, but the sort that had worked well enough in the past and could be transported across the bay on a scow in calm weather.

Yet even with their own wells most of them still liked to get their drinking water from the old well in the field, and from habit and thrift they had kept their rain barrels and cisterns, so as not to waste what had always been a bounty.

When Dave came back, they were through supper. On the way in he leaned over the bean pot on the counter and breathed deeply. "Have some, Dave?" Joanna said.

"I can't." He took one of his antacid pills. Jamie came down the back stairs whistling, wearing some of his Christmas finery; all of which, including the scent, his parents had agreed he would never put on.

"Even Solomon in all his glory was not arrayed like one of these," Nils said.

Dave asked with interest, "Is that some of the perfume that makes women go mad with desire?"

"I dunno," said Jamie. "I haven't tried it out yet."

"Well, let me know," said his uncle. "If I decide on a new career as a swinger, I'll need all the help I can get." He took another antacid pill.

"Especially when it mixes with those wintergreen things you're always crunching," said Nils. "The combination ought to make you irresistible."

Jamie stood in the sun parlor doorway pulling on his jacket, grinning, and Dave said, "Stop making fun of us old fubs, boy."

"Speak for yourself, Dave," Nils said. Jamie laughed. "Goodnight, everybody." He disappeared.

"Something tells me," said Dave, "that he's not headed in the right direction."

"If you mean Rosa, no," said Joanna. "Haven't you heard about Randy's new lobster-buyer? The boys don't bring her roses, they sell their lobsters to her."

"That so? Randy used to toll 'em in with a drink on a cold day. What's she use?"

"Hope, I guess," said Nils.

"That boy looked more than hopeful. I never saw him so lit up. Shines like a glass bottle."

"Well, I guess she likes him as well as she likes anybody," said Joanna cautiously. "Of course she's only been there a couple of days."

"Come on, brother, let's go shoot some pool." Nils got up from the table. "I've been over and built a fire."

"All right." He sniffed the air. "Lingers a mite, doesn't it? He'd better not get downwind of his hockey buddies. Might shake 'em up some."

Joanna wasn't interested in television tonight, and when the kitchen was tidied she turned off the generator and left a small lamp burning for Nils on the kitchen table, and went upstairs. Rory had gone to the clubhouse with the men.

She read seed catalogs and made a list by lamplight, with a window slightly open on the side away from the wind. The southwest breeze had freshened, and poured through the spruces with a sound like the rote on the shore. It drowned out everything else, including the varied voices of generators. This was such a pleasure that she couldn't waste it, and put out the lamp and lay in the dark listening and thinking. She remembered how the wind and water had sounded when she stood in the meadow that afternoon, and wished that she and Nils could build a cabin down at Bull Cove where they would stay summers. They could find a spring somewhere; there was always fresh water trickling over the rocks. The nights would be quiet except for the sea just beyond the doorstep, or the wind in the trees like tonight, and the sunrises would fill the cabin. The only difficulty would be that it was such a long way to the harbor and his boat. Young Jamie Bennett, who with his wife Pleasance had set up housekeeping in a cabin at Bull Cove in 1827, hadn't any such inconveniences. He could beach his wherry at high tide and never mind the breakers.

They'd moved across from Brigport, and at first they'd been all alone on what was then known as South Brigport, or the South Island. For her and Nils to be alone at Bull Cove would be like living on a separate island from all the others. She knew with one side of her mind that the cabin at Bull Cove would probably never happen, yet the trips she and Nils had taken had once seemed hazy, romantic impossibilities. They had seen Sweden and Norway, they had seen the Devonshire coast from which Jamie Bennett's family had come. So why not a cabin at Bull Cove? He could have the dory on a haul-off, with an outboard, for running around to the harbor. She had lived all her life on this island, in three houses, but had never yet had the sea at her doorstep.

It hadn't taken young Jamie long to start calling it Bennett's Island. There was a photograph of him taken in his prime by a Limerock photographer just after the Civil War ended; a handsome man in his late sixties, king of his island and looking it. He had lived a long, energetic life. Her father could just remember him down on the harbor beach looking over the cod the hired fishermen brought to the splitting tables; at ninety, his brown hair not gone all white yet, he was saying to a gaunt boy from Bucksport, "Give me that knife, son, and I'll show you how to dress out a codfish."

Her thoughts moved drowsily from old Jamie to young Jamie, *that* young Jamie and her young Jamie and thence to Nils and herself drinking in their morning coffee on the rocks of Bull Cove on one of those perfect June Sunday mornings. Wild rugosa roses, eider ducklings—

She heard low voices downstairs and realized the men were back and having something to eat. After a little while the voices stopped, and Nils was coming quietly into the room. "I'm awake," she said. "You didn't play very lor

"Guess what." He undressed in the dark.

"You had a visit."

"They came up to play their records and dance. They had the house to themselves, and so they had to come up to the clubhouse."

Still bemused by the cabin, she could be kindly. "Well, in all fairness, there's that good dance floor, and it's Saturday night, and they're young."

"I suppose so." He got into bed and they moved together. "Some of those convulsions they were going through up there looked as if they were trying to shake the baby loose."

"They might even believe it was possible. They call it Dracula."

"Poor little tyke, might be better for him if he doesn't make it." He hugged her to him, kissed her, and yawned.

"Did you leave them up there? With a *lamp?*"

"They're jumping up and down by the light of my five-cell flashlight. Cheaper to replace the batteries than the clubhouse. Hugo's back, by the way, but not our son."

"I wonder what he's doing."

"Worried about him?" Nils asked.

"No! I'd just like to see him with Bronwen, being a sovereign person, not his father's and mother's child, Ellen's kid brother or Linnie's older one."

"We might be surprised."

"I don't know. I hate to admit it, but he doesn't seem to manage very well with girls. I think Rosa appreciates him, but she's not looking at anybody yet and I don't know when she will."

"Or else she'll pick out the same kind as Con Fleming."

"Some neat little man you can wear on a charm bracelet." She groaned. "What a waste. The Cons dazzle and the Jamies are lost in the glare . . . He did take Bronwen for a long walk last night," she added hopefully. "They sat on the cemetery wall and looked at the stars. Didn't talk much, he said."

"Maybe that means action."

"Being prejudiced, I don't think the Brigport Boys stand a

chance beside the Bennett Islanders. Being objective, I know that Hugo's one of the dazzlers, and Jamie could be lost in the glare again."

"Well, he was pretty optimistic tonight, going by the looks and the scent of him." Nils gathered her to him. "Nothing like having the house to ourselves, is there?"

5

*F*ebruary went out with one long shriek, the worst blow of the winter, prophesied by a ring around the moon and Jupiter within the ring. It began as a northerly and shifted in the night to the northwest. The long seas plunged past the southern end of Brigport, buried the breakwater, and smashed their way straight into the harbor. The boats fought, bucked, and reared at the ends of their mooring chains, while the spray flew off the crests like blowing smoke and froze on the decks and washboards. There were clear skies and a paralyzing cold that worked through every layer of clothing and the flesh and then burrowed into the bones. At Brigport, the harbor being in the lee, there was little to worry about, while at Bennett's, though the moorings held, everybody expected something to give way because the boats had become so heavy with ice.

There had been a full moon and an abnormally high tide at midnight, and when the wind came off northwesterly the seas swept the wharves clean up to the fishhouses. Traps went, ballasted or not; coils of rope, buoys, laths, oilcans, a wheelbarrow, crates, tubs, barrels—everything that had been left outside, considered safe, joined the monstrous mess bobbing in the rockweedy surge. Terence Campion's bait shed was washed off the end of his wharf. Skiffs filled and lost their oars, if they hadn't been tucked under the middle seats. Linnie's dory, tied at the top of the beach by the Sorensen fishhouse, had been roughly thrown about, but her lines held.

As soon as the chaos was discovered at first light, the

clean-up began. Many of the wives and all the older children turned out to work with the men, but the screaming wind and the cold made it a long and wretched job. All that the seas had thrown over the beaches, into the road and the marsh, was hard enough to clear of freezing rockweed, but then there was everything that had washed in under the wharves, the loose laths and the tangles of warp; buoys, crate covers, oars.

One worked till hands and feet were numb, warmed up in a fishhouse or a kitchen, changed gloves, and went out again. On the surface the islanders were philosophic. They were used to this kind of violence. They knew they would ache come nightfall—they ached now—with all the dragging and the pulling and the unsnarling, all the trips up and down the slippery beach and over the ledges, all the carrying. But at least they would have saved a good deal. It would be a while before the seas flattened out enough for them to go out and look for their traps, but at this time of year the pots were in deep water, safe from being smashed against the rocks. Instead, they could be dragged across the uneven bottom by the force of the water, sometimes for a mile or more, and wherever there was a canyon or a "deep hole" they could disappear into it. If the warps weren't long enough, the buoys would never show again.

The men made the usual jokes about savings on income tax, but there was an ache to get out there and *look*, an ache as genuine as the one in their backs and legs and hands. The wind died down, surf no longer buried the breakwater, but it still roared ashore along the west side, and roiled and hissed and glittered all the way to the mainland. Then gradually it let go and began to flatten, and one morning they woke up to an almost-quiet. Jamie went out with his father, expecting a long day of searching for buoys and shifting heavy wet four-headers back to where they were supposed to be.

Suddenly, what with the new silence and the boats gone out, the place felt like a deserted village to Joanna. She knew the children were over there in the schoolhouse, she knew other women were getting their washes onto the lines, but she felt somehow left high and dry, like a trap tossed halfway across the marsh and left there unclaimed. She'd worked hard on the salvage and now she was in no mood to be relegated to home and washing.

She went down to the wharf on the off chance that there might be something she could do around there. If not, she'd go over on the west side to see if anything new had come in. The older children had been going there after school everyday to salvage anything worth using, but today she'd be ahead of them.

Rosa had *Sea Star* at the end of her wharf, with the engine running. "I thought you'd gone out too," Joanna said. "I couldn't see her from my kitchen window. "

"Nope, I'm late this morning. I must've overslept because it was so quiet all of a sudden." She started down the ladder and Joanna, while liking her, fiercely resented her possession of her own boat and her own person.

Halfway down the ladder Rosa stopped. "Come on with me! Four eyes are better than two to spot buoys if mine haven't all been carried to Spain."

"Girl, you just let me take Rory home and get my jacket," Joanna said jubilantly. "Anybody who tries to stop me will get mohaggled." She expected Phoebe to be waiting for her on the doorstep; the girl hadn't had her nose outside during the bitter winds. But she wasn't there, and the radio was blasting away in Dave's kitchen at the volume usual in his absence.

The Nova Scotia boat was beamy and comfortable, seeming to find her own easiest way between and across the swells. Joanna enjoyed watching Rosa aboard *Sea Star;* she was like the boat, big but not burdensome, leisurely but not sluggish. *My twin,* she sometimes called the boat, not entirely joking. She'd been sloppily overweight a year ago, and Con Fleming had left her so raw, and she had tried so hard to hide it, that her self-consciousness had hurt Joanna just to see it. Her gray eyes had often been red-rimmed and set in a wide, defiantly stupid stare like a wall behind which she could disappear. Now, with the scar of Con Fleming dealt with, or at least

protectively scabbed over, she was no longer a compulsive
eater, but hard and flat of belly and bottom; she might have
still been given to long thoughtful stares at times, but usually
the gray eyes showed humor and an ingenuous friendliness.
She was a handsome, healthy, self-possessed young woman.

Now, as she helped wherever she could with handling pots,
Joanna tried to imagine her and Jamie working together, understanding each other perfectly without words, one indi-
visible unit. It was all too easy, and she forced herself to
relinquish the picture before she could become addicted to it.

The weather was still cold, but without the wind the sun
was warm, and the distances had a hazy, tender blue. The two
women didn't talk much. It was enough for them to be on the
water. Rosa found one string of hers nearly intact, about a
half-mile southeast of where the traps were supposed to be,
but there were lobsters in all of them. She hauled and baited
them and carried them back. In two other places she found
only a few of her buoys, and they cruised around looking for
more. In the Rock Channel they saw Owen's *White Lady* and
Rob Dinsmore's boat together as the men worked to undo
a snarl where some of their gear had dragged together. The
men glanced around and waved briefly.

Rosa pointed at the broad stern of Rob's boat, where the
name was lettered in an artistic arch. "Isn't that the best damn
name for a lobsterman you ever saw?" she demanded.

The name was *Beautiful Dreamer.*

When they got back to the harbor, Joanna was ready to go
home and make housewifely motions. Sometimes she thought
that being out in a boat was as satisfactory in its own way
as making love.

The men put in a long day, and when they came up to the
house in the late afternoon they walked as if their boots
were made of iron. Phoebe came in on their heels.

"Where's Daddy?" she demanded imperiously.

Jamie ignored her. Nils, getting his boots off in the sun
parlor, said, "He'll be right along. They've had a lot of lug-

ging and looking all day today." Phoebe leaned against the wall and looked sulky. On his way to wash up Nils put his hand on her shoulder. "Come on, dear, sit down and have a mug-up with us. Mince pie right out of the oven."

"I hate mince pie."

"Elegant manners the kid's got," Jamie said to his plate. Phoebe narrowed her eyes murderously at him, but appealed to Nils with plaintive sweetness.

"Freddy's working his guts out for that mean little twenty percent. Uncle Nils, he's so tired at night he can't see straight. I don't think it's *fair!*"

"Twenty percent of a season's average is a good chunk of money."

"But he isn't getting *anything* right now. Anything that *matters!*"

Nils said nothing. It was a waste of time to answer Phoebe sometimes. Joanna pushed the mail across the table to him and he tore the wrapper off *The National Fisherman.*

"I have my baby to think of," Phoebe wailed. Jamie's head came up.

"Then why don't you just think about it and keep still? Knit a few booties. Hem a few didies. First thing you know you'll be tipping your old man into an early grave, and then who'll take care of your baby?"

"Freddy could make a good living if he just had the chance!"

"Ayuh? Way I heard it, his kid brother's doing a staving business this winter, musseling with that boat and outboard Freddy couldn't bother to salvage. When the kid isn't clamming, that is, at ten dollars a hod."

Her face reddened and contorted, the helpless struggle for a retort was cruelly visible. Jamie added a final twist. "He's even bought himself a new Honda."

"Where do you get all this dirt, anyway?" she cried. "From Bronwen Jenkins? Well, I suppose she could've made out with half of Port George, she's done it everywhere else!" she jeered.

"But I didn't know you ever took time to *talk*. That must be when you get tired of all her other talents!"

Jamie looked imperturbably at her. Her voice thickening with sobs, she shouted, "I bet she knows a lot of different ways to do it!"

She ran out. "Who'll get me first for making Baby cry?" Jamie asked. "Uncle Dave, or Tight-arse-and-pull-up?"

"Neither," said his father. "They're too tired, Freddy's even lost his Gee-zuss. But don't pick on her."

"She asks for it."

"Ignore her. She's too young for you to bother with."

"She's a brat, Jamie, but that's all she is," Joanna cautioned him. "She's really only about ten. Try to remember that."

He raised his eyebrows and lifted spread hands in a gesture of innocence, looking ridiculously like his Uncle Owen. "What did I do in the first place except tell her to shut up? That's a privilege of seniority. She's lucky I didn't wash her mouth out with soap and water." He grinned at his mother. "Anyway, Ma, it ought to keep her out of your doughdish for a while."

"I'm not sure of that, and don't call me Ma."

Nils stood up. "Come on, let's get those traps off before the tide goes." On his way past her he patted her shoulder and said, "Good pie, Ma." He kissed her before she could speak.

"Is that any way to carry on in front of this pure young dog?" Jamie asked.

"You speaking for yourself or Rory?" said his father.

Joanna watched them go, followed by the dog. They walked alike, held their heads and swung their arms the same way. In a houseful of blonds she had never felt a stranger; it was a special private delight to her that Nils's children were as fair as their father.

After supper that night Jamie went to Brigport for the first time since they'd started clearing the storm damage. He dressed for the occasion, but he would be carrying his rubber boots and work clothes aboard the boat in case he stayed the night with the MacKenzies. Joanna gave him a dozen eggs to make up partly for all the breakfasts he ate over there.

"Don't you think I ever kick in toward the grub?" he asked in exasperation.

"Never mind, tell Hannah it's a present from your mother."

"All right. Thanks," he added as an afterthought.

"Look out, you might dislocate your jaw some time speaking up so recklessly," Nils said from behind his paper.

"Well, at least I said it, didn't I?" Jamie asked. "I can't help it if I'm moderate."

A little while later, when they were deciding whether they wanted to watch television or to read in bed, Hugo came in with Tommy Wiley, Owen's young helper.

"Where's the big man?" he asked.

"Gone to Brigport. Why not you?" Joanna asked.

"The ice is going, so I've got nothing to do over there, seeing as I didn't get the new girl. I'm glad one of us from Bennett's got her, but I wish it was me."

"Come on now, you always get the girls," Nils said. "How about sharing the wealth?"

Hugo leaned in the kitchen doorway looking both nonchalant and decorative. Tommy gazed at him from under his hair with näive admiration. "You're right," Hugo said generously, "old Jim needs the experience. The Navy didn't do a thing for him that way, you know ... We're going up to Ralph's. Rosa's coming along like a hill of beans with the banjo."

He left with Tommy faithfully at heel. When from the dining room windows they could see the flashlights bobbing across the dark field by the windbreak, Joanna said softly, "So Jamie's really got a girl. I hope she appreciates him."

"It didn't take her long to make up her mind. It's that snow-covered Alp business, remember?" He yawned. "I'm too tired to stay up. You want to go out, Rory?" He stood in the doorway while Rory nosed around the front dooryard, and Joanna came up behind and put her arms around him. They leaned comfortably and sleepily together. Dave's lights shone through bare rose bushes, the Big Dipper hung immense over Brigport.

"But I hope it's more than the blue eyes and the mysterious silences, and that smile like yours that he doesn't flash around too often," she said. "I want her to think he's special because he hasn't a scrap of guile, and he wouldn't know how to pretend. He never compromises, and he meets all opposition head on, but in spite of that he can be loveable if you give him half a chance—"

"It doesn't smell like winter anymore," Nils said. "Not like spring, either. We should be like the Lapps, and have eight seasons. We do anyway, come to think of it."

"Aren't you listening to me?" She squeezed him around the ribs. "All right, I talk too much. But listen, I'm not marrying him off and trying to decide what I'll wear to the wedding, honest."

"*Good*," said Nils. "Now let's go to bed."

6

*J*oanna and her brother Philip's wife, Liza, took a walk down to the Eastern End one afternoon and had coffee with Steve's wife. The day was springlike, with glittering aquamarine distances, a smell of earth, and cries of crows and gulls above the brown fields and unusually tranquil coves. A day without wind was rare enough to be hoarded, not thrown away in a rush. They walked home slowly through the woods, unwilling for the long afternoon to finish. When they came through the Eastern End gate to Hillside, they went out onto Windward Point, where they could look down into Schoolhouse Cove and see Owen's *White Lady* at the wharf below them. He and Tommy were landing trap stock; the lobster smack had brought out a load today. The last few bundles were piled on the wharf as the women descended the steep path by the workshop, and went out on the weather-worn planks.

"*Good* afternoon, sisters mine," said Owen. "Finest kind of a day, isn't it?"

"We'll pay for it," said Tommy, mightily hefting a bundle of laths onto the wheelbarrow.

"Hark to the Ancient Mariner," said Owen. "Leave 'em be, Tom. You and Richard can wrassle all that stuff under cover by and by. How'd you like to take her around to the harbor and put her on the mooring?"

"Ye*sir!*" Tommy sprinted happily across the wharf and aboard the boat. Owen cast off the lines while the boy started the engine, then stood with his hands on his hips watching while *White Lady* cautiously backed away from the spilings and turned and headed out around Windward Point. Tommy looked back and waved; they could see his smile.

"You've made his day," said Joanna.

"Yep. Have a seat." He waved at a dry lobster crate, and he sat down on another one. Joanna tried not to look too intently at him, but he didn't seem to be out of breath. "Tommy's a good boy," he said. "Willing little cuss, and handy as a pocket in a shirt. If it wasn't for him and Richard doing most of my trap-building, I'd be sure as hell tempted to go in for wire."

"They say there's a lot of advantages," said Joanna.

"Ayuh, they *say*." He shrugged. "Richard wants to try a string this summer. We'll see how they go. What are you thinking, Liza Jane? That's a mighty long, thoughtful look. You ever get homesick for New York?"

"No! Even though it's getting toward my favorite time of the year there. I'm thinking a long thought about long hair. If Tommy were blond he'd look like Veronica Lake. Remember her?"

"Oh, God, yes! ... One of these days Tommy's going to start wearing it in pigtails or I'll take the sheep shears to him, before he scalps himself aboard the boat. The hauling gear's likely to make a snatch at him."

"He does keep it nice and clean, though," Joanna said.

"Brushes and combs like the Lorelei. I never saw anything like it. I don't miss the girls forever washing their hair, not with Tommy keeping himself beautiful. But he's a decent young one, he could be doing a lot worse than fussing about his hair. He doesn't ask to go over to Brigport and hang around, and I wouldn't let him go anyway. So when he goes in to see his folks it's like a trip to New York for him, except it's safer."

"And he always acts so glad to get back," said Joanna. "Comes up the wharf all one big grin. 'Hi, Mrs. Sorensen! Did I miss anything?'"

"He loves the island as much as any of us. Maybe more so

because he doesn't take it for granted, like the ones who were born to it. Of course—" he paused, and from decades of experience Joanna recognized the signals—"when he gets interested in *one* girl, instead of the whole bunch as a rare species of wildlife, it's hard telling what'll happen. These bashful ones can surprise the hell out of you."

"They certainly can," she agreed cordially, now sure of his drift.

"It's a big help to them, the way times have changed." He looked out to sea. "They don't have to make witty talk. They don't have to stand around first on one foot and then the other, waiting to give her a box of chocolates or a mess of short lobsters. Or *stockings*. Once, if you gave her a pair of silk stockings you could walk her home, with maybe a few extras."

"I didn't know you ever had to bribe women, Owen," Liza said innocently. "Not from what I've heard. I thought it was the other way around."

Joanna burst out laughing. Owen gave his sister-in-law the smile that had once made things very easy for him indeed, and probably still could, if he cared to make the effort. "Oh, I wouldn't say that," he said modestly. "It wasn't all that simple. You expected some preliminaries. God, that was half the fun, wasn't it? Now it's: 'Hello, my name's So-and-so,' and it's into the sack and away we go." He began to sing, " 'Row, row, row your boat, gently down the stream—' "

"I'm keeping very quiet," said Liza, "because Sam's only fourteen, but every day he's that much older."

"So is Richard," said Joanna distinctly, and Owen stopped singing. "You know Richard, Owen's son? Next year he goes away to high school. He's already handsome and outgoing."

"A chip off the old block," said Liza.

"Only better-looking and with a lot more charm than his father had at fourteen, believe me. And times have changed. Little fourteen-year-old girls don't stand around waiting for the ice cream cones and the offers to carry their books. Some of them are even taking their mother's pills. Now *there's* an advantage, because then Brother Owen wouldn't have to worry about—"

"All right, shut *up*, damn it!" Owen shouted at her.

"If you've been trying to gowel me about Jamie, you're wasting your breath. Nils and I aren't so innocent as to believe we've got a twenty-five-year-old virgin for a son. He makes his own living, pays his own way at home, and lives his own life. Whatever he does at Brigport, as long as it's not criminal, is no business of ours. I don't know about it, and I don't *care*."

"You can't prove that," he challenged her.

"I don't have to. You can't prove otherwise."

"You mean to tell me, the way you were brought up and the way you brought those kids up, that you're not losing sleep about his bedding down with that girl?"

"First," she said composedly, "I don't know if he *is*, and you don't know either. And second, you sound as if you're so jealous you can't stand it."

"I *am* jealous, damn it." He was half-laughing. "I'd like to be twenty-five again, the way things are today."

"I thought you just said you didn't want any woman handing herself over without a conquest first."

"We're not talking about me, we're talking about *you*. Can you look me in the eye and tell me you don't care about your son spending his nights with a girl you don't know?"

"Would it make it any better if it was a girl I did know? I can look you in the eye—I'm doing it right now—and I'm telling you that he's living his life now, and I'm living mine, with Nils."

"And you don't care," he persisted.

"Why is that so important to you? If I worry about any of them, it's Linnie because she *wants* to be in love, she's *ready* to be in love, and she could really be hurt. I was married when I was her age, but she seems so damn' young to me. Maybe I seemed that young to Mother and Father, but I didn't *feel* it."

"She probably doesn't feel it either," said Liza.

Owen sat in silence, looking down at the wharf planks between his feet. "Listen, honeybunch," she said. "I don't really believe that Richard's going to be seduced the first week of high school."

"The next week," he said morosely.

"Holly'll be there to keep an eye on him."

"Good God, *Holly!* Talk about *Linnie* being in love with love!"

"They're Laurie's kids as well as yours, remember," she said unkindly. "That should give them some ballast. If you're lucky maybe they'll be like Jamie and wait till they're twenty-five to cut loose."

"Thanks."

"I think you've ruined his day," said Liza.

"He brought it on himself."

"I think I'll go home to my wife," said Owen, getting up. "She fell in love with me because she thought I was wonderful, and she still does."

"He said modestly," said Joanna. The three walked back along Windward Point together. Owen was very quiet and dignified. "Sorry if I riled you," he said to Joanna.

"I wasn't in the least riled."

"Your cheeks got pretty red. Your voice rose."

"Oh, shut up!" she said. "Go tend to your fan club." They separated, laughing; they could annoy each other, they could jab on purpose, but never hold a grudge afterward. As the middle two in a family of six, they had always had a special closeness, which had been all belligerence once but had grown out of that as they had grown, witnessing each other's agonies.

"I don't know what that conversation on the wharf did for you two," Liza said, "but if it's all the same with you, let's leave off the *O tempera, O mores!* bit. I'd like to think cozily of Sam being only fourteen and wanting a horse."

"Are you getting him one?"

Well, seeing as he'll be going to high school next year—oh dear God, there we go again. Let's really forget it! I've not had him all his fourteen years, you know. Only four of them. I'll probably be a perfectly hellish mother the first time he looks at another female, even if it's not until he's thirty-five."

They laughed, but Joanna said, "No, you won't be that kind. You're not half so clutching as you could be."

"Give Philip credit. He flattens me when hysteria threatens. Ah, look at them," she murmured as they came in sight and sound of the afternoon ball game in the well field. Tommy had joined it and was running bases with his hair streaming out behind him and Tiger charging at his heels, Rory barking, and everyone yelling.

"They're all safe right now," Liza said. "While we're looking at them, they're *safe*."

Joanna didn't get a chance to talk privately to Nils until they went to bed that night. Jamie had called him aboard the boat and said he wouldn't be home to supper, but it was one of those evenings when someone kept dropping in. Nora and Matthew Fennell came down across the field, Vanessa Barton walked around the harbor to borrow something to read, Charles Bennett had an errand at his fishhouse and stopped in.

They got to bed finally, and she said, "Owen began plaguing me today about Jamie."

"What about Jamie?" he asked drowsily.

"Oh, this love affair. *Supposed* love affair. He thought I was going to get all defensive and mother-henny. I told him that whatever the story was, it's Jamie's business."

"Is that what you really think?"

"In public, yes," she said. "In private—I don't know. What do you think?"

"Don't tell me you want me to make up your mind for you."

"No, I just want your honest opinion."

"I don't have any opinion," he said, "because for all we know they may be spending their evenings reading aloud.

He can read to her from *The National Fisherman* about last year's herring catch, and she can improve his mind with James Russell Lowell." He hugged her close to him. "You feel as good in your birthday suit as you ever did."

"So do you. But Nils, listen, it's close on to twelve, and in that apartment in Fowlers' building your son is probably in bed with Bronwen Jenkins. So what do you think about it?"

"Well, they've got a nice evening for it—I don't know, Jo. I don't like the whole picture nowadays, but Jamie's a part of the times and he's a self-supporting adult. I suppose I'd be disgusted and ashamed if he'd been bounding from bed to bed like a sandflea since he was fifteen. But I know he's been pretty lonely sometimes. So how can I come on like the ghost of Grampa and say *Thou shalt not?*"

"They don't take time to find out if they're in love," she complained.

"Let's not talk about it now, huh? Or even think about it. If there's one place in this house where the kids aren't allowed, it's their parents' bedroom. After they're born, of course. Before that we couldn't do much about it."

"You know what?" said Joanna. "For a man of few words, you talk an awful lot."

7

*J*amie didn't come home again until late the next day, after hauling. He baited up, changed his clothes, and left again. He was good-natured and uncommunicative. He did not come home that night, and apparently went out to haul from Brigport the next morning.

"Leave the kids to their play," Nils said, "as long as they leave us to ours." She laughed, but after he left she found she was spending too much time feeling apprehensive and angry for no clear-cut reason. The sensations concerned Jamie and Bron, but she couldn't be sure what they meant. Am I *jealous?* she wondered in dismay. Am I turning out to be *that* kind of mother? It was like discovering the symptoms of something fatal.

It was time to get out of the house. She put up a lunch and went out the back way with Rory. She locked the house, a regrettable necessity these days with Phoebe living next door. It was an open-and-shut day, dazzlingly bright one moment, the water all a blinding sparkle, and then clouds blew over, black enough to spit snow. She and the dog crossed the meadow to Goose Cove, and went over the rocks as far as Bull Cove. As children, generations of Bennetts had searched the woods above the cove, prying up boulders or just digging at random, always in hope of discovering some traces of Jamie Bennett's cabin. He and Pleasance must have been exceptionally tidy, because none of their descendants ever found anything they'd thrown out or left behind at Bull Cove when they moved to the newly built Homestead.

Joanna poked around now, and entertained herself by laying out a floorplan for her and Nils. She and Rory shared lunch and then went farther along the rocks toward Sou'west Point. Out here she was free of everything but herself. She took the sense of freedom home with her, amiably disposed toward everyone and especially generous toward Jamie. She wanted only for the girl to be as much in love as he was; otherwise that fine bloom he was wearing these days would go as fast as mist on a windowpane.

She could hear the afternoon ball game before she came out around the barn. Rory tried to make up his mind whether to go and join it or take his elderly bones into the house. He finally went off toward the noise at a dignified pace, but with his tail alert. She crossed the yard with an escort of hens, who all tried to crowd through the back door with her. The house was unlocked, and Jamie was in the kitchen, brooding over the teakettle on the stove as if willing the water to boil.

"Hello!" she said cheerfully, putting her satchel on the counter and beginning to unpack it. "Enough water in there for me too?"

He made one of his ambiguous sounds, which in this case she took for *yes*. "What a day I've had," she said. "I didn't bring home half the shore, it just looks that way. And the stuff I had to leave behind—it kills me. Time was when I'd have brought all I could lug and more, and that would kill me too." She went over to the sink to rinse out her thermos bottle, telling him about the shattered plywood dory she'd seen. Turning around to better describe it to him, she got the first glimpse of his face.

His mouth was swollen, there was a scrape on his nose, both cheekbones were puffy and blackening, and one cheek had a cut.

"Good Lord! What happened to you?"

"Would you believe slamming my face into a wharf?" He had to speak from the side of his mouth. His eyes were cold and wary.

"No," she said. "Who hit you?"

He turned away from her and reached for the canister of teabags. While he was working the tight lid off, she saw his knuckles. He put a teabag in a mug, and dangled another one until she took a mug off the shelf and held it out to him. He carried the mugs to the table and came back for the boiling teakettle, all in this silence of hostile resignation. Resignation because he couldn't escape her questions, hostile because he didn't want to answer them. Then you shouldn't have come home, my boy, she thought. The earlier vague anger came back, strengthened to rage. She felt it in her stomach, seeing the marks on his face and hands.

She said, "You've been in a fight. About what?"

"Nothing much."

"Some of the boys resent you being with Bron, and ganged up on you. Is that it?"

He didn't deny it. "Only a few of them. Enough for me to handle all right. Bron got in a few licks with a piece of stove wood." He couldn't smile very well, but the cold went out of his eyes. "Then somebody heard the row and called the constable, and Randy came charging down to protect his property, and they took off. But I could have managed them." It wasn't boastful, it was a simple statement of fact. She thought, Well, at least I had my day on the shore before I had to find this out.

"Where's Bron now?"

"She went in on the smack today."

"Did she quit?" She hoped so, no matter what Jamie felt for her.

"Not *her!* She didn't go in to bellyache to the old man, either. She had business. She'll fly out tomorrow."

"So in the meantime we're honored with your company," she said. If it sounded spiteful she really didn't care. She had a wild energy, as if she wanted—no, *had* to shout at him, strike out in all directions; she was doing well to keep her voice down, spiteful or not.

"You'd better take out your teabag," he said gently. She did so; her hand was not trembling, though it felt shaky.

"Who were they?" she asked, keeping her eye on the mug.

"It doesn't signify. They won't bother me again."

"I don't believe that," she said, "as long as they think you're poaching . . . Did you loosen any teeth?" He shook his head.

"Didn't your face hurt while you were hauling? And your hands?"

"Some." He moved his shoulders slightly. "It's not so bad now."

"You haven't been at the MacKenzies all these nights, have you? And don't shrug at me," she added. "I know now why that used to drive my father and mother crazy. Jamie, I don't like this situation, and I'm pretty sure your father doesn't." The mention of Nils seemed to bring him into the room, helping her to slow herself down.

Jamie's grimace was necessarily one-sided. "He made that clear when he came alongside this morning, with a few well-chosen words like, 'You could have had your skull bashed in or your throat cut.'"

"Well, you could have. I've heard about these accidents. Jamie, you've never in your life had trouble over there, except when you used to squabble with the MacKenzies."

He half-grinned, then winced. "The green apple wars."

"Jamie, are you in love with Bronwen?" He set down the mug and gave her a steady look over his bruised cheekbones. It was neither sheepish nor defiant.

"If you're not," she said, "then you're helping yourself to something just because it's there, with no responsibility. Just taking."

"What's the matter with that?" He sounded honestly puzzled.

"How does Bron feel about it?"

"She's responsible for herself. I'm responsible for me. The trouble with you, Marm," he explained with infuriating tolerance, "is that you can't imagine going to bed with a man you weren't in love with and married to, and all blessed by a preacher. Times have changed. You and the old man might as well be a century apart from me."

"Thanks," she said sarcastically. "And don't call your father 'the old man.' "

"Sorry. But nowadays people can admit it's possible just to have a lot of fun without thinking 'this has to be the one I've been saving myself for.' "

"Well, back in my dark ages they had fun like that too. A good roll in the hay has always been a good roll in the hay. Times haven't changed that much, and people haven't. It's still possible to victimize, and to be a victim."

He sipped more tea. "And which am I?"

"I don't know. Your father and I would like to think that our son wasn't taking advantage of some girl who happened to be in love with him, or think she was." And vice versa, she thought, but I'll never offer that insulting suggestion.

"I didn't seduce her, if that's what you mean."

"I didn't mean that." She couldn't imagine his seducing anyone, but she could see him being seduced. "I just want to remind you that nobody gets anything for nothing, and sooner or later something has to be paid. Maybe the beating is just the first installment."

"The wages of sin?" There was that ghostly but annoying resemblance to Owen again, as if he were making fun of her in the same way Owen had.

"The wages for human behavior," she said, stung both by his irony and the likeness. "You'd better be pretty sure you know what Bron thinks before this goes much further. What she *really* thinks. She may be hoping for more than you know."

"That scare you, Marm?"

"I wouldn't want to see either of you badly hurt, and I don't mean something like last night, though that could have turned out a lot worse, as your father said. I'll tell you, Jamie, if you two were in love and wanted to get married—fine."

"Marriage is for somebody who wants to start a family. Marm, neither of us wants to make a commitment, as they say. We're free and clear, with no strings. What's wrong with that? We meet halfway, as equals. We know what the risks are, and we can walk away with nobody hurt."

"You're just a little too smug, my boy. You'll excuse me for being skeptical. However—it's no skin off my nose, but it's quite a bit off yours already."

He had to laugh at that, even though it obviously hurt, and she was able to laugh with him. The depth of her relief after her first reactions surprised her. She felt a return—almost—of the sense of freedom that had buoyed her up for most of the day; an expansive lightness and airiness because the situation was no longer secret with either of them.

"Anything else I can help you with today, Marm?" he asked.

"Now that you've set me straight, you mean? Kindly brought me up to date, educated me, and so forth? Yes. You can tell me what you're going to say to Linnie when she finds out about this."

That knocked away the complacency. He said belligerently, "She's nineteen, she's going to college, she's not ignorant!"

"I know all that. But no matter what other people do, it's what goes on inside the family that counts. She still cares about what we think and do. You're her older brother."

"Why should I have to be an example for her, when the first time she thinks she's in love it'll be away all boats? It wouldn't matter a hoot in hell what I'd been doing or not doing! Back when she was seventeen, for God's sake, if Edwin Webster hadn't been a man of principle—"

"Oh, you admit that now, do you? You used to think he was a sex fiend."

"Well, I was pretty numb myself in those days."

"Let's think about *now*." She made fresh tea for herself, and sneaked a glance out the window toward Dave's to be sure Phoebe wasn't on the way. There were times when a private and uninterrupted conversation in this house was impossible.

"I've got to bait up," Jamie said warningly behind her.

"I've heard that before. It always comes in handy." She returned to the table. "Jamie, just think of Linnie for a minute," she said reasonably. "You said, 'the first time she thinks she's in love.' Would you rather have her go to bed with a man for love, thinking he's in love too, or for fun, because she's hunting and choosing as an equal partner?"

This time his wince wasn't for hot tea or a raw lip, and he quickly suppressed it, but she had seen it. She pretended she hadn't. "I can see a couple of kids the same age being swept into this thing," she went on. "I know what it's like, Jamie, believe me. I haven't forgotten. But she's meeting a lot of older men. Once sophistication used to mean starting to smoke, taking your first drink. You had to do it, even if you hated the taste of tobacco and liquor, and never kept it up afterward. Nowadays it's something else."

He set his mug down so hard the tea slopped. "I'll talk to her. I'll tell her that when she's earning her own living she can live her own life. Until then, it's your rules. And in the meantime if I find out she's diddling with anybody I'll break both their necks. How's that?"

"Jamie, for heaven's sake! I don't want you doing your parents' chores for them! That's for me or your father to tell her, except for the last part. I don't think we'll say *that*. All I want you to do is think about what you're going to answer when she says, 'You're doing it, so why shouldn't I?' "

"That's what I'm going to say! Besides, I'm a man. So it's different."

"Oh, the triple standard!" She began to laugh, and the color came up under his skin and darkened his cheekbones even more. "One for you, another one for Bron, and still another one for your kid sister. Hey, I think we're going backward instead of forward."

"Dammit," he said furiously, "it *is* different for your kid sister. It *should* be!"

"What if Bron's somebody's kid sister?"

He shoved back his chair and got up. He was going through the door to the sun parlor when she said, "Jamie." He stopped and waited, without looking around.

"Promise me one thing," she said.

"*What?*"

"That the minute you see Linnie next week you don't grab her by the shoulders and say, 'Are you going to bed with some cheap son of a bitch?'"

His head ducked forward, he made a sound between a choke and a sneeze, and then looked around at her, trying not to laugh, trying to hold onto his belligerence and the comforting heat of self-justification.

"Serve you right if I did."

8

The day the two college students were due home for their March break, the weather was showery and breezy, but not enough to keep the men in. Everyone went out except Steve, who walked up from the Eastern End to collect a new propeller sent out on the mailboat. The children were in school, and the only women waiting in the store were those who lived close by.

Joanna leaned against the counter by the cash register hearing, without listening to, the conversations around her. Mark and Steve were in the back room looking for rubber boots in Steve's size. Behind the post office window, Mark's wife padlocked the mailbags. Steve's Argo lay behind the stove, adding a robust tang of wet dog to that of the fire. Louis, the store cat, sat immense and pontifical on the counter, studying Argo. Water sloshed and gurgled around the spilings under the building, and sometimes a brief hard shower beat on the low roof, and hit the windows like handfuls of gravel.

Joanna was still uneasy about Linnie. She wasn't sure if she was doing her child an injustice or trying to keep herself from being caught out as an unsuspecting fool. Maybe it came down to a simple matter of being prepared for the worst while hoping for the best; then you could try to decide what "the worst" was, and this led you back to the starting line again, and the theory that the middle years of humankind would be a lot happier if, like the rest of the animal kingdom, you ceased to recognize family ties as soon as the young were able to feed themselves and learn the basic facts of self-survival.

Of course there was a simpler alternative. You could learn how to be less of a worrier, and more of a fatalist. *For this is wisdom; to love, to live,/To take what Fate, or the Gods, may give.* It was a great motto for survival as long as you didn't remember too clearly the rest of the verse, and Linnie reading it aloud to her last summer after discovering *India's Love Lyrics* on Laurie's poetry shelf.

The door opened and Phoebe came in, wearing a pink slicker and sou'wester. She smiled shyly around at everyone.

"What are you doing out in *sneakers?*" Maggie Dinsmore scolded her. "And not even socks!"

"I never thought." Phoebe's manner was earnest-small-girl.

"Well, you should think for the baby's sake, if not for your own."

"Poor little Buster," said Phoebe tenderly, patting her belly. Marjorie Percy winked at Joanna, who said, "Whatever became of Dracula?"

"*What,* Aunt Jo? *Who?*"

"I think I heard the whistle." Joanna went out. Phoebe was saying, "It's either Frederick David or Tamara Kim. We can hardly wait! Our own little baby!"

Joanna shut the door firmly and said a short dirty word, which she saved for moments like this and never used in any-one else's hearing. She walked down through the long shed to the open wharf. The water splashed noisily below, and the skiffs bounced at the moorings. The gulls picked around on the shore and ledges left exposed by the tide. Her exasperation with Phoebe had disappeared in the shed, and now the nibbling anxiety about Linnie vanished. She became her-self in the purest sense; it was like slipping back into her own skin. The transition was familiar to her, yet always shook her with the joyous astonishment of return. And it never lasted long enough.

The sky brightened as if the sun suddenly shone through

opalescent glass, the gulls turned pure white, wet roofs blindingly reflected the light. *Clarice Hall* whistled outside Eastern Harbor Point and came rolling through the tide-rip. She had radar and other amenities, but conservatives on both islands swore that she wasn't half the boat old *Ella Vye* had been; she'd pitch and wallow in seas that wouldn't give a dory a rough ride. And the boy would wear her out in a couple of years. The same things had been said about *Ella Vye* when thirty or so years ago she'd replaced another boat.

Mark and Steve came down through the shed with the others trailing behind them. Link maneuvered the seventy-foot *Clarice* into place across the outer end of the wharf, the men secured the lines, and the girls climbed the ladder. Joss, Owen's daughter, had brought along a midwestern friend who had visited before. They departed rapidly for Mark's house, or for a discreet clump of spruces on the way to it.

Linnie came up, talking over her shoulder to the deckhand and engineer, who were one. "I'm going to get you for that, Duke," she threatened. "I may just take a course in diesel engines and get your job away from you."

"I'd pay for it, just to see the day when you've got a load of passengers who didn't make it to the rail, and missed the bucket. That cabin won't remind you of no garden of lay-locks."

"I'll have things a little better arranged than you have, my man!"

Grinning, he took the tarpaulin off the cartons piled on the forward hatch. Linnie and Joanna hugged each other, Linnie greeted everyone else, and by that time her bag had come up, and she and her mother went home to lunch.

"What are you getting Duke for this time?" Joanna asked.

"Oh, you know Duke. He can't figure out what a girl wants to study mathematics for. He says I'll never get a man that way, they'll all think I'm too smart. And *I* said, 'What makes you think that's my big aim in life, to get a man,' and *he* said, 'That is what wimmen are born for, Miss Lady,' and *I* said, 'Well let me just put a flea in your ear, *Sir!*' And we were off. And you know what he said to me just before I went up the ladder?" She stopped in the path. "With this face like a wet week, and this real sorrowful tone he said, 'I never knew you was one of those Wimmen's Libbers, after the way you was raised.' As if I'd turned into a prostitute."

They both laughed and went on toward the house. "I've half-a-mind to try that diesel business, just to see his jaw drop when I show up to work," Linnie said. "Not that Link would give me Duke's job or that I'd want to take it from him, but maybe I could be an extra hand some summer."

"Holding the buckets," her mother suggested.

"Yuck," said Linnie. "That's what it would be. He'd never let me near that engine of his. It's his child. Talk about sublimation!"

After an extended reunion with Rory she ate a large lunch, talking about campus affairs and personalities and the most recent demonstration. Roger Forrester was conspicuous by his absence, as in her letters. Afterward she went to her room for a nap and Joanna went back to the store for groceries and mail. Mark and Helmi were alone in the quiet of early afternoon, and she had some coffee with them. The weather cleared entirely while she was there, and when she got back to the house there was a note against the sugar bowl, saying that Linnie and Rory had gone for a walk.

It was what they all did whenever they came back to the island, as if to prove to themselves that it was still there.

Joanna saw Phoebe starting out and watched to see her go down past Philip's and turn right, which meant she'd be going around to the far side of the harbor to Kate Campion's. Sure of having the house to herself for a while, she mixed and baked a batch of the thin crisp molasses cookies both children liked. Linnie came in the back door just as her mother was taking the last sheet out of the oven. At the same time Jamie came in the front way, and she hugged him with all her might. For years he'd been fighting off her ardent strangleholds, but today he returned the embrace and she was so astonished that she stood off without being shoved, and stared at him.

"You've been practicing!" she accused him. "So it's true, all that stuff I heard on the boat!"

"Tell me about it," he invited. "I'd like to know what's going on in my life." He took a warm cookie.

"You've muckled onto the lobster-buyer, and half the men on Brigport are feather-white about it. Some of them tried to beat you up." She narrowed her eyes, nodded her head. "Yup, I can see the traces."

Jamie leaned against the counter eating his cookie.

"Look at him!" Linnie appealed to her mother. "Talk about *conceited!* Boy, he must think he's something on a stick. Young Lochinvar come out of the west, and so forth."

Jamie took another cookie and headed for the door. "Hey, *Lillebror*," Linnie called after him. "Joss and I are going to throw a big party at the clubhouse, a real old island time for everybody, kids and all. So keep it in mind, huh? We brought back some new records, and—"

"Records, hell!" Jamie came back. "We'll have some real music. I've been promising Bron. When are we having this swahray?"

"Tomorrow night?" Linnie sounded uncertain, as if Jamie's metamorphosis were a little overwhelming.

"Finest kind," he said blandly. "Weather's supposed to be good for the next couple of days. Full moon too. You'd better round up your music today." He went out, starting to whistle before he was through the door.

" 'Haste to the Wedding,' " said Linnie. "Does that tell us anything?"

"Not the way he's talking," said Joanna. Linnie moved to where she could watch him go down to the shore.

"I don't believe this," she said reverently. "Boy, do I want to get a look at *her!*"

"Oh, he's blossomed," her mother said dryly.

"Aren't you happy for him?" Linnie came back and took a cookie.

"Yes—at least I suppose so. But when you've been a parent this long you know it's never safe to say, 'Well, this is it, and isn't it nice!' "

"Didn't you feel that way about Ellen and Robert? I was crazy about him."

"But you were only ten. When Ellen wrote and told us she was going to marry him, your father and I weren't very happy. We thought the world of Robert, but he was too old for her."

Linnie was dimmed. She put down her half-eaten cookie and said in distress, "I never knew that."

"You weren't supposed to."

"Well, did Ellen know how you and Father felt?"

"No, and if you ever blat it, I'll keelhaul you. I'm only telling you now because you're old enough to realize that we don't automatically turn off our concern about our kids when they come of age. Even though I sometimes think it would be an ideal answer." She smiled at Linnie. "Don't look so worried, honey. We were wrong about Robert, and Ellen was right. The doubt went long ago. Ellen knew what she was doing."

"Ellen always knew," Linnie said glumly. "I'll bet she never made a real mistake in her life."

"I'll bet she *did*. She's not perfect, love."

"If she did, she made them when she was living away from home, so she could cover them up."

Joanna felt a disagreeable bunching-up in her midriff. "I suppose that's the best way to plan your mistakes," she said lightly.

"Did you ever make any?" It came out probably louder and bolder than intended, propelled by a supreme effort of courage.

"Oh, Lord!" Joanna looked devoutly at the ceiling. "Don't remind me!"

"Terrible ones?" the girl persisted, in the habit of bravery now.

"They seemed terrible to me at the time, but I managed to

survive them, outgrow them, whatever you want to call it. It happens to most people."

"Well, that's a hope," Linnie said gloomily. She went to stand at the harbor window, a silenced and shadowy figure against the late-afternoon brightness outside. Joanna began to put cooled cookies in the crock, waiting for something; another question, an answer to her own unspoken one, anything. It was there, she was sure of it. It had been with them right along.

A few years ago she could have put her arm around Linnie and said casually, "What's on your mind?" and got an answer. But now the sense of armed, or at least walled, boundaries was strongly with her. The long fair hair that she used to braid, or periodically cut because of the spruce pitch tangles, was a woman's hair now, and the droop of shoulders and tilt of head was not that of a discouraged or worried child who could be quickly reassured.

Suddenly Linnie said, "Father's coming in! I'm going down to meet him, and then I'll see about the music."

She grabbed a handful of cookies on the way. "I hope he's bringing in some lobsters!" she called back. The door slammed. She ran across the dooryard, her hair blowing back in the wind, shouting "Hi, Freddy!" as she went around him and left him gazing after her with delighted astonishment. He came on up the path grinning, and went into the house happily shaking his head.

"You and me both, Freddy," Joanna said aloud. "What *you* need, Joanna, is a good cup of coffee." Nils would be wanting some anyway. She made a fresh pot, and sat down with hers as soon as it was ready. She put her feet on another chair and ate three cookies, and reflected that if an eider duck could think, what an immense relief must be hers when the ducklings grew too big for the blackback gulls to pick off and were beginning to exercise their wings. No need to say in time, "You're on your own, kids." They knew it, and never came back with drooping heads and shadowy eyes, wanting the comfort of Mama and Papa without the advice.

9

They had a supper of warm boiled lobster, with salad and hot biscuits on the side. Jamie ate with them. He and Linnie talked about the party while their parents listened in bemused silence. He left for Brigport while they were still sitting over their coffee, and had probably gotten no farther than the gate when Linnie whispered loudly, "And he isn't even *gormy* about it! He acts as if he's been doing this all his life!"

"Doing what?" Nils asked.

"Spending his nights where he's spending them," she said in a normal voice. "Not with the MacKenzies." She gave him a cautious sidewise look, testing the weather. Nils was amiable.

"Where'd you hear that?"

"On the boat, of course. Where else?"

"You and Duke must have had a high old time when you weren't fighting about rights for women," said Joanna.

"Duke knows everything that's going on," Linnie bragged.

"And a lot that isn't," said Nils. "How'd he start out? 'I surmise'? That's his new one-dollar word."

Linnie giggled. "Nothing so fancy. He said, 'Seems like your brother's playing house with the new lobster buyer.' Well, if I hadn't known it was a girl, that would have shaken me up some. But I was shaken up anyway. Jamie not only going steady, but moving in with her! I just can't get over it. Can *you?*"

"We don't seem to have any choice," her father said.

"I think you're both being just great not to throw fits all

over the place and act as if he's going to hell in a handbasket. Because, after all, he's doing the sensible thing."

Nils poured more coffee. "Well, don't get any ideas. Concentrate on picketing buildings. Or better still, on your schoolwork."

Linnie decided not to take the subject further.

The girls spent the next morning in their home kitchens, baking pans of brownies and other confections. There were also volunteer contributions from other sources. The Dinsmore children were sent around to be sure that everyone knew about the party. In the afternoon Joss and Gracie came over from Hillside, and went with Linnie to the clubhouse, where they filled the lamps, swept the dance floor, and got the small kitchen ready for making coffee and fruit punch. The day was chilly with prospects of freezing that night, so at suppertime Nils built a fire in the big old potbellied clubhouse stove.

The children began to collect up there before dark. When Joanna and Nils crossed the field, the moon was rising over the woods, a perfect cosmic orange suspended in azure light by a supernatural cord. In the lane they met up with Philip and Liza, and Dave. Violin music came dancing down toward them, as Ralph Percy warmed up in "The Devil's Dream." It could very well have been the dream of all of them; island children had heard the tune from the time they were in their parents' laps, and even when they were not yet born, but present.

Joanna's reaction was always the same. First the instinctive response that had made her drum her feet on her highchair footrest when her father whistled jigs and reels for her; then for the growing child there had been the almost unbearable excitement of the whole long day preceding a dance night. And then, much later, the music became the killing stab. It hadn't killed, but for a long time she'd expected it would.

Tonight as they came in sight of the lighted windows and open doorway where the music came tumbling out, she put her hand through Nils's arm, and he pressed it hard against his side until she could feel the ribs and body warmth under his sportcoat. *He knew.*

Philip knew too, beneath the jokes with Rob Dinsmore and Foss Campion on the porch. Dave, silent, knew too. Yet should time suddenly reverse in some terrifying way, the scene appearing through the lighted doorway would be different for each of them.

For her, it would be Alec who was playing "The Devil's Dream." It was true that the drowned ones were always with you. If it weren't Alec's long brown head tipped over the fiddle, Fort Percy's thick freckled hand would be making the bow dance, instead of his younger brother Ralph's. If you narrowed your eyes and looked through a blurring screen of lash it could be Young Charles swinging Gracie in the Portland Fancy, and not his brother Hugo. And if Young Charles and Fort were there, old Gregg's clarinet should be singing a duet with the violin.

The jolt of *déjà vu* lasted only for a moment and, as always, she recovered quickly from it.

"What are we waiting for?" Nils said in her ear. She turned her head and met his eyes. The creases were deeper around them, but they hadn't changed. There was no lurch of dislocated time here. She tossed her coat onto the nearest bench and took her place opposite him at the end of the line.

Eventually everyone on the island had come. Small children skimmed around the edge of the dance floor like minnows in a tide pool, or perched on the benches, temporarily hypnotized by the dancing and the music. Almost everyone was dressed up for the occasion. Phoebe was all in pink and white like a birthday cake, and she must have spent half the afternoon washing her own and Freddy's hair, and styling his curls. He looked like half a dance team until he actually danced, when he displayed his particular style of fumble-footed enthusiasm.

Jamie and Bronwen had arrived sometime during the first waltz. Joanna didn't see them come in; suddenly they were among the dancers. Jamie looked stern but he danced as competently as if he'd been doing it ever since he could walk. Bron wore a yellow-flowered dirndl, and her hair was held back from her face by a wide yellow ribbon. She seemed to be moving in a trance of happiness; whether it was because she was in Jamie's arms, or loving the homemade music, Joanna couldn't guess.

Hugo was playing the accordion for the waltz, with Rosa playing the banjo. The dancers went round and round the hall like skaters to the old tunes, the later ones, and the new waltzes the musicians had been learning. The two Campion families were on the floor, with Foss piloting Helen like a tugboat managing a liner. The Fennells, the Dinsmores, the Percys were all there. Dave, looking rejuvenated in the lamp-light and very pleased with himself, led Gracie with a debonair formality. Richard danced with his cousin Robin, Steve's daughter, the two of them deadly serious and Richard obviously counting. All the Bennett brothers were on the floor with their wives. Joss was helping young Sam to propel her around the course; he came only to her shoulder but was immensely proud just the same.

Linnie kept smiling broadly at Jamie and Bron past Tommy Wiley's hair, but she couldn't get Jamie's eye. At the end of the dance she pounced, and he was trapped into introducing the girls. Linnie took Bron by the hand and brought her across to Joanna and Nils. Jamie looked after them, shrugged, and went outside with Matt Fennell.

Bron was shorter than Linnie, who gazed down at her with doting pride as if at an adorable toddler. "Here she is," she announced. "Nobody told me how cute she was!"

"How did Duke happen to leave that out?" asked Joanna. "Hello, Bron. Come and sit down. Don't you look nice!"

"After my working clothes, you mean?"

Nils said, "Lobster-buyers never used to show up at the dances in petticoats. I don't know if those were the good old days after all. How are you doing over there, Bron?"

"Very well, I think. Randy's satisfied, anyway."

"Then that's what counts."

"Did you see my father and mother waltzing?" Linnie asked her. "All *she* needed was a train. You know how they hold them up fastened to one wrist, and I can't decide whether he should be in white tie and tails or one of those gorgeous uniforms."

Nils put a finger on her nose. "The secret of our happy marriage is that the waltz is the sexiest dance there is." He went off to play pool. Linnie said with appreciation, "He's always surprising me."

"It's plain to see we've got to look for good waltzers," Bron said. "I hope they aren't all taken."

"Jamie's terrific!" Linnie was still astonished by him. "And I don't know when he learned! You're the reason he's here, Bron. Usually he just plays pool, or stands out on the porch with the ones who pass the jug around, or they drink beer and throw the cans into the juniper, the slobs. Not that Jamie gets loaded," she added hastily. Bron grinned, and Linnie said with an envious sigh, "What dimples."

"Ignore them, will you? I used to be called Dottie Dimple, and I loathed it and the dimples too. And I still don't like being short. When I get to teaching I'm afraid my kids won't take me seriously."

"You look *perfect* with Jamie," Linnie assured her.

There was a crashing chord on the accordion that startled everybody to attention, and Hugo struck up "Here Comes the Bride." Darrell Robey from Brigport, all big nose, grin and deep blush, stood in the doorway with a girl hanging onto his arm with both hands. She looked at once terrified and delighted. They were being shoved from behind; there was a burst of ribald laughter from the porch, and Darrell, still grimacing and scarlet, kept saying, "Hey, knock it off, will ye?" The girl pushed her face against his shoulder. From inside the hall another group converged on them, and Hugo put down the accordion to join in.

"Is *Darrell* married?" Linnie asked incredulously. "Old

Bashful Darrell? Last year if I *spoke* to him he almost swallowed his adam's apple!"

"He's married all right," said Bron. "They came out this afternoon. They got married last week and went on a trip to Montreal. Pretty, isn't she?"

"She looks familiar." Linnie got up to see better.

"She's Eloise Paisley—"

"Oh, sure! She's an almost–Sea Goddess from last year's Lobster Festival."

"You make her sound as if he'd got her at a rummage sale," said Joanna.

"She got *him*, if you ask me," said Linnie cynically. "Well, I'm a hostess so I'd better go say something. But I can tell already what she's like. Poor Darrell!" She left them.

Hugo had been the first to kiss the bride and now they were all doing it, spinning her around, twirling her from one man to another while Darrell was anchored in one place by heavy-handed congratulations. The bride was squealing happily.

Jamie was nowhere to be seen. "He's standing outside, sneering," Joanna said to Bron. "You'll see that a couple of his uncles are kissing the bride, but none of that nonsense for young Sorensen."

"His uncles have real charm," said Bron, "but Jamie's got the most."

"I always thought so. After his father, of course."

A man cut away from the confusion and headed toward them. "That's Ivor Riddell," said Bron. "Doesn't he sound like a Thomas Hardy hero?"

"Yes, and I like his seadog whiskers."

"Grampa calls them grass about the bows ... Gives him a dite more chin than he's really got. Riddells mostly come to a point."

Riddell bore down on them. He wasn't tall but he looked to be tough and wiry, his cheekbones sharp. His brown beard and hair were thick and well-groomed. He wore a blazer over a green turtleneck jersey, which made his eyes very green, tartan slacks, boat moccasins. "Behold the gentleman lobster-man," said Bron. "He baits not, neither does he plug. He merely steers the boat, and picks off the herring scales with tweezers, one by one."

"Behold the lady lobster-buyer," Riddell said. "If you dressed like that on the car, Bron, especially on windy days, the Riddells would never get a lobster from Brigport."

"I'm doing all right in my jeans and boots. After all, I wouldn't want to really hurt *your* company. You've got to pay for that fancy boat and the Bar Harbor-type residence you're building on Pirate."

"It's just an ordinary little cottage to put my family in this summer," he protested to Joanna. "And believe me, I know lobstering from the bait butt *up*. I had my first traps out when I was knee-high to a scupper. But this one's always had her ax out for me." He patted Bron's head. "If I were younger or she older, our grandfathers might have married us off to each other to form an empire, or tried to, and the thought of it still gives me nightmares. I wake up thanking God for Angie and that wedding ring." He held up his hand to show it. "You have to be the Bennett sister," he said more seriously.

"I am. Joanna Sorensen now."

"I know your husband, and most of your brothers. And your son, at least in passing. And that pretty blonde girl—"

"My daughter Linnea," said Joanna.

"I'll have to apologize to her for crashing the party. I came out from the mainland this morning to check on the work at Pirate, and bring the men some supplies, and the newlyweds rode out with me. Well, they've had no peace over there all day, as you can imagine. Tonight I invited them and the gang out for a moonlight sail, hoping to quiet things down so the kids can get some time to themselves when we get back. And one of the boys said there was a dance here tonight. I didn't realize it was a private party."

"Not that private," said Joanna. "It's just an island get-together. You're all welcome."

"It's nice of you to say so. You know," he said soberly, "I feel something deeply personal for both those youngsters. I've always known the Robeys, and Eloise used to be our baby sitter."

Hugo was going back to his accordion, Ralph to his fiddle, and Linnie shouted over the confusion, "Choose your partners for March and Circle!"

"Hey, she's got good lungs as well as pretty hair," said Ivor admiringly.

The bride and groom were shoved into position as the first couple. Darrell's blush looked like a permanent red varnish, his grin fixed and anguished. His wife was pleased with all the attention and seemed not to notice his misery. She was long-legged, very slender and graceful, with flying dark hair and curly bangs above a narrow, delicate, laughing face.

Good Lord, Joanna thought with delayed shock. *Darrell.* How had he ever caught her? He hadn't finished high school because he couldn't stand it on the mainland; he was as wild and shy as a gull or a seal. He was a good hockey player, but Joanna had never seen him on a dance floor until now. Like Jamie, he'd always preferred to look on.

"Dance with me, Bron?" Ivor pulled Bron up into line behind the bridal pair, displacing another couple who protested but had to give way. Tommy Wiley came to Joanna, but before he could speak Richard took a slide down the hall, caromed into Tommy, and grabbed Joanna's hand.

"Hey, come on, Aunt Jo!"

"Just a minute." From nowhere, seemingly, Owen's big hand came down on his son's shoulder. "You're getting above yourself. You ask a lady for a dance, you don't gaffle onto her like a caveman."

"Heck, Aunt Jo doesn't need all that fancy stuff."

Owen turned him away. "Come on over here and cool down your impetuosity."

Tommy, trying not to grin, asked for the dance and was accepted. As she took her place she saw Jamie in the doorway, scanning the scene as if he were looking for a missing pot buoy in a choppy sea. Spotting Bron with Ivor, he disappeared again. Dave led out Phoebe, and Freddy went off happily to a group of Brigport teenagers who didn't know the dance and were noisily occupying a corner. Just as the music started Joanna had a glimpse of his hand resting familiarly on the small of the nearest female back.

Vanessa and Barry Barton formed a set with Joanna and Tommy. It was a long dance, and when it was over Joanna sat down with Van, and Barry went off to the pool room. Their three-year-old daughter slept heavily in young Cindy Campion's lap, thumb in her mouth. "Thanks, Cindy," Van said, taking the child into her own lap. "I'll do as much for you someday."

Cindy was flaxen-fair and snub-nosed like her Finnish mother. "That's a long time off," she said. "I'm not going to get married till I do a lot of other things first."

"Good for you," said Van. Cindy left to get a drink of punch. "I hope she remembers that," Van said. "Kids have a choice now. I never thought I did. But I was some ignorant. I didn't know beans."

She was better-looking than she used to be when she first came to the island, a tall, gaunt, resentful-young woman in an old raincoat. Joanna had finally established contact with her through books; if it could be called contact, that tenuous, safe conversation about favorite writers. People had been sorry for Barry, who was hard-working and good-natured, because there were days and days when Van never got up, or else she went off early in the morning and stayed all day. But whenever Joanna met her face to face, her pity for Barry would disappear under the shock of meeting those strange yellow-gray eyes. This woman was in torment.

There had been times when the sight of someone running or a knock on the door after dark would be like a fist driven hard against Joanna's belly. *Vanessa is dead*, the messenger would say. *She is drowned*. Or, *She has shot herself*.

Of course it hadn't happened and probably never would, because of the child asleep in its mother's lap. Van's expression now, though remote, was not haunted. The child had the same thick ginger-colored hair and yellow-gray eyes, and when she was awake she was as charmingly alert as a little fox. When Van had been that age, she was already an abandoned child; it must have been worth the universe to her to hold this one in her arms as she could not remember being held by her own mother.

"I didn't know beans," she could say now, indulgently, as if there had been nothing so very terrible in her life. Well, Joanna knew what it was to outlive a nightmare.

The next dance was another waltz, and Owen came to Joanna. "I've lost my wife to the Crown Prince of Riddell," he said. "Come on, Jo."

"You ask a lady for a dance, remember? ... I'm resting after the last dance. That Tommy swings like a demon, and Ivor's almost as bad. Take Van. Give me the baby, Van."

Owen didn't speak. He stood looking down at Vanessa without any discernible expression, and Van looked up at him as if her brain had gone blank and her face matched it. There was a tightening at the back of Joanna's scalp, as if the ghost of those old bad premonitions were touching her there. She almost said bluntly, "Don't you two *speak?*" But she stopped in time.

"I've got to take Anne home," Vanessa said quietly. "Any minute now she'll wake up howling." He made a small stiff inclination of the head, his dark face wooden, and then he walked away. He went toward the door, but then changed his course and headed for Rosa. He said something that made her laugh, and they began to dance. He didn't look in Vanessa's direction again. She spoke to a passing child.

"Will you tell Barry I want to take Anne home now?"

She used to knit trapheads for Owen when she first came,

maybe they'd had some disagreement about that. Or maybe Owen just didn't like her, though he'd never mentioned it in Joanna's hearing. Maybe he thought she bullied Barry. Or, Joanna reflected with amusement, she was indifferent to his charm and he couldn't understand it.

Nils came toward her saying, "Sounds like our kind of music." He held out his arms and she moved into them. "Good night, Van," she said over her shoulder. Van was startled by the sound of her name, as if she'd gone away while she was still sitting there. When Joanna saw her again, from across the hall, she and Barry were leaving. The child's head lay against her father's shoulder. He went out first, smiling, proud of his baby, saying goodnight to everyone nearby. Vanessa paused in the doorway for an instant and looked back, but at what or at whom among the dancers, you couldn't tell.

Then she was gone.

The party went on in the old style, contredanses alternating with waltzes. The records would come out later, when most of the older people had gone home. After an intermission with coffee and punch, there was a Liberty Waltz. Joanna started out with Dave, but after the first Grand Right and Left she was firmly embraced by Randy Fowler.

"What are *you* doing here?" she demanded.

"Is that any welcome to an old admirer? Well, I was owlin' around the harbor, and I thought I'd take a moonlight sail over to the South Island and join the party." He was stoutish now, double-chinned, a respectable husband and father, but his sparkle was unquenchable. "I was hoping I'd get the bride, but *this* is better. My God, Jo, time was when I'd be out of my mind with it. As 'tis, t'aint bad."

"I'm glad you brought your wife with you," she said severely.

"By gorry, try to get away without her! She's some jealous. Makes me feel real young and desirable. She watching me now?" He craned his neck.

"She doesn't know you exist. She's dancing with Charles."

"Ayuh, she always liked him. But supposing you and I was

to scoot quick out that door, she'd know it. Got eyes in the back of her head. What are you laughing about?"

"You and me scooting out like sixteen-year-olds."

"Listen, all the scooting out and jumping into the bushes isn't done by the kids these days, anymore than t'ever was. I can tell you things that'd make your hair curl. And speaking of that, your boy's doing all right for himself." Jamie was decorously circling the floor with Gracie, looking resignedly into space while Bron seemed to be enjoying Owen. "He snubbed up some of our fellers with a round turn," Randy said, "and they didn't take kindly to it."

"So I hear. I don't like it much."

"Oh, hell, it's just a few of them. One's way too old to be chasing after her, and he's married too. But he's grumbling around like he had a chance till Jamie showed up. And there's a couple of young ones who think he's poaching, but she'd never give 'em a look even if Jim warn't around. They aren't worth a you-know-what in the snow. Bright girl, that one. Schoolteacher."

"I like her," said Joanna. "I'd just like to think there won't be any more trouble."

"Oh, that. Mike and I took care of 'em. I'm not having my place stove up, and they know it."

But there are other ways, she thought. Some things never change. Randy went rambling on. "Whit Robey, the damn' fool, dragging his wing like some old rooster. He'd ought to be hanging by the gills somewhere to cool off. I told him he was a disgrace. That young girl ain't going to look at him, if he was the last man on earth!"

"All join hands!" Owen sang out. Randy gave her a burlesque-soulful look and a squeeze around the ribs before he released her. "There!" he said. "At last I did it."

10

*J*oanna and Nils left the party at the end of the Liberty Waltz, and took a walk down to the harbor. Away from the clubhouse, with the insulation of spruces between them and the music, they entered as if into another dimension the immense white silence of the night. There was a flood tide shining at the tops of the beaches and shifting restlessly about the wharves' planking. The boats seemed to float unnaturally high, above the water instead of on it. The breakwater beacon was a feeble spark and the stars were dimmed almost out of existence by the intensity of light.

"No power plants," Joanna whispered. "Remember when it was always like this?"

With their arms linked, they went around the shore as far as the big anchor half-sunk in the corner of the marsh above the beach, and crossed the marsh to where the schoolhouse stood small, white, and solitary, its face to the moon. They went up on the seawall and contemplated the twinkling tide that filled the arc of Schoolhouse Cove, and watched the glittering rush of the swells breaking on the outer ledges. The buildings of Hillside gleamed against the black hill away to their left. South of the cove, the Bennett Homestead showed whitened gables against a pallid sky.

As it always did, the moon made a mystery out of the familiar. The dance they had just left, the clubhouse and everyone in and around it including their own children, could have been nonexistent except in dreamlike memories of another world. Or as dreams themselves, perhaps. Nils kept Joanna's arm through his, pressed against his side, anchoring her securely. His bare head was white in the moonlight, like the roofs and the rocks. She wondered what he was thinking, and if she were as much of a mystery to him.

A dog began to bark up at the Homestead; Charles and Mateel were just getting home. The dog quieted quickly and Joanna imagined the shaggy little mongrel terrier rushing in happily ahead of her family. Light appeared in the kitchen windows, fiery gold.

Without speaking, they went back across the schoolyard past the stark shadow of the swings. The bell glinted secretively in the belfry. It always had, for Joanna, the waiting, attentive silence of something alive.

Back at the harbor the Binnacle was lighted now, the Dinsmores were home. A group came down past the well; Owen and Laurie, Philip and Liza, Steve and Phillippa. Richard, Sam, and Robin were chasing round and round the field, tripping each other up. They wanted to go for a walk while their parents stopped at the Sorensens'.

"No borrowing a skiff to go rowing, understand?" said Owen. "You've got years ahead for that. And don't go making a racket where people have gone to bed. And no rampsing out on Fern Cliff."

"I was going to say something," said Philip mildly, "but you got it all said first. Mind yourself, Sam. I want you back at the house in an hour."

"Yessir!"

"I suppose we should say something to our daughter," Phillipa said to Steve. "So she won't feel left out."

"Hell, I was including her," said Owen, making a snatch at Robin's nose. She dodged, chuckling, no longer the dignified waltzer. She had the black Bennett hair and her mother's gray eyes, full of moonlight now. The three ran toward the shore, leaping after their shadows with ecstatic energy.

A lamp burned in Dave's kitchen and they could see him

reading at the table. Owen went over and knocked on the window. "Turn out the watch below!" he shouted. "All hands on deck!"

"Aren't you ever going to grow up and *shut* up?" Dave shouted back.

"Not while I can breathe. I only left the dance because they started playing those goddammed records. Randy Fowler was moaning about how he used to be able to dance all night and go to haul before sunup. He says, 'Ain't it hell to grow old?' I told him to speak for himself, I'm not growing old and I wouldn't admit it if I thought it."

"Who you trying to convince?" asked Dave.

"Come on over to the house, Dave," Nils called.

"I'm dryer than a cork leg," Owen said. "And no sense asking these two for any of the hard stuff, they only dole it out if you drown yourself or witness an ax murder. So we'll have to settle for coffee."

"One thing, it'll be better than what the kids boiled up tonight," said Philip. "My spoon stood right up straight in it. I'd swear they learned how in a lumber camp."

"I'll be over as soon as I blow out my lamp," Dave said.

As the others settled down in the dining room, Steve said happily, "We've drunk a good many cups of coffee around this table."

"Don't start sounding like an old codger," said Owen. "We can do without the nostalgia."

"I saw you spinning the bride around," said Joanna.

"So did I," said his wife.

"Oh, she's just a paper dolly," said Owen. "For my money there's a hell of a lot more to Bron. I hope Jamie doesn't let her get away."

"She's done something to him," said Liza. "I got him in the Liberty Waltz and he was practically suave."

"Well, he's willing to fight for her, we all know that," said Philip.

"Let's hope he doesn't have to tonight, with all those

lamps," Joanna said, making a joke of it for the rest of them. Alec's death had begun in foolishness, innocent enough, but there was liquor involved. It could come like that, suddenly, innocently, with no real harm intended—or with the intention hardly realized and then afterward the defiant triumph, *Well, the son of a bitch had it coming.*

"They've probably blown out all the lamps by now," Steve was saying.

"If it was any warmer, half that gang would be out in the bushes," Owen said. "I should've told those kids not to go back to the clubhouse. God knows what they could trip over besides empty vodka bottles."

The children were back almost on the hour, and the evening broke up. In bed Joanna told Nils what Randy had said. He was amused about Whit Robey, and told her not to worry about the others. "We can't keep our hand over him every minute. He's out of his own territory and he's got to keep his wits about him, that's all. Might be they've had enough, anyway."

"I'm not being one of these overprotective mothers, I *hope*," she said indignantly.

"I know you aren't," he gentled her, and gradually they fell asleep in the moonlit room.

The early morning was cold, fair, and quiet except for the gulls and crows, and the sounds of engines warming up. The tide pools among the dark buffalo-humped rocks reflected the sky's subtle shift from coral toward blue. When Joanna walked back to the house, one song sparrow was singing in the spirea bush outside Dave's front door. From inside came the frantic thumps and exclamations that meant Freddy was getting up in a hurry. Without glancing in, she imagined Dave grimly eating his breakfast while the war went on overhead.

Linnie was scrambling eggs and frying bacon. Her hair was in two braids, and she looked leggier than usual in her old lined jeans and deck boots. Her much-darned khaki wool turtleneck was a World War II relic picked up at a Brigport rummage sale one year, and cherished ever since.

"Jamie's coming back to take me out to haul with him," she said. "Isn't it unbelievable?"

"What is?" Joanna took a fresh cup of coffee and a warm doughnut to the table.

"His taking Bron home, and staying. Imagine us being so calm about it. Or *are* you calm? I can't tell about Father and I don't dare ask."

"You don't sound very calm yourself," said Joanna.

Linnie turned scrambled eggs onto her dish and ringed it with bacon. "I'm not! I've been excited ever since I got over being shocked. Because I *was*, at first. I guess that's the first natural reaction. I mean it's built into anybody like me, with my background and all, until I stop to think about it." She sat down at the table and contemplated her plate with appreciation. "Too bad to break up that composition, but I'm ruthless. Oh boy, I'm starved, and I had a big open lobster sandwich about one-thirty this morning, too. All by my loneys down here, by candlelight. No, Rory helped me." Rory pressed his chin harder on her knee.

"I just can't help wondering what kind of lover Jamie is," she said. "Terrific, probably."

Joanna said quickly, "Any fights last night?"

"Nope. Once they started plaguing Darrell. Everybody kept cutting in and getting her away from him, but when he began to get worked up, swallowing hard and looking as if he'd either burst into tears or go berserk, they cooled it. I think *she* was disappointed. I can't think why she ever married Darrell," she said candidly, "unless she's pregnant. He's a good kid, but she's used to a lot of action and attention. I guess his folks aren't very happy about it. Lad MacKenzie told me when he walked me home. He's a good kid, too, so I walked *him* down to the wharf, and saw all the Brigporters off." She sighed happily. "What a night! Full moon on Bennett's Island. Perfect, except—" She stopped.

"Except for what?" asked Joanna, bracing herself.

"There's something I have to tell you. I don't know if Uncle Dave'll complain or Phoebe'll come weeping and wailing. But I was terrible to her last night."

Joanna relaxed and said, "How terrible were you?"

"Awful!" said Linnie with enthusiasm. "She was so jealous of all the attention Eloise was getting, and Freddy was buzzing around that little Bradford twerp who ought to be named Lolita, so poor Phoebe had to do *something*. She was going on and on to me with the married-woman bit, as if she'd not only discovered marriage but invented it, and *then*—" Linnie put down her fork to give the moment its full dramatic due. "*Then* she said to me with that smarmy little smile, 'You must be really desperate sometimes, to be your age and have nobody.'"

"Oh, Lord!"

"So I said, 'Do you think, Phoebe Sorensen, that everybody's so desperate they have to scrounge around at fifteen to get somebody to marry them? Boy, *that's* desperation! That is The End, and not the Living End, either. A dead end, and you're stuck in it, kid. And you know it!'"

"And then what?" asked Joanna. Poor Dave had been sitting here enjoying himself; what had he met when he went home?

"Phoebe's eyes were out on sticks. She was sucking wind, trying to think fast, and while she was still speechless I said, 'And you'd better put a choke collar and leash on Freddy.' I said it good and loud but he never even heard it, he was so busy trying to make it with a fourteen-year-old who'll never reach the ninth grade without a baby under her arm. Anyway, Phoebe rushed out, bawling."

"She might have fallen down and hurt herself on the way home," Joanna said.

"She didn't. I went behind her, but she didn't know it. She boohooed and cussed all the way home. Such *words!*" She giggled. "She hates my effing guts, by the way."

"Oh, Linnie," Joanna said with a sigh. "I know she's a pest and a malicious one, too, but she's a lot younger than you are, and it's not her fault she was raised as a True Princess."

"Then it's time she found out she's not royalty. You know her and her tears. If they'd all been saved up and let loose together, it would be the second Flood."

There were times when Linnie was definitely more Bennett than Sorensen. "Anyway, it made my evening," she went on. "She didn't come back again, and Freddy never went home till the last gun was fired. He was in a frenzy amongst all the goodies. A moth driven mad by the flames."

"Maybe you should be sorry for them," said her mother. "Maybe you weren't too far wrong with your desperation speech. They could be frantic, both of them, underneath all that foolishness."

Linnie was quiet, her chin on her hand, the other hand caressing the dog's ears. She looked out across the brown field toward the spruces of the lane. "I wouldn't be surprised," she said at last. "But if she'd only keep her mouth shut. She asks for trouble."

"I know," Joanna agreed. "I start out with the best intentions to be a good aunt, and in about two minutes I want to spank her . . . *Do* you feel desperate, to be going on nineteen and have nobody?"

Still looking out the window, Linnie answered in the same neutral tone. "I felt a little desperate after I broke off with Roger."

"How did that happen, or shouldn't I ask?" Joanna hoped she sounded interested but not avid.

"Oh, it was that stupid weekend when I was going to work so hard with my skis!" She turned back to her plate, gave Rory a piece of bacon, and finished her scrambled eggs. Joanna felt that she was giving herself ways to keep busy while she talked, but that she wanted to talk. For herself, she didn't move a hand or shift an elbow, for fear of breaking some unseen filament of communication.

"And I'm such a numbhead, I thought he had the same idea.

At least consciously I thought so," she corrected herself. "Maybe I knew something different underneath, but wouldn't admit it to myself. But I had to admit it finally. He didn't lose any time making himself clear, and he's about as subtle as the stink of last year's bait." Her laughter was rueful and adult. "For about twenty-four hours I had a big war with myself, trying to keep from hurling myself at him and saying 'Take me, I'm yours!'" She stretched out her arms and dropped her head back. "But the fact that he'd picked up a new pupil in nothing flat was a big help to my will power. I howled myself to sleep, and when I woke up the Great Enlightenment had come in the night. I was free!" And she sounded jubilant.

"Marm, he had a line that was so ancient it was like an old piece of potwarp that's been caught around the foot of a spiling for about five years, and it's all gunk and slime, and frayed out. He told me he loved me, but if I didn't care enough about *him* to make the relationship total—those were his very words—he was deeply hurt and he couldn't see any future for us."

"On or off skis," Joanna suggested. Linnie smiled, but her cheekbones were flushed, and the rims of her ears. "In other words, if I didn't put out, he'd cut out. Well, I may be a naïve island kid, but I don't think any of us islanders are that naïve about the facts of life. And boy, was his technique rotten! I've had better propositions right around home."

"*Really?*" They both laughed.

"I think I was as mad about being considered gullible as I was hurt. Then, the next day, somebody asked me why I was hanging around the dorm instead of being out on the slopes with Superski—or Superstud as he probably prefers to be known—and I sort of shrugged, and after that I began hearing things. Well, Roger has but one aim in his life, and it's not his degree. It's to bed as many women as he can. Preferably virgins."

"Collecting maidenheads instead of scalps," said Joanna.

Linnie whooped. "I love that word! It's a lot nicer than hymen. Sounds poetical instead of clinical." She gazed thoughtfully at her mother. "Calling things by different names does make a difference. I can't call Bron Jamie's housekeeper, because it's her house, but I'll call her his mistress. It's like the difference between *Playboy* and Shakespeare."

So this far we have progressed, Joanna thought; to find out that Linnie is still blessedly Linnie, and that one could be thankful Jamie wasn't a dedicated collector of maidenheads. "Listen, what about your lunch?" she asked.

"Oh my gosh!" Linnie pushed away from the table, dislodging the dog's chin. "Sorry, Rory. What can I use for sandwiches? I finished up the lobster."

"There's cold pot roast, or canned corned beef—you always like that. Do you want doughnuts, filled cookies, or turnovers?"

"One of each, and we'd better put in extra for Jamie. Does Bron fill his dinner box or does he do it himself?"

"I haven't the slightest idea about his domestic arrangement." Joanna rinsed a thermos bottle with cold water.

"Marm, you're really being cool about this," Linnie said.
"I'm not so cool as I look."

"I know you and Father must have been stunned to have Jamie fall so hard, and then just move in with her, right in the face and eyes of everybody. My old square Jamie. He's always been such a Puritan." She opened the can of corned beef. "I wish Rosa would take him. But Bron's fun, and she's intelligent, and she probably won't get pregnant, or give him VD—"

"Now that is something I hadn't thought of. *Thank* you. Butter or mayonnaise?"

"Mayonnaise. Marm, you shouldn't have to think about VD," she said merrily. "Jamie's been in the Navy, and he should know the ropes. Hey, that's pretty good. Navy—ropes—" She slapped sandwiches together while her mother filled the thermos bottle with milk. "If Uncle Mark would give me a job on the car this summer, maybe I could toll in some Brigporters who couldn't make it with Bron." Joanna gave her a sidewise look and Linnie laughed. "There isn't one

I'd give a tumble, or let tumble me. I'm going to be very fussy about where I bestow my maidenhead."

"Your what?" Jamie was in the kitchen doorway, borne in on cold air, bulky in oilclothes. "Aren't you ready yet, for God's sake? You were in such a pucker to go, I thought you'd be down on the wharf waiting for me ... Got you a hake," he said to his mother. "Left it outside."

"Good morning, *Lillebror!*" Linnie kissed him. "I can just see the bloom, or should I say the blush of love—"

"There'll be a blush on your bottom if you don't get down aboard that boat just as tight as you can jump." He turned around and went out with a thump of rubber boots and stiff rustle of oilclothes. Linnie pulled on a long-tailed flannel shirt.

"Thanks for the hake," Joanna called after him. "Linnie, you can't talk about Phoebe not knowing when to keep her mouth shut."

"I know, I know." She collected kerchief, gloves, and hooded oil jacket, and took the lunchbox from Joanna. "Thanks, Marm. See you."

11

*J*oanna corned the hake in a kettle, to cook for supper that night, and went upstairs to tidy her and Nils's room. Linnie's room was in a state of inspired disorder, which was her own affair.

With the windows wide open, and a chilly but springlike breath coming in along with the gulls' voices, she wondered how it happened that she was the only one in the family left ashore on this fine day. But if she'd gone with Nils she'd never have had the talk with Linnie, which had been like finding Jamie safe in that February dusk. You could roll voluptuously in deliverance as in a meadow of summer grasses. Until next time, which at this moment of euphoria was never going to happen.

At least she could spend most of the day outdoors, and she had the whole island to choose from. But when she came in from tending the chickens, Phoebe was trundling a load of clothes across the yard on a wheelbarrow.

"Rory, let's escape," she said to the dog, but she still felt so good that she couldn't turn the girl away. She'd been letting her use the washing machine, but had made it clear that Phoebe should consult with her first about the most convenient time. It was obvious from Phoebe's expression this morning that she wasn't consulting anybody about anything. Sometimes I wish Linnie didn't have quite so much to say, Joanna thought. If I'd describe any of my children as mouthy, she's the one.

She went out to help lift the heavy basket. "Hello, Phoebe," she said cheerfully. "You're up early on a beautiful day."

"By the time Daddy and I get Freddy started, I might as well stay up. He was some groggy." She looked at her laundry basket with loathing. "I could care less about washing."

This expression always made Joanna want to say, "Oh, you mean you do care, and wish you didn't?" However she asked kindly, "Don't you feel well?"

Now comes the storm about Linnie, she thought. But Phoebe surprised her by blurting out, "I'd feel fine if I wasn't —if I wasn't—" she broke off and looked down at herself. "And I've got four lousy months go go! And *then* what?"

Oh, Phoebe Ann. You poor kid. "You'll love the baby when it's here," Joanna said. "And it ought to be a pretty one, if it looks the way you did. Freddy must have been a nice baby too."

Phoebe made a small grumpy sound and turned her head away. Her hair was tied up, and the back of her neck looked forlorn and childish.

"Well, let's get your wash started," Joanna said, "and then we'll have a mug-up. Did you eat any real breakfast this morning?"

"No," Phoebe said in a cracked little voice. She sniffled, and squeezed up wet eyes. Joanna felt like putting her arms around her. If I could always feel this way about the child I'd be a truly good person, she thought, but then Phoebe isn't always this appealing. Which would make no difference to a truly good person, I suppose.

She wasn't really ready for a mug-up, after two breakfasts, but she made some hot wheat cereal, with raisins, while Phoebe loaded the machine in the bathroom. If Phoebe refused it, she'd chill it and fry it for someone's breakfast tomorrow. Phoebe came out with pink nose and eyelids. Subdued and docile, she poured milk on the cereal and began to eat, while Joanna sipped a glass of her own cranberry juice and worked on a plan for her vegetable garden. Phoebe ate hungrily about halfway through her portion. Then she said into the silence, "I wish they hadn't made me marry him."

It brought Joanna to attention. She looked quizzically at the girl, who stared back at her, sulky and defiant. "Well, it's true. They *made* me. I wasn't in trouble, everybody knows that. This girl that was on the pill got extra for me, so that's how I kept out of trouble. I never got pregnant till I was three months married, and that's what makes me a good girl." The eyes of tear-washed blue were innocent of sarcasm. "I didn't *have* to get married," she insisted.

"But you wanted to, Phoebe," Joanna said. "It was the great love of the century. We all heard about it, we couldn't help hearing."

"I *thought* I wanted to," the girl said doggedly, "but how did I know what was good for me and what wasn't? When I walked out of the house they should have dragged me back."

"They couldn't tie you up or lock you in your room, you'd only have run away again."

"Then they should have kept dragging me back. When I shacked up with Freddy, Dad should've come after me if he had to haul me out by the hair. They were responsible for me, weren't they? So why'd they let me do it?"

"Oh, come on, Phoebe," Joanna said. "I've seen you in action when you were set on having your own way come hell or high water. There was no living with you."

"Okay, I admit it!" She nodded her head vigorously. "But whose fault is it? *Whose fault?*" she demanded. "Look, they despise Freddy. They despised him then! So why didn't they fight? No, they wanted to get rid of their rotten kid, *me*. That's what. They made me a rotten kid, and then when we had the fight and I rushed out of the house and found Freddy, I kept waiting for them to show up to get me. But they never did."

"You'd have fought them tooth and nail—"

"Never mind that! They were *supposed* to come!"

"Your sisters did."

"It wasn't any of their business! I'm not *their* kid."

"Well, didn't your parents hold off quite a while before

they signed the papers? Hoping you'd change your mind and come home and go back to school?"

"*Hoping*," she said in contempt. "Why didn't they do something besides hope? I was only fifteen, for Pete's sake! No, what they were hoping for was that I *wouldn't* change my mind. I was their honest-to-God juvenile delinquent and they could hardly wait to get rid of me."

Joanna wanted to make some sort of protest, but with a great effort she kept quiet and listened.

"Then they took over the wedding," Phoebe said grimly. "They could have told us to get married by a justice of the peace in his office—that's what Freddy's folks wanted. But *no*. Big deal. Have to ask this one and that one. Do it right. *Make* it right. Turn me back into a virgin overnight . . . You heard everything else, Aunt Jo; did you hear I backed off at the last minute? I got so nervous I was throwing up, and Freddy was scared I was pregnant." She grinned maliciously. "But Daddy told me that after all I'd put them through I was going up before that minister if he had to drag me up there by the scruff of the neck. Yes, dear sweet Dad. Aunt Jo, why couldn't he have got tough like that *before?*"

"I don't know, Phoebe," Joanna said.

"If Linnie'd done anything like that when she was fifteen, you and Uncle Nils wouldn't just let her go like that."

"I can't imagine it," Joanna admitted.

Phoebe went back to eating cereal. "Well, they may have thought they were getting rid of their rotten kid, but they've still got me. *And* Freddy. *And* dear little Dracula."

"*Poor* little Dracula is more like it," said Joanna.

She said passionately, "I *do* want it, most of the time! And you know I was always a very good sitter. My sisters trust me with *their* babies. Freddy wanted Dracula stopped when we found out, but I said, Never! I don't believe in abortion. And Freddy's never going to lay a hand on *this* baby! I hope it's not fussy at night, that's all. He hates to have his sleep disturbed."

Joanna felt a little sick. She couldn't really imagine Freddy battering a baby, but most child-beaters didn't look the part. Of course this could be just one of Phoebe's more dramatic touches... And Alice will be watching, she assured herself.

"Aunt Jo, do you think men really go for mathematical girls?" Phoebe was now asking, in a rapid return to her usual self. By the time she'd wheeled her wet laundry home to hang out, Joanna had to remind herself, as she'd reminded Linnie, that the girl was more to be pitied than blamed.

She and Rory finally left for their walk; out into the Homestead meadow, then off to the right and up through the old orchard in the woods to the cemetery. Clearing away the winter's harvest of broken limbs as she went, she followed an old trail up a steep rise through the spruces. It was cold in their shade, but the light southwest breeze sometimes tossed down to her a gust of resinous warmth, and she passed through patches and stipplings of strengthening sunlight.

Far overhead the gulls circled on the wind. She stayed in the woods, wandering from one familiar spot to another. A huge, solitary pudding stone on which she used to stand and shout, an ancient gray birch that had survived another winter and whose scaly and peeling bark she used to imagine as a dragon's hide. There was a prowlike outcropping of granite ledge, with a deep plunge below it, which had been a vessel at sometime or other for almost every child on the island who could imagine standing bravely on a pitching bowsprit to look for land ahead. There had once been a clear view of the shore from here, but the slope had filled in since she was small, so that the water sparkled between moving boughs, and broke heard but unseen on a stony beach.

Rory puttered contentedly around, finding fascinating scents even though there was nothing more than mice for four-footed wildlife in the island woods. They went down to the shore finally and she sat on an immense white-bleached timber rolled up by the winter flood tides to the top of the beach, and ate her bread and cheese and orange. Robins and sparrows picked in the rockweed, sea ducks rode the glinting swell offshore. The water splashed pleasantly around the rocks. She had sloughed off Phoebe's shoddy, depressing atmosphere long ago.

She went back around the shore by the rocks and up over the slope among juniper and bay to Mark's back door. No one was home. From the northern end of the house she could look down on the wharf; the lobster smack *Caroline Jenkins* was at the car, taking crates of lobsters aboard. Everybody was out to haul today, with only skiffs left on the moorings.

She went down the path and into the store, where Rory lay down behind the stove with a sigh. Helmi was keeping store, knitting a sweater for young Mark; she and Joanna talked placidly of complicated stitches and getting the gardens in. Sometimes, hearing such talk, Joanna felt like the woman in the nursery rhyme who didn't know herself and wondered if Helmi ever felt the same, remembering conversations in the past when the appearance of placidity was likely to be a frozen silence capping a potential explosion. They went from gardens to books, and when Linnie came in, they were both startled.

"For heaven's sake," said her mother. "What are you doing in this early? More trouble with the engine?"

"Nope. Everything's fine, but I got tired of it," she said airily. "I hitched a ride home with Barry. He was limping in with a warp in his wheel." Rory got up stiffly to meet her and she bent down to kiss his head. "Can I charge a couple of candy bars, Aunt Helmi?"

"Help yourself. *You* got tired of being aboard a boat?"

Linnie went around behind the counter. "Oh, it was getting boring out there. He wouldn't let me plug lobsters, and we disagreed on measuring a couple, and I couldn't put bait on to suit him either. You know how fussy he is." She slid open the candy case door and got her bars. "So I decided I'd rather work on my own gear than stand around watching him like a summer complaint. I can have the shop to myself right now too."

She wrote down her purchase on the pad on the counter,

and left. Joanna went out behind her and stopped her at the corner of the building. "Did you two have a fight?" she asked in a low voice.

"*No!*" The disclaimer came a little too fast.

"Come on, Linnie. I know all about it. Owen and I hardly spoke a peaceful word to each other until we were grown-up with families of our own."

"Moth*er*," Linnie said. "I did not have a fight with Jamie. And Bron does pack him a good lunch, by the way, so I didn't have to leave him any of mine!" She grinned, waved her lunchbox at Joanna, and went away whistling. The whole departure was a little too well arranged. Joanna went back into the store.

"There's something," she said to Helmi. "All I can think is that maybe while on the surface she approves of Jamie living with Bron, underneath she's really shocked, and she might have said something to him."

"I'm glad Young Mark is only eight," Helmi said.

"Well, maybe by the time this batch of little ones grows up there'll be a swing back to the old ways. Really old ways. Chaperones."

"Arranged marriages," suggested Helmi. "I look at that son of mine playing in a tide pool or fishing off the car and I *know* he'll never be able to pick out the right woman."

"You'd better get used to that, because you'll still be thinking it when he's twenty-one."

She gave Linnie a little time before she left for home, remembering from her own youth how hard it was sometimes to get a chance to sulk, cry, or swear in private. Whatever had happened aboard *Valkyrie*, it was between brother and sister, and none of her business, no matter how curious she was. The things that my father and mother didn't know about us, she mused. And how much they must have guessed.

Linnie was already in the fishhouse. She had changed into overalls and was now heading up the five new traps she'd built during the Christmas holidays, eating her lunch as she worked. She had thirty traps in all now, fishing them around the island in summer from her dory, with a six-horse outboard for power.

"I hope this upside-down hake mouth works for me the way it does for Hugo," she said. "Or else he's doing a lot of lying. Tomorrow I'm going to paint buoys."

She was keeping the door open to let in the sounds of gulls and water. "Doesn't it sound like spring, the way they sort of ring over the harbor? It must be love songs, because this is the only time they sound exactly like that. And there's that salty, rockweedy smell you get right now, too. I don't know how Joss is going to stand it when she goes away to work in some reference library."

"What about yourself?" Joanna asked.

"I've got two years before I have to worry about it. Then I may decide to become a full-time lobsterman like Rosa." She glanced sidewise at her mother, mischievous, "What would you say?"

"Lobster *person*," said Joanna.

"You're really thinking, 'If you feel that way about it, darlin mine, you can quit now and save us a few thousand.' "

"What I'm thinking, darlin mine, is if you go lobstering you'll be fulfilling your mother's earliest ambition. We'd just like you to try something else and see something else first."

"I've got it all figured out. I could have a gang of traps out, and be a tax accountant. Then I'd have the best of both worlds. I could do everybody's taxes here and maybe get some clients on Brigport."

"Sounds good," said Joanna, seeing no need to suggest that any lobsterman who couldn't figure his own taxes probably preferred to keep the whole matter a deep secret between him and his mainland lawyer.

"How does corned hake strike you for supper tonight?" she asked.

"I've been dreaming of it since this morning," Linnie said with a convincing display of greed.

12

*J*amie didn't come back that day, and for a wonder Linnie didn't comment on it. Her enthusiasm about the corned hake was blatantly overdone, and it was a relief when she went out after supper to go over to Hillside. Joanna didn't tell Nils about the early return. If the two had a scrap, they'd make up the next time they met.

"Can I go to haul with you tomorrow?" she asked Nils.

"Mm." He was getting his news program and knitting trapheads at the same time.

"Want me to knit too?"

"No, this twine is mean stuff. Make an applesauce cake instead. We'll take it with us tomorrow."

"How can you think of food after that meal?"

"It's tomorrow's food," he said reasonably.

She made the cake double-size, pleased to be doing it for him and happy about making a day of it with him tomorrow. They were asleep when Linnie came home. In the morning she got up while Joanna was making a lunch for herself and Nils; she was quiet, and had only toast and coffee. "Get what you want for lunch," Joanna told her. "There's cake for your dessert or mug-up, however you want it. I'm taking along some extra; I thought we might give Jamie a hail and pass him a big enough whack to treat Bron."

"I told you Bron packs a good dinner box, Marm," Linnie said. "What are you trying to do, compete?"

Nils was filling his water jug at the sink. He glanced around

at her and she fidgeted uncomfortably. "Well, I was just trying to keep you from having your feelings hurt, that's all.
He might refuse it."

"I can't imagine that," said Joanna. "But if he does, I
promise I won't throw myself down on the platform and
pound my heels and yell, 'You like Bron's cake better than
mine!'"

Nils laughed, but Linnie was not amused. After Nils went
out, she stood around uneasily watching her mother's prepara-
tions. Suddenly she said in a loud defiant voice, "I guess I'll
go too."

"I thought you were going to paint buoys."

"Oh *well!*" Linnie said haughtily. "If you two want to be
alone—"

"At our age, and isn't it disgusting? Oh, get your clothes
changed. I've got enough food for three here."

Linnie didn't bother to make even a token protest. She was
so eager to go with them that her mother was touched. We're
lucky that she still wants to be with us, she thought.

They went along the west side and out around Sou'west
Point, and then toward the east. That warmth that had come
from the south yesterday lingered. If it wasn't quite spring,
it was not winter either, but one of Nils's Lapland seasons.
The breeze sprang up again as the sun climbed, so lightly that
the water wasn't ruffled, but spangled with flakes of fire. The
bow of the boat tossed them into the air in prismatic showers,
and there was never an end to them. When you looked back
toward Bennett's with its soft dark fur of woods, and over the
western sunlit bay to the hyacinth-blue island of Monhegan,
you had the illusion that this was the start of an endless summer day.

There could be a blizzard before the week was out, and
today would turn very cold when the sun went down. But for
now they were fine. The boat lifted on the summits of the
swells and coasted toward the glossy valleys below. She and
her passengers were as much at ease in their element as the
rafts of eider they saw. They came to Nils's first buoy, and

as he gaffed it, he said, "Who's baiting and who's plugging? Make up your minds."

"We'll keep swapping," said Linnie instantly. "Marm?"

"I'll bait. With all this help, your father'll be lucky to get a decent day's work done." Vigorously she stabbed the bait iron into a fatly stuffed baitbag.

After a couple of hours' work they were south of Pirate Island, and they saw *Valkyrie* a little distance to the north of them, circling up to a buoy. Beyond him a dark red Brigport boat was cutting away to the northeast. Pirate Island was not a ridge from here, but an imposing heap of terra-cotta-colored stone.

Nils turned *Joanna S.* toward *Valkyrie* and put on some speed. Joanna got out the foil-wrapped pan of cake, and enjoyed the ride until she became all at once aware that something was missing; something had been overlooked, omitted, or had withdrawn of its own volition. Startled, she looked around the cockpit, her mind inarticulately questioning until she saw how Linnie stood apart from her and Nils, alone in the stern, her arms folded, and her head turned obstinately away. She was staring out at the empty eastern horizon. Her lip was tucked under her upper teeth.

Oh my, they *did* have a good one, Joanna thought, abashed. I wonder if he asked her what I told him not to ask her. *Kids!* Wait till I tell Nils.

Valkyrie rolled in her own wake, turning her side to the seas, and Jamie gaffed a buoy that came up light to his hand, only a short length of warp and glass toggle hanging to the end of it.

They all saw it. Nils's face gave nothing away, and Joanna realized that she was not surprised. She turned again, and caught Linnie's wince.

"So that was it," she said.

"So what was what?" Too late, the dazed innocence as if she'd been startled out of a daydream.

"It happened yesterday too, didn't it? And Jamie sent you ashore."

"Nothing was cut yesterday. They'd been hauled, and dumped with the doors open. Seven anyway. Then he said he'd bait-iron me if I told, and he took me across to Barry."

"Well, you didn't tell," said Joanna. "I'll make sure he knows that." Linnie sighed and looked down at her feet. Joanna went back to Nils and put her arm through his. "It started yesterday," she said. "It's Whit Robey, most likely. Randy told me he's been hanging around Bron."

"She's a real addition to the community, isn't she?" he said.

They circled up alongside *Valkyrie*. Jamie was gaffing another loose buoy. He gave them a bleak look that should have shriveled them into nothing. It swung to Linnie and she said angrily, "I never told!"

"No, we just came over to bring you some cake," Joanna said. One corner of his mouth twitched slightly. Not really wanting to, he hooked his gaff into the other boat's rail, holding her close and at the same time keeping the two boats from bumping.

"How many cut off?" Nils asked.

"Eleven so far that I've picked up, and those two are swimming free." The two green and white buoys, one about twenty-five feet ahead of the other, were gliding swiftly along with the wind and the tide. "Going home to Bennett's," Jamie observed with a cold smile.

With identical turns of the head the men looked toward the dark red Brigport boat. The man in the cockpit was an anonymous bulk. A trap seemed to shoot up from the water and leap onto the washboard.

"He the one?" asked Nils. "Whit?"

Jamie shrugged.

"Maybe we'd better go talk to him," said his father.

"*No.* Not with the women aboard."

"We'll go into the cuddy and not even breathe," said Joanna. "I know you don't think we can keep quiet, but we can."

"It wouldn't amount to anything but more of that Robey bullsh—"

Nils said, "A little conversation in the right place and at the right time sometimes works."

"We'll talk," said Jamie, "but not now. Let the bastard go on laughing for another day."

"All right. But I'd advise you to have a couple of witnesses along, or Whit will be having you arrested for assault if he has to make the bruises himself."

Jamie smiled. "He'll never get the chance." The two boats rocked gently along together, the riders silent, watching the distant boat at work. Finally Nils said, "The last thing we need is a trap war."

"We're not going to have one," Jamie said.

"He bothered any other strings?"

"No, this is the only spot where we come anywhere near. He'll probably say I was the highbinder who fished over the line and he was just teaching me a lesson." Some inner spiral loosened in him, his smile came easier. "I hope he hauled those traps and left the doors open before he cut 'em off. I hate like hell to think of those big four-headers down there full of lobsters."

"I'm sure no Robey would miss a chance to make a few extra dollars," said Joanna. "Does he sell to Bron?"

Jamie laughed. "Marm, there's just no way she can tell my lobsters from his."

"Lately you and Linnie have been treating me like the backward kid sister," said Joanna. "I was just wondering, for another reason."

"She could refuse to buy from him," Linnie said. "*I* would."

"So he'd just go over to Merrill's car. Bron's in the business of buying as many lobsters for Randy and the family firm as she can. This hasn't anything to do with *her*." If that's what you're thinking, he might as well have added. "Whit just felt like pushing me, that's all. I'll set him straight. I'm going back to work."

He took away his gaff and the two boats instantly moved apart. Jamie put his engine into gear and took off after the floating buoys. Nils turned *Joanna S.* in a wide arc and pointed her at the Rock.

"I forgot to give him his cake!" Joanna said.

"Never mind, it served its purpose," Nils said. "Let's take a sail. It's a pretty day for it."

"Are you trying to calm me down, or yourself?" she asked. He smiled, and spoke over his shoulder at Linnie. "Come up here, Old Go-to-Loo'ard!" She came unwillingly, and he stepped away from the wheel. "Steady as she goes. Aim her for the northern end."

She cheered up at once. "Captain Bligh over there never let me *touch* the wheel."

They ate lunch in the lee of the Rock. The sun shone strongly enough on their sheltered position so they could shed caps and outer jackets. A coastguardsman hauling his traps from a peapod kept looking toward Linnie's fair head as if she were his mark. "I wonder how long it'll take him to come alongside and say hello," said Joanna.

"He may be old enough to enlist, but he looks about sixteen," Linnie said severely. "And he's *short*. I can tell."

"Give him a kind look," advised her father. "The short ones need it."

"I'm not the Red Cross, or the Salvation Army either."

They stayed away from the subject of the cut-off traps until Joanna set out the cake. "All right now, tell me about Whit," Nils said.

"Randy told me about it when we were dancing. He thinks he's got the boys flattened, but he says Whit's making a fool of himself."

"He's so gross," said Linnie. "I mean, he actually doesn't see a bit of difference between him and Jamie! As if Bron would even *look* at him! Well, cutting off a few traps isn't going to do him any good."

"It's not going to do your brother any good either," said Nils, "if he cuts some of Whit's and then Whit whacks off a few more, then Jamie cuts again, and then Tom Robey gets into it. Then Bruce thinks he has to side with Jamie, and *he* gets rimracked—"

"All right, all right! I get the message!"

"If I hadn't wanted give Jamie a piece of applesauce cake," Joanna said, "we probably wouldn't have known anything until the war was in full bloom. Dammit, I've just got to the place where I can accept Jamie and Bron as a fact of life, and now *this*. So what do we do?"

"We don't do anything. He does it." Nils began to fill his pipe.

"Back down?" Linnie exclaimed. "Give up his girl to pacify some old lecher?"

"No," said Nils, "but he can stop living in two places. He's a Bennett's Islander, not a Brigporter. He can move home and court the girl in the old way, then marry her. He can build a house down on Sou'west Point if he wants to be remote. But if she's good enough to sleep with, she's certainly good enough to marry. Once she's not dangling before their eyes like a fresh herring before a flock of gulls, they'll accept the situation."

"Jamie and marriage." Linnie made a face. "I can't see it."

Nils gave way to irritation. "Never mind whether you can or not. They're the ones concerned. There's no getting anything free, and I thought we'd brought you children up to realize that. Your brother thinks he can have the girl for nothing. I suppose it's known as living your own life, but before he gets through, the rest of us are likely to be paying for the experiment." He stood up. "I'm going back to work," he said, exactly as Jamie had said it earlier.

The coastguardsman made it while Nils was up on the bow taking up the anchor. He passed the time of day in a down-east accent and was respectful to Linnie's parents without being able to keep his eyes off her. He was indeed short, and rosy and juvenile in appearance, but Linnie was charming, and in something like five minutes she knew his name, rank, place of origin, and the name of his family's dog. They left him waving happily from his double-ender.

"How'd the dog get into it?" Joanna asked.

"I always ask. It's a good safe subject, and talking about their dogs makes them feel secure when they're away from home."

"So you're not the Red Cross or the Salvation Army, huh?"

The rhythm of work and tide and weather controlled the rest of the day. Joanna knew that when she was on shore again the *Now what?* syndrome would take over, fight it as she would. There hadn't been any trap trouble with the big island for a long time; in fact, for the past few years the men had been loosely allied against the purse-seiners who spoiled the islanders' stop-twining, and the attendant carriers whose un-caged propellers sliced off so many pot buoys. But trap trouble could spring up anytime, unless nobody was fool enough to rush in on either side, and that was too much to hope for.

All right, when I step ashore I'll worry, Joanna thought, but out here—no. I won't waste this.

When they were almost home, heading up the west side, they drank the last of the coffee and ate the last of the cake. "You keep this trap business under your hat," Nils said to Linnie. "Least said, soonest mended. I'll talk to your brother."

"How do you talk to him if he doesn't come near?"

"I won't chase him over there as if he were about twelve and a runaway, but I can catch him out on the water. We can wind up this mess before anyone knows it even began."

"Maybe," Linnie said skeptically. "I know you can do just about anything, *Fader*, but—"

"You just keep on holding turn, my girl. We don't have trap wars anymore. It's too expensive."

When Nils worries it's time to worry. He was apparently as unclouded as the sky; Linnie gave in, and when they reached the wharf she was unclouded too. Dave and Freddy were working in the fishhouse, Rosa was heading traps on her wharf, and Linnie went around there. Nils took the boat out to the mooring and Joanna went home. The afternoon game was going on, but Rory preferred her company to watching the neighbors' dogs run bases and pounce on the ball whenever anyone fumbled a catch. He even managed a few skittish bounces as he accompanied her to the door.

The instant she was inside, she hated the house. It was not depression that hit her, but a positive charge of frustrated indignation. She washed the thermos bottles, muttering, "That cussed Whit. But if Jamie were behaving himself it would be somebody else's traps." Rory listened intelligently. "Why does there always have to be some damn thing to worry about?" she asked him. "You get them raised, and you ought to be able to have five minutes to yourself when you dare to take a long breath and say now they're on their own. But *no*, they—"

"Who you talking to, Aunt Jo?" Phoebe appeared in the kitchen doorway.

"Don't you ever knock?"

"At my uncle's house?" Phoebe looked incredulous.

"At anyone's house. Do you need anything?"

Phoebe's eyes widened, she said with conspicuous sweetness, "Just to visit with you and Uncle Nils—"

"How about making it another time? I'm about to take a bath." It was a lie, but in self-defense. She tried to soften it, but Phoebe was already leaving. She went out with her head very high and marched down toward the wharf, ignoring the frantic excitement of a home run.

She met Nils on the way and snubbed him. When he came into the house, he said, "Uncle Nils just got a look that would curdle cream."

"My fault. I'm sorry. But do I have to have Phoebe and hot flashes both?"

He wrapped his arms around her and put his face in her neck. "If our kid hadn't been with us today I'd have had my way with you out there."

"Thanks for making me feel so desirable, but I'm in a rotten mood, so let me rave." He released her and began to wash up at the kitchen sink.

"I was holding forth to Rory about Whit and Jamie, and Little—well, I won't use Owen's term, but you know what it is—pops up in the doorway. God knows how long she'd been

listening, so it may be out about the traps. She's probably telling the whole waterfront about it by now."

"Not if Linnie can help it." He was undisturbed, or apparently so.

"She can't very well strangle her younger and pregnant
cousin, especially with the father and husband right there."

"Well, it'll be no great harm done, I suppose, if it is nosed
around, as Maggie would say."

"Blast these kids anyway!" Joanna erupted. "And I don't
mean just Phoebe, but that son of ours! When we were his age
we had responsibilities, we weren't so blindly self-centered.
We had some respect for our parents and the way they
brought us up. Damn it, I've been going round being calm and
liberal and objective for long enough, and it's not my nature."

"It sure isn't. And rage becomes you. Always did." He put
an arm around her shoulders and they leaned companionably
against the counter. "Know what today's motto for parents is?
Survive. And we will."

"I always believe you, Nils, but if our son starts acting like
a go-to-hell Viking—"

"We'll survive that too."

She turned and took his face in her hands and kissed him.
"Come out with me to Fern Cliff tonight to watch the moon
rise? No kids or mosquitoes this time of year."

13

The next day was open-and-shut, with intervals of cold breezy sunshine and then quick hard squally showers, soon over. Sometimes snow mixed with rain. But almost everyone went out, and Linnie had the fishhouse to herself to paint buoys in; her colors were yellow with large orange circles and a red stick.

Joanna went to the Sewing Circle at Nora Fennell's, and returned home across the field in a pounding rain. When she came into the house, shedding rain gear in the sun parlor, she could smell the wood fire in the Franklin stove in the sitting room. Rory lay on the hearth rug, and Nils had pulled the sofa up to the fire. He was smoking his pipe and contemplating the flames.

"Isn't this nice?" she said happily.

"Lock the doors and then come in here and sit down."

She went slowly, hoping her chill was from the cold rain and not a premonition. "Where's Linnie?"

"Gone around to the harbor to the Campions', the last I knew. I don't care if she hears this, but I don't want Phoebe dropping in out of the everywhere into the here. It's all right, nobody's dead."

"Then tell me before I pass out." She sat down beside him.

"I caught up with Jamie," he said. "I made a beeline for him when I saw him where we caught up with him yesterday. Before I reached him, a snow squall hit so I lost sight of him. When it passed, I was about fifty feet from him and he was cutting off one of Whit's buoys."

Nora's cranberry tarts were making her sick. She tried to be as quiet as Nils. "Where was Whit?"

"Nowhere in sight. Turns out he's laid up today with a bad back, he must have outdone himself yesterday. Wonder he didn't hire guards for his gear, but I don't think that crowd even trust one another . . . I asked Jamie what he was doing, and he said he was only cutting off as many as Whit had cut of his—no more. I said I was sure Whit would appreciate the justice of that."

"What did he say?"

"My sarcasm was wasted. I got one of those Scandinavian silences you like to talk about. So I told him what he should know already. Never mind what an outlaw like Whit does, the rest of us are supposed to know better. We don't have room these days for private vendettas unless we're ready to drag everybody else in and make it war. If he wants to lose all his own gear, that's one thing, but he's got no right to involve anyone else, and he knows damn well this can't be contained between him and Whit."

"Did that make a dent?"

"Well, I think something got through," he said.

She said angrily, "Nils, if I didn't *know* he was bright, sometimes I think if he had any more brains he'd be a half-wit."

"He was carrying a rifle on the shelf, and I told him to put it in the cuddy and not take it out until he gives it back tonight. He nodded, so I took that for a promise."

"He'd have borrowed it from Bruce," she said. "Wouldn't you think Bruce would know better?"

"They're friends. Young Matt would have done the same. They might argue with him about it but they'd let him have it and hope to God he wouldn't use it. One shot through Whit's hull and he's in court for assault with a dangerous weapon and anything else Whit could accuse him of. And Whit would likely be lucky enough to have a witness along."

"Probably Tom. One would lie and the other swear to it. How many of Whit's had he cut off?"

"Six, he said. Fourteen more to go. They do things up in

nice round numbers. When I left him, I never looked back. I'm trusting and hoping like hell that he stopped right there."

"Did you say anything in all this about his courting and marrying Bron?"

"That was at the end, after the rifle. It didn't rate the flicker of an eyelid, or a nod. Maybe a blink, but I couldn't be sure ... Could you stand Bron as a daughter-in-law?"

"I like her, but we're not the ones to be suited, are we? Could she stand *us*? I don't mean just you and me, but the whole kit and caboodle. She'd be falling over an in-law at every step."

"They can always build themselves a cabin down at Bull Cove, like the other Jamie."

"No they can't because that's for you and me." She laughed at this expression. "No, I'm not cracking up. It's just a nice relaxing dream I have of us retreating from the roar of the crowd and the power plants."

"Why don't we retreat to Green Ledge?" he suggested. "Or I could hire out to Ivor Riddell and then we could live on Pirate Island with a few thousand medricks."

Joanna lay awake that night seeing the scene as Nils had described it, but with a few relentlessly glittering touches added by her own imagination; the blinding descent of the snow squall cutting the boats off from each other, then its fast departure and the flash of the knife in sudden sunshine. Whenever she saw the knife in the act of cutting she felt a spasm in her stomach. It was one thing to hear about it, God knew she'd grown up with it, but another to see her son in the actual act. Because Nils had seen and had told her, it was the same as if she had been there. She certainly saw it plain enough, over and over, as she lay awake that night.

Going by the rough but workable justice of these island places, he had a right; but to insist on that right for his own satisfaction, no matter how many other people might be un-willingly dragged in, was wrong. Moving in with Bron was nothing compared to this.

Whit's behavior was no excuse. Her brothers had tangled a few times with Whit's branch of the Robeys, and now she could understand her parents' disapproval and anxiety.

I wish I could tell them, she thought, how every year something else is added to what I know about them. It's not so much a generation gap between our children and us as it is a responsibility gap. Ellen knows it already. Jamie and Linnie'll find out someday ... When I was Jamie's age I had a child almost old enough for the first grade, and I worked in a fish plant to support her. He is living, in some ways, like a child himself; an only child with plenty of money who thinks about what *he* does and what *he* wants, and not about how his behavior can ricochet off the rest of us, and finally hit where he never expected it to.

Nils slept deeply by her side. A hard day's work was the best narcotic; he could keep his worries for the daylight hours, and sleep at night in spite of himself. She was too hot, and she got up and was immediately chilled. She put on her bathrobe and slippers and found her way through the house in the dark. Linnie slept well too, she always had.

Joanna lit a lamp downstairs, made cocoa, and got out Dickens' *Our Mutual Friend* for a reliable tranquilizer. She folded herself up in Nils's Morris chair with a blanket around her and sipped and read, peaceful again. Rory sighed in his sleep, the Ansonia clock that had been Nils's grandmother's pride had the same sturdy reassuring tick as one of the clocks in the Homestead. As a child she would wake in the night from a frightening dream and listen for it, and then feel safe to go to sleep again. We have all these talismans, she thought, that convince you the earth hasn't suddenly exploded itself out of orbit ... One of her great-grandmothers had worn her hair in long curls, in the fashion of the 1860s when her first child was born. Feeding at her breast, he had learned to reach up and fondle one certain curl as he sucked. When she wanted to wean him, she'd cut off the curl and tied it into his crib, within his reach.

We never do grow up, Joanna thought. I have Dickens,

cocoa, the clock. Who am I to call Jamie a kid? ... She went
back to bed eventually and curled against Nils's oblivious back
with her arm over him, and soon fell asleep, thinking of the
rim of dark, and I shouldn't want to take this away from
Jamie either.

Sunday was quiet, cloudy, and mild. In the early morning
when she let Rory out she could hear the bantam rooster
crowing up at the Homestead. A flock of early robins who
had arrived overnight were picking their way across the dun-
colored fields, which were now showing in some places a
shimmer of green, if you looked hard enough.

The pearly softness and the earth scents were deceptive: if
you started pulling away the spruce banking and looking for
the first sign of daffodils, you were tempting Providence. A
blizzard wasn't unheard of, let alone snow showers like yesterday's ... With sleep, and now the arrival of pleasant daylight,
last night's haunting had become as insubstantial as snowflakes
themselves when they fall into the sea.

Though he wasn't going out, Nils was up early for his leisurely Sunday breakfast. Linnie came downstairs singing, " 'O!
Sälla land, O! Sköna strand,' " in honor of the day.

"Guddag," she said to both her parents. "Did I tell you that
I'm going to Sweden?"

"Before dinner?" asked her father.

"Next summer. You know I've always wanted to go. I decided this morning I'd better make up my mind while it's still
there."

"Sweden or your mind?" asked Joanna.

"Oh, the famous wit of the Bennetts! I can make my fare out
of my traps. I wonder if Jamie'd go with me. Do you think
Swedish girls go mad about blonds or prefer dark men for a
change?"

Ralph came over with his tractor rig and plowed up Joanna's garden, then drove up to the Fennells' to do the same.
Linnie got her clothes ready for her return to college. The
island children collected at the schoolhouse at ten for Sunday
School, taught by volunteers; Philippa usually came up from

the Eastern End to play the hymns on the old cottage organ, and Maggie Dinsmore led the singing.

In the early afternoon a steady warmth came through the layers of mother-of-pearl cloud and the wind still hadn't risen enough to disturb the spruces; the rote on the outer shores was still there, everlastingly so, but one had to consciously listen for it, like holding a shell to the ear. Older children disappeared on long beachcombing walks toward Sou'west Point. Linnie, wearing overalls over an old plaid flannel shirt and with her hair tied back out of danger, coppered the bottom of her dory, and sanded the bruises the storm had left on the strakes. Nils worked on the wharf, tying new bright blue warps onto traps while Joanna painted his buoys; she had a steady hand for the striping. They could savor the exquisite peace of a day without wind all the more because Dave and Freddy were out. Yesterday they hadn't finished hauling through, as Dave's indigestion had become too bad. It sometimes reached new heights of performance during a long day alone with Freddy.

Rosa worked on the next wharf, also putting on new warps, her rope a deep pink. "This color is so gorgeous," she said, "too bad it'll get all messed up."

"There speaks the woman of it," said Nils.

"He can talk," said Joanna. "He chose this blue to match his eyes; you know ... If I had a nickel for every buoy I've painted in my life, I'd be a rich woman today."

"Did you really get a nickel?" Rosa asked. "I got a penny apiece from my father and thought I was a rich kid."

Beyond Rosa, Ralph Percy and his boys were painting a skiff. Beyond that, Hugo had brought his boat *Finest Kind* in beside the Bennett wharf, and was tuning up her engine. He and young Matt Fennell had doubled up with their fathers for the winter fishing, but they would be going alone now. Matt's boat was on the harbor beach beyond the wharves, and he was getting her ready to be painted. Children played on the beach, and around the harbor. Foss Campion was building the new front doorstep his wife had been fighting for since last fall.

Terence Campion and Barry Barton were putting up Barry's new CB antenna.

"Well, I'm done." Linnie came around the fishhouse with the can of copper paint and brush. "How do I look? All copper freckles?"

"Not bad," Joanna said.

"The darn stuff flies so." She went into the fishhouse.

"I'll fasten that cover down," Nils called after her. "Nobody else ever gets it tight enough."

"Yup!" She came out cleaning her hands on a rag dipped in kerosene. "I guess I'll go home and wash up, and then go over and see how Hugo's doing. Sounds as if he keeps pulling a dragon's tail over there."

She met Joss and Gracie on Philip's lawn, and the three girls went up to the house together. They came back in a few minutes, called to Joanna and Nils, and went on over to Charles's wharf, where Hugo's engine was now enthusiastically shattering the hush. *Finest Kind* backed out with a roar and a swash, and took off across the harbor, not quite wide open but causing enough turbulence to set all the moored boats rocking and sending the gulls protesting into the air.

"Well, I guess it's officially spring," Rosa called over to Joanna. "The Wild Colonial Boy has gone to sea." When the engine sound grew faint beyond Long Cove, the silence came sweetly back.

" '*O! Sälla land, O! Sköna strand*,' " Joanna sang under her breath. She was wondering what was still suspended, what other shoe was about to drop. Nils may have convinced Jamie that trap-cutting led nowhere, especially with a rifle aboard, but if Jamie'd slashed off only one of Whit's traps, Whit wouldn't be likely to let it stop there. And on Jamie's own admission, there'd been six cut off; fourteen to go, to make it trap for trap.

She remembered Whit in Mark's store one day, drinking soda and smoking a cigar, leaning back against the counter with his barrel chest and beer-pod thrust out, holding forth expansively about a couple of Riddell fishermen who'd been trying to keep him and his brothers off the Pirate Island grounds. He had a drawl that grew more pronounced each year in direct ratio to the increase of summer people on Brigport who considered him a genuine find.

"No young rooster is goin' to tell old Whit where he can fish. I sot those pots in good faith where I wanted 'em sot, and that's where I callate to keep 'em."

"And supposing they callate different?" Mark asked. Whit gave him a theatrical wink and said, "Then we'll just have to wait and see, won't we?"

The long cold war, which occasionally heated up, never touched the Bennett's men because they didn't fish anywhere near those grounds. This particular flare-up ended when Whit fired a rifle through somebody's cabin without stopping to look closely at the two men in the cockpit. One of them was a coastal warden. Being arrested and actually standing trial after a long career of doing as he and the other Loud Robeys pleased was such a shock to Whit that when he received a suspended sentence he actually thanked the judge. Out of court he made some emotional comments about the Riddells' lack of honor in hauling the law into an innocent little misunderstanding, but the fear of jail kept him in order for his year of probation.

"Good faith" was one of his favorite expressions, and never required any relationship to what he was doing at the time; he just liked the sound of it.

"Whatever he does," Mark said after Whit left the store that day, "he does in good faith that he won't get caught."

That time his faith had let him down badly, but when his probation was over he was as devout as ever. So he could blandly cut off Jamie's traps practically in plain view, knowing the evidence was too circumstantial; even if Jamie saw him with the knife in his hand, it was only one man's word against another's. By the same token he couldn't prove anything against Jamie either, without a witness.

But damn it, Joanna thought, striping a buoy, he won't leave things where they are now, even if Jamie's willing to.

All because of little Bron with her round face and her little rump in tight jeans, who won't give the old whoremaster the time of day.

Oh, shut up, Jo. You like the child. Or why don't you just admit you wish she hadn't got this cute idea about being a lobster buyer and that Randy hadn't gone along with it? Yes, I do wish it, she said defiantly, and felt a little better. She came back slowly to her surroundings. It felt as if she'd been away for hours, but Rory still slept on the warm planks, Nils was moving around in the fishhouse, whistling softly to himself. *O! Sälla land, O! Sköna strand.* Linnie had gotten them all off to a good start this morning.

Rosa was now over on the Percy wharf. Tiger was barking up in the field, the foolish, puppyish bark reserved for Liza's cat, who was mousing in the tall tangled dead grass. Tommy was rowing Owen out to *White Lady*. *Finest Kind* suddenly became audible again in the unseen distance as she came out around Ten Pound and headed up Long Cove. The gulls took to the air over the cranberry bog behind the beach, circled in a crowd over the spruces on Eastern Harbor Point. The air was full of the engine's sound magnified by the echoes hurled back from the rocks. Nils came out and stood by Joanna, watching the boat round the point and cross the harbor full tilt.

White Lady got the full force of the wake and Owen's head appeared over the washboards. He shouted something, easily guessed, while Tommy appeared to be picking himself up off the platform. Charles and Philip were out on the end of the Bennett wharf, and Joanna knew Hugo was in for something more when he got within earshot.

Hugo headed directly for the Sorensen wharf. Only Linnie was with him now, and Joanna thought, incongruously, The other shoe has dropped.

14

*S*he was too cold for fear; her hands were steady as she balanced her brush across the open can of paint and took off her gloves. She and Nils walked together to the end of the wharf, stepping carefully over Rory. The engine stopped and *Finest Kind* slid in with a bubbling rush. Linnie was wiping her eyes on her sleeve.

"Jamie's all right!" Hugo yelled hastily. The cold began to ease up. She moved her fingers cautiously as if they'd been half-frozen.

"Thanks," said Nils. "What's happened?"

Linnie came up the ladder. "Jamie's boat sank, right there in the harbor! Somebody did it. She's lying on the beach like a wounded gull—poor *Valkyrie*—" She was ready to cry, and Joanna put her arm about her.

"She's not at the bottom of the harbor then, and Jamie with her."

"No, but it's the way she *looks*." She blew her nose. Hugo was explaining to Nils what had happened.

"Drew Bradford was rowing out this morning before it was hardly light—you know how he likes to get a head start with that old Redwing of his, and his mooring's right handy to that spare one of Randy's that Jamie uses. Well, there she was, half-sunk. The water was already over the engine." Rosa and the Percys came down the wharf, and Hugo repeated the news for them, and again when his father and uncle arrived. With everybody walking around and over him, Rory woke up and joined the group.

"Drew went in and got Jamie up—" out of bed with Bron, Joanna thought—"and by that time a couple of other fellers were down at the shore. They towed her in and beached her beside the old Fowler dock."

"Does he know how it happened?" Nils asked Hugo.

"Sure. Hoses been cut. His radio and fathometer were smashed too. I don't know about anything else. Jamie's standing around not saying a word, but he's some white."

"He looks as if somebody'd tried to kill his wife or his child," said Linnie.

"Well, as long as he's safe," said Joanna, "that's the important thing." The paralytic cold had given way to that fine inner trembling, but her voice sounded firmly matter-of-fact. "Where are the other girls?"

"They're taking a walk till we get back."

"What's he going to do now?" Nils asked Hugo.

"Well, he's got the water out of her and he's going to have Josh work on the engine. Otherwise he never said aye, yes, or no."

"He's not going to leave her there for another night," Nils said. "I'm going over right now. Hugo, you can set me aboard."

"Not without me," said Joanna, "and I don't give a hoot in Hades if he doesn't want his mother showing up." She went down the ladder after Nils, and Linnie followed her. Rory stared yearningly down at them and Joanna said, "It's all right, Rory. Stay."

"Give a shout if you need any help," Charles called.

"Ayuh, we'll turn out the fleet," said Ralph.

"You mean all the might and force of the Bennett's Island Navy?" Joanna asked. "That'll make 'em tremble in their boots."

"Damn right!" They all laughed on the rebound from the blow, all but Rosa who had said nothing the whole time. She stood to one side, leaning her elbows on a trap, her chin in her hands, her face expressionless.

Linnie, feeling better, decided to stay with Hugo when her

parents transferred to Nils's boat. While Nils was casting off his mooring, *Finest Kind* left the harbor a little more decorously than she'd entered it.

"What in hell's going on?" Owen shouted across at them. "Tommy damn near split his skull open!"

"Somebody sank Jamie's boat!" Joanna called back. "Is Tommy bleeding?"

"No, but he's got a blue Easter egg. You tell Jamie from me it doesn't pay to mix pleasure and business."

"He ought to know it by now without being told," Joanna said. Nils put the engine into gear and they headed out of the harbor.

They reached Brigport harbor at a slack time of day. Only a few boats were out, and there wasn't much activity around the shore. Most of the dwellings on Brigport were well away from the harbor, except a few summer places perched among the rocks and spruces apart from the working section, and these were still empty. The store was closed.

Bron wasn't on the car; she wouldn't need to be there until the men were due back in. At Tim Merrill's car, Nils tied up beside *Finest Kind*. They walked around the shore by a narrow track that wound over and around ledges, and squeezed between workshops and fishhouses. They went past the outside steps leading up to Bron's apartment, but there were no sounds of life from it. The gulls' cries over the harbor intensified the sensation of actual vacancy, as if everyone had gone away and was not really up on the island recuperating from Sunday dinner.

They went around the corner of the roomy old building where the apartment was, and down onto the beach between it and the store. *Valkyrie* was upright against the wharf, looking surprisingly the same as usual. Somehow, having been put out of commission, she should have at least looked wounded. Hugo was there with Jamie, Bruce MacKenzie, and Bruce's younger brothers; Tim Merrill, who was the Sorensens' age; Drew Bradford, a much older man; and a boy with an Indian headband, long hair and strings of beads hanging outside his sweatshirt. Joanna remembered the headband and hair from the party.

Jamie saluted his parents with a wintry smile. "I thought you'd show up," he said.

Everything was low-keyed. Greetings were casual. When the civilities were over, the men stood discussing the boat in unhurried murmurs. "Bad business, bad business!" Drew Bradford kept murmuring, shaking his head. He and Tim left, the boy with the headband politely took himself out of the scene; Bruce and his brothers went, promising help if they were needed.

"I guess we ought to see where those girls have got to," Hugo said. "Come on, Linnie."

Joanna sat on the gunnel of a dory while Nils and Jamie examined the destroyed equipment, discussing it in overquiet laconic words. Finally they came away from the boat and Nils took out his pipe and filled it. Jamie stood with his hands in his pockets, looking at the beach stones at his feet.

"What are you going to do now?" Nils asked between puffs on his pipe.

"Josh's off to the main for the weekend. He'll be back tomorrow and we'll get to work on the engine."

"You're not leaving that boat here another night," his father said. "They can drop boulders into her from up on the wharf and smash through her platform. Or they can douse her with kerosene and burn her right under your nose." His gaze moved away from Jamie, upward toward the windows of the apartment. "And if you just happened to see or hear something, and rushed down here, there could be one less lobsterman in the world."

Jamie's face reddened. "What about Josh working on my engine?"

"Take the boat to the mainland. Get the engine cleaned up and the radar and fathometer replaced. But if you insist on keeping her over here another night—"

He stopped. It was not often that Nils issued an ultimatum, but one was implicit now in his pause.

"I suppose you're right," Jamie said grudgingly.

"As soon as she floats we'll take her. We've got a perfect chance."

"I guess I'll go walk around." Joanna said, not sure whether they even heard her. She went up the beach and on to the worn turfy slope by the store. Bron stood there as if waiting for her. She wore her work jeans and deck boots, and dark blue Norwegian sweater.

"Hi," she said huskily. "Can I give you a cup of tea or something?"

"I'd love a cup of tea," Joanna said. It was the truth, re- action had left her not quite shaky, but on the verge of it. They went up the outside steps to the apartment. It was one big bright room, finished in a light plywood paneling, and simply furnished. There was a schoolhouse stove for heat, with a new lobster crate for a woodbox; a wide double couch made up with a wool tartan blanket for a spread. Bron heated water on the little gas range in the kitchen area. If she was nervous, she wasn't going to show it by making aimless conversation, and Joanna felt the same way.

The place was neat, the only clutter the pleasant one of books lying around, and some record albums by the little por- table player at one end of a long plank table drawn up to the windows that looked over the harbor.

"I've never been up here before," Joanna said. "It's a lovely place."

"I guess it's noisy in summer, though." Bron was getting out mugs.

For some reason the room reminded Joanna of the cabin at Bull Cove, which would probably never exist except as an escape in her mind, and she felt something almost like envy, or even resentment, as if something had been taken away from her. It was so unreasonable, and therefore upsetting, that she hastily picked up a paperback book and began leafing through it. The leaves flipped over by themselves to a bookmark and she saw a marked verse.

> *The sunrise blooms and withers on the hill*
> *Like any hillflower; and the noblest troth*
> *Dies here to dust. Yet shall Heaven's promise clothe*
> *Even yet those lovers who have cherished still*
> *This test for love;—in every kiss sealed fast*
> *To feel the first kiss and forebode the last.*

It moved her as some poetry could, and she closed the book quickly feeling as if she'd intruded on someone's deepest privacy. She had been consciously trying not to see this room and this bed as the place where Jamie and Bron made love, but now she had no defenses. The poem touched her for more than the usual reasons, it gave her and Bron a relationship, or at least a connection that was *not* Jamie and the fact that he was the son of one and the lover of the other. Even if it were no stronger than a spider's silk thread, it joined them as two women who had much more in common than Jamie.

Bron stood back to her, pouring boiling water into a squat brown teapot. In her jeans and sweater she looked hardly more than a child. But when she turned and came to the table carrying the tray and the diffused white glow of the day shone on her face, it showed that she was no child, and that she was tired.

They sat down at the table. "Bron, who does Jamie think did it?" Joanna asked.

"Wait, I've got a tin of shortbread—"

"Never mind for me, the tea's fine."

Bron sat where she could look down past the wharf and at the men around the boat. "He hasn't said a word about it. In fact he's hardly said a word about anything since Drew came and told him. That tea must be ready." She began to pour.

"What a nice fragrance," Joanna said. "What kind is it?"

"Lapsang Oolong. Somebody gave it to my mother, but she doesn't go for anything fancy." She smiled, but the earlier, merry smile seemed to have been extinguished. This one hardly suggested the dimples in her round cheeks.

When she took sugar her hand trembled slightly, and because she still kept staring out the window the spoon clicked against the edge of her cup and spilled a few grains.

"I wonder if it was Whit," Joanna said.

Bron's head came around. "*Whit?* Why? Besides, he's practically helpless with a slipped disc, or something. He skidded in his bait shed the other night."

"Maybe he hired someone to do it. The boys who ambushed Jamie that time. Or maybe they did it on their own . . . Don't mind me, Bron, it's the first chance I've had to think since we got the news, and I have to think out loud sometimes. I can't do it in my husband's presence because it drives him out of his mind."

"I didn't know anything could do that to Mr. Sorensen."

"*I* can. It's a kind of accomplishment, if you want to look at it that way."

"Why did you think of Whit first hop out of the box?" Bron asked.

"Didn't you know that Jamie and Whit have been having a little private trap war? And Jamie got mad enough to take a rifle to haul with him?"

"No, he never told me." Her dismay looked genuine. "And he never acted any different."

"Well, it's just been going on for a few days. It's a modest little war so far, but when Whit gets over his ailment I don't know what will happen. Don't let on to Jamie I told you."

"I won't. But—" She picked up her cup, looked into it, then set it down again. "Mrs. Sorensen," she said, "maybe you know that Whit's made some pretty blatant passes at me."

"Yes, I heard that. It's typical of him."

"Well, I didn't ask anybody to defend me. I handled it myself and I thought he got the message, the same as some of the boys. But it could be that you think I'm to blame for the trap-cutting and what's just happened to *Valkyrie*, as well as the ambush." She was blushing, but valiant. "If I weren't here, none of these things would have happened to Jamie. That's what you think, isn't it?"

Joanna hoped she wouldn't blush herself, but she felt like it, remembering earlier thoughts that day. She sipped tea, trying to get her words in order.

"It's true about your being here," she said. "Maybe these things wouldn't have happened. But that doesn't make it your fault. Jamie could have gotten into trouble all on his own. In fact, he did this time. He knew what quarter the wind was in. Bron, I hope I never blame anybody else for whatever roofs my kids manage to pull down on their own heads."

The stiffness left Bron's mouth. She looked away.

"Besides," Joanna said, "Whit was about due to break out. He fishes right up to the line and over it if he can, and sometimes I think he starts things just for the hell of it. Rites of spring or something."

Bron laughed, not very successfully. She drank half her tea and put it down. "Look, stay and finish yours, please, but I have to get out to the car. The smack's coming, Sunday or not."

"I'm just about through, so I'll go with you. It was good, Bron. Thanks. Just what my twittery stomach needed."

They separated at the brow of the beach. Bron gave a quick almost furtive glance at the men, but nobody looked her way. She went on past the store and disappeared. Joanna walked down the beach. The tide was already up to *Valkyrie*'s stern.

Bron came out past the store's outbuildings and onto the big dock, where her double-ender was tied to a ladder on the side toward the beach. She looked small and lonely walking the length of the wharf, unnoticed by anything except Joanna, and the gulls, who took off from the spilings as she approached.

Jamie, at least wave your hand at her, Joanna silently urged him, but he didn't get her signal. Bron went down the ladder, the peapod slipped around the corner of the high stone dock, and disappeared.

15

When *Valkyrie* was in her home harbor, on her own mooring, Jamie asked Hugo to take him back to Brigport. So the girls rode back again, and some children this time. Joanna left Nils to give information to the other men, and went up to the house to put the teakettle on. There was no sign of Phoebe, and that was a relief. She was warmly received by Rory. "Rory, the only thing I worry about with you is how much longer we'll have you with us," she told him. "I'm glad you didn't understand that, but your eyes look as if you did, damn it." She felt stuffed with tears. "Come on in. I'm tired, that's all."

Nils was tired too. It showed not in the way he walked into the house—he always moved at the same pace, neither fast nor slow—but in exasperation. "How much does it take to convince him that's no place for him?"

"I'm glad he went back, Nils. He's hardly spoken to Bron since Drew turned him out this morning."

"Are you encouraging this now?"

"Here, have a good strong cup of coffee to hold you till supper's ready. I'm encouraging him to be decent. I talked to her, and she wasn't fussing or whining. But I wouldn't be surprised if she thinks he blames *her*. She needs some re-assurance."

"If he's blaming anyone, he knows where to fix it." Nils sat on the kitchen stool beside the counter. "As Grampa said at least once a week and usually more than that, 'What goes over the devil's back comes back under his belly.' I'm not excusing the kids who jumped him, and God knows I've no use for Whit. But Jamie had no business in being where he was. He knew in himself he was doing a wrong thing, moving in with the girl, and he thought he could get away with it. Does he think he's invisible? Or immune? He looks at me and I swear I can't guess what he's thinking. Or if he's thinking at all."

There was no answer for that, since Joanna often had the same reaction.

"Now it'll likely cost him his winter's work to get set up again," Nils went on. "And if the boat had stayed there another night it might have cost him a hell of a lot more."

"All I'm hoping right now is that he won't go around making accusations and getting his face pushed in," said Joanna. "If he'd wait to see what his friends pick up, the truth's bound to surface after a while."

"Like a dead body," said Nils dourly.

"Not that it'll do him any good to know, because he'd probably think he should get revenge." She stopped peeling potatoes. "You know something, Nils? For the quietest one of our children, he's been the one to keep us in the most suspense."

"Exciting, isn't it?" said Nils. The strain broke, and they both laughed.

Linnie went up to Rosa's after supper, and at the edge of dark Dave came across the yard with twine and needles, to talk about *Valkyrie* and relate what he'd picked up about it during the day on his boat radio. Nils turned the conversation to something else and later they watched a movie made on location on the coast of Ireland. After the movie Joanna set out a mug-up. "When's Alice coming, Dave?" she asked. "Has she got her replacement trained yet?"

The corners of his mouth turned down. "She doesn't even *have* a replacement. I hear they still teach bookkeeping and accounting in the school, but I'll be damned if you can find somebody who wants to knuckle down and work. What these kids need is to live through a depression, without us having to share it with 'em." He laughed, but the sound was rusty and labored. "We had a hard enough time just keeping clothes on our backs and grub in our stomachs. Row a peapod all day for a handful of fifteen-cent lobsters and think you'd done well. On shore you couldn't find a job for love or money. Now they burn rubber as if they owned Firestone, and drink like old hands, smoke pot and swallow pills because life is so goddam dull, they've got to get their kicks somehow. By eighteen they're a bunch of has-beens." He pressed a knotted fist hard into his midriff. "And the only way they know how to cook is to drown everything with pizza sauce."

"Have a glass of milk to calm down your gut, Dave," Nils advised.

"The hell with that. This custard pie ought to do just as good." He swallowed, and shut his eyes. "Ah, cool," he sighed.

"Cool, man, real cool," said Nils, and they laughed.

"One thing I can say about those two," Dave said earnestly. "I don't think they're on any pills. She'd better not be, by God. Last thing we need is an idiot baby. They were into the marijuana, that damfool kid of mine was trying it out at fourteen, but when I took Freddy on I said, 'No more of that. If I ever smell it on you, you're out for good.' And there's no booze either, not while I'm guaranteeing their bread and butter."

"Well, they don't seem to be pining away," said Joanna. "This is a good healthful life they're living."

"But I don't know how long it'll last. We're going in for Easter and her checkup, and when they come back he'll have forgotten everything he's learned from me. It won't take him more'n a weekend to lose it. And she'll be tossing her head as if she was doing me a favor by coming into this low-class ghetto. I shouldn't be talking this way about my own kid, but *Gee-zuss!*"

"Careful, you're catching something from Freddy," said

Nils. "Seriously, why can't you let them go their own way? Do you think they'll just down and fold their hands while they quietly starve to death?"

"Not quietly. Never anything *quietly*." He looked over his glasses at them. "Alice says the same as you, and if it was just those two, I'd do it in a minute. But there's the baby. Left to themselves he'd have her racing all over hell and gone on the back of a motorcycle." He threw up his hands. "Nope, can't do anything but what I'm doing, because of the baby."

"Well, nobody can argue with that," Nils said.

Rory had been walking around looking for crumbs, and now he went out into the sun parlor and scratched at the front door. "I guess Rory and I'll take a walk in the moonlight," she said to the men. She put on her loden coat and went out with the dog.

Most of the generators were shut off for the night and houses were dark. So she and the dog walked in near-silence around to the anchor and across the marsh to where the schoolhouse caught the first light of the rising moon, then back to the harbor. The grass crisped with frost underfoot, and the air was cold in her nostrils, but the marsh scent was there, as everlastingly a part of her experience as the damp, fishy, salty smell in the covered part of the big wharf. In the summer, both the warm spongy black earth of the marsh and the cool slippery planking of the shed had been as familiar to her bare feet as the Homestead floors.

So how about some new experiences for your second half-century? she asked. Like a doorstep opening out on Bull Cove and the full moon? Well, until she got it, the old ones would be good enough, like the view of the boats in the harbor as she came back to the anchor and, for a bonus, a boat coming in, red and green lights gleaming jewels against the deep blacks, velvety grays, and odd moving bits of glitter that belonged to this hour of moonrise.

This could have been a transient, a small dragger like

Gemini looking for a spare mooring or a place to drop anchor. But, without hesitation she came on among the moorings, and she headed for the wharves. The tide was so low that when Joanna came out between Rosa's and the Sorensen fishhouse she couldn't see the boat, but she could hear the engine. They must have just made it to the ladder at the end of Nils's wharf.

She could look out along the wharf through an alley between rows of traps, and see Jamie appear at the top of the ladder. He put down his zipper satchel and reached over the side for whatever else was handed up to him. The boat backed out from the wharf and Jamie stood watching. When he turned away from the ladder, Joanna stepped back behind Rosa's fishhouse into a wiry tangle of rose bushes.

The boat, probably Bruce's *Hannah Mac*, was going across the harbor now, so softly that she heard Jamie's feet on the loose pebbles between the buildings. Then the fishhouse door opened and shut.

Ignorant of all this, Rory had been nosing at the foundation of the Percy fishhouse. Joanna apprehended him as he came around the corner. "Let's go home and find Father," she whispered. She got him away before he could pick up Jamie's scent and dig at the door. She walked home with the moonlight in her face, cautiously savoring comfort, looking forward to bed and sleep. There were a cot and blankets and sleeping bag upstairs in the fishhouse where Jamie had often turned in when he came home late from the hockey games, so he had a place to lie down in and keep warm, if he didn't want to come to the house. She would not wonder, tonight anyway, why he was back.

Crossing her dooryard she could look into the lighted kitchen and see Nils washing the mug-up dishes. How could I ever come home to a house without him in it? she thought. The moonlight turned dull and very cold. She went in quickly behind the eager dog.

"Oh, what a tidy man," she said, hugging Nils from behind.

He turned almost roughly and embraced her, kissing her throat and then her mouth. She put her arms around his neck. "Not only a tidy man," he said.

Rory pawed at her foot, stood off, and barked. "It's cookie time," Joanna sighed. Rory barked with more fervor. Joanna released Nils and was released, and reached for the dog biscuits. "Jamie's back," she said. "Bruce brought him over. He's in the fishhouse now, but he may be waiting till the light goes out."

"That cabin of yours at Bull Cove looks better and better. Let's turn this place over to the kids." He was not smiling, but she knew a change had set in at the mention of Jamie's return, like a shift in the wind or the turn of the tide, known by instinct before it becomes an obvious fact.

Linnie made a noisy entrance. "Hi, everybody!" she called from the sun parlor. "Anybody been out in the moonlight? It's some gorgeous!" She came into the kitchen. "Hello, my darling Rory Mor." She kissed his head with a loud smack. "How was everybody's evening?"

"Fine," said her mother. "How was yours?"

"Oh, simply arregorical, as somebody or other used to say. How did that word get into our delightful island patois?"

"It came from one of the hired fisherman in our grand-fathers' time," said Nils. "They lived in the little camps that used to be between the marsh and the beach, beyond the anchor."

"You're looking very handsome tonight, *Fader*. So are you, *Moder*. Why don't you two try again and see if you can get us a black-eyed baby?"

"In case you haven't noticed," Joanna said, "it's too late."

"Do you suppose if I married one of my Bennett cousins I could do it, then? It would have to be either Hugo or Pierre, because Richard and Stevie and little Mark are too young. On the other hand, I *could* go looking up Great Uncle Nate's grandsons. They aren't too bad if we go by those pictures we keep getting—"

"Would you mind waiting until after you graduate before you start out on this safari?" asked Nils.

"Linnie," said Joanna. "Your brother's back. He's down in the fishhouse and we think he'd just as soon have nobody but Rory welcome him into the house."

"Oh, good! I guess nobody got him, then. We were worried. He was really on Rosa's mind . . . I'll brush my teeth and be gone in a trice. Why not a twice? Or a once?"

She went into the bathroom. When she came out she said, "Hey, Rosa's composed a new song. It's called "The Ballad of the Sad Lobsterman," and the chorus goes like this:

> 'Oh, the lobsterman's song is sad and long,
> With never a word of hope;
> For every lobster that comes over the side,
> You won't get much for his sweet inside,
> And you'll have to spend it on Bait and Gas
> And coils upon coils of Rope!' "

Both parents applauded. "Thank you. Next time I'll do *Carmen*." She ran upstairs, calling goodnight.

Jamie didn't come in while Joanna lay awake, which wasn't for long. She knew that he was home on the island where he belonged.

16

By breakfast early the next morning, Jamie still hadn't come to the house. "If I was a nice sister I'd take him down a cup of this super coffee," Linnie said.

"You'd be an even nicer one if you left him alone," said Nils. "He had a hard day yesterday."

"Wouldn't you rather be waked up by me with coffee than by Freddy rampsing around below?"

"They're not going out today."

"Maybe Jamie's trying to get up his courage to tell us he's engaged," Linnie suggested. "For him to tell anything personal is like pulling out one of his own teeth, or peeling off his own fingernails."

"Do you have to, at this hour?" Joanna left the table to start putting Nils's lunch together.

"You know what I mean." She became purposefully vague. "Do you think it's a good idea to pressure anybody into marriage like that?"

"Like what?" Nils pushed away his plate, and folded his arms on the table.

"Well, you've told him to fish or cut bait, haven't you? Ever since all these things started happening because he moved in with Bron?" She kept busy with her scrambled eggs. "*Actually*, it's what any parent would say. It's what *I* would have said once, before I realized that an alternative lifestyle is possible, and Jehovah isn't going to come out of a cloud and strike people dead for living together before marriage."

"Well, somebody's giving your brother a few licks, if Jehovah isn't," said Joanna.

"*Actually*," Nils said, "living together isn't something new in this family. Your Uncle Sigurd lived with his housekeeper for years before she surprised them both by getting in the family way."

"Aunt *Leonie?*" She forgot to be politely patronizing.

"Aunt Leonie, and not long before you were born," said Joanna. "It was practically the last minute for her. Quite a shock, too. But for heaven's sake, don't ever mention it."

"I won't, but I just can't imagine Aunt Leonie! Uncle Sigurd, maybe, but never *her*. Well, that explains the way they are with poor Gunnar," said Linnie. "No wonder he wants to run away to sea, even if it's by way of the Maritime Academy."

"Let's get back to your brother," said Nils. "I didn't tell him he *had* to do anything. I reminded him of a few things that might have slipped his mind, that's all." He got up from the table. Bemused, she watched him put on his rubber boots and windbreaker, pick up his watchcap and lunchbox, kiss Joanna and leave. Almost stern with her preoccupation, she went to the sink window and watched him go through the gate.

"One thing I admire about my parents," she said without turning her head, "is that they know who they are and what they expect of us. There's no doubt in their minds, which leaves none in ours."

Joanna, clearing the table, said, "I don't know whether I should spoil the image by admitting this, but the doubts and fears and worries are always there. It's a part of the human condition, I guess. There are times when our life is like Barney's brig, both main tacks over the foreyard."

"What I mean is, you know you're our parents, and that we're your kids, and you're not afraid of us." She turned from the window, and began to help with the clearing. "Probably I'll do plenty of things in my life that you won't like, the way Jamie's going now. But the worst thing that could happen to us would be for you and Father to stop being yourselves. If you ever accepted anything we did without a word, what would we have to come back to?"

It was the sort of statement that could turn you smug if you didn't watch out.

"Remember that," Joanna said. "The next time you object to any of my opinions I'll remind you that I'm simply being true to both of us."

"Good!" Linnie smiled at her. "You know, last night I was coming back to the house, and I saw you and Father through the window, right there. I wasn't being a Peeping Tom or anything, but I couldn't help seeing you, and you were like lovers." The color flowed up through her throat and face. *"Passionate* lovers. And after all these years! I felt it when you were dancing the other night, only last night the message was a lot stronger. You and he are absolutely separate from us—that part of your life, your *real* life, is in a different world. *We* know you as Mother and Father, but the way you know each other, the way you are when you're alone with each other . . . Well, you know an awful lot you aren't telling, and I'll never find out, no matter how long I live." Her voice trembled and her eyes glistened with emotional tears.

"Oh, Linnie," Joanna said. She put her arm around the girl. "What your father and I know is that we love each other and we've done so for over half our lives. You can't possibly know about that when you're still so young, but it *can* happen for you. What I wish for you, more than anything else, it for you to have something this good when you're fifty."

Rory barked outside and they saw Jamie coming across the yard. "Speaking of love," said Linnie flippantly, "here comes the Casanova of the Coast." She gave her mother a short but fierce hug. "Thanks," she muttered, embarrassed now.

Jamie and the dog came in, Rory pleased with himself and Jamie terse. "Morning," he said. He set his dinner box on the counter and went on into the bathroom to wash. Joanna and Linnie raised eyebrows and shoulders. "The Lochinvar of the Lobster Pots," whispered Linnie. "Romeo in Rubber Boots."

"Shut *up!*" Joanna whispered back.

Jamie looked a little hollow about the eyes, but he ate a good breakfast. Nobody tried to make conversation with him and Joanna hoped he appreciated that. Linnie went up to make her bed. Joanna drank another cup of coffee at the table with Jamie, but worked on her list of spring projects and unnecessarily rearranged her vegetable garden. When Jamie had finished, he carried his dishes to the sink, and tidily wiped up his crumbs. Then he went to the stairs and shouted, "Linnie!"

"What?"

"You girls want to go in today? Matt's towing my boat in. There's a perfect chance over, and tomorrow it's coming off southeast and blow like a man."

Linnie was silent. "Talk about agonizing decisions," Joanna said.

"You've got an hour," Jamie called. "Be down on the wharf by quarter past seven if you're going."

"Oh gosh," Linnie said forlornly from out of sight. Jamie brought his kit bag in from the sun parlor and got out his shaving gear and disappeared into the bathroom again. Linnie came downstairs, looking anxious.

"I can't decide. I'd be going in tomorrow on the boat anyway, and I hate to lose even one day of my vacation, and it's perfect today already, but of course it's a weather-breeder. And I know what the bay's like in a southeasterly, and I guess I'd better go see what Joss and Gracie want to do."

She went out and Rory with her. Joanna was washing the breakfast dishes when Jamie came out after shaving. "We'll be staying in a few days, Marm," he said on his way upstairs for clean clothes.

"I expected you would. Have as much fun as the law allows." She'd have liked to ask him how Bronwen was, but even if she could have sounded unconcerned she'd have re-reived no satisfactory answer. *All right* was as much as she could expect.

She went out to attend to the hens. The early morning was mild even in the shadows of the barn and woods, and last night's frost on the grass of the field was melting to a rainbow sparkle as the sun struck it. There was still time for snow-storms, they could have an Easter blizzard, but they were on the other side of March hill now. The birds knew it, from the gulls to the nuthatches, and the hens crowding around her feet were excited not just by her presence and cracked corn.

It was a day to take her lunch to Sou'west Point. That reminded her to go in and pack lunch for the voyagers. They'd be in Limerock before noon, even with slow traveling because of *Valkyrie* in tow, but they'd be famished before they were halfway.

While she was assembling ingredients on the counter, Linnie returned, all doubts gone now that she'd made up her mind. She ran upstairs to pack, meeting Jamie on the way. "Cross on the stairs, means a fight," she warned him happily, "so watch out . . . Bron going in too?"

"As far as I know she'll be buying lobsters as usual." Out in the kitchen he took a plastic jug of drinking water from the refrigerator. "Look, Marm, we're not striking out for the Azores. You've got enough soul-and-body-lashings there to last a week.

"My rule is, whenever anyone starts across the bay, load 'em down as if they're going away to starve. Besides, it's a good way to clean out the cupboards."

His mouth curled up on one corner in the same way his father's did. "See you at the wharf." He went out carrying his bag and the jug, his good jacket under his arm.

As usual when anyone made a special trip in, others decided to go along. Young Matt's wife was there, Rosa had to attend some business with her Seal Harbor property, Hugo was going as a matter of course. A little crowd collected on the Bennett wharf; Owen had gone to haul, but Laurie and Richard had time before school to see Joss and Gracie off. All the harbor children were there, some of the women, and Freddy was happily officious about handling the lines. Phoebe sulked because she wanted to go in *now*, and not wait until her father was ready to go in for Easter.

Out in the harbor *Peregrine* picked up *Valkyrie* and went past the southwestern end of Brigport. In the fair, calm morning and full sunlight it was possible to make out the undulating dark blue line of the mainland twenty-five miles away.

The women talked a few minutes, and then Linnie went across the marsh toward the school, trailed by children. Joanna refused an invitation to coffee with Liza and hurried home to get her own lunch together and herself away from the house before Phoebe trapped her. She'd be on the prowl today and in a foul mood, thinking of all the fun she was missing.

17

*T*he perfect day had been a weather-breeder, all right, but the blow the next day was a short one. By late afternoon the sun was out, and if the ground was too wet for marbles and a little too skiddy for baseball, there was a fine breeze for kite-flying. Rosa returned on the Thursday boat, and Jamie and Hugo came out on Saturday with the young Fennells aboard *Peregrine*. When he went to haul again, using his father's boat, he came home and sold his lobsters to Mark as he'd always done. At the end of a week he had still not gone to Brigport, even to see Bruce.

"I can't help wondering," Joanna said to Nils in bed.

"Forget it. Whatever it was, it must be over."

"I want him to have a girl, Nils. I don't want him to get into the habit of loneliness. I wish I knew about Bronwen. It's important to me to know how he's behaved in this. What if he's decided she's bad luck for him, and simply dropped her, like this?" She snapped her fingers. "It's been plaguing me all week. I keep remembering how she looked over there."

"Maybe they've had a fight," said Nils sleepily, "and they'll make up after a while. Whatever it is, we're not likely to know. Jamie's Jamie. What is it they like to say nowadays? Somebody's a very private person. Well, that's what Jamie is."

"Too damn private to suit me," Joanna grumbled against his shoulder. "There are times when it's like having this very polite boarder. Startles me when he calls me Marm."

Nils chuckled. "Forget the boarder then. Just think about us."

"Yes." Lovers, Linnie said. She couldn't tell Nils, he'd have been embarrassed. But she treasured it.

A few days later when she went to the store in the afternoon she saw Randy Fowler's *Osprey* tied up at the lobster car, loaded with wet traps. Randy was in the store with Mark, drinking soda and eating crackers and rat trap cheese.

"Isn't this the long way home with that load of gear?" Joanna asked him.

"I'm just putting off the evil hour," he said despondently. "I can't stand the sight of that harbor now that I'm anchored fast in it. Felt like I'd renewed my youth when I threw those pots overboard in February. Now the long pretty days are coming, and the spring spurt, and I got to go back on the car again."

"Where's your buyer?" Joanna asked.

"Fool girl's up and left me. Christ, I only gave her the job to please Noll, he's used me right all these years. But she's got a good head on her, and she ran things fine, so I got spoiled." He opened another can of soda with fatalistic desperation, as if it were another fifth of whiskey. "Trouble is, she's female, and got normal female instincts, but I'd have thought a girl who's grown up in the business wasn't about to fall arse over teakettle for some young tom in rubber boots. The ones from away, sure, they think it's all so damn romantic. But I thought she'd know better."

"Well, love goes where it's sent, they say," said Mark.

"Ayuh, even into a cow turd. I know that. But love don't mix with business." He laughed suddenly, and winked at Joanna. "Not that I haven't had my share of trying it, before I got married and respectable." He rubbed Louis's broad head. "I hope you don't take offense at what I said about your boy. It's no insult. I'm partial to cats."

"No offense taken," said Joanna. "So Bron's gone. I'm sorry."

"Well, you've got your boy to blame for that, I guess. But it's likely for the best. Too many bad marriages these days . . . Always were," he corrected himself. "Takes a special

breed of woman to be an island wife, too. He knows that.
This fetcher Darrell's lugged home—by the time the summer
people've come and gone, that bird'll be flown too. You wait
and see."

"Jamie couldn't wait to take Bron to bed," Joanna told
Nils. "Then when she became a liability he couldn't wait
to drop her." They'd seen Phoebe leaving the house, so they
knew it was safe to speak out loud in broad daylight on private
matters. "I don't feel very proud of him right now."

"He's so cautious he probably never mentioned marriage,
and I don't think he bedded her against her will," said Nils.

"You don't like it any more than I do."

"I never liked any of it, except Bron herself. I didn't think
much of her being so easy, but I liked her. Seemed an honest,
straightforward kind of youngster."

"I wish I could look at this as a noble sacrifice Jamie's
made to save everybody's skin, not only his own," said Joanna.
"Now don't tell me I can't have both ends and the middle. I
know that."

"I was only going to say it's over, and forget it."

"I'm a woman, I identify with Bron, so I can't forget it. On
command, that is, like somebody under hypnosis. But I am
not going to brood," she assured him. "What do you think of
planting the bush beans where the spinach was last year?"

The call came for Jamie that *Valkyrie* was ready, and he
flew in from Brigport, intending to paint her before she was
launched. The smaller children made Easter decorations in
school, rabbits wearing dresses and overalls, and baby chicks
wearing flowery bonnets. The older girls drew a fresco of
lilies on the blackboard. Even the boys liked coloring eggs.
After school each day they rehearsed their Easter service.

David Sorensen took Phoebe and Freddy across to Port
George in *Phoebe Ann*. Tommy Wiley went with them;
Owen had given him a week off. The three high school stu-

dents came out on the Saturday boat, a trip both foggy and
choppy but not by island standards a bad one. This year
Easter coincided with their spring vacation, and they came
ashore damp but exhilarated, as if they had a world of free
time before them, not just a week.

Joanna hoped that Jamie would look up Bronwen ashore;
that there'd been some arrangement between them that they'd
kept to themselves, letting the older people think as they
pleased. With all there was to do at this time of year, with
all the expectations and promises of spring, she was still
disturbed at times by the fact that Jamie could have simply
dumped Bron. This led to a new anxiety; was Jamie capable
of forming a strong attachment, or would he never let himself go that much, never give anything away, and grow more
and more into himself as time went on? The picture of him as
a silent, unyielding, solitary old man haunted her in the early
hours when one is most likely to be haunted. With sunlight, or
at least daylight—even a stormy dawn—and her first cup of
coffee, she would call herself a fool. She was so ashamed of
her fantasies that she wouldn't tell Nils. Instead she would
repeat to herself what he had already said to her.

Jamie's Jamie, and we have to accept him as he is. A very
private person, as they say ... Yes, she would eagerly agree,
and why do I insist that what works for us has to work for
him? Randy Fowler was probably right when he said Jamie
had made the right decision. A cautious son could be a great
comfort to parents, the way things were these days. The way
things had always been, any day, she corrected herself, wondering how her father and mother had survived raising five
sons.

The children's Easter service was a great success and they
had a pretty day for it, which was unusual. At times April
was hardly distinguishable from winter.

It was time to take away the banking, and the vegetable
seedlings were beginning to grow on windowsills. The first
herring of the season hit the harbor. Nobody did anything

about it; Jamie was captain of the seine gang now, as much as there was a captain. Owen, who had sold him the outfit, was the one to spot the action, when he rowed out to his boat at dusk to get something he'd forgotten.

He came directly up to the house where Joanna and Nils were sleepily preparing to close down for the night after a long day. "Where in hell is that boy of yours? The harbor's full of herring, but everybody's down on their arse watching damn-fool TV because he's not here."

"He's painting his boat, which you know very well," said Joanna.

"He's had four good days to paint her, and he sure as hell isn't painting *tonight*. He's off on a spree somewhere."

"I hope he is!" said Joanna angrily. "Good God, look at yourself at his age. What were *you* up to?"

"That's beside the point."

"It always is when you don't want anyone to remind you of it."

"Oh, calm down, both of you," said Nils. "Sit down and relax, Owen."

"I can't relax, dammit! Not with those herring out there and my outfit high and dry!"

"You sold Jamie the outfit, remember?" said Nils. "And those aren't likely to be the only herring this year."

"Well, they could be," Owen argued. "It's happened like that in the past! He's probably hired a car and driven to Portland to see some X-rated movies, while the herring come and go."

"You impossible *Puritan!*" Joanna said. "Besides, you don't have to go all the way to Portland now for dirty movies."

Owen whirled around in his pacing and jabbed a finger at her. "Maybe he's got his girl pregnant and he's having to marry her. Right this minute. Ever think of *that?*"

"Well, at least it would save me having to decide what the groom's mother is going to wear."

Nils was shaking his head. "You know what he sounds like,

Jo, tramping up and down and waving his arms and raving? I'd swear Grampa's possessed him. I keep expecting him to break out in Swedish cussing."

"Did he really cuss, Nils?" Joanna asked.

"I don't know, but it sure sounded like it. We'd all run for cover when he cut loose."

Owen swung around, glaring at them; then his frustration broke up in laughter. "Oh, what the hell!" He dropped into a chair and stretched out his legs. "Sure, the boy deserves some fun. He's too solemn for his own good. But it's times like now when I wish I hadn't given it up. When the frost goes out of the ground and the wind starts smelling like spring, I get so damn homesick for the days when we chased herring up and down the coast . . ." His gaze lengthened as if he were seeing distances through the house walls. "Setting out on fine evenings, with the seineboat behind and a string of dories in tow, jogging along in the sunset waiting for the dark . . . Christ, there's times when I don't know myself anymore."

They were silent; there was nothing to say. After a few moments Owen said in a slow, heavy voice, "The year I had to give it up—it was the same year we almost lost Barry Barton right in the harbor here, remember?" The words fell of their own weight like rocks, and rings seemed to spread out from them in widening circles. Without knowing why it happened—the images came so fast—Joanna saw Vanessa at the clubhouse party with the child in her lap, looking up, and Owen standing before her, both faces gone impassive as if they'd been simultaneously stunned into vacancy. The reaction she'd had then came back now, much stronger. Then, as Owen slapped his hand down hard on the table and stood up, the pictures went as rapidly as they had come.

Rory was barking at Owen's noise, and Owen said, "You're right, old Cap'n. That's enough nostalgia for today."

I'll get back to it later, Joanna thought. I'll try to take it apart. But she knew she didn't really want to.

"I'd better get out of here before old Gunnar really grabs

aholt," said Owen. "This is the time of year when he was on the prod."

"I'd have said that time of year was twelve months long," said Nils. "Have a drink. Hot coffee, cold beer—"

"Nope. Holly's brought home some new cutthroat card game we're all supposed to play tonight."

"I'll bet you were scared she'd bring home a boyfriend with hair to the waist and draped with whiskers and beads," Joanna jeered.

"The day she does that, *he* leaves by way of my boat, and *she* doesn't go back to school. She can knit trap heads and bait bags for her pocket money, and learn to keep house."

"Grampa Gunnar *has* got him!" said Joanna. "Somebody ought to warn Laurie."

Owen gave her the most radiant of Bennett smiles. "Oh, I'll shed the old devil between here and there. In the bosom of my family I'm clever as a kitten."

Nils and Rory walked across the yard with him, and Joanna finished setting the table for morning. The picture of Owen and Vanessa returned, but she wouldn't give it houseroom. She had enough pesky obsessions now without adding another one, created out of nothing but an imagination that seemed sometimes never to have gone beyond adolescence.

Nils dropped his book and fell asleep before she did, and she was absorbed enough in her reading not to think even marginally about either Jamie or Owen. But she couldn't coast gradually into sleep because she had to rouse up to blow out the lamp, and then she lay in the dark wide awake, seeing Barry and Vanessa as they had first appeared on the island. Barry was as brisk and friendly as a terrier, Vanessa arrived like a captive in chains.

She was different now, at least outwardly. You would never really know her, yet she had become a part of the island fabric and would leave a hole if she should disappear. Barry was more of a man now, less the bouncing overage juvenile . . . The looks, or lack of them, at the party had meant nothing except that Van didn't like Owen and he knew it. He didn't charm every woman he met, even if there was a myth to that effect. He might make some hackles rise, and who knew what was in Vanessa's past that set her against men like him?

She went to sleep finally, relaxed in the certainty that any unanswered questions about the Bartons didn't concern her in the least.

18

*J*amie, apparently unmarried, came home with *Valkyrie*, and if he had looked up Bron, nobody was going to know it. *Valkyrie* had a new engine, far more powerful than the damaged one. True to form, he hadn't bothered to mention it beforehand. He and his crew, Ralph, young Matt, and Hugo, began immediately to get the seine ready for stopping off the harbor.

"I think we can safely say that if he has one passion it's herring," Joanna said to Nils. Jamie, sleeping in his own bed at night and going out from the family wharf to haul, behaved as if he'd never been away. As far as anyone knew, no more of his traps had been bothered. Dave returned, bringing only Tommy with him. Tommy looked strangely pallid, as if his vacation had been strenuous. He was wearing dark glasses and was unenthusiastic when Richard and Sam ran down the wharf to welcome him. Someone asked him if he was sorry to be back, and he replied fervently, "I'm some *glad.*"

That's the most he's said since we left Port George," said Dave. "I don't know whether he's worn out from sowing wild oats, or if he's in love." Dave crossed the yard that night to have fish chowder with the Sorensens, and Joanna asked him if Phoebe and Freddy had given up. She tried not to sound hopeful. The hope was for his sake; he looked much better than when he'd gone ashore. If he was going to be alone, she'd be glad to have him eat all his meals with them, and she'd see that he ate the right things.

But he sighed. "Nope. Freddy was trying his brother's new motorbike and showing off like one of these stunt riders at the county fairs. Bounced off and sprained his back."

"How long will it lay him up?" asked Nils.

"Oh, he's not laid up—not that one. I think the only time he's lit anyplace is when the bike threw him. But he's not supposed to do anything heavy for a few days ... Might's well enjoy it while I can," he said, brightening. "Something about this time of year. 'When the hounds of spring are on winter's traces.' Remember all that poetry Miss Ashley used to read to us? We sat there twitching as if we had fleas, but you know, the stuff stayed with us. With me, anyway."

They were moving gear nearer to the island all the time, as the lobsters moved in, and by summer they'd be fishing close to the rocks. Joanna went out with Nils one morning to set a load of dry traps around the Outer Ledges, and then they went on to haul some in the Rock Channel. Nils turned on the radio to ask Dave how he was doing. They could see him farther off to the southeast. There was a light roll, and *Phoebe Ann* rocked as if she were a cradle.

"Finest kind!" he called back jubilantly. "My God, this is some peaceful out here! I dunno but what I may subsidize my man to keep him ashore! ... I got a pot on the washboard here, I'll talk to you later."

"Never mind, nothing going on anyway," Nils answered. He was coming up to one of his own buoys and had to gaff it, so he didn't bother to turn off the set. The illusion of silence over the sea was always destroyed by the radio-telephone, because there was so much conversation going on, some informative, some foolish, some neighborly. Joanna half-listened, the bait iron poised, watching Nils pick out and measure some big broad-backed dark green beauties. Suddenly she became aware that Darrell Robey was calling and he sounded upset.

"Listen," she said to Nils, "Darrell's in trouble."

"Where are you, Darrell?" a Brigport voice responded.

"West side of Pirate Island. Got a warp in my wheel, and

there's some old baister of a surge on down here. My wife's seasick. Christ, I never *saw* anybody so seasick!" He sounded desperate now.

"Ain't you got a piece of salt pork on a string for her to swallow?" someone teased.

"Hell, he ought to be able to think of something better'n that to take her mind off her guts," another voice broke in. "*I* could."

"Shut up, you sons o' bitches!" Darrell exploded. "Look, I'm not asking anybody to tow me in! Ain't somebody decent enough to take *her* in? I can jog in slow by myself, but I want her on solid land while there's still something left of her!"

With more sympathy one of the others said, "It'd take me half an hour to get where you are. You could be pretty near home by then."

"Me too," someone else said. "Seems as if there ought to be somebody nearer."

"Maybe Eloise is pregnant," Joanna said to Nils. "That would really scare her."

"Somebody's off there to the southern end." Darrell sounded breathless. "It's *Valkyrie*. Hey, Jamie, you listening?"

Far off, someone snickered. "Got her back, has he? He better keep her out of harm's way in the future."

"I never trusted that kind of cooling system in a boat. It's likely to fail when you ain't looking, and leave your arse in a sling."

Nils glanced over his shoulder at Joanna. "Don't be so flourishy with that bait iron, you'll be stabbing yourself."

"Who's flourishy?" she snapped. Nils grinned and she shrugged, reminding herself of Linnie. "It's over and done with."

"*Bonny Eloise* calling *Valkyrie!*" Darrell sang out. "You got that fast new engine, Jim! How about running my wife home? She's some sick!"

There was a long pause. Then Jamie said, "All right, I'll pick her up."

Darrell was touchingly grateful. "I'm much obliged, Jim."

"Ayuh." It was flat and final.

"The reluctant Good Samaritan," said Nils.

"He probably doesn't want to look at Brigport Harbor again for a good long time." She wondered if he would miss Bron on the car; if guilt or indifference would keep him from looking up at the windows over the workshop. Well, it was nothing to dwell on. It was over and done with, as she'd just said.

In the late afternoon Charles and Owen came up to the house looking for drinks, hot or cold. As the year warmed, the sessions were moved out to the table in the sun parlor, looking across the slope of lawn to the woods. Joanna still yearned for a table with a water view. The cabin at Bull Cove might be fantasy, but she could say to herself devoutly and often, *If I live long enough* ... And the promise made her feel positive. In the meantime, there were moments when the view across to the woods pleased her, especially after the warblers began to come, and she would keep her binoculars and Peterson on the table beside her cup. No room for that now when the men came in, filling up the place, but she'd rather have them than not. Jamie and Hugo appeared a little while later, and there was a naturalness about this, like a return home. The boys helped themselves in the kitchen and came out to the table.

"What happended to *Bonny Eloise* out there?" Charles asked Jamie.

"You mean the girl or the boat? One got a couple of warps in her wheel, and the other one got seasick. There was quite a roll down there, and I guess he thought she wouldn't last till he got home, at the rate he was crawling."

"You have to clean up your boat afterward?"

"Nope," he said seriously. "I guess she didn't have anything else to heave. When I put on some speed and she got that cold wind in her face, she revived. Looked all right by the time I put her on the wharf."

"He got pots down there?" Owen asked.

"No, but a lot of other guys have. He'd taken her down there on a ride, close in so she could see the new cottage Ivor's having built. He was gawking too, so he managed to run right through a place where the traps are thick as spatter. Even his cage didn't do him any good. He was cussing out some of his relatives." His mouth twitched. "I told him I didn't know he knew so many words, and using 'em in front of his wife too."

"She's probably heard them all before," said Hugo cynically. "He didn't get her out of a convent."

"I suppose the clan's going to get all they can before Ivor starts setting out," said Nils.

"Makes you kind of glad Brigport would never let us set a trap in the water down there," Owen said. "Now we can all sit back and listen to the cries of anguish."

"The way I heard it," Hugo said, "they think Ivor's the one who'll be crying. They figure they've got squatters' rights on those grounds."

"Rather them than us." Charles took his mug out to the kitchen for more coffee. "The Riddells are rich enough to keep setting out new gear till the Last Trumpet."

"Did you ever hear that the Mafia's bought into some of the big lobster companies?" Hugo asked brightly. "Maybe Ivor will put contracts out on the ringleaders."

"Stop that foolishness," his father ordered. "And if you've dropped any gear within a mile of that place, you move it damn quick, or you'll be sliced off by one side or the other just to keep you from laughing too hard."

"How's Bonny Eloise doing?" Owen asked. "The girl, not the boat. Life as a lobsterman's wife beginning to take its toll? She aged any since the party?"

"All I know is she was green around the gills and then she pinked up a dite."

"You probably never even looked straight at her," said Hugo. "A perfect chance to show the charm Bennett's Islanders are famous for, and he passed it up."

"I can tell you another thing Bennett's Islanders are famous for," said Jamie, "but my mother would make me leave the table."

Joanna thought, He sounds contented enough with life right now, but at what cost? *Whose?* Owen leaned forward, dark eyes gleaming.

"Tell me something, Jim. When you took the bride home today, did you take a swing around Randy's car for the sake of auld lang syne? Or couldn't you bear to?" He shook his head and fetched a theatrical sigh. "My, but she was a sweet little armful to swing in a square dance. Cute as a bunny rabbit."

As if nothing had been spoken, Jamie said, "Well, time to get back to work." He got up and Hugo did too, saying, "Thanks for the mug-up, Aunt Jo."

After the boys went out Owen asked with mock concern, "Did I hit a sore spot?"

"That's what you were hoping for," Joanna accused.

"He looks older. Experienced. There's a different light in his eye. He still looked innocent when he came home from the Navy, but no more."

"Anybody around here who was still innocent at twenty-five would have to be retarded," said Charles. The men laughed and shoved back their chairs, and returned to the shore. Joanna was clearing up the dishes when Laurie came in the back door of the sun parlor. She was flushed and out of breath. She put her finger to her lips, looked out the front door, and then came back to Joanna, smiling at her mystified expression.

"I feel like a secret agent." She dropped into a chair. "Whew! I wanted to get here without creating a sensation, so I had to come around through the meadow. Richard's the nosiest critter on earth except when Holly's home, and then there's a struggle for supremacy. So I had to dodge the two of them."

"Cheer up, we're in luck. Phoebe hasn't come back yet, to pop in while you're telling me you're leaving Owen for some haker you've been meeting secretly off Schooner Head."

"How'd you ever guess?" Laurie clasped hands against her breast.

"I'm getting to be an expert at it. Tea, coffee?"

"I could use a strong hot cup of tea." Joanna brought it to her and she sipped cautiously, but thirstily. "Oh, that's good. Just what I needed. Look, before anyone *does* come in —is there any way I can talk to Jamie? I have to do it now, if it's possible. Otherwise, I'd just like to sit here and comfortably wilt. Wow, I've got to lose ten pounds, or Owen will be swapping me off."

"Jamie's just gone back to the shore," Joanna said.

"Which is where I don't want to talk to him. Jo, this is awfully important," she said. "Would you ask him to come up here? Then I'd just as soon tell you why."

"All right. I can hardly wait."

Down at the wharf Dave had just come in. Jamie was mending tears from their first set in some seine spread out on the beach near Linnie's dory. She went to him through the dryly rattling beach pea vines and spoke to him in a low voice.

"Your Aunt Laurie's at the house and she wants to talk to you. Can you leave that a minute?"

The flat wooden needle went in and out to make the time-out-of-mind knot, the left hand and fingers were crooked in the fisherman's way through centuries. "What's she want?"

"She didn't tell me, but it's important."

One knot, then another one. He hated to leave a job he'd just started. She waited, listening to the men's voices from the wharf.

"All right," Jamie said finally. He put his work down and walked home with her.

"I won't waste your time, Jamie," Laurie said at once. "I'm worried about Tommy. He's taken to camping out and it's not fit."

"Where?" Jamie was amused, but politely so.

"Oh, up on the hill with a pup tent and his sleeping bag. And you know it's still damp and cold in the woods."

"Maybe he feels adventurous," Joanna suggested. "If he's got a sleeping bag he's warm enough. Maybe he met a girl on the mainland and he wants to be alone to think about her."

"If he has, he's mighty love-sick then, because he's hardly eating, and Tommy was always a great trencherman. No, he's got something worrying him. Even Richard's noticed. How can he miss it?" She looked exasperated. "Owen tried to talk to him aboard the boat, and Tommy promptly got seasick. And you know that Tommy *never* gets seasick, no matter how rough it is."

"What have I got to do with this?" Jamie asked.

"He likes you and he looks up to you. You're enough older for that, but not too much older. You're the same generation, but you've been around."

"Have I?" That slow-coming smile, like his father's, could be quietly devastating if he knew how to use it, and not just on aunts.

"Come on now!" said Laurie. "A couple of years in the Navy represents the peak of cosmopolitan experience to Tommy. He's losing weight, too, from not eating, and he was skinny enough to begin with. We've been wondering if he's got some girl in trouble."

"What, at Easter?" Joanna protested. "Would he know *this* quick?"

"Don't forget he was home over Christmas. Oh, dear. Even if he's old enough to start a baby he's certainly not old enough to be married. He may be twenty and a rooster in some respects, but to me he's about as downy a chick as Richard."

"He's got a mother and father to worry about him," Joanna said.

"I know. But he's been with us for three years and he's one of the family. Jamie, if you could only find out," she implored him. "Whatever it is, he'll be a lot better off for telling it."

"All right," said Jamie kindly. "Where is he now?"

"They haven't got in yet. But he takes off right after supper with his flashlight and his radio and his book. You could corner him in his camp. You go through the pasture gate and up over those ledges to the left. You know, the flat place where Richard and Sam had their tent last summer."

"I'll go over tonight then."

"I'll be grateful forever."

"That won't be necessary," he told her solemnly, but then he smiled again, and Joanna thought of Bron, and wondered whether the memory of that smile was pleasure or torment.

19

She had a chance to tell Nils about Jamie's errand, and then Dave came across the yard for a supper of fish and potatoes. The potatoes and squash had grown in Joanna's garden, the fish salted in a crock after Nils and Joanna had spent a brilliant October Sunday catching codfish off the Rock. She had made the piccalilli. No one raised a pig on the island these days, so the salt pork, now transmuted into crisp translucent scraps, had come from Brigport. "Shouldn't eat that, but by God I'm going to," said Dave. "Can't do any more harm than pizza sauce."

Jamie went out at dusk. The men knit on trap heads and watched television. Joanna used to knit heads once, to help support herself and Ellen after Alec died. Tonight she worked on a sweater for one of Ellen's children. They took to the shores like sandpipers whenever they could come, and one of them was showing an interest in the violin. Alec would have adored them, Joanna thought, but she could not imagine Alec as a grandfather any more than she could see Jamie in the part. They called Nils "Grandfather," which in its own way was just as strange. I must ask him sometime if he thinks *Grandmother* fits me, she thought with amusement.

Still, she liked it from the children; it was like possessing a title.

Jamie came in before Dave left, and watched the last of the movie. When his uncle had gone, they waited for him to volunteer information but, being Jamie, he didn't. He got himself a glass of milk and a handful of cookies.

"Well, did you or didn't you see Tommy?" Joanna finally asked.

"Ay-up!" He drank some milk. "Found him all bundled up in his pup tent reading by flashlight. I asked him straight out what was eating him, and he was so startled he told me. Poor little bugger thinks he's got VD."

Even Nils straightened up on that one. Jamie drank more milk. "Hardly dares go into the house for fear of infecting somebody. I told him I didn't think that was likely. Won't use the bathroom. I wonder if they've noticed that. Got himself a latrine in the woods. He thinks he's the worst sinner that ever was, and he's scared foolish."

"Has he got anything to worry about?" his father asked.

Jamie shrugged. "I'm no expert. I didn't offer to make an examination and a diagnosis." He laughed. "That would make a scene to discover, wouldn't it? Biggest scandal to ever hit Bennett's Island. So *that's* why Jamie Bennett can get along without girls!"

They all laughed. Jamie shared a cookie with Rory. "I asked him about sores, he's got nothing like that. Lot of discomfort, though. Getting real painful to make water."

"But where does he think he got it?" Joanna asked.

"He was out on a party while he was ashore, where there was a lot of pairing off. He had a few beers, and with Tommy it only takes one to make him think he's the man who broke the bank at Monte Carlo. Well, he had more than one, and he ended up on a couch with a girl, and he thinks they made out, but he hasn't seen her since, so he's not sure."

"I hope he doesn't get an urgent summons from her papa in a couple of months," said Joanna.

"Likely she wouldn't know who it was, the way he described the party. He swore she was a nice girl, so he couldn't believe she had anything like that. So I asked him what a nice girl was doing at a party like that, besides putting out—which he knew she was doing with somebody else before she and the beers wrassled him onto the couch." He stopped to eat and drink again. "If he's got anything, she's the one."

"What did you tell Owen and Laurie?" Nils asked.

"Nothing in the house, with Richard and Sammy and Holly standing around. I said I was on my way back from the Eastern End. Uncle Owen walked down the road with me, and I told him. He won't let on to Tommy. I'm taking the kid over to Stonehaven tomorrow to the doctor. For the public I'm borrowing him for the day to help me load some spruce laths I'm getting over there."

"Well, let's hope it's a false alarm," his father said.

"From what I've been hearing and reading," Jamie said grimly, "it wouldn't surprise me if he did have something. The kids are passing it round and round, and some of them are a lot younger than Tommy. And the so-called nice ones are pretty damn generous with it. Well, I got her name out of him before he could stop to think, and *that* little disaster is going to be nailed."

They left early the next morning. No one else knew about it in time to think up a good reason for a ride to the big island fifteen miles to the northeast; Tommy in his misery and shame didn't need any more company. The day was cool and cloudy, with a light northeast breeze and a smart chop. It wasn't enough to keep the men in from hauling, and with a day to herself Joanna went down to the Eastern End. She and Philippa dug dandelion greens in the field, trailed by Steve's dog, several cats, and a duck and drake. There were times when the Eastern End seemed as remote from the harbor as a separate island, with only two houses on it. Steve's helper had lived in the other house but he had quit and moved to the mainland when his wife became pregnant and it looked like a difficult nine months ahead.

They were making the house over to Eric, Philippa's son by her first marriage, so that no matter where his work took him he would know he had a permanent home on the island of his heart. "There's plenty of room for the other children's needs, and Eric will be wanting a place before anyone else," Philippa said. "I wouldn't be surprised if he brought a girl home to meet us this summer. I just have this feeling. But any new wife is an unknown quantity, even if you knew her before."

"Even your own kids are," Joanna said.

"Don't I know it! So the house isn't to go out of the family. If he ever has to give it up, it can't be sold except to us, for whatever he's put into it. Of course, we're all hoping for the best."

"Universal family motto. *We hope for the best.* How do you say that in Latin, to make it sound classy?"

"I don't know, we'll ask Eric when he comes."

"He could probably say it in Greek and Hebrew, too. I'm glad he's coming this summer, girl or not."

In the late afternoon she had her greens all cleaned and soaking in cold water, and was upstairs changing out of grimy jeans and sneakers when she saw *Valkyrie* coming up Long Cove, with a bone in her teeth and white rooster tail streaming behind. Joanna and Rory were down at the wharf by the time the boat was in the harbor. Neither David nor Nils was in yet, but Rosa came out from her fishhouse, and Ralph came around from his wharf.

"Hey, I thought you were bringing back spruce laths!" he called as *Valkyrie* came up to the spilings with the new engine purring.

"Couldn't find them. Guess I was misled." Jamie shut off the engine, and went up on the bow. "We went all over that island on a wild-goose chase."

"Where'd you hear about them, anyway?"

"Couple of Stonehaven guys talking on short wave. Here." He tossed a line at Ralph. Tommy came up the ladder.

"You'd ought to know better than to pay attention to that. Might have been those two I heard talking one day about running a whorehouse. One of 'em said he wouldn't make any money because he'd be his own best customer."

Tommy, reaching down for the carton that Jamie handed up, laughed uproariously and nearly fell off the wharf.

"You'd almost think he knew what I was talking about,

wouldn't you?" said Ralph. Tommy laughed even harder. It was obvious he had nothing to worry about.

"I hope Jamie paid you for your time, Tommy," Joanna said. "Don't let him get away with anything. I hear he has fishhooks in his pockets."

"Oh, he took me to dinner in the best place over there, and I picked out the fanciest grub on the menu."

"Didn't fob you off with a hamburger, then," said Rosa.

"Nope! Hi, men!" he shouted as Richard and Sam arrived.

"Gee, why didn't you stay to the movies?" Richard asked enviously. "We would've."

"We had better things to do than that foolishness."

"And besides, they don't show any filthy ones over there," said Ralph.

"Anyway, we had to bring a passenger back as far as Brigport," Tommy said. "Here, Rich, grab aholt. Your mother gave me a list, and that's her stuff."

"You mean you went around the store and picked it all out?" Sam and Richard were convulsed. They fell together, cracking heads.

"What do you think it was, you numbheads, *underwear?* It was sewing stuff and I gave the list to the lady ... You helping, Sam, or just standing there making idiot noises?"

"I'm helping, I'm helping."

"Here." He loaded them. "See if you can lug this across the island without dumping it all out between here and there." He picked up a stuffed plastic shopping bag. "Thanks, Jamie," he said earnestly. "It was a great day. Look, if you do find out anything about those spruce laths, or whatever else you need a hand for, just let me know."

"I will," said Jamie. Tommy and the younger boys went off between the fishhouses to the road, loud and ebullient. "Well, I'm heading home for a good cup of decent coffee before I put the boat on the mooring," Jamie said. He leaned down and took hold of Rory's ruff. "How are you today, Brother?"

Rory's eyes fixed on Jamie's with amber bliss. "How about

a mug-up?" Jamie asked him, and Rory started for home.

The afternoon was chilly but there was a smell of green-ness and growing. "It's strangely quiet around here," Joanna remarked as they passed Dave's house.

"Phoebe's ambushed me so many times right about here that I automatically go way off on a starboard tack," Jamie said. "The way Rory still sheers away from the place where the firecracker went off when he was a pup."

"Just listen." They stopped in the path. "That house must be sitting there gently throbbing with relief, like a tooth when the ache is dying down. Did you ever hear Freddy looking for a saucepan in the cupboard, with Phoebe scream-ing directions at him?"

"Hey, maybe we can notify her doctor that Bennett's Island is a might dangerous place for her to be in her condi-tion."

"Oh listen, out of sight should be out of mind. Forget her, and tell me about Tommy." They went on again. Rory waited on the doorstep, too gentlemanly to show his impa-tience.

"Well, he was so drunk with relief when he came out of the doctor's office that I never did get the straight of it except it's not VD. It's a bladder infection, near as I can make out, and the doctor gave him a shot, and some pills to take. He's to drink gallons of water and go back next week. And not catch cold in the meantime. The main thing is, it's got nothing to do with women."

"No wonder he ate such a dinner."

"Yup, he made up for the past week. I guess Doc Summers gave him a little talk about the dangers of free love, and I followed it up." They went into the house. Rory managed a few prances toward the kitchen. "I told him I didn't expect him to live like a monk, but at least he could be careful about jumping in and out of the sack. He was so delirious he prom-ised everything. After dinner he was bushed, so he went aboard the boat and crawled into a bunk. I borrowed a pickup and went looking for spruce laths, just so as not to make a liar out of myself. No dice, but I did hear about a good piece of twine cheap."

Because of Tommy, Joanna'd heard more from Jamie in two days than in two weeks before. She was both gratified and amused. "Who was the passenger?" she asked.

"Huh?" He was washing his hands at the kitchen sink and turned a blank face toward her.

"Tommy said you had a passenger for Brigport."

"Oh!" He went back to washing. "Eloise Robey. She'd been to Limerock to see her folks, and came out on the ferry. She was going to call Darrell from there, till she met up with us in the restaurant and hitched a ride home."

"Do you want a sandwich or something sweet?"

"One of those doughnuts'ill be fine." He dried his hands and took one from the jar.

"How's Eloise doing?" Joanna asked. "Did she say? Life out here must seem pretty dull to an almost-Sea Goddess."

"Well, she's no dumb kid, you know," he said seriously. He watched her pour boiling water into the top of the pot. "She knew what she was getting into. Pretty well knew, that is. I guess you can't always tell."

"I always thought Darrell was too bashful even to cast a shadow, but he must have a lot more to him, to be able to sweep such a beauty off her feet."

"Darrell's not what he seems." He didn't go on with it, which made it sound cryptic and profound; it probably wasn't meant to be.

"Who is?" she said. "You didn't happen to see Bronwen the last time you were on the main."

There, it was out and, surprisingly, he didn't cut her off. "Is that a statement or a question?"

"It was a hope that you'd pick it up. I just wondered what became of the great romance, that's all."

"Never was one as far as I know. Look, I'm going back to Brigport for the night. Bruce told me this afternoon he's bought Ally Bradford's outfit at a bargain, but some of the twine needs mending and rehanging. I'm going to help him so he'll be ready by the next dark."

She sat down at the table with him while he had his mug-up. She was always happy for him when he talked herring and was actively engaged in seining them, because these were the times when she could be sure that *he* was happy; he became something and someone else then, a distillation of the ancestral blood of generations of Scandinavian and Devon fishermen, not her and Nils's child but the inheritor of hundreds of years of experience.

In a little while he took *Valkyrie* out of the harbor again, passing *Joanna S.* coming in. He waved to his father and went on past the breakwater beacon, heading across the fast gray and white chop. He would pass between the southwest end of Brigport and the Thresher, then go up the northern side and anchor off the MacKenzies' shore.

"Good Lord," Nils said with asperity, " 'Once bitten twice shy' doesn't apply to him, I guess."

"He was too excited about twine, even somebody else's. You could tell he can hardly wait to get his hands on it. And the boat'll be right under their noses there. With Bron gone there's no reason for anybody to try anything now. Whit's still hobbling around with a cane. The other kids liked Jamie well enough in the winter, during the hockey games."

"*Some* of them did. To a few others he's still a Bennett's Island bastard. Well, it's up to him, isn't it? Tell me what happened to Tommy today."

20

It was now May by the calendar, though on the island it was still more of a charming idea than a fact. The schoolchildren hung handmade Maybaskets to everyone; a few crocuses showed, there were some new birds, and the azure stars of scilla burst open among the rocks at the edge of the Sorensen woods, confirming the idea as a potentially workable one.

Phoebe's and Freddy's time ashore had stretched out to nearly two weeks. Joanna fed David whenever he'd come to a meal, but he had begun refusing, making jokes about being so spoiled he wouldn't be able to stomach Phoebe's cooking. "I may have to take it over in self-defense," he said.

"He's not eating enough," Joanna complained to Nils. "And I'll bet he's white as the underside of a haddock under that tan. He probably needs iron."

"He's got chronic indigestion and he'll have it as long as he's got those two," said Nils. "If they took off for Alaska to live he might get shed of his bellyache, but he'd come up with something else." She started to protest and he put his finger on her nose. "I'm not brutal. I know my brother, that's all. There's absolutely nothing we can do about the way he runs his life."

On the morning after the Maybaskets, everyone went out but Dave. When Joanna hadn't seen any signs of life over there long after Nils and Jamie left, she went across the yard to see if he was all right. He was at the table in the neat kitchen—he and Nils had special tidiness genes, she said—

drinking tea. His face was drawn and grayish, but he smiled when he saw her.

"Hi, Jo! Summer complaint hit me in the night, so I'm staying in today."

"Rushing the season, aren't you? ... Remember when we'd always say it was the ground water running into the well when we'd had a lot of rain?"

"I still don't think that's so far off." He was obviously speaking with an effort. "I'm going back to bed. A few hours' sleep'll set me right. I've been awake since midnight and on the run."

"How about some Kaopectate?"

"Thanks, Jo, but I figure I'm more sleepy now than anything else."

"I'll get out then and not pester you. I'll send Nils over when he comes in and maybe you'll be ready for something light then."

"You know me," he said cheerfully. "I'll be ready for a five-course feed by then."

Damn it, she thought fiercely on the way home, if there's nothing we can do about these things, why do we have to watch? Why do they persist in suffering right under our noses? Forget it, Nils said. Well, it's *your* brother, she told him silently. She did her washing, and when that was all out on the lines she put up a lunch and went up across the field to see what Nora Fennell was doing. Nora was dismally prepared to clean closets, but could be easily led astray this morning. With their two dogs they went down toward Sou'west Point, in no hurry; the steep stony beaches were too full of interesting and possibly useful débris. The prevailing southwest wind whipped up a light surf. There was always a swell down here, always the deep, slow, glistening seas pouring over the ledges.

They ate their lunch in Old Man's Cove, where fresh water ran down from some mysterious source to fill a rock basin where the dogs could drink. The loom of Sou'west Point was still ahead of them, but they decided to leave it for another day, and worked their way slowly homeward, carrying what they could of their loot.

"I'll never outgrow this," Joanna said. "I swear I won't pick up one thing and I always stagger home loaded like a packhorse, and hope to get it stashed away behind the barn before Nils sees it."

"Oh, do you meet up with that too?" asked Nora, and they both laughed.

It wasn't quite that bad; Nils appreciated a driftwood fire in the Franklin stove as much as she did. She'd also found one of his buoys, and a perfectly sound varnished oar with rowlock still attached. "I hope no harm came to the owner. I always used to be afraid of finding a body all wound up in the kelp after a storm," she said. "But I never did. Nobody has in my lifetime, though it's happened long ago."

"Cheer up, it could still happen to you."

"Thanks."

She came into the backyard and stopped to feel the sheets for dryness. The hens clustered sociably around her feet and impeded her progress toward the back door. Rory was good-humored when they got in his way, having known most of them since they were just out of the egg. In the house he went to his blanket and lay down with a sigh. She emptied her basket of driftwood into the woodbox beside the Franklin stove, and went back to the kitchen to rinse her thermos bottle.

School wasn't out yet, and the village was quiet. The harbor was rippling and shimmering in the pale sunlight. But much closer there was something foreign and intrusive to draw her eye away from the distance.

"Oh Lord," Joanna muttered. "They're back. Who brought them?"

Phoebe was walking up from the shore. She had on new slacks of particularly intense blue and a plaid smock top, which vibrated in several different directions. She'd had her

hair cut off into a sort of thatch. She carried two of the in-
evitable plastic shopping bags. Freddy was coming behind
her with a loaded wheelbarrow. He stopped on the road and
had a shouted conversation with someone out of sight; many
gestures, much merriment. Then, with the wheelbarrow, he
came on smiling happily to himself. Phoebe stopped at the
doorstep and watched him approach.

"Maybe he bought a new motorcycle," Joanna said to Rory,
who beat his tail on his blanket a couple of times but didn't
bother to open his eyes. She went out to take in the washing.
She was folding a sheet when Rory began to bark. The
chickens ran squawking in all directions as Freddy came slamming out through the back door.

"For heaven's sake, Freddy!" she exclaimed.

Then she saw his terrified face. *Phoebe*, she thought at once.
Miscarriage. This quick? I just saw her! When he said "Dave,"
she couldn't make sense of it at first.

"He's some sick!" the boy gasped. "I think it's a heart
attack!" He gulped as if trying not to throw up. "*Gee-zuss!*"

Every man who would otherwise be near at hand was out
today. "Run and get Mark," she said. He tore off around the
house; for once he wasn't in rubber boots. She went in through
the sun parlor, saying to Rory, "It's all right, go lie down.
Stay." Her hands and feet had gotten cold, and her head felt
light. This was how things happened. Dave could be dying,
and she wouldn't know how to stop it. None of them would
know.

When she went in, the first thing was the smell of vomit.
The next was Phoebe, standing stiffly against the wall, staring;
she couldn't take her eyes off her father even to glance toward
Joanna. Dave was sagging half-off the couch, and he had indeed
been very sick. The odor in the overheated room was over-
powering. The front of his shirt was bloody, and so was the
mess on the floor. He was tallowy white, shining with sweat,
his eyes shut, and he was obviously in great pain.

"Phoebe, go in the other room and sit down," Joanna said,

but the girl didn't move. Joanna went around the substance on the floor and lifted David's feet gently and put them on the couch. He said faintly, "I'm all right. It's not my heart ... Cold, though."

Not your heart, but something awful, she thought. "Get a blanket, Phoebe."

Still no motion. She turned to go into the next room to find a blanket, and met Nils and Mark coming in the back door. Freddy was behind them, panting, big-eyed. When she saw Nils's face and heard his whisper "*Davie!*" she wanted to put her arms around him, which wasn't needed right now. She went on into the next room and found a blanket folded on a cot there. She brought it out and Nils took it and began to tuck it around his brother. He was almost as pale as Dave.

"Looks as if you've got yourself an ulcer," Mark said heartily, "and it's just erupted."

"Like Vesuvius," Dave whispered without opening his eyes.

"Well, we better get you ashore."

"Not in this mess. Not like this. *Please.*"

"All right, Davie," Nils promised. "We'll do the best we can without rousting you around too much."

With a wail, Phoebe doubled up. "Freddy, take her into the other room," Joanna said. Looking as if he'd been ordered to pick up a rattlesnake, Freddy approached her, and her wail became a shriek. David tried to sit up, and Joanna took Phoebe by the shoulders and pushed her into the next room. She opened the front and let the fresh air pour through. "I've got such pains," Phoebe said between chattering teeth and bending over. "I think I'm going to lose the baby!"

"*Gee-zuss!*" Freddy wilted into a chair. Phoebe drowned him out with her next cry. It could be all dramatics, it could be genuine fear and nerves, it could be premature labor. Why didn't I go all the way to Sou'west Point and miss all this, Joanna mourned. But then I wouldn't be near Nils now.

"Freddy!" Nils called, and Freddy shot out of the chair. "Yessir!"

"Go down aboard my boat and see if you can raise Jamie. Tell him we need him."

"Yessir!" Freddy left by the front door, leaping the four steps in his enthusiasm. "He doesn't care about me!" Phoebe howled.

"Listen, we've got to get both you and your father to the mainland, that's what everybody's trying to do. So you sit quiet here. Are you bleeding?"

"No, but what if I—"

"We'll stop at Brigport. There's a nurse, remember." She'd just remembered it herself, with silent hosannas. Bruce Mac-Kenzie's wife, if she hadn't gone off on a visit somewhere. No, Jamie'd mentioned her yesterday, hadn't he?

"We'll need an old door to carry him down to the wharf," Mark was saying when she returned to the kitchen. Dave looked dead on the couch, she was afraid to watch for his breathing. "There's one over in the barn," Nils answered. He was ladling water into a washbasin. "Show him, Jo, and get some newspapers. We've got to do something about this mess before everybody tramps through it."

On the way out they met Marjorie Percy. "What's wrong? What can I do?"

"Dave's very sick," Joanna said, "but Nils is tending him. You can try calming Phoebe down. She thinks she's having it."

"Oh God," said Marjorie. She went in by the front door.

"What do you think, Mark?" Joanna said to him as they went through the gate.

"I'm scared to think. This is something new to me. He could be bleeding to death inside." They said nothing else. They found the spare door in the barn, and Joanna dusted it off. Mark laid it across the wheelbarrow to take back. "I'll leave this on the doorstep and go down to fill Jamie's tank when he shows up, if that whirligig's got hold of him," he said.

"Listen, Mark, why don't you call Brigport and see if Hannah MacKenzie can go with us, or give us some advice, or something."

"I'll do that."

She went into the house and collected a supply of old newspapers, cleaning rags, and a carton to put the trash in. Liza came in while she was running off a pail of water. "What's going on? Is it Phoebe?"

"Dave." She gave her a brief description. Liza was admirably laconic. "Sounds like a bleeding ulcer all right. What can the rest of us do?"

"Maybe supply hot-water bottles?"

"I'll tell Maggie." She helped Joanna carry her supplies across the dooryard, but didn't offer to go in.

Valkyrie and *Finest Kind* came in first, *Girl Kate* behind them. In the kitchen Nils had managed to get the bloody shirt off Dave and was sponging his face and chest. Joanna spread a thick layer of newspapers on the floor. "We'll take care of that later," she said.

"Marjorie found a clean shirt for him," Nils said. "I don't want to move him around, but Dapper Dan insists."

"He wants to impress the nurses, that's all."

"How'd you guess?" Dave whispered.

"Because you're such a ladies' man at heart, remember?" Joanna told him. "Can you manage alone, Nils?"

"*This* I can, but . . . You're going in with us, aren't you?" He straightened up to look at her.

"Yes. Of course." She realized suddenly that Nils believed his brother was dying before his eyes. She put her hand on his arm and squeezed. "I'll leave you two alone and spare Dave's girlish modesty. I'll go pack for us."

Phoebe was huddled in a chair sobbing and pulling tissues to pieces. "Can you find out which bag has her pajamas and toothbrush and so forth?" Joanna asked Marjorie.

"I heard you," said Phoebe peevishly. "I know which bag it is." Marjorie winked at Joanna, who nodded and left. "I want Freddy!" Phoebe wailed after her. "Make him come in here!"

The first children were showing up from school, the Percy boys hurrying home to change their clothes before the afternoon ball game. They were innocent yet of the disaster. They spoke politely to Joanna and she sent them down to Mark's wharf to find Freddy and tell him he was needed at home, at once. "And tell them *I* said so," she added.

"Ay-yup!" They went off at a run, racing each other. Tiger took off noisily after them. Joanna went home to pack for Nils and her. Rory lay tranquilly on his blanket, undisturbed since Freddy's outburst. Liza would attend to his supper and keep him for the night.

The men were coming up from the shore now, walking fast. She watched from her own doorstep while they carried Dave out on the couch mattress and laid it on the door. Once they were on their way to Mark's wharf, where there were no rows of traps to impede the necessary maneuvering of stretcher from wharf to boat, she went back into Dave's house calling, "Okay, kids, let's get moving!"

Phoebe was howling like a frustrated five-year-old. Marjorie said in suspiciously mild tones, "Freddy thinks he won't bother to go along."

"Oh, he does, does he?" Joanna felt a great liberating burst of rage. Marjorie stepped neatly sidewise and let her pass. Phoebe crouched on the edge of a chair, hugging her middle with folded arms. Tears streamed from her swollen eyes; her mouth was square. Freddy sat on the stairs, looking both scared and defiant.

"What do you mean, you think you won't bother to go?" Joanna asked him.

"I'd be more good here! Somebody ought to stay here and look after things, somebody to haul the traps!" he cried eagerly.

"*Somebody* is going along to look after his wife. Get up and start moving, or I'll help you up and I know just how to do it."

"Yeah, but—"

"*Freddy.*"

He got up. "Gee-zuss," he said under his breath. "What if she—"

"All the more reason for you to be along."

"She's not bleeding," Marjorie said to Joanna. "I think it's all nerves, myself."

"Can you walk, Phoebe?" Joanna asked, "or do you want Freddy to wheel you down in the wheelbarrow?"

"*No!*" Phoebe rose, gasping dramatically, but remembering to pick up her box of tissues.

"Lean on Freddy," Marjorie suggested. Freddy winced, and stared at Phoebe as if she might explode if he touched her. She looked back at him with contempt.

"Don't worry! I wouldn't let you touch me with a ten-foot oar. You just better be along, that's all. *You just better.*" She hiccuped, groped for another tissue, and blew her nose. "You *want* me to lose Dracula, don't you?"

"I never said that!"

"You did too, when you wanted me to go out on that Honda!" Squabbling, the two went out. Phoebe forgot to hunch over and clutch her middle, and began freely waving her arms.

"God bless our happy home," Marjorie said to Joanna. "Well, it's better for her to be mad. This has been a terrible shock to her."

"Oh I know. I've only thought of Dave himself, and Nils, but I guess it did hit the poor little wretch."

Liza and Maggie came to the wharf with hot-water bottles. Helmi brought down extra blankets. Mark had called Brigport, and someone would bring Hannah MacKenzie out to meet them off the southern end; she'd be prepared to travel with them if necessary. He would call Alice as soon as they were on their way. Joanna remembered to tell Liza about Rory, and at the last mintue Kate Campion came running down the wharf with two thermos bottles and a square tin.

"Just a little heartening for your stomach," she said.

The day's chop had flattened out, and when Bruce met them off Brigport, the two boats hardly rolled together as Hannah came aboard. She went into the cabin at once with Nils to take a look at Dave. Phoebe, crouched on a crate in the stern, began to snuffle again, and Freddy was both frustrated and exasperated, but didn't dare leave her to join the conversation over the washboards as Bruce waited for his wife.

"I guess we won't see you tonight then," Bruce said to Jamie.

"Guess not."

"What's he missing?" Joanna asked.

"Oh, Linda Pierce is throwing a big birthday party bash for Elmer. Wanted all the hockey ginks there. Made a special fancy cake and all."

Jamie looked unimpressed. "Well, I hope your uncle comes along all right," said Bruce sympathetically. "I guess a party's the last thing you're interested in right now."

Hannah came out of the cabin. She was a plump girl with kind eyes behind big glasses; her manner was pleasantly optimistic rather than overbearingly cheerful. "I really don't think anything'll happen, but I'll ride in with you if you'd like," she said to Nils.

"I would like," he said. He was extremely quiet about it.

21

They reached the public landing in Limerock a little after five. The ambulance was waiting, and Alice's car. There were only a few people around at this time of day, most of them youngsters, and a police officer was there to keep them out of the way. Alice stood on the float with the ambulance crew as *Valkyrie* came alongside. She was a small, lean woman, always smartly dressed and groomed; she was proud of herself as a business woman. Right now her lipstick stood out gaudy and dry against the pallor around her mouth.

The instant the boat grazed the float, she came aboard and knelt beside Dave. "Well, you *have* got yourself in a mess," she said harshly.

"Sorry, Bud." Dave's whisper was hardly audible. She put her hand on his forehead for an instant, then stood up and nodded at the ambulance crew. They and Hannah exchanged a few brief technical questions and answers that might as well have been in a foreign language. The rest stood out of the way, and even Phoebe was awed into silence. Once the stretcher was on the way up the ramp, Hannah following, Freddy leaped onto the float as if about to take wing. "Mama!" Phoebe cried, and launched herself at Alice, who braced for the impact. "I've had such terrible pains! I'm going to lose my baby!"

"I don't think so, Alice," Joanna said. "She was scared to death at first, we all were, but she and Freddy have been arguing and eating all the way over, so I don't think any-thing's wrong. Hannah doesn't either."

"We had one of those false alarms last week," said Alice. "They come in handy sometimes." She patted the girl's shoul-der. "Hush now. We've got enough to worry about. Nils, Jamie—will one of you drive my car if I go with the ambu-lance?" Her voice was stretched to such a thin level that Joanna kept expecting it to rip.

"Sure, Alice, you go along," Nils said, "and we'll see you at the hospital." Her mouth almost trembled when she thanked him. She ran up the ramp. At the top she turned and called back, "Will you drop the kids off at my aunt's? Phoebe'll tell you where."

The ambulance drove up toward Main Street, and the policeman got into his cruiser and left. The spectators still watched *Valkyrie* and the other people, as if expecting new action at any moment. One showed up in a skiff from farther along the shore, and rowed back and forth past the boat like an anticipatory gull.

"Hey, why can't I call up a friend of mine to come and get Phoebe and me?" Freddy suggested.

"I'm doing what your mother-in-law asked me to do," said Nils. "After that, it's out of my hands." Freddy looked desolate. Phoebe said nothing. She was so forlorn now, drained by her terrors and helpless angers, that Joanna took her into her arms and cuddled her for a few moments, and Phoebe didn't resist.

"This has been awful for you, but they'll take good care of your father now. So let's get you to your aunt's, and you can lie down for a while and then maybe come to the hos-pital."

"All right," said Phoebe meekly.

Jamie stayed behind to find out about a mooring; the hopeful gull waited to be hired to row him ashore.

After Main Street, the side streets were empty and peaceful in their fresh May greenery. They left Phoebe and Freddy

with their great-aunt, an older version of Alice; Phoebe hurried into the house, Freddy hung back, heavy-footed, and
looked yearningly over his shoulder at the car. When the door
had shut behind him, Joanna said, "Clap of doom for Freddy.
He thinks he's going to the guillotine or the gallows when he
has to do something he doesn't want to do."

Nils was gazing straight ahead. He didn't start the car
directly, and she moved closer to him and put her hand on his
knee. "How are you, love?"

"Oh, so's to be up and about." He gave her a slight smile.
"I'm glad you came."

"So am I, but I'm not much help. I can't take off any of the
burden. It's no use saying *Don't worry*, I know that much."

"Listen, you're here, and that's everything," he assured her.
"I can see you and touch you. And we got him alive across
the bay, we had a good, smooth, fast ride, and a nurse along.
We've done all we can." He started the engine. "Do you
want anything before we go to the hospital?"

"No, that hot tea Kate sent along was a big help."

When they drove into the hospital parking lot they sat
quiet for a few minutes more, as if getting their resources
together. Robins sang loudly in the surrounding elms. Otherwise the place was deserted at this hour. "I ought to call
Sigurd," Nils said, "but I don't know how much help that'll
be to Alice, the way she feels about him anyway. Who needs
him moaning *Allsmäktig Gud!* in the waiting room every five
minutes?"

"Let's wait till we find out how Dave is," she said. "Then
call him."

"I knew you'd have an idea. That's what I have a smart
wife for. I'm not too smart myself at the moment."

She turned his face toward hers, and kissed him. A boy
cutting across the blacktop on his bicycle whistled at them.
"Now he'll go home and tell about these old coots smooching
in the parking lot," she said.

"What old coots? I don't see any."

She laughed, and then had a frightful sensation, as if some inescapable terror had just shown itself to her and then ducked back into hiding until the next time. And who knew when that would be? She was short of breath and said in a fast light voice, "Nils, about the time Alice came aboard and saw Dave, I decided that I'm going to tell you at least once a day that I love you."

Alice sat alone in the waiting room. Her back was rigidly straight, her ankles neatly crossed, her hands clasped on her bag. Her eyes were fixed on a point on the opposite wall. She might have been in church, concentrating on the sermon. When the presence of the other two got through to her, she gave each a short nod.

"They've set up the IV and they've started the blood work." She sounded as impersonal as an employee giving a bulletin. "Hannah tells me there's quite a bit of that, before they can start giving him blood. She says there's nothing I can do for him tonight, but I'll stay at Aunt Cora's just to be near." She talked a little faster than usual, the only sign beside her pallor that she was simultaneously keyed up and wrung out. "This has been coming on for a long time, but I thought it was chronic indigestion, more fool I," she said with arid bitterness. "Well, if they can stop the bleeding and get him through this, there'll be a long convalescence, and *I'm* in charge now."

To keep her diverted, Nils asked, "Freddy taking over the whole outfit, then?"

It worked.

"I'm not *that* much of a fool!" she said. "There'd be nothing left of the gear *or* the boat in three months! *No*. His father and I can go halves to feed them and pay the rent on something for them. Nothing fancy, but they'll have the necessities till Freddy gets going on his own. And that's that." Her cheekbones flamed, her eyes sparkled. "I'm tired of Phoebe running our lives. We didn't ask her to quit school and move into a trailer with Freddy. She wanted him—

couldn't draw a breath without him—well, she's got him, and she can't have both ends and the middle too."

The hands were so tightly fastened on the bag that they were whitening. "I know just what happened today. I gave them plane fare for Brigport against my better judgment, but they had to get out of town. He borrowed his brother's new motorcycle again—*took* it, really. Went joyriding, and smashed it up. It's a wonder he didn't have her with him, and a wonder he wore a helmet and didn't bash his brains in. What few he's got," she added dryly. "The brother's been looking for him, to beat him up. So I sent them back to the island today, instead of making them wait for the mailboat, and they must have barged in and told David the whole rotten mess, and started *this*."

"I don't think so, Alice," said Joanna. "He'd been sick in the night. He looked bad this morning—so white. I know now it must have been from losing blood. But he told me it was summer complaint. Phoebe walked in and found him the way he was."

Alice looked at her with those bright staring eyes. "Jo, don't ever let your kids become more important than your husband, and don't let *him* put one of them ahead of *you*."

"We can't," said Joanna. "We need each other for aid and comfort."

Alice's laugh was raspy. "You're lucky. Well, maybe this mess will turn out to be a blessing in disguise. It'll be our last chance. Our only one. If he lives," she added bleakly, and then returned to her silent concentration on that invisible point opposite them.

The sight of Jamie coming down the corridor was like the first glimpse of the island looming out of a gale-torn sea or one of those surprise snowstorms that sometimes enlivened a trip home across the bay. She wanted to go and meet him with open arms, but she was restrained by the thought of their mutual embarrassment.

"I borrowed a car," he said. "How are things?"

"They're making him comfortable," Nils answered.

Jamie was as close to being fidgety as his mother had ever seen him. He put his hands into his pockets and took them out. Finally he said gruffly, "I'm sorry, Aunt Alice."

Surprisingly she reached out and took his hand. "Thanks for bringing him over, Jamie."

"That's all right. I was some glad of that new engine."

"I hope you didn't do her any damage, driving her like that."

"Nope. It's what's she's built for."

"I'm glad of that," Alice said with unusual softness. She released his hand.

"What are you folks going to do?" Jamie asked. "Staying in?"

"Yes, till we're sure Dave's on the mending hand," said Nils. "If you want to go home, go ahead."

"You know where Hannah is?"

"Somewhere around," said Joanna. "You'll have a lovely chance home. It'll be moonlight pretty soon." She was terribly homesick, as if she'd been away from the island for weeks; as if it had become inaccessible to her; as if she'd been driven into exile.

"Go ahead with him if you want to," Nils said.

"No! I'm worried about Dave too, you know." She was disturbed by his suggesting it, and then decided he'd been sure of her reaction, but wanted to hear it just the same. We've both lost part of our hide today, she thought. Got this awful cussid *mortal* feeling, somebody or other used to say.

Hannah came in. "Hi, Jamie! Your uncle's looking better already. You'll get a peep at him before you leave," she told Alice. "Just don't get hawsed up by all the plumbing."

"You want to go home with me?" Jamie asked her.

"A moonlight sail with Jamie Sorensen? I'd be out of my mind to refuse." She gave Alice a pat on the shoulder. "Mr. Sorensen couldn't get better care anywhere else in the world. So try to get a good sleep tonight so you'll be all fresh for him tomorrow."

"I don't know how to thank you," Alice began.

"I'm already thanked, just by seeing him into Dr. Bell's hands."

Aching to escape for a moment, Joanna said, "Nils, let's walk to the car with them. Be right back, Alice." Alice nodded without speaking.

Dusk was settling in. Nils stood with his hands in his pockets, looking up and down the street, but she knew he wasn't seeing it. The last few hours were so deeply embossed on his vision that everything else must move only insubstantially across it. "Hannah, we can't thank you enough," he said.

"Oh well, it's the same as I told Mrs. Sorensen. I got my thanks a little while ago when Dr. Bell took hold. I didn't really *do* anything, you know. There wasn't anything I could do."

"You gave moral support," said Joanna.

Unexpectedly Jamie took his father's arm and squeezed it. "Keep your cool, *Fader*." Also unexpectedly, he kissed Joanna's cheek. "Get some rest."

"And you have a good trip home and a good party." Watching them go, she felt that longing catch in her throat like tears. They were going home, and she couldn't even think, Tomorrow morning we'll be going. It was monstrously self-centered of her, and she wouldn't give it houseroom. But the thing still lay in ambush, and she wanted Nils home on the island, as if the daily ritual were the spell to preserve them from harm.

"He's a good solid dependable kid when you need him," Nils said.

"Yes. I suppose we oughtn't to growl when he doesn't always act like the Rock of Gibraltar." It brought Bronwen to mind, and to think about something else besides Dave and Alice was like escaping from a straitjacket, or as she imagined it would be.

They went back in, feeling duty-bound to stay by Alice until she told them to go. Nils would want a look at Dave himself, or at least some word from the doctor, before he would leave. Where would they stay for the night anyway? When she needed to move around again she'd see about getting a room somewhere.

Valkyrie was on her way home. Don't dwell on that. Nils questioned Alice about her job. How could he think of things to ask? Her own mind was dulled down to a few sparks; a bed for the night, Bronwen, *Valkyrie* crossing the night sea, the island under the rising moon.

"Mama!" someone said huskily. "How is he?" It was Signe, the daughter who lived in Damariscotta. "Is he *dying*, Mama? When Phoebe called she was hysterical. Oh, *Mama!*"

"No, he's not dying," Alice said remotely. "At least I don't think so. I'm waiting to talk to the doctor." Nils sat the girl down in his chair, and told her what was going on.

"Thanks, Uncle Nils. That Phoebe! I should have known better, but the way she talked it sounded as if he were practically dead when they took him off the boat." She put her arm about her mother's braced shoulders. "Anna's coming down from Bangor. Thank God Ed's driving her, because she'll be crying the whole way and she'll be a mess when she gets here."

"Well, she'd better behave herself in here," said Alice snappishly. "I've got enough to contend with without you young ones throwing fits. Who's taking care of *your* young ones, by the way?"

"Their father. Oh, Mama!" Signe was half-laughing, half-crying. "If you were ever any different, I don't know what we'd do." She turned then to kiss Joanna. "Hi, Aunt Jo. You look wonderful sitting there. Unflappable, you and Uncle Nils both."

"Don't kid yourself," Joanna said. "Uncle Nils maybe— Aunt Jo, never. She flaps like a shirt on a handspike."

"You could have fooled me."

"You two can go now," Alice said abruptly. "I won't be alone now, and you must be about ready to crawl under the kelp, as Dave says. Look, you take the car and go stay in the house at Port George. There's plenty of food on hand, help yourself to whatever you want, and you can feed the cat." A change came into her parched tone. "He won't know what to think when I don't come back tonight. His food's on the shelf in the entry, and be sure to give him some milk too. Please," she added.

Signe smiled. "We all know who comes next to Dad," she said. "Bobby Shafto."

"Well, he's an old cat!" Alice said defensively.

"Mama, we all love old Bobby," Signe assured her.

The half-hour ride through the May dusk to Port George was restful after the last few hours. The house stood by itself on the outskirts of town, spruce woods behind and saltwater across the road. It was immaculate outside and in, fussy with ornaments, handwork, and photographs. The bobtailed cat was a friendly and comfortable presence. Like Bobby Shafto in the song, he was fat and fair, and a useful distraction when you found yourself trying not to look at David's chair and his special magazine rack, and his boat models. He's not dead, Joanna kept telling herself, but she and Nils were both waiting for the telephone to ring. They could not easily shed the day's terrors; the weight was still heavily upon them.

Nils made a pot of coffee at once, and called Sigurd in Fremont. Joanna found a container of homemade beef stew in the freezer, and it provided a good and heartening meal. Sigurd drove in while she was washing up the dishes. He was still yellow-haired, and running to fat. He had stopped drinking some years back, but he didn't need liquor to become emotionally intoxicated. True to form he cried, "*Allsmäktig Gud!*" when he saw Nils, and exclaimed, sighed, or groaned it quite often thereafter. He was indefatigable in the vitality of his distress, and when he'd worked off the worst of that, his good spirits were as exhausting as his bad ones. Joanna left the men alone in the kitchen after a while and went up to Alice's room with the telephone book, to try and reach Bron. Nobody answered at Ferris Jenkins's number, and she turned on the table television set Alice had at the foot of the bed and tried to watch a play for half-an-hour before trying again. It wasn't a very good one, but Alice had no books up here—she wasn't much of a reader—and the windows looked at the woods. She went into one of the other rooms and watched the moonlight over the sea, thinking how foreign and out of joint she felt, with cars going by between her and the salt water; it didn't even seem like the same ocean she knew.

When she tried the Jenkins' number again, a young voice answered and she thought at first it was Bron. Her disappointment was painful when the girl said, "I'm Charley—Charlotte, that is. Bron's sister."

"I'm Mrs. Sorensen, from Bennett's Island," Joanna said. "I had to come in from the island, and I wanted to say hello to Bron and tell her we miss her."

"I know she loved it out there," the girl said politely. "I'll leave a message for her. She's in Boston this week."

"Thank you very much. It was nice meeting you, Charley."

"Nice meeting you too, Mrs. Sorensen.

So that's that, she thought, hanging up. End of something that was most likely never intended to happen in the first place. So I'll forget it.

Downstairs Sigurd was reminiscing between massive bouts of laughter. Could he have brought a bottle along after all? But all she saw was his coffee mug, and the few crumbs left of the coffee cake she'd heated for dessert. Bobby Shafto clung to his broad thigh, blissful with all the male company and noise.

Nils looked quenched with fatigue by the time Sigurd left, singing in Swedish something better left untranslated.

"That man out-Bennetts the Bennetts," Joanna said. "Let's go to bed."

22

$\mathscr{D}$avid responded quickly to treatment, and now the long recovery lay ahead. He would not be going back to the island. Nils and Joanna could leave on the mailboat two days later. In the meanwhile, anyone who could think of an errand called the Port George house to make requests and read lists, so Alice's car was pretty well loaded when she took them to the wharf at seven in the morning. Her thanks were dry and sparse, like vegetables trying to grow in a dusty garden plot, but they knew she meant them. She would be out later to clean the house and collect personal belongings. Much as she disliked the island and hated the trip, she would not let anyone else do the work.

"At least you'll let us put you up," Joanna said.

"Well, yes," she conceded, and even smiled a little, as if to acknowledge the ridiculous extent of her obstinate self-reliance.

The kitchen had been scrubbed when they got there, and Joanna never found out whom to thank. Jamie and Nils started taking up Dave's gear, the others helped, and in a few days all the traps were lined up at the head of the beach between the fishhouse and the store. Moving it to Port George waters would not be discussed until he knew what he would be able to do.

May was the month when the ospreys began to pipe and circle high overhead, watching for fish. The lobster smack brought out crates of fresh alewives and the lobsters hungrily responded. The days were long, exhausting, and productive.

It was the time for setting out halibut trawls, but not for setting out garden seedlings that could be still destroyed by frost; no one ever counted the wild strawberries by the show of blossom.

The seining crew had already trapped enough herring in the harbor for a good supply of bait, and the factories were eager for all they could get. Right now the price was good. If it should be a big herring year along the coast the price would drop, but the boys would still make money.

Over on Brigport the younger Robeys and Allards always had priority in the harbor, but the MacKenzie boys were doing all right so far in their own cove; Jamie had helped them the first few times and stayed all night afterward, the way he used to do after the hockey games. When he was back on Bennett's he lived as he always did. It irked Joanna that she hadn't been able to reach Bronwen but, swept along toward summer, she began to think the call would have been unsatisfactory anyway. Bron would never have admitted being dropped by Jamie, even if Joanna were insensitive enough to ask. So it was over, and forget it. Between lobstering and seining Jamie seemed happy enough—if that was the word for his usual attitude. *We must take him as he is*, Nils would say.

" 'And a bird overhead sang Follow,' " Liza recited. " 'And a bird to the right sang Here; And the arch of the leaves was hollow, And the meaning of May was clear.' How's that?"

"Perfect," said Joanna. "Reminds me of the orchard." They sat on the end of the Bennett wharf with their legs dangling, waiting for Nils and Philip to finish baiting a halibut trawl, when they would all go to set it. It was late afternoon. Sam and Richard were out with their outboard dory, under orders to stay away from Cindy Campion's skiff as she rowed Robin Bennett around the harbor. Ralph's boys were helping him bag up. Rosa had *Sea Star* beside her wharf and was doing some painting inside the cuddy. Jamie was aboard *Valkyrie* at her mooring; he'd just come in from hauling and was

doing some housecleaning before rowing ashore. Young Matt
Fennell was rowing in from *Peregrine* toward Mark's wharf
where a cluster of children were fishing hopefully for harbor
pollock. Hugo was rowing to the ladder beside Joanna.

All the boats were in, so the sound of another one coming
at full speed up Long Cove created a mild curiosity among
the adults and the children. Everyone was watching for the
first glimpse of her past Eastern Harbor Point.

"Cindy!" Terence Campion yelled between cupped hands.
"Get in close to shore!" Liza looked for Sam, and saw the
boys poking around without power in the shadow of the
breakwater, well out of the way.

Bonny Eloise came charging into the harbor, throwing
water like a breaking wave. Cindy turned the skiff's bow
expertly into the deep, fast furrows of the wake and kept it
there. Across the harbor by the breakwater, Richard grabbed
for the oars to turn and steady the dory. The boat came
roaring on, and adult curiosity became annoyance. Philip and
Nils left off baiting the trawl and came out on the wharf.

"What in hell goosed *him?*" Hugo called from his skiff.

Darrell was heading straight for *Valkyrie.* On either side
of him everything rocked in the turbulence. It looked for an
incredible minute as if he were going to ram Jamie. "Nils,
he's gone crazy or he's drunk!" Joanna shouted, getting up.
But suddenly he stopped the engine and in the silence the
surf of the wake splashed on shores and wharf spilings and
they could hear the boats rocking. Ralph ran around to help
Rosa hold *Sea Star* off. "Marriage sure turned *him* into a wild
man!"

Bonny Eloise ran down on *Valkyrie* with the speed of her
momentum, and as the sides knocked together Jamie went for
his gaff to fend the other off. But before he could reach it
Darrell had leaned across and grabbed him by the front of
his shirt. Jamie chopped at Darrell's wrist, and the other
man had to let go.

"If you've got anything to say, come aboard and say it,"
Jamie said. It was heard distinctly above the wash.

"All right, I will!" He jumped into the other cockpit, bringing a line with him and made it fast in a ring in the stern deck, while Jamie stood watching him. Darrell turned quickly and pitched into Jamie with both fists. Caught off balance, Jamie fell backward out of sight with Darrell on top of him.

Nils was down the ladder and into Hugo's skiff faster than Joanna had ever seen him move. The outboard across the harbor started up, and the dory shot out from under the breakwater, made a sudden turn toward the lobster car where young Matt Fennell was wildly beckoning, took him aboard, and headed for *Valkyrie*.

"Philip, he *is* insane," Joanna said to her brother.

"Jamie can take care of himself," he answered, but he didn't look away from the scene in the harbor. Jamie had managed to throw Darrell off and pull himself up. This time he was braced for the attack, and the encounter was fierce and fast. Matt reached the boat first and climbed aboard, Nils and Hugo arrived a few moments later. The boys in the dory shut off the outboard and sat back to watch.

Nils said something not audible as far as the wharf. It didn't work and he seized Jamie's arms from behind, while Matt tried to hold Darrell. Matt was solid, but he couldn't subdue the skinny Darrell; it took Matt and Hugo both just to get his arms behind him. Nils released Jamie, who walked astern and looked away from the rest, out past the breakwater toward the horizon. Nils followed and spoke to him, gave up after a few minutes and went back to where Matt and Hugo were trying to calm Darrell without letting go of him. Nils attempted examining the marks on his face, but Darrell jerked his head back violently. Finally they let him go and he climbed back aboard his boat and went out of the harbor at top speed. The men stood in *Valkyrie* for a few minutes, looking after him, talking and shaking their heads. Then Matt went back aboard the dory with the boys. Nils returned to Jamie and was obviously telling him to get into his skiff and come ashore. Finally Jamie nodded, but still didn't move. Nils came back in with Hugo, and when they were halfway to the wharves, Jamie pulled his skiff alongside *Valkyrie*.

"I think I'll go back to the house," Joanna said. "Whatever that was all about, he won't adore finding his mother waiting on the wharf. It's bad enough to have his father mixed up in it."

"Yep, you might as well lay out the Band-Aids and put on the teakettle," Philip said. "And I'll get back to baiting trawl just as if I didn't give a damn what was going on."

"I often wonder how Father and Mother kept their sanity," Joanna said. She walked home fast. Her thoughts were chaotic with nervous expectancy. Jamie was manifestly safe, but why the attack? It had appeared as meaningless as a lunatic's assault on a random passerby.

They came in a few minutes, escorted by Rory as if it were some ceremonious occasion. Jamie was bleeding from superficial cuts, one on a cheekbone and one over an eye. "I'm all right," he muttered. He had a puffed upper lip. His right hand was red about the knuckles and he had a lump on the back of his head where he'd hit something when he went down.

He sat in stoic silence while Joanna applied first aid to the cuts and gave him ice cubes in a towel to hold against his lip.

"What about this place on the back of your head?" she asked. "Are you dizzy, sick-feeling? Seeing double or anything?"

"I didn't hit hard enough for a concussion," he said around the ice cubes. "It's nothing. I'm all right."

Nils was saying nothing, and Joanna became uncomfortably conscious of the quality of his silence. The teakettle was boiling and she turned off the gas.

Nils said softly, "Do you want to have it out now or later?"

"Now," said Jamie. There was nothing either pathetic or repentant about him in spite of the Band-Aids and the cold compress held to his mouth.

"Why did he jump you?"

"He thinks I've been fooling around with his wife." Admirably direct.

"You're getting yourself quite a reputation. *Were* you fooling around with his wife?"

"He's a bastard," he said harshly. "He's a couple of centuries too late. He thinks a woman's his possession to show off like his boat; or she's like a dog to come when he snaps his fingers, and kick when he feels like it."

"I asked you a question," Nils said. "*Were* you fooling around with his wife?"

"I don't call it fooling around. If he doesn't like it, it's his own fault. He drove her to it."

"*What's going on?*"

"We're going to be together."

"You're *what?*" Joanna hadn't meant it to explode like that.

"I take it you've already been together, as you put it," Nils said.

"And she had to tell him, damn it! I told her to let me do it, or we'd do it together. But she's too damn' honest for her own good." He started to get up. "I'm going over there. I hope he didn't belt her before he came after me. If he did—"

His father put a hand on his chest and pushed him back into his chair. "I want to get this straight," he said. "Why is Darrell in the wrong because you laid his wife? I could take up the time to think up a nicer term for it, I suppose, but I'm in no mood for that."

Jamie went red. The invisible wires began in Joanna's legs. It was like the day when she had believed it possible for Jamie to be lost, the similarity was sickeningly *there*. Nils and Jamie had had arguments in their twenty-five years together, but never a confrontation like this.

Jamie put the icy compress on the counter. "What's happened between her and me doesn't matter," he said deliberately. "We figure he's lost his rights, the way he's treated her. When I ran into her on Stonehaven that day, she was leaving him. She'd gotten a ride to Stonehaven with somebody and was going to Limerock on the afternoon boat. She was in terrible shape, shaking, and trying not to cry—" He stopped as if overcome by the memory. Then he went on with increasing vehemence, a phenomenon in itself.

"I talked her into coming back and giving him another chance—yup, I was the son of a bitch who did that!" he said savagely. "I told her some of the Robeys were odd, but all us islanders are odd, and she'd get him tamed in time. I talked to her all the way back, goddammit, and she was all set to do her part. Next thing, he's drunk as a coot at Elmer's party, the night of Uncle Dave's mess. Crazy first, and then abusive. He finally passed out and I borrowed Bruce's truck and we took him home. She was all to pieces, trembling, crying again—" He clasped one hand with the other hard, wincing because the knuckles were sore, and the sight started a sympathetic pain in Joanna's midriff.

"I took her out and walked her around for an hour or so in the moonlight. We went down on the northwest side, and she began to calm down. She had the key to Professor Macomber's cottage, so we went in there and she made some coffee."

Does she carry the key around her neck? Joanna wondered. Hysterical, and yet she remembers to take this key?

Jamie had to look away from them finally; even if he couldn't escape, he'd make the attempt. He turned his eyes toward the spruces and new-leaved birches where Joanna watched for birds. "So after that—after that night," he said in a low voice, "we decided what to do, but we were going to wait till she heard from Professor Macomber. He's going to Europe this summer, and she wrote to him about somebody wanting to rent the cottage. Then we'd talk to Darrell together." He started to get up again. "Only she didn't wait. He must have done *something*, the bastard! She'd never have told him unless he beat it out of her."

"Or else she wanted a little excitement of her own, to take his mind off herring," Joanna suggested.

He ignored that, staring into his father's face as if he hoped beyond reason to find something there which was not. "You can see why I've got to get over there. She may be hurt, and who the hell'd care? His folks didn't want him to marry her, and the rest of the women are jealous of her looks."

Oh, Jamie, Jamie, Joanna mourned. To hear this coming out of *you*, of all people.

"You aren't going anywhere until we get the rest of this story," Nils said, too gently. "If all hell breaks loose around our son, we have a right to know why. You're going to rent the Macomber place and move in there with her? In her husband's own territory?"

"Well, I sure as hell can't bring her over here!"

"Good God, how much is the man supposed to take?" Nils exclaimed. "He was half out of his head today. What's already happened to you over there, what happened to your *boat*, when the girl involved was single?"

"Darrell won't do anything," he said with grim confidence. "He's had his explosion and that'll end it, because he knows he'll never get her back now. He's not the vindictive type, like some of the Robeys."

"That makes it nice for you," said Joanna. His brief glance at her said that sarcasm was beneath his contempt when his whole existence was in upheaval.

Nils went on, "Supposing some of the vindictive Robeys decide to be vindictive for him? You've already had some of it, just a taste. Whet your appetite for more, did it?"

Jamie shrugged.

Keep quiet, Joanna said to herself. Don't shout at him even if you feel like it, and you do. "Couldn't you wait," she asked, "until she leaves him legally?"

"That would take months. No. We aren't waiting. Life's too short."

"You're shortening yours by the moment, it seems to me," said his father. "I asked you a question a while back and I got no answer. How do you know his friends and relations won't give you a real shivaree this time? If the place is burned down with you in it, or you get knocked in the head or maimed for life, it'll be just a bad accident due to liquor and high spirits."

This time Jamie didn't bother to argue, but surveyed his father in polite silence. Evidently everything was well worth losing for love. But *Valkyrie?*

"You could lose the boat altogether this time," Joanna observed.

"I'm keeping her right there below the cottage where I can have an eye on her." He sounded reasonable and entirely ordinary, as if nothing were out of the way. "Anybody mind if I go up and change my clothes now?"

Impassively Nils made a slight gesture of dismissal. Jamie got up and left them. Joanna's resolution to be calm shivered on the brink of dissolution. She called after him, "You dropped Bron rather than chance a trap war!"

"This is different." He went on upstairs. His parents stood listening to his footsteps. When he had reached his room, Nils said in a low voice, "Come on." They went out the back door, Rory with them, and across to the barn. The tame chickens followed them in a sociable group. They went out into the alders a little way, to a granite outcropping where the sun struck warmth into the gray rock. It had been Nils's playhouse and then his ship when he was a small boy. They sat down, and the hens picked around them in the dead leaves.

"If all flesh is as grass," Nils said at last, "he's doing a hell of a lot of haying."

Joanna put her arm through his. "Let's neither of us beat our breasts and moan 'Where have we gone wrong!' "

"We don't have to blame ourselves, no. But that boy was almost crying out there, and I don't think Jamie's one little dite ashamed of himself."

"Why should he be? From his viewpoint, I mean." Rory rolled ecstatically on his back, kicking his legs and growling. "He thinks Darrell's already lost her, and there's something in that—you can't take a woman away from a man who's got a good firm hold on her. I'm not defending him," she said quickly. "I'm so mad with him that I'm working like hell to try to see it from his point of view."

"His point of view should be the same as ours," Nils said. "She's a married woman, whether she likes it or not."

"You know how Jamie is about injustice," said Joanna. "If he really believes she's being abused—"

"He's probably the only one."

"That's what I almost said to him. But she probably cries very artistically, her eyes don't get red and her nose doesn't get stuffed up the way common peasant noses do. You can see I'm not really being objective."

"That's a relief." He put his arms around her. "Right now I don't want to be reasoned with. These two decide on the basis of a lot of sweet talk and one tumble on a mattress that they've got love everlasting, so to hell with the consequences. Our son, with our training, turns out to be about as morally bright as Freddy. I'm leaving the girl out of it. He's twenty-five years old and it's not likely she raped him."

"Well, there's rape *and* rape," said Joanna.

"Spoken like a Bennett. *Owen* Bennett." They kissed. "When I was ten or so and standing on the bridge steering among the icebergs I never thought one day I'd be kissing a beautiful woman out here." He kissed her again and she spoke against his mouth. "Don't let him upset what we have. Remember our motto. *Survive.*"

"I'll remember." He stood, and pulled her up with him. Rory, who'd given up rolling and had been lying on his back with the sun on his belly, got eagerly though stiffly to his feet. "I'm going back and finish baiting trawl."

"Maybe Philip's finished it."

"Then you and I and Philip and Liza will go out and set it."

The house was quiet when they went through it, picking up jackets on the way. They both glanced involuntarily at the ceiling, but they didn't mention Jamie. When they were walking to the shore, they saw *Valkyrie* going out past the breakwater.

Everything around the harbor looked the same. The children were still out there in their boats; Ralph's boys had finished baiting up and had been allowed to row their father's skiff. It was ordinary and peaceful, and yet it was joltingly different; the very air still shook with the after-vibrations of a violent dislocation or displacement. But he's not dead! she protested to herself. Keep remembering that... If Darrell isn't waiting for him with a shotgun, she added cynically.

The completed trawl tubs waited inside the Bennett fishhouse, but nobody was around. While Nils rowed out to bring his boat in, Joanna went to Philip's kitchen door. "Ready?" she called.

"Just waiting for the skipper," Philip answered.

Neither he nor Liza asked any questions. When the trawl was set, and they were going home in the saffron light of sunset, Nils told them. "Jamie's moving into Macomber's cottage with Darrell Robey's wife."

Even Philip, least perturbable of the Bennetts, was startled. Liza said, "Oh, my God! Jamie with a married *woman?*"

"Unless he's changed his mind in the last hour," said Nils.

"I'm sure you're not as calm as you look," she accused him. "Either of you. He's not my son, but I'm sick to my stomach."

"We're not calm," said Joanna. "Maybe we're still in shock. Oh, we'll live through it, so don't get all fussed up on our account."

Philip looked back across the shimmering slopes of water to where the red-and-white kegs marked the trawl anchors. "Jamie," he murmured. "Well."

"The perfect comment," said Nils. "Let's leave it at that."

23

*J*amie came in the next day and sold his lobsters to Mark, then went across to the Sorensen wharf to bait up. He wasn't about to give up his own good bait, herring he'd caught and salted himself. He didn't try to avoid his father.

"Well, I think I may be a little proud of him for that," Joanna conceded. "How was he?"

"Polite." She couldn't tell whether or not Nils was being ironic. "I asked him if he was still intending to stop off the harbor here, and he said he's turning the rig over to Ralph for the summer."

"If he's willing to give up that for her," Joanna said slowly, "I feel as if the wind has really been knocked out of me, on top of not much sleep last night. I guess I kept on believing he'd be back here seining as usual even with this great love affairs going on."

"Well, he won't be," said Nils. He left to go with Philip to haul the halibut trawl, taking Sam and Richard this time. They got two big halibut and sold one to Randy Fowler at the store in Brigport, and cut up the other one for sale around the island.

There was a quilting session the next afternoon at the Bennett Homestead, and everyone turned out for it, even Rosa, who could do fine sewing if she chose. Joanna walked alone to the Homestead, wanting privacy to think. Her mind was made up, but she had to decide what to say. She knew that some form of the news had traveled around the island, but it would be easier on everyone if she spoke of it first, gave the straight facts, and let that be the end of it as far as she was concerned.

The others could chew it over among themselves till the end of the world, as long as she didn't have to hear it.

When everyone had settled down to work around the quilting frames, she said, "I'd like to say something." The instant quiet was very flattering, she thought sourly, then knew she was being unfair. "We're all like one family here in lots of ways—I mean, it's impossible to keep secrets, and this isn't one anyway. Or it won't be, just in case any of you have missed it until now. Darrell Robey's wife has left him, and she and Jamie are setting up housekeeping in the Macomber cottage."

The silence lasted while everyone tried either to be very busy or very attentive. Then Helen Campion, whose large face was always flushed, became an even darker, distressing, purple-red.

"*Your* son!"

"Weird, isn't it?" Joanna agreed. "Of course we've already had a dress rehearsal, you might say."

"His new wife?" young Mrs. Matt asked wonderingly.

"I don't think he had an old one," said Joanna. There was a nervous ripple of laughter.

"I can't believe it about Jamie," said Kate Campion. "She must have hypnotized him. Boy, talk about seduction!"

"You know what the Bible says about the strange woman," Maggie Dinsmore said seriously.

"The Bible also says a lot about committing adultery," said Helen Campion.

"It's the married partner who commits adultery, isn't it?" Rosa asked, her voice husky and shy.

"But it's all called fornication!" Helen was agitated. She took off her glasses and wiped them, and her eyes were watering. "Joanna, I'm surprised at you and Nils! Letting him do it! Disgracing you in the face and eyes of the world!"

"What can they do?" Vanessa asked. "He's a grown man."

"They can refuse to condone it!"

"How do you know we're condoning it, Helen?" Joanna asked good-naturedly. "We aren't. But there's nothing we can do about it."

"You can turn your backs on him. Cast him off till he casts *her* off."

"Jamie's always been so levelheaded," Philippa said. "He's just on a wrong tack, that's all. He'll come back on course after a while."

"As if that's all there is to it!" Helen cried. "No sin, just a wrong tack. And you with a minister for a son!"

Philippa concentrated on quilting. "Oh, Aunt Helen, relax," said Kate. "If something like the Trojan War doesn't start up from it, it may be over and forgotten a year from now."

"Thanks, Kate," said Joanna. "I like your *If*. It's very reassuring."

"Cold comfort," suggested Helmi. Surprisingly this brought laughter. Helen Campion was still upset, but Liza asked her for news of her son and daughter and their families, and calmed her down to the point of getting out the latest snapshots of the grandchildren. Soon she would no longer be so horrified by Jamie's public immorality, and by tonight she would comfortably believe that Joanna and Nils were writhing with humiliation. It might be one big family on the island, but it wasn't always a friendly one.

Jamie stopped coming home to bait up. Perhaps he was made uncomfortable or embarrassed by working side by side with his father. He still sold to his uncle, and gassed up there, but came and went without any side trips home. He would be getting bait from the MacKenzies, probably herring they'd seined when he was helping them with the outfit. Joanna doubted that he was going with them on a regular basis; if Eloise had him cornered, he wasn't going to escape with the boys, even to work. Joanna kept her malicious thoughts to herself, but was convinced that Eloise would even be jealous of herring. On fine days she was seen aboard *Valkyrie* as Jamie hauled, which effectively kept any of the family from approaching him, except, of course, Owen, who came around by the house afterward to tell Joanna.

She could have done without this and tried to act bored and sleepy; that was easy enough because she kept waking in the middle of the night to think about Jamie, and then again before dawn, when she couldn't fall asleep again. She couldn't arouse Nils and hand it all over to him, or have them be enraged together and work through the storm to the other side and a temporary stretch of fine weather; when Jamie stopped coming home to bait up, Nils had stopped mentioning him.

"I thought you'd want to know he looks pretty good," Owen said. "Be a hell of a shame if he went to all this trouble and ended up looking as if he'd been dragged through a knothole."

She faked a yawn and said, "Watch it. No obscenity, please."

"Who's obscene? She was laid out on the bow deck, but she hustled right down to be sure I didn't pass him any secret messages. Hung onto his arm and rubbed her cheek on his shoulder and batted those eyelids up and down at me. He reddened up some."

"I can imagine, if you were watching them with that expression." She was sickened by the picture, by the girl's insolent possessiveness and Jamie's compliance. But Owen wouldn't be allowed to guess.

"You know," Owen said, "by the time Darrell decides to get rid of her she'll have been playing pussy-in-the-corner with three or four other chumps besides Jamie. So you won't get her as a daughter-in-law. You ever hear anything from the Jenkins girl?"

"No, and I tried to reach her when we were in about Dave."

"Nice girl," Owen said. "But I can see why this one's got him in a cleft stick. Speaking loosely." He grinned. "She can't help giving it off any more than she can help breathing. She's in love with herself, and that kind, male or female, attracts lovers the way syrup does ants."

Owen irritated her because she knew his sense of mischief, but she had to come out with something, since she couldn't say it to Nils.

"All right, so there'll be three or four other ones. That doesn't set Jamie free, you know. He won't just shrug his shoulders and say, That's that, and walk away without a scar. Owen, for this to be going on with Jamie is like seeing him with a fatal disease."

"You underestimate him. He's tough. He's not that baby you washed and diapered and set in his high chair. Sure, it'll hurt, it'll gnaw at him, but he'll live through it and learn something." His tone was harsh, his look inimical. Men against women, she thought with morbid humor. "You're never too old to learn, they say. The lessons get harder as the time gets shorter, but there's no letup," Owen went on. "It's not what happens to you when you're twenty-five, it's the punches you take at fifty that kill."

She thought he meant the heart attack, and couldn't think of anything to say. But when the silence became full of needles she said, "Eloise will be more than just a gnawing pain. Jamie's not ordinary."

"None of us are. Extraordinary, every last one of us."

"He's not like any of us. He's not even like Nils. Nils has an inner compass. I'm not in the least sure about Jamie. Everyone says he's so levelheaded. Well, they *did*, but they can't be saying it now . . . These youngsters who suddenly blow their brains out—how many of them are described as calm and levelheaded? And then they kill themselves and you realize that all the time they were in hell with no claws"—

Angrily he interrupted. "If you think Jamie's going to blow his brains out over this one, you're crazy. By the time she's moved on to the next one he'll know she's not worth it." He shoved back his chair with a deliberate hard scraping over the floor and stood up. He dropped a hand heavily on her shoulder. "Don't waste your time worrying. Just figure he's getting a liberal education."

"What am I supposed to figure about Bonny Eloise?"

"Oh, go on hating her. Good for your liver, keeps it shaken up."

The talk had been a help and for a little while it reduced the enormity of the thing that had happened in their lives. But when Nils came home she realized the illusion. How could you not see something as tremendous when it was being so obviously ignored? It was the first thing in her life she had not felt free to mention to Nils; and this new timidity and uncertainty ate at her like a secret pain. And when it was temporarily quiet, there was always the worry about something happening over there.

Alice came out by mailboat to pack up things in the house. She'd always hated the trip, but she was more afraid of flying across the bay. This time it was a miserable chance across, a stiff easterly wind taking the *Clarice Hall* on the side all the way. Alice had been sick, and she was white and staggering when Duke assisted her onto the wharf. She didn't look as if she would make it to the house through the whipping curtains of rain. But she refused to be steered into the store to rest for a few minutes and have a cup of tea.

Walking gave Alice more color in her face and vigor in her voice. "I never once had a decent trip out on that mailboat," she said. "That's why I put my foot down at the first. David had to choose between the island and me. I never made a touse when he gave up teaching for lobstering, but I'd be damned if I'd move out to this place."

"Well, he really loves his house at Port George," Joanna said tactfully. "So I guess he made the right choice."

"But nobody thought so at the time. Including you."

"We live and learn," said Joanna.

Alice gave Dave's house a sidewise look as they passed it but said nothing. When they came into the other house she said approvingly, "You have done a lot since the last time I saw the place."

"Which was when Uncle Eric died, and they brought him out here to the cemetery." Joanna took Alice's raincoat. "Yes, we've done a bit in nineteen years. Get those wet shoes off, I've some slippers here. Rory, go lie down now." Alice didn't care for dogs.

ELISABETH OGILVIE   (204)

"I was going to be stiffnecked and camp out across the yard
there," she said, "but a chemical toilet and no running water
never was my idea of gracious living."

She ate a bowl of hot chowder and then went to work, refusing help. "Listen, I am so *glad* to be getting him out of here,
it'll be no job at all."

"Well, it's warm in there anyway. I built a fire. The minute
you feel tired, come on back over and have a mug-up."

The weather cleared in the late afternoon. Alice had her
packing done by supper time, and settled down with her cro-
cheting to watch a crime program to which she was addicted.
The boys stopped off the harbor and made such a good strike
that they called for a carrier. The herring was taken out in the
morning, and Nils arranged for Alice to go home aboard the
carrier. The day was mild, fair, and still. The gulls and shags
paddled hungrily around the seining operation, while the
medricks screamed and dove.

"It's not the island itself, Jo," Alice said, while they were
waiting. "When it's like this it reminds me of that poem Dave
likes—'Earth has not anything to show more fair.'"

"Or: 'Where every prospect pleases and only man is vile,'"
said Joanna. "Grampa Sorensen's favorite hymn when he was
mad with everybody."

Alice smiled. "I never met the old man in the flesh, but I
feel as if I knew him. Oh, it's real handsome out here sometimes, but it's not always summer and strawberries, and there's
that twenty-five hellish miles. I was afraid to raise kids out
here even if everybody else had done it. I was sure *we'd* have
the fatal accidents, or pneumonia in the middle of a hurricane,
and so forth. Well, look at you all, and look who's had the
fatal accident. Named Phoebe Ann."

"Oh, Alice, she's not the worst kid in the world," Joanna
protested. "She'll settle down sometime. And I don't know as
where she was raised made any difference." She was thankful
they hadn't had sixteen years of Phoebe on the island.

"No, it's *who* raised her," Alice said grimly.

"Well, right now Nils and I aren't exactly bursting with pride."

"About Jamie? You can't call him a juvenile delinquent."

"No, but the ghost of Gunnar is putting a lot of other interesting names in our mouths." They both laughed. "Nils says *Survive*. You get Dave well so he can enjoy his garden and the Grange again, and"—

"Keep Phoebe off his neck," Alice broke in. "I've got my work cut out for me, because when she cries he's a gone goose. When the baby comes I may be able to swap a couple of one-way tickets to California for it. Or Pago Pago."

In the afternoon Philippa came up from the Eastern End, and she and Liza and Joanna went to the cemetery to work. The old orchard, shut in by a surrounding wall of tall spruces, was showing blossoms here and there in its lake of heat. Strawberry blossoms and violets had appeared with the medricks, and wild pear petals fell in the slightest tremble of breeze. Birdsong was loud in the trees. The women knelt on the warm earth, clipping and trimming around the family stones, loosening the earth around the perennial plants. Their talk was restful and desultory.

With the constant wash on the shores of Goose Cove below them, and the susurrus of the wind in the spruce tops, and the usual distant hum of boat engines carried unevenly on the wind, they didn't hear Charles coming with his power mower until he was in sight at the far end of the orchard.

"Oh Lord," Joanna said. "Charles's new toy."

"He must have shaved a strip all the way from the Homestead," said Philippa. They sat back and watched him come up through the broken pattern of light and shade under the apple trees. The noise racketed back and forth between the spruce walls, and Charles looked supremely absorbed.

"What a handsome man," Liza said. "You don't usually notice it so much in Charles as in the others, because he doesn't laugh so much."

"Well, he's happy now," said Joanna. "Too bad he didn't

get a riding mower. Then nothing on the island would be safe."

He paused outside the granite gateposts, but didn't turn off the machine. "Good afternoon, girls!"

"Time was when you could hear the birds around here," Joanna shouted at him.

"What was that?" He turned it off.

"I said, Why don't you go back to sheep for keeping the grass down?"

"Don't be so reactionary." He leaned against a gatepost and took out his pipe. "Don't let me disturb your labors. I can get in there later and work." He watched them for a few minutes and then said offhandedly, "Pierre's coming home this summer. Staying ashore for three months."

"You and Mateel must be so happy," Philippa said.

Charles admitted that, cautiously. "I'm going to have him and Hugo shingle the roof. I hear Eric's coming home, too. We ought to work up some business for him. Too bad to waste a minister."

Philippa waved the clippers at him. "Let me tell you right off that he doesn't expect to be asked to preach just because somebody thinks his feelings will be hurt if they don't."

"But it still puts us in a hell of a position. If nobody asks him, he'll think nobody gives a damn."

"I like your language, considering the subject," said Liza.

"Well, to tell you the truth, Eric's not too sure of his pulpit performance yet," Philippa said. "He thinks he's a lot better at counseling. Besides, he says he'd feel self-conscious preaching to a select audience consisting mostly of relatives who keep remembering him when he was eight."

"Too bad we can't have a few marriages lined up for him. But nobody believes in marriage anymore around here, except as something to shoot at."

"Are you talking about Jamie?" Joanna challenged him. She sat back on her heels.

"Not necessarily. I don't know what actions Hugo's up to

when he goes ashore. I told him if I ever found out he was running around with a married woman, I'd drag him home by the seat of the pants and shake hell out of him on the way."

"Well, I can't see Nils doing that with Jamie, or Jamie cooperating." Joanna went back to clipping; it was a great help to have something to do. "If he were underage—yes. But not now."

"When he gets his bellyful he'll be home," said Liza. "Likely to be her with the bellyful," said Charles. "You'd better get him out of there before she's in the family way. He'll never be sure if it's his or not. Can't tell who else's been comforting her."

"Oh, Charles," Philippa reproved him.

" 'Oh Charles' *what?* I've seen that kind before. We all have."

"You're no help," Joanna told him.

"All I know is," said Liza, "that in a couple of years we're going to clap Sam into a barrel and feed him through the bunghole till he gets past the awkward age."

"Which is anywhere between sixteen and sixty-five," said Charles. "Look at me! If I go ashore without Mateel she's positive I have to beat off the women with a stick."

"Listen to him," said Joanna. "Conceited."

Later she and her sisters-in-law walked back to her house through the May wind and scents, leaving Charles happily mowing. She felt better in herself, *with* herself—more natural —than she had for days. Some things remained the same, and you had to remember their importance. *Priorities* was the word nowadays. First things first. When Jamie was a baby and then a child, he had priority. Now it shouldn't be so.

They washed up and sat down to hot tea. When Liza left, Philippa stayed a little while longer, going over the bookcases, and Joanna asked her what Steve thought about Jamie's behavior.

"You know Steve. All he said was that he remembers when he was twenty-five." There had been a girl the family had never seen, had never even heard of until it was all over. "And he hopes you and Nils don't get too depressed about it."

"We *won't.*" She was almost savage at the thought of Nils's silence about Jamie. "But you can't simply forget it. There's the plain truth that Darrell was almost out of his mind when he came over here that day. How do we know it can't happen again, only worse? He could break out with murder next time."

At least Philippa didn't make one of those token protests. Joanna went on. "And along with his brooding, Darrell must take an ungodly amount of plaguing at the shore. Jamie's already built up a backlog of bad feeling over there because of Bronwen. Talk about fools rushing in! This is what we have on our minds constantly besides the moral question, and I don't know which is worse."

She wanted to say, *The worst thing is that Nils and I aren't talking about Jamie anymore.* But it was nothing she could say to anyone except Nils who, if she insisted, would simply answer, *There's nothing to talk about.*

"And there's the other question," she said. "How much does a child owe his parents? How far should he honor his father and mother without sacrificing his own rights? Is it honoring us to keep us in this stew of anxiety, or is that our problem, and nothing to do with him? That's what he'd tell us. He practically has."

"Maybe he feels he's honoring you by being honest," Philippa suggested.

"Maybe he does," Joanna agreed, "and we've tried to honor him by treating him as his own person. But where's the line?"

"Those questions won't bedevil him until he's a parent himself," said Philippa.

24

She had not yet told the girls about Jamie, and it made letter-writing difficult. She felt that she was lying to them by letting them think that everything was the same as usual for this time of year. But if the affair turned out to be short-lived, they might not need to know about it until it was all over.

She sat at her desk in the sitting room trying to write at reasonable length to Ellen, uncomfortably aware that Ellen could sense her restraint. Why not tell Ellen? She put her chin in her hand and gazed toward the harbor. The day was diamond-bright and the wind blew hard from the northwest, piling surf over the end of the breakwater, and the boats were all uneasy at their moorings as the seas rushed in through the harbor mouth. No one had gone out to haul. It was hard to keep one's footing, and there was too much tide running and too much dazzle for finding buoys. Nils was out in the barn making renovations in the hens' quarters, and Rory was lying in the sunny lee of the back doorstep.

She was thinking that Macomber's Cove on Brigport wasn't much of an anchorage for *Valkyrie* in this weather when Jamie appeared in her line of vision like an apparition. He had apparently come around from the shore, and must have entered the harbor before she'd began to watch it. He was carrying the suitcase he'd taken with him and she thought with solemn, cautious thanksgiving, He's coming home. It's over.

She didn't move; she wouldn't rush to greet him and show too plainly what she felt. He looked well, but thinner and older, as if he'd suddenly taken a long leap far ahead into maturity. He looked more like his father than ever. Now she wanted to move quickly, to hurry out and tell Nils, but she made herself stay where she was. Jamie came purposefully through the gate, no reluctance or hesitation there, but that's how Jamie would be; when it was over, it was *over*, and no looking back.

"Ahoy the house!" he shouted in the sun parlor. "Anybody home?"

"In here," she called back. She went out to meet him. He'd remembered to take off his cap instead of merely shoving it back on his head; Nils had always insisted on that, and the little gesture pleased her. "Well, hello!" she said.

"How's everything, Marm? How are you?"

"Fine. How are things with you?"

"Couldn't be better!" he said heartily, and there was that swift ghostly resemblance to Owen. He was reaching into his hip pocket and brought out his billfold. "I came over to pay my board. Guess I'm late, huh?"

"You don't owe any board, you haven't been eating at home."

"But I brought my dirty clothes."

Joanna forgot how she was supposed to look and sound, but not the caution. "For me to do and for you to take back?" she asked gently.

"Yep. No hurry, though. I'll come and get them in a couple of days."

"Can't Eloise do your laundry?" She was still gentle.

"There's no machine at the cottage. Where's Rory? He all right?" He was looking around.

"Rory's fine. So is your father. Isn't there any water at the cottage either? I used to wash your father's clothes by hand. I had a couple of tubs and a washboard, plenty of rainwater and yellow soap."

"She wasn't brought up that way," he said innocently. Nils came in the back door, and Jamie, without any visible self-consciousness, said, "Hello, Father."

She didn't look around. "Jamie's brought his washing home. Next time we'll have our business sign up."

"There won't be a next time," said Nils. "You've moved out, you've moved out all the way. This isn't a laundry and it's not a hotel either, where you can check in and out at your convenience. Put your money back in your pocket and take your dirty clothes with you."

"I guess I'd better take the rest of my clothes too," Jamie said, after a long pause during which Rory scratched and growled in frustration at the back door.

"I guess you'd better." Nils turned to Joanna. "Come on out and see how you like the improvements on the old ladies' home."

"Why don't you ask the residents?" She was sick enough to retch as she followed Nils out. She had thought nothing could be worse than Jamie's first departure, but this was different and far more devastating. If Nils hadn't come in, she and Jamie could have had it out, and even if he'd stalked off in a rage, it would have been far better than this granite finality.

How could Nils keep on talking carpentry after such a scene with his son? How could be maintain a poise that she knew to be false? She looked where he pointed and saw nothing. Suddenly she said in a low shaky voice, "Nils, you've slammed and locked the door on him. He's so proud, he'll never return to us now, even when he realizes she's made a fool of him."

"She hasn't done that. He's managed it all by himself."

She turned back toward the house and he said in soft warning, "Joanna, don't go in and apologize for me."

"I would never do that!"

"He's your child, and nothing like this ever happened before."

"He's your child too, and you're my husband, and the two of you have just—I don't know how to describe it, but—" Her head began to ache, and she was very hot. "Now she'll look all the better to him. He can justify himself all over the place."

"Come here." He sat down on a sawhorse and beckoned her over. She perched unwillingly beside him, wanting only to run somewhere from this killing combination of depression and rage. "This is what he's chosen," Nils said. "He can't live in both places as it suits him. He knows what the story is. When he's done with this way of living he's welcome to come home."

"But after today he won't, no matter what. He's as stiff-necked as you are. Nils, do you realize what he's going through if he's really in love with her?"

"*Love?* I suppose he thinks that's it. All this foolish yarn about rescuing a maiden in distress, and Darrell turning out to be the dragon. But she's a married woman. If it's love, it'll last while she gets free."

"Well, he's certainly not seeing straight, whatever it is, and if it's love as he understands love, he's half in agony, half in bliss, and everything we say is a slap or a slash. We've become the enemy, Nils!" Her throat clogged, and he put his arm around her. "We shouldn't be locking him out—we should feel sorry for him, as if he's suffering through some disease—"

"Were you sorry for him when he came in with his dirty clothes?"

"No," she admitted, "I felt like hitting him. I thought he had one hell of a nerve. Knowing how we feel about this situation, he comes rampsing in all smiles and expects me to do his washing."

"All right, then. Whether he's suffering from love or stupidity, we don't have to suffer it with him. He had no business looking at a married woman in the first place. Why should *we* make all the adjustments? Nobody worried that much about us, and we came through. How about us preserving the integrity of *our* lifestyle? I got that phrase out of a magazine," he added. She was forced to laugh.

"Love me?" he asked. "Even when you don't like me?"

"When don't I like you as well as love you?" she challenged.

"A little while ago."

"Oh, that. It was foolishness."

When they went in, Jamie was gone. She was conscious all day of his newly emptied room, as of a disturbing presence in the house. That night she made herself go in and look into the closet and empty drawers. He had really made a clean sweep. Some of the morning's desolation came back, but not so strong, because she and Nils had talked out there on the sawhorse.

We are still his parents after all, no matter if he is an adult, she thought. But even though she left his room quickly when she heard Nils coming upstairs, she knew that now she could mention Jamie without being rebuffed. So she didn't feel the need.

They made love and later they talked, relaxed and dreamy in the dark. "I don't want to deprive Jamie of anything like this," Nils said. "You don't know how much I want him to have something good of his own, not just in bed, but a whole life. But there's the right and the wrong of it."

"When we were young it was different. Everybody had to work so hard for what little there was to earn. These kids today are almost what we thought of as the leisure class."

"Gentleman lobstering," said Nils. "We struck it rich after the war, so they've got both the advantages and disadvantages of our prosperity."

"And when we were kids it was the rare girl who went the limit. Oh, there were plenty who *did*, but it wasn't taken for granted. Now it's the rare girl who doesn't. It makes it damn' easy for the boys to skip from flower to flower. I always knew Jamie'd crash like Humpty Dumpty, and when I thought it was Rosa I felt so safe."

"Are you blaming her for not taking him?" Nils asked.

"Good Lord, no. I'd never criticize anyone who knows enough not to jump in with both feet. It's no use anyway. She's not fixated on silent Swedes the way I am."

The disturbing presence of the vacated room had withdrawn to a non-threatening distance. "Anyway," she said, drowsily floating, "by the time this mess runs its course, everybody will be talking about what somebody else's kids are doing."

"If we don't get a trap war out of it," said Nils, "and if Darrell decides to be resigned, and if some of the ones who resented Jamie taking over Bron don't resent him playing house with the almost-Sea Goddess—yep, it'll all be the same a hundred years from now."

25

*J*amie still occupied most of Joanna's thinking when she was alone, no matter what she was doing; she alternated between anger and sympathy, remembering what it was like to be in love. Sometimes she let herself go in rage against the girl who had seduced him with her tears. But she knew that Jamie had to be a willing partner to seduction. And what if Darrell really was a house devil beneath that gawky, ingenuous shell? Maybe Eloise had a right to leave him. But she had a family to go to, out of Darrell's reach. How afraid of him was she, to set up housekeeping with another man right under his nose? And Jamie had been so cold-bloodedly sure that Darrell would accept it. So how much of a brute did *that* make him? Whenever she arrived at this question she lost sympathy for Jamie all over again.

When she was with someone else, Jamie was always standing at the edge of her mind, as he had stood in the sun parlor that day, watching his father with blue eyes, asking nothing and yielding nothing. Jamie had gone away then, but he never went away from the shadowy eaves of her consciousness. He would be there when she woke suddenly in the night, simply standing and looking, and a hideous apprehension could set her heart to thudding inside her rib cage and bring out sweat on her body; she would be obsessed with the idea that if anything happened to him that persistent spectral image of him would be the final one to carry all the rest of her life. She would want to ferociously shake Nils awake and say, "You did it!"

But just as suddenly she would be horrified by this impulse, and moved almost to tears by the innocence and vulnerability of his sleep. This tendency to tears irritated her; she'd never been an easy weeper. She'd get up and find her way downstairs by flashlight, and the instant she was in motion the extremes of panic, rage, and guilt were gone. Sometimes she put her loden coat over her bathrobe, and pulled on her boots, and went out to walk around in the night, across to Schoolhouse Cove. She sat on the sea wall and looked at the stars, companioned by the swing of the Rock light, and listened to the silence, which was enhanced by the far-off clamor of gulls excited by a school of herring. If it was rough she'd watch the white lines of combers rushing toward the beach, and luminously breaking all around its long arc. The ocean-scented wind dampened her clothes and curled her hair, and the sound of the tumbling stones and sucked-out gravel was as familiar and reassuring to her in its own way as the sound of Nils's breathing. It was a part of the island's breathing, and in these moments alone the island would return to her as if they had been separated for a long time.

Back to the house, and Rory's tail drowsily hitting his blanket, she would light a lamp and make a hot drink and read until she was floating with drowsiness.

It was a rare night when she didn't have to work her way through the cycle, and she suspected that Nils also lost more sleep than she was supposed to know. But they didn't discuss it, because there was nothing more to be said. If the men passed each other when they were hauling, she was pretty sure there was no contact, but she didn't ask.

Nobody brought up Jamie now, not even Owen, and this unnatural restraint could make her fractious, and even humiliated for herself and Nils, as if they'd become objects of pity. She was sometimes tempted to snap at them, "For heaven's sake! You can say his name, he's not in jail, he's not dead!"

She didn't. She did write the news to Ellen, saying she didn't want Linnie to know until she'd finished her school year, so her last few weeks wouldn't be knocked all out of kilter. Ellen wrote back, "E. sounds like the worst kind of spoiled brat.

If Jamie's really lucky, Darrell won't divorce her. I'd hate to see him legally tied to her. Now he's still got a chance to escape, even if she leaves a few scars. Right now he's probably happy as a clam at high water, so don't you and Father spoil your days worrying about him."

Joanna hadn't referred to the possibility of actual physical danger; this particular anticipation belonged to the parents. She thought again about the eider ducks who presumably stopped worrying when the ducklings were no longer small enough to be gobbled by blackback gulls or snatched from below by seals.

She and Nils rose early one Sunday morning to go fishing, and were out of the harbor before any other house showed signs of life. Liza's cat and Rory saw them off in the sunrise. They sailed out toward the Rock to try the place where they'd had good luck before. The same coastguardsman came out to haul his traps, probably because he recognized the boat. He rowed his peapod alongside and was disappointed not to see Linnie, but was polite to her parents.

They didn't do well on this spot so they moved toward another favorite shoal, where they caught some big pollock and a cusk. Peaceful as the day brightening into its full sapphire splendor, they jogged up the bay. Nils dressed the fish and Joanna steered, and they were followed by gulls in a blizzard of beating wings. They stopped at another shoal far to the east of Pirate, baited their lines again, and did as well here as they wanted to do. With this batch dressed and laid by, the washboard cleaned up, the last gulls flown, they ate their lunch and cruised on toward the northeast. Behind them their own islands became the cloudy isles of dream or poetry, and ahead of them lay foreign headlands purple as grapes or iris.

"Let's go to Isle au Haut sometime," Joanna said.

"We can go right now. We'll never have a better chance."

"No, I mean start out early in the morning and travel as the sun rises. The way we did today. But maybe I don't want to go," she contradicted herself. "It was always the Magic Mountain to me and I'd like to keep a few illusions. Once you land on the place, it's never the same again."

"Your brother Owen would have a good answer for that."

"You aren't Owen so don't try it," she said severely, and they laughed.

After a time they turned and headed back, cutting in to pass close to Pirate Island. "Take a turn around the landing and let's look at Ivor Riddell's new place," she said. Amenably he swung the wheel over and they headed up the west side of the island. *Victrix* was rocking in her own wake as Ivor set wire traps from the stack on her broad stern. The high, grating cries of hundreds of medricks could be heard even over the two boats' engines. There were two children in the cockpit with Ivor and one of them pointed at the Sorensen boat; Ivor waved emphatically, his smile showing white in his beard.

"He looks like a movie star playing a lobsterman," Joanna said. "With his big fancy boat and all."

"Jealous?"

She jabbed Nils in the ribs and made him jump. Ivor slid another trap overboard, paid out bright yellow warp, and the boy tossed out the red-and-green buoy. Then *Victrix* circled without haste to the idling *Joanna S.*

"Out sporting?" Ivor called.

"You could call it that," said Nils. "Like a nice fish for your supper?"

"If it's cod, no, thanks. Wife found a worm in one once, and that finished it."

"How about a pollock?"

"Finest kind! Now you're talking my language." Nils passed it over, and the girl, about eleven, shuddered dramatically.

"Yuck!"

"We hate any kind of fish," the boy said proudly. He was a little older than the girl.

"You hate anything you can't cover with ketchup or

chocolate sauce," their father said. "They don't even like lobsters," he said to Nils and Joanna. "Can you imagine that?"

The children smiled complacently.

"But that's good," said Joanna. "Otherwise they could eat
up a lot of the profits."

"Say, I never thought of that!" said Ivor. Their smugness
wavered a bit.

"Speaking of profits," Ivor went on, "I wonder how long
these'll last." He put his hand on the nearest trap. "I'm betting
they'll clean 'em out tonight. Well, there are plenty more
where these came from, and I can keep on setting until they
get damn' tired of cutting. As soon as I can, I may move into
the cottage and protect my property with a rifle."

"Well, let's hope it doesn't come to shooting," said Nils.

"Hey, come ashore and see the cottage. The workmen have
flown in for the weekend." He was jovial and insistent. "Put
her on my other mooring there—that's where I'm going to
keep a little twenty-foot fiberglass beauty for hauling close
to the rocks. I'll put this baby on her own mooring and take
you ashore in the dory."

"You want to?" Nils asked Joanna.

"We're out on a spree, might's well see the sights real
close up."

"All right then." He turned *Joanna S.* toward the empty
mooring. Ivor made *Victrix* secure, then came for them in the
dory, standing up and pushing on the oars, a child in both
bow and stern. It was a short trip to a deep narrow bit of
beach, the only usable beach on the island, and not always easy
or safe. Today, even in very light winds, there was a frill of
surf on the shingle.

"That's a good dory," Joanna said, when she stepped ashore.
"Some of them are pretty tittle-ish."

"She's supposed to be mine," the boy said, surprisingly.
"My great-uncle gave her to me. I worked on her all winter."

"I did a little," the girl said. "When he'd let me."

"You two going to have traps out this summer?"

The little girl, who had Ivor's green eyes and thick brown hair, widow's peak and all, looked as she had at the mention of eating fish, but the boy said seriously, "I'd like to, but my mother thinks it's kind of dangerous."

"I'm going to be a model," the girl said. "First I'm going to win the Sea Goddess as soon as I'm eighteen, and that'll give me a head start. I want to live in New York and be on TV. You know, like those girls who show off their hair, and jewelry, and cars—"

"And how to clean the toilet bowl," the boy said. She looked ready to cry. The boy turned solemn dark eyes on Joanna. "I think my mother will let me have traps if my father says it's all right. I'm a good swimmer. I took lessons. I think I would like to eat a lobster that *I* caught."

"Yuck!" cried his sister. Greedy for Joanna's attention, she talked fast. "Our baby sitter we used to have was almost Sea Goddess once. She's beautiful. Then she went and married a *fisherman*," she said in disgust.

"What's the matter with that, dummy? Mr. Sorensen's a fisherman. So is Dad."

"But he doesn't have to be."

He looked at Joanna and shook his head. "She's nuts."

The cottage was all natural wood and windows, with a big central fireplace for burning driftwood. The stove and refrigerator would run by propane gas. "And we'll have oil lamps and candles," Ivor said. "I hate those g-d generators ruining the summer evenings. And we'll have an outhouse, but the classiest outhouse on the coast." He laughed and rubbed his hands.

"It's beautiful, and your view is too, and I'd like to be here in a storm," said Joanna. "What does your wife think about it?"

"She hasn't been out yet. I tried to convince her last night that she should come today, but she was afraid it might blow up rough, or rain, or something."

"Gosh," the boy said, "a picnic out here would be more fun! Way up on those rocks you can see halfway to Spain, maybe more!" He took off up the rocky slope behind the cottage; the future model was already on the summit. Beyond them the birds screamed and swirled.

"Don't go near the medricks!" their father shouted.

"I wonder if the flounders still come into Spanish Cove," Joanna said.

"Listen, feel free to come down and fish for them whenever you want," Ivor said fervently. "I'm just interested in keeping those Brigport brigands away from my grounds."

On the ridge the children moved vividly and vehemently against the sky; they seemed outlined with light.

"They love it," said Joanna. "You may even be able to wean them away from ketchup and chocolate sauce out here."

They all laughed. Ivor offered them cold drinks, then wanted to make coffee or tea in one of the old camps he was using as headquarters, and seemed disappointed when they refused.

"Maybe when you're all moved in we'll come down," said Joanna "If your wife realizes she has neighbors who'll come calling from five miles away, she might like it better."

"Yes, sure," said Ivor. "That's all she needs. Thanks again for the fish." He thanked them again when he rowed them out to the boat. He went back in again immediately to get the children and finish setting pots.

"He doesn't seem too sure about his wife," Nils commented, coming back to the cockpit from casting off the mooring.

"No, he didn't even want to talk about her. He must be disappointed. It's too bad, because this place is wonderful in the summer, and if she doesn't let the kids come to stay it'll be a crime against them."

"Maybe she's got a phobia about open spaces," said Nils.

"And maybe she's selfish and spoiled and can't do without her car and a houseful of telephones and being seen downtown everyday. I hope she's decent enough to come out and at least take a look at this cottage he's built for her."

"Well, don't work up a case against the poor woman sight unseen. Ready to go home?"

"I guess so. It's been a great day." And it had been. She had hardly thought of Jamie the whole time. The ache was always there, but dulled. It would begin to grumble and threaten when they went into the house, and when she passed the open door of his room, but it wasn't like a toothache over which you had no control, she thought; she would not let it flare.

26

Night after night during the dark of the moon the boys stopped off the harbor and caught herring. One and sometimes two carriers stood off the harbor mouth waiting for the right tide for loading. The gulls called day and night, shags paddled brazenly in the pocket; medricks, like swallows, were almost faster than the eye. The islanders who preferred corned herring to the redfish cuttings brought out by the smack had full hogsheads in their bait sheds. Anyone who loved fresh herring to eat could always get a bucketful. Nils salted down a batch in the big earthenware crock that had been used for herring since his grandfather had first acquired it. They would eat Swedish pickled herring and onions with their baked beans next winter, and freshen herring to eat with boiled potatoes and the dandelion or shore greens put up this spring.

It was the kind of herring season Jamie might have dreamed about, and his absence from it cruelly emphasized his alienation. Of course he would get a share of the money, because he owned the outfit. But for him to be taking it without laying a hand to the twine, without being out there in the nights with the others, was as astonishing as his love affair.

They were doing well at Brigport too, but he wasn't going out with the MacKenzies, either. This bit of news came by way of a carrier skipper who'd been in the store when Nils and Joanna happened to go in together.

"Where's that yellow-headed boy of yours?" he asked with amiable curiosity. "How come he's not out there in the thick of things? He made a couple of sets with the MacKenzies a while back, but I ain't seen hide nor hair of him since, neither here nor there."

"He's doing something else this spring," said Nils.

"Ayuh? The way he acted, I didn't think he knew there was anything else in the world."

He found out there was, Joanna said silently, afraid that if Mark should catch her eye she'd explode into foolish giggles, and Nils would think she was hysterical. But Mark looked admirably remote, as if he were counting the number of gulls perched on the harbor ledges and fishhouse ridgepoles.

If there was a soreness in Nils because somebody else besides Jamie helped him lug his herring into the shed, it never showed in outward marks around his mouth or his eyes. The rhythms of the season carried him and Joanna along. She set out the vegetable seedlings after the danger of late May frost had passed, hoed the furrows for the seed potatoes and carefully placed them, planted seeds and onion sets, put back the low wire fencing to keep the hens out. She did not think ahead as she usually did to eating the Hubbard squash and Green Mountain potatoes in the winter, and wondered if Nils too practiced this rigorous censorship as he salted herring in the crock.

The Owen Bennett family went off to Joss's graduation, leaving Tommy in charge of Hillside. Linnie returned home by mailboat that same day, euphoric as she always was at the beginning of summer. In that she hadn't changed a bit since she'd started the first grade. Nils was out to haul, and at lunch Joanna began to tell Linnie about Jamie and Eloise. She had only a faint hope of making the story brief and unemotional; Linnie would be ruthless for details.

But Linnie stopped her almost at once. "I know it," she said with unusual restraint. "I just didn't say so in my letters because I didn't want to prod you and Father about it. If you didn't mention it, why should I?"

"Good Lord," said Joanna. "I forgot about the Brigporters at school. Somebody wrote the news, I suppose."

"Yes." She said nothing more about it. She was not only

unemotional but downright flattening. If Joanna had wanted to ask just what she'd heard, she received no encouragement.

"I'm going down to freshen up the name and numbers on my dory," Linnie said, with a return to her natural ebullience, "and then I'm going to bag up, and on the high tide tonight we can launch. And tomorrow I'll set out a load of gear."

"Good," said Joanna. If Linnie had decided to ignore Jamie's affair or at least keep quiet about it, her mother should be thankful, but she had the feeling that she was the one who'd been shut up.

Linnie, Nils, and Ralph slid *Dovekie* overboard at high tide, around sunset, and Linnie invited Joanna for a ride while she tried out her engine. It was good having Linnie coming and going again, noisy as Ellen and Jamie had never been, talking college, lobstering, and men all in one glorious muddle, and if she'd matured enough to realize they just had to live around Jamie, Joanna was proud of her.

When Joanna and Nils went to bed, Linnie was playing pool at the clubhouse with Tommy and Hugo. In the morning she came downstairs saying she was starved, and ate a large breakfast. Then she rested her elbows on the table and looked sunnily from one parent to the other. "I've got a full tank of gas, and it's flat calm, so I'm going around to Macomber Cove to see Jamie."

Nils went on sipping hot coffee. "I thought you were setting traps this morning," Joanna said.

"I can do that any time. I want to catch him, and it's the first Sunday in June so he can't go to haul, right?" She watched her father.

Over to you, love, Joanna thought.

"Right," said Nils. "No Sunday hauling ... You'll never have a better chance to set gear."

"Don't you want me to go see Jamie?" Here it came; yesterday's passivity had been for Linnie's own purposes.

"No." Nils was unruffled.

"I'm of age!" She got up fast. "I can go even if you don't want me to!"

"Yes, you can go without permission," her father agreed. "We'd rather you didn't."

"Why?" she asked belligerently.

"He's made it plain he doesn't need the family. He ought to have a good chance to do without them."

"His parents, yes, but not *me!*"

"Thanks," said Nils.

"Oh, you know what I mean! When you're trying to live your own life your parents can make you feel guilty just by *existing!* They don't have to say a word, they just have to *be*. It's different with a—a sibling."

"We know that," Joanna contributed. "We didn't grow up in isolation booths, we both had siblings, dear. But we think that right now Jamie should be left strictly alone."

Linnie's hands gripped the back of her chair. "He's been so good all his life, so solid and so square—and I mean *square* —that you can't forgive him for surprising you by going really wild. I won't say something *bad*, because it isn't bad. He has to be really in love to act like this, and real love can't be bad, ever."

"It's not a case of forgiving or not forgiving," Nils said. "Sure, we're surprised. We're offended too. And ashamed. We didn't know we'd raised a son who'd move in with a married woman, and in her husband's own territory, too."

"To add insult to injury," Joanna put in, "and if you take that phrase apart, it's a pretty potent one."

"Well, he couldn't very well bring her over here to you, could he? You should have been understanding no matter what he's done, but you've driven him off, made him an outcast—"

"He's cast *us* off, seems to me," said Nils. He left the table abruptly, and went into the kitchen.

"Remember the talk we had back in March, Linnie?" Joanna asked. "And you wanted your father and me to remain true to our principles?"

"It's different! I didn't mean *this!*"

"You can always say you didn't mean *this*, no matter what

it is. Linnie, you weren't here. You don't know the condition
Darrell was in, you don't know how your brother looked and
sounded. It was—"

"Never mind, Jo." Nils came back to the table and faced
Linnie across it. "We don't have to justify our behavior to
you or to anyone. We're your parents."

"I never thought you'd pull that one on me, *Fader*," she
said scornfully. Her eyes were full of tears.

"Look, *älskling*," he said. "We've always been pretty
reasonable, so you can't forgive *us* for being what you call
unreasonable. Now you do as you please. You know what
we think, we know what you think, and that's the end of it."

She kept her head up as if she were trying to keep the tears
from running over. "All I want to know is, if I do go, will I
find my bags packed and put out by the gate when I come
back? Will I be requested to never darken your door again
if I go see *Lillebror?*"

"No," said her father dryly, "but he's likely to request it
of you if you call him *Lillebror* in front of his woman."

She said with an unsteady little laugh, "I'll be careful not
to." She went back upstairs, and Joanna began to clear the
table. Nils carried out some dishes and put his arm around
her waist. They looked at each other without speaking, and
then moved apart as Linnie came back down, carrying the
Irish fisherman sweater Joanna had knit for her last Christmas.
She took her yellow oiljacket off its hook. "See you later,"
she said diffidently.

"It's supposed to breeze up southerly, so don't take any
chances coming back," her father said. "Jog round to the
harbor and call Mark, and I'll come and get you."

"Thanks, but I'll get Jamie to bring me." She went out.
Rory walked part way with her and she stooped down and
kissed the top of his head, as she'd been doing ever since he
was a puppy. Then she went on with her free-swinging, lanky
stride, her rain jacket hooked by a finger over her shoulder.
They watched her through the sink window.

"I wonder what *she'll* take up with," Nils said.

"My sunny Swede isn't turning cynical, is he?"

"It goes with the job."

"And how do we act when she comes back?" Joanna asked. "Do we listen greedily to everything, as we're starved for news? Or do we just let her run on and pretend we aren't interested? Or do we farm off in different directions and leave her high and dry?"

"You intend to brood over it all day?"

"Nope," she answered cheerfully. He laughed and pulled her toward him and kissed her.

In the late morning they went up through the Bennett meadow to the Homestead. Hugo was building a skiff in the barn. The men stood around out there, and Joanna and her sister-in-law made the rounds of Mateel's flower and vegetable gardens, and they looked for signs of green strawberries on the point. Later they all had coffee and coffee cake. The threatened southerly breeze whipped up, but when they got back to the harbor, *Dovekie* was already on her haul-off. Linnie wasn't in the house.

They never had Sunday dinner at noon, so Joanna went to work setting out the pepper and parsley plants Mateel had given her, and Nils replaced some weak boards on the walk that led out from the back door between the lilacs. Rory took an equidistant position so he could keep an impartial watch. The hens divided their attentions between Nils, the dog, and Joanna's frustrating fence. The scent of opening lilacs was blown unevenly about, the white-throat sparrows and robins sang. I am nearly contented, Joanna thought, digging with bare hands in the warm friable soil. I could purr, if only I couldn't think.

Rosa came along by the windbreak, between whose trunks the harbor sparkled, and stopped at the garden. "If you want to know where Linnie is," she said, "she's been at my house, and now she's gone for a walk to Barque Cove."

Joanna sat back. "Is she all right?" Rosa's face was a

shadowy blurr because of the soft yet dazzling cloudiness behind her head, but her voice expressed both her reluctance to carry tales and her concern for Linnie.

"Well—you know she went to see Jamie?"

"Yes." Joanna got up, brushed her hands off on the seat of her jeans, and stepped over the fence. "Sorry, Ernestine," she said to an old Rhode Island Red who almost hadn't got out of her way. "Come on over where Nils is, Rosa. He ought to hear this."

Nils stopped carpentering and took out his pipe. The three sat on the end of the doorstep, with the lower plumes of purple lilac nearly brushing their heads, while Rosa talked. "I was down on the wharf when she came home, around ten. Lad MacKenzie brought her over and towed the dory. There was a real chop and that boat of his is a wet one, so they were ducking spray when they came into the harbor, and laughing. They were having fun, it looked like. Well, they fastened the dory on her mooring and then he put Linnie on the wharf. She thanked him and seemed happy as a lark. The minute he started off and she turned away, she burst out crying."

Joanna knew she was going to flinch, and almost stopped the reaction in time. Nils had his pipe to take up the slack; a man could always pretend he couldn't get it lit.

"Nobody else saw her, all the kids were in Sunday School. I took her up to my house to let her get it out of her system. Hey, please," she begged, "don't let on I told you. But I thought you ought to know."

Nils gave up tinkering with his pipe. "What happened over there? What did Jamie do?"

"It wasn't so much what he did as what he didn't do. She wanted to show him she was loyal and understanding and everything, and she wanted to get him over here to see *you*, even if she had to fake being sick or something. She was sure she could make it work. Well, you know Linnie when she's sure of anything."

"But it didn't work," said Joanna.

"No. Jamie was either embarrassed or mad, she couldn't tell which, but she felt there was this thick wall between them. And he wouldn't bring her back even when she said she was scared to go out between the end of Brigport and the Thresher with the wind coming up southerly. He told her to go along to the MacKenzies' cove and get one of them."

"He sat right there and told her that, did he?" Nils asked very softly.

"Yes, but Eloise was the worst thing—she wouldn't even tell him that he *should* help his sister. Linnie says she'd have refused it, if he offered just because Eloise told him to. But she sat there with her arm through his, and with this little smile all the time as if to say, See what power I have over him."

"So she went along to the Macs," said Joanna.

"First she thanked Jamie, and she says she *thinks* his ears got red, but she's not sure." Rosa smiled. "She was hurt, but mostly mad. She howled it all out of her system, and called them both all the names she could think of, and now she's gone over to Barque Cove. I've spent so many hours over in Barque Cove myself, I almost grew fast to one particular rock." She looked apologetically at Nils. "I hated to dump all this on you."

"Glad you did," said Nils. "I wanted to know how it worked out. We had a little touse about it this morning."

"She was all set to believe it was true love, like Lancelot and Guinevere, or the other pair that drank the love potion on the ship coming from some place—you know—"

"That must be what happened on the trip back from Stonehaven," said Nils.

"And they thought it was just plain old root beer," said Joanna.

"Wow, I'm keeping away from that stuff," said Rosa. "God knows where I could end up."

"How does Linnie feel about the great romance now?" Joanna asked.

"Eloise is a tramp and Jamie's a blockhead. I hold her it was mostly poor judgment on Jamie's side, and I know all about that. I've made some awful damfool mistakes and had to live with them afterward, and there's nothing that can make your guts crawl so bad. I said she should start pitying Jamie, because he's going to need it." She took a long deep breath of lilac and stood up.

"Take some with you," Nils invited, getting out his jack-knife."

"Thanks, but I've got plenty up there and my catbirds are back looking it over, just like in Seal Harbor."

"Have dinner with us tonight," Joanna suggested.

"I'm going over to Kate's. Besides, when Linnie comes back you won't need me around."

She left, and they didn't discuss what they had just heard. Joanna didn't know whether she was glad to be vindicated, or disturbed because Linnie had been so hurt. A mixture of both, she guessed. She went into the house and made a chocolate bread pudding with meringue, Linnie's favorite.

Linnie came home late in the afternoon, not seeming to have cried but with a careful air of elderly poise. "I've been over on the west side," she said. "I've decided to be engaged to the island, if I'm not already married to it. As soon as I get out of these clothes I'll set the table." She ran upstairs. When she came down again, in lighter slacks and a short-sleeved shirt, Nils was sharpening the staghorn-handled carving knife with a steel.

"I always love to see you do that," she said reminiscently. She began laying the silver. Suddenly she straightened up and said, "Well, I went and I came back. I guess I'm glad, because now I know there's nothing to go for, and I'll stop thinking about it."

"That's what your mother and I have had to do," Nils said. "I guess we'll all just stivver through it somehow."

There was no more discussion. When they sat down to the table and Nils was carving the meat, he said, "How about setting your traps after supper? Or are you planning on lugging them out three at a time?"

"Hey, I'm not that proud!" Linnie came to life. "You coming too, Marm? Maybe he'll give us a sunset sail around the island."

27

The high school students returned home for the summer. The eighth graders, Sam, Richard, and Robin, graduated from the island school, with all the children taking part in the exercises. Everybody was invited, and there were refreshments afterward. As if it had been considerately holding back for the graduates' sake, the fog came the next day and stayed. It burned off over the island by noon every day, and the sun shone with a blue-white heat from a gauzy sky. But the island could have been some mountain village set high as Everest in a sea of cloud. Brigport remained invisible. The Rock was heard, but not seen, day and night.

Occasionally the mountain effect was lost when the fog withdrew a hundred feet or so offshore in the middle of the day, and revealed a moat of satiny blue barely darker than the sky, dark-speckled with eiders and their ducklings. There was no wind, so the wash over the ledges was lazy and quiet. The sweetness of the rugosa roses growing wild everywhere hung in the moist air. Wild strawberries ripened deep in grass that hardly ever dried.

The children who had traps out were frustrated, and the mourning was loud and repetitive. Though their traps were set in close to the rocks where the big boats couldn't go, so they could have been able to touch shore anywhere—at least always keep it in sight—the fog could suddenly crowd in again and blot out everything. It was considered that people had enough to worry about without wondering if their children were chugging blindly toward the mainland twenty-five miles away, or toward Spain three thousand miles out.

Linnie was surprised by the fog several times. She would shut off her engine and listen and wait. She would smell the humid fragrance of the roses, or the warm reek of rockweed in the heat, and use this for her compass, rowing *Dovekie* toward it until the land loomed enormously off her bow. Another time she heard the voices of children sent to pick strawberries on the steep open slopes of Sou'west Point. She tipped up the engine and rowed *Dovekie* home, in and out of coves, so as to keep the land in sight; enjoying herself, perfectly at home with herself, no matter what might have been bothering her when she set out and would be waiting when she set foot on shore.

She didn't talk about Jamie. "I'm not going to let him ruin *my* summer," she burst out once from a long silence.

With the fog they felt even farther away from him. Before that he was seen out hauling, even though he pretended not to see anyone and kept his radio off so no one could call him. Matt went alongside him once but not twice; Hugo, more persistent, occasionally chased him down, and said afterward that Jamie's vocabulary had been reduced by Eloise to two words: Yep and Nope. He had stopped bringing his lobsters to Mark, and the fog imposed an isolation in which the distance of miles and years was implicit.

On one of the days when the cloud didn't lift, and the daytime fog was as wet as rain, Joanna carried a plate of filled cookies down to the fishhouse, intending to make coffee there. Nils had a fire going and Rory slept beside the stove.

"What do you know?" Nils asked her with an odd quirk to his mouth. "*Valkyrie* just cruised in out of the fog and tied up over at Charles's. I wouldn't have seen her if I hadn't been out on the wharf."

She felt a spasm like the start of intestinal cramps. It almost doubled her up but she held herself straight and said lightly, "Did he see you? Did he wave?"

"He looked toward the wharf."

She had to be satisfied with that. "I wonder what he wants," she said. "It's too much to expect he's taking an indirect way home." She began sorting nails on the work-bench, and the only sounds were the spruce lath ends snapping in the stove and the gulls walking around on the roof.

"I wish we'd have a good smashing cracking *hell* of a thunderstorm and clear this mess out of the air," she said gloomily.

The door was flung open. "Hi!" Linnie's hair hung straight and wet. "Jamie's over at Uncle Charles's! I'm going over to find out why and then I'll tell you!"

"Thanks," Joanna said, but the slam of the door drowned her out. "I was going to tell her not to bother, he'll tell us what he wants us to know."

"There's only one thing he could tell us that I want to hear," said Nils.

But knowing Jamie was only a little distance away made her painfully uneasy. She wanted to see him for herself, even if the experience left her more uneasy. Nils smoked his pipe and seemed inhumanly absorbed in sorting his cultch. Rory scratched at the door, and Joanna let him out and went out behind him. He picked up Linnie's tracks and followed; in a few minutes he'd be at Charles's fishhouse. Why shouldn't she walk over there too? *I came in to say hello*, she would say. He'd say hello back, and her overture would drop to bottom like a pail lost in the well. All right, dammit! she thought. She went out on the wharf. The tide was very high, almost on a level with the planks, silver gray dissolving into fog so you could hardly tell where one left off. Moisture fell lightly on her face.

Valkyrie lay off the end of the Bennett wharf looking twice as big as she really was. No signs of life there except for the gulls. Fog completely erased the far side of the harbor, but children's voices echoed in the woods on Eastern Harbor Point. The nearer silence bothered her like a tangible threat, but she knew it was only because she longed to see Jamie and he was within physical reach, but still withdrawn and hidden from her, and not just by fog.

A boat was coming invisibly into the harbor and feeling her way slowly toward Mark's wharf, also invisible. The hesitation rhythm of the underwater exhaust was unfamiliar to her. When she was younger the sight and sound of a strange boat would send her around to the big wharf to see. It was nothing to her now, yacht, transient fisherman, or whatever. She went back inside to Nils, ready to flame up at the drop of one of those blasted five-penny nails of his.

"Or take up smoking a pipe," she said resentfully.

"Huh?" He sounded preoccupied.

"Never mind, I'll lay in a stock of lollypops and Tootsie Rolls. You'll get sick of the sight, but it'll give me something to chew on beside my thoughts." She pulled another coffee can toward her. "Freddy sure left chaos behind him. I wonder how he's doing in Port George. No, I don't. I keep holding the thought of our cabin at Bull Cove. The world forgetting, by the world forgot."

"But not by the IRS," said Nils.

There was a hard fast rap on the door and they both jumped; it flew open as if kicked and Ivor Riddell stood there. His orange oilclothes were shining with wet, and moisture dripped off the rim of his sou'wester. His beard was flattened by the mist.

"Hello, Ivor! Nils said. "Come on in and steam a little."

"Can't stop." He snapped off the words, hardly moving his lips. He looked all around the fishhouse, and without turning his head; it made him appear tense and furtive. "I'm looking for Jamie."

"You'll find him in the Bennett shop," said Nils affably. "That's the last one down."

"Thanks." He shut the door before anything else could be said. Joanna moved to where she could see him go out onto the road, and then said, "What was all that for? Do you think he's going to ask Jamie to fish Pirate Island on shares?"

"Could be. Jamie can't be too comfortable over there, and if Ivor offered him one of the places on Pirate they'd be all set until cold weather, with only the Riddells for neighbors during the summer. What more could true love ask?"

"I can't see Jamie fishing for somebody else, when he's always been his own man, and made plenty of money at it, too."

"He'd do staving around Pirate, even on shares. He stopped being his own man quite a while back."

"Ivor was an awfully funny color," Joanna said, "or else International Orange doesn't go with his complexion and green eyes. Leaches the color out of them." She tried to go on sorting, but it was no use. "Oh, come on, Nils! Let's not be proud. Why should everybody else get everything first-hand? Even Rory's there, for heaven's sake! And we'll never get anything from *him*."

Nils surprised her. "All right."

The Bennett fishhouse was crowded. Linnie, Hugo, and Sam perched on the steps up to the loft. Charles was pouring coffee into mugs from the tall blackened agate pot that lived on the potbellied stove; Philip sat on the workbench, whittling lobster plugs. Ivor, his sou'wester off and his oilcoat open, stood with his feet apart as if braced on a tilting deck, his hands behind his back. Joanna kept Jamie for the last; he stood up when his parents came in, nodded at them, and sat down again on the nailkeg. Rory came graciously to meet them.

"Well, look who's here," said Charles. "Come on in and find yourself a place to light. We're having a caucus."

"I thought only crows had those," said Joanna. Sam giggled, and Linnie groaned.

"Coffee?"

"Not any of yours, thanks," said Nils. "No offense intended."

"You did intend it, but I'll leave it lay. Ivor, you feeling courageous enough to try my special Fishhouse Brew?"

"No, thanks." He slashed the words off as if he were slashing the tail off a fish. He does have an odd color today, Joanna thought. "I've got business with *you*," he said bluntly to Jamie. "You may want to hear about it in private."

"I don't think so, whatever it is."

Ivor's green eyes coldly ranged the room, not missing anyone. They returned to Jamie and stayed.

"You all know I've had a cottage built on Pirate," he said. Jamie looked back at him, politely attentive. "Some of you have been ashore and gone through it. Well, the carpenters finished up about two weeks ago and I took them back to Limerock. I haven't been near the place in this fog mull till yesterday. There was an extreme high tide and it was flat calm, so I brought out some stuff for the cottage."

Jamie was beginning to show puzzlement. The rest were listening so intently that the snapping of wood in the stove was as loud as a firecracker.

"Well," Ivor said, "to make a long story short—" he wet his lips—"my cottage was *flat*. Burned to the ground. All that was left was the chimney. A thirty-thousand dollar job was cold ashes."

"*Jesus!*" Hugo exclaimed, and Sam dramatically hissed something. Philip stopped whittling.

"My God, Ivor!" Charles said. "What happened? They leave oily rags in a closet, something like that?"

"Well, after I got my legs and my wind back, I went up to Brigport. I expected to lose some gear, but I never thought any of the local crooks went in for arson. I posted a notice in the store offering five hundred dollars reward for information—I figgered somebody would sell his own grandmother for that. Then," he said with sardonic satisfaction, "I went back aboard my boat, and waited."

"Hey, I'm sorry about your place," Jamie said, "but what's it got to do with me? You said you have business with me. What kind?"

"Just hold your horses. I'll get to it soon enough." Joanna was beginning to feel something like the spasms again. Philip hadn't resumed his whittling, and Charles had forgotten his coffee. The three on the stairs weren't moving.

"I've got me a witness who knows who did it," said Ivor. "Didn't know it at the time, naturally, but it's somebody who could put two and two together and get the right answer."

"Well, that lets out half of Brigport," said Hugo.

"Shut up," Charles growled at him. Something was breaking in Jamie's face, but it was a false dawn; puzzlement closed in darker than before.

"It was all right a week or ten days ago. I can't remember just what day it was."

"It was the fifth of June," said Ivor with a kind of steely triumph. "Fog lifted a while in the afternoon and you took your girlfriend out for a little sail around Pirate Island, and you went ashore."

"We did," said Jamie.

"My witness says you're the one who set the fire."

Joanna started forward, but Nils grabbed her arm and forced her back. Across the fishhouse Linnie pushed past Hugo. Jamie was on his feet, red with astonishment. "Somebody's crazy! *You're* crazy! Why would I burn your place down?"

"Everybody resents my moving onto Pirate because you've all had those grounds pretty much to yourselves since the old man stopped putting fishermen out there."

"I never fished Pirate," Jamie protested. "None of us ever did from here."

"That's right, Ivor, and you know it," said Charles. "That was always a Brigport berth, when they could get away with it."

"Yup, and they got away with it for far too goddam long. But this one's a Brigport fisherman now, or should be, way I hear it." His grin was more like a show of teeth. "Shacks up with one girl over there, drops her and then steals another man's wife, a young girl that's still a bride. I'd say that kind of criminal'd be capable of burning anybody out, wouldn't you?"

"Jamie's no firebug!" Hugo said loudly.

"My witness says different."

"Who is this witness?" Philip's slow deep voice.

"I'm not naming any names. It's somebody who went ashore with him on Pirate, and who'll swear he carried one of those heavy grocery store paper bags with him. They separated and the other party walked up toward the nesting area, but the medricks started dive-bombing her so she went back to the skiff. He wasn't there, but when he did show up he didn't have the bag, and he said 'That'll take care of the son of a bitch.' "

Jamie looked white enough to faint, but Nils wouldn't let go his lock on Joanna's wrist. Jamie sat down heavily, his mouth open, staring blindly at the man. Linnie came and stood behind him and put her hands on his shoulders.

"If she'd known then what he'd been up to," Ivor went on, "she might have been able to stop it, but she never guessed. Well, fog shut in thick as dungeon that night, and nobody saw the blaze, but that's when it had to be."

Hugo said softly, "If that's love, give me hate any day."

"She's a filthy little liar," said Linnie. "What's she trying to do, make a fast five hundred?" Her fingers dug into her brother's shoulders, but he didn't notice.

"I know her from way back," said Ivor. "She used to be our sitter. I believe her."

Charles cleared his throat. "You can leave now, Ivor. You've made your point."

"So now you can close ranks and forget it, is that *your* point?"

Nils spoke up. "Our point is that none of us believe it. You'll have to have more of a witness than that."

"Listen, the Bennetts may be little kings on this island, but when they cross into somebody else's territory the immunity ends. You'll see." He jammed on his sou'wester and went out.

The quiet left behind was thick with surmise and embarrassment. Jamie sat staring at nothing. Philip slid off the bench and said, "Well, this won't buy shoes for the baby or pay for the ones he's wearing. Come on, Sam, back up to the shop."

Sam came reluctantly down the steps and around Hugo.

"Some baby," Hugo said. "What size you wear now, Sammy? They'll have to fit you out with herring boxes without topses, like Clementine."

Sam chuckled. Philip put a big hand on his shoulder and gently shoved him toward the door. He's thanking God, Joanna thought wryly, that Sam's still practically an infant.

"Talk about a nest of vipers," Charles muttered.

"I'm going over and beat the truth out of that one," Linnie announced. "I haven't been hauling traps for nothing all these summers."

"Jamie, come on home and have a drink," Nils said. "We need to talk."

Jamie roused himself. "I've got to get back."

"She'll keep. Come on."

Jamie rose stiffly, as if he weren't even sure of his legs anymore. Hugo said softly, "What in hell's her reason?" His cousin turned toward him, bringing up a doubled fist. "*Shut up.*"

It was a silent walk home in the thick, raw mist. Only Rory was enjoying himself, delighted to have the whole family together. Joanna was reminded horribly of a walk back from a new grave. But she was glad at the same time that they'd been with Jamie when his blue skies crashed in on him.

At the house Nils told Jamie to get out of his oilskins, and took down the whiskey bottle and glasses. There was a tacit agreement that Eloise was not to be mentioned except favorably, which was going to make the discussion very difficult.

The four sat down at the dining room table. Nils waited until Jamie had his drink, then he said, "Now tell me what Ivor's got to go on."

"Nothing but that goddam paper bag! He couldn't have heard her straight, or he's made up the whole thing for some crazy reason of his own. *I've* no reason to want to get rid of him! I'm no Brigport fisherman, I'm a Bennett's Islander. The reason I came over here today—" he moved his glass in tight little circles on the table, watching it. "I wanted to talk to Uncle Charles about buying a piece of land to build a house on. We're getting married as soon as the divorce goes through, and I want to come home."

"With *her?*" Linnie interrupted loudly. He ignored her, and her father gave her a displeased glance.

"The divorce started yet?" he asked.

"No. He won't agree yet to get one or let her do it. But he will," he assured both parents with an eagerness Joanna found almost unbearably pathetic. "Once he gets it through his head there's no chance of her coming back."

Nils nodded. "What did Charles say?"

"You know how he always figures that morally the land's heirship property, even if it's in his name. He said I could have a piece if the family agrees."

"Sounds like organized crime," said Joanna.

Jamie managed a very faint smile. "Who's the Godfather?"

"I don't know but we could use him right now to take care of Ivor." The atmosphere had perceptibly changed; it was easier to breathe, even to move.

"Let's get back to him," Nils said. "It wasn't you, and he swears it wasn't an accident—"

"Which it could very well have been," Joanna put in.

"I suppose it's no use saying he did it himself, for the insurance," Linnie suggested. Nobody paid any attention to that.

"Let's say it's arson," Nils went patiently on. "It would have to be a Brigport man unless some mainland enemy of his ran all the way out here in the fog to do it. But that's unlikely. So what about a Robey? Whit or Tom? They're the logical ones ... What we want to know is why he says this girl is his witness and that she's swearing it was you."

"He's lying," Jamie said at once. "He's going to get somebody's hide for this, and if he can't find the right one, it doesn't matter who he nails." He got up. "I've got to get back there. He hasn't talked to her. I'd know."

"Was she away from you this morning?" his father asked. "Did you go out to haul?"

Jamie hesitated. Joanna saw the hand close on the back

of his chair, the knuckles shining like knobs of polished bare bone. "She went to the harbor for the mail. What are you getting at?"

"Just that he could have seen her," Joanna soothed him. "Even if they didn't any more than pass the time of day."

"Sit down," said Nils. "We're not through here yet."

Jamie sat down. He looked gaunt and drawn, the color like stain on his cheekbones. "If he *is* lying about her," Nils said, "he's going out on a limb. She could sue him, or threaten to. *You* could."

"Maybe there's something he's blackmailing her about," Linnie remarked. "Forcing her to tell this yarn."

"*Jesus!*" Jamie was on his feet again. "I'm leaving now. Thanks for the drink."

"Come down off your high horse and answer some questions," said his father. "Was there a paper bag?"

"Yes. We had some food for a cookout. We had a little fire in the rocks by the beach. I burned up the bag with the other trash before I drowned the fire."

"Did you go into the cottage?"

"No. It was locked, and I woudn't have, anyway. We could look in all the windows. If anybody did set the fire they must have started it under the deck."

"Did you separate at any time?"

"Now what are you getting at?" Jamie asked desperately.

"The truth, if possible. Could you have gone back to the cottage without her?"

"I could have, but I didn't. He had it all mixed up—*I* was the one who walked up toward the nesting area. She was looking for wild strawberries on that slope above the cottage. We were apart maybe half an hour. I got back to the skiff first, not her."

"What about saying, 'That'll take care of the son of a bitch'?"

"Father, you'd be marvelous in court," Linnie said. The two men ignored her.

"That's his creative thinking," Jamie said. "Rounds the

story off. All he bullied out of her was the fact that we were separated for a little while."

"Well, he'll need more than that to take you to court," said Nils. "But he can make one hell of a stink about you. Not that you haven't raised one already all by yourself."

"Any suggestions about handling him?" Jamie asked sarcastically.

"Yes, not that I expect you'll follow them. If stupidity was a crime, you'd deserve a life sentence." Jamie blushed instantly to the hairline, and Joanna herself recoiled from Nils's frigid self-possession. But this was what enabled him to take charge of them all.

"After you try to find out how Ivor got his story, you ship your girl home to her parents to wait for the divorce, and you come home here. Camp out in the fishhouse, if you can't stand your parents."

Jamie waited a moment, nobody spoke, and then he left. Linnie ran out after him but he ignored her. She came back, blowing her nose. "Rosa was right about pity. I'm going up to see her." She took off at a lope.

"I don't want him going back over there now, in this mood," Nils said. "He knows she's lied, no matter how hard he swears Ivor was the liar. But I can't stop him and I can't chase him. God in heaven, Jo, I don't know what to do." He turned to her despairingly, and she held out her arms.

"Maybe Philip would go," she said into his neck. "I know he would."

"We'll see." His voice was muffled by her hair. They stood in the embrace as if they'd each sink if they separated. Linnie and Rosa came by the window, and then they moved reluctantly apart.

28

"Well!" Joanna said loudly. "You men had your whiskey, I'm having a good strong cup of tea. "Marm, Father," Linnie called as they came into the sun parlor. "Rosa says she'll go over and see what's going on."

Rosa was embarrassed but courageous. "Maybe I'm ramming in where it's none of my business. But he'll hate whoever shows up on his tail, and it might as well be someone outside the family."

"We'll be much obliged," Nils said courteously. "It shouldn't be his father or one of his uncles. Thanks, Rosa. How about this fog?"

"I'll go straight to the harbor, I guess, and strike out on foot. If anybody's nosy, I'll say I'm going to see Hannah MacKenzie."

"Can I go with you?" Linnie asked.

"No," Rosa said placidly.

"I'd like to say something to that Jezebel. I could blister her ears off without even touching her."

"Nobody's going to do anything like that, least of all you," said her father.

"Well, at least I can see Rosa off, I *hope*."

"And I'm on my way right now," Rosa was halfway out the door. Linnie caught up with her and was talking emphatically and waving her arms in Bennett style as they became phantoms in the fog and then disappeared in it.

The teakettle was filling the kitchen with steam. Nils turned off the gas and interrupted Joanna's reverie at the window. "How about that cup of tea? Want an aspirin or something?"

"No!" she said crossly. "I'm fine. Just murderous. And, oh yes, ready to thank God on my knees because Phoebe isn't around with all this."

"The silver lining."

"I've got to do something strenuous while we're waiting," and I don't want to leave the house. So I guess I'll do some more baking."

"Have your tea first. Sit down and rest your face and hands," said Nils.

"Do I look as if I'm about to slip my mooring?"

"No, but you might as well admit you're scared about what happens when Jamie meets up with her. *I* am."

She protested, "He'd never—"

Nils put up his hand. "Don't say it. You can't be sure about anything. You can just hope."

"If he looks savage enough, she'll think of something to say. She probably started working on her story as soon as she left Ivor. He doesn't want to believe she's done this to him, so he'll believe anything she tells him."

"What in hell *could* she explain?" Nils demanded.

"Maybe she thinks she could make five hundred fast, the way Linnie suggested, and the lie wouldn't hurt Jamie because nobody could really prove anything. It's the way Phoebe would reason. She'd offer to split the money with him and think that would make it all right." Her head was beginning to ache, starting at the back of her neck. She said wearily, "My murderous instincts are squeezing my arteries, or whatever they do. I'll take the aspirin and the cup of tea."

Linnie came in again, savagely pulling off damp clothes and kicking her boots the length of the sun parlor. She assuaged her homicidal instincts by three cups of tea, and three slices of homemade bread, with rhubarb sauce. Then she offered to chop walnuts for the cookie recipe Joanna had chosen because it was so complicated and time-consuming. Nils went back to work in the fishhouse.

In about an hour and a half, Rosa and Nils came in together. Joanna wasn't going to ask a question until Rosa got
out of her oilclothes, but Linnie couldn't wait. "How is he?
Did you see *her?*"

"No," said Rosa. She looked worn out. Nils took her wet
things and hung them in the sun parlor, and Joanna poured
a cup of tea for her and set out some fresh cookies on a plate.
Rosa sipped thirstily at the hot tea but ignored the cookies.

"Well," she said finally, putting down the cup. "First,
Hannah was at the store with the pickup, so I didn't have to
go looking for her. She didn't know anything that was going
on, just that the cottage burned down but not about what
Eloise told Ivor, and about him coming down here today and
so forth. And she didn't think anybody else did. They were all
saying it must have been Whit or Tom. When I told her, she
nearly drove off the road into that brook with the forget-me-
nots, and she came out with a lot of words I didn't think she
knew." Linnie giggled with nervous excitement. Nils sat with
his chin on his hand, listening without expression. Stomach
cramps agonizingly contracted Joanna's midriff but she made
herself sit still.

"She drove me right down to Macomber's, or as close as
the truck could go, and she waited for me, and I walked down
there alone. *Valkyrie* was at their wharf, so I knocked at the
back door. Nobody answered, and I'd just figured that he
was somewhere on the island looking for Eloise when I heard
something drop inside, so I went in."

She cupped the mug in her hands and looked into it.
Quite apart from her preoccupation with Jamie, Joanna
thought something has hit Rosa hard.

"He was standing in the bedroom," she said finally. "He'd
bumped against a chair and knocked it over ... He was a
wreck. Without saying a word or making a motion, he was—"
She shook her head angrily against a sudden spurt of tears;
they had never seen tears in her eyes before and she was
exasperated and ashamed. "I *know,*" she said with difficulty.
"You see, I know."

"I guess I'll have a cup of tea myself," Nils said, getting up. "How about you, Jo?"

"Oh—sure—I'll get it." She went out to the kitchen. Linnie stayed at the table, but began talking nonsense to Rory.

"It's all right," Rosa said strongly. "I'm not going to throw a fit. The place was a wreck too, because she'd moved out fast while he was over here. Bureau drawers were hanging out, cupboards open, stuff dropped everywhere. Besides the original mess; well, she never did list housekeeping among her accomplishments when she ran for Sea Goddess."

"I'm glad she never got it," Linnie said viciously.

"Maybe if she had, she'd never have taken up with Darrell," Joanna said. "Well, where did she go when she moved out, Rosa?"

"I asked Jamie, and he just shrugged and sat down on the edge of the bed. I tried to talk a little courage into him but he didn't even hear me." Why didn't *we* go? Joanna cried silently. We're his parents, at a time like this we'd have counted for something . . . But she knew that the pity and love which remembered him as a baby wasn't what he wanted or needed now.

"I went back and told Hannah, and she drove me around to Darrell's little house at Popple-rocks Cove. He wasn't there, but his sister—you know Phillida—was in there; she's been cleaning for him once a week. Darrell was down at the harbor building pots. She said Eloise had just taken off for the mainland with Ivor."

"And to spend that reward fast!" said Linnie. "Boy, she didn't waste any time, did she? Oh, wouldn't I love to get that one by the neck, and twist and twist, and—"

"Hush up, Linnie," said Nils. "Well, it was going to be rough on him anyway—I'm glad she got out of there before he came back, or it could have been a lot worse."

"Phillida was about ready to burst, so we got the full effects. Darrell'd been home for a mug-up, and Eloise came tearing in to get some gear she'd left behind when she moved out. She was weeping all over the place. Phillida wasn't impressed by that, she said it was just to keep Darrell in line because he gets all upset when she cries. She was claiming she had to run away while Jamie was out of the house because he was so mean and vicious, nobody knew how bad—"

"The same things she said about Darrell," Joanna said. Rosa nodded.

"Anyway, he was all set to take her back, and Phillida was wondering how she could prevent it, short of shooting Eloise where she stood. But she said she was going home to her folks and never coming back. Ivor Riddell was starting for the mainland right now and she was going in with him. Doting Darrell drove her down to get her stuff from the Macomber cottage and then to the harbor, and Phillida squeezed herself right into that pickup with them, just to make sure Eloise got aboard the boat. She was all ready to do a little secret wrist-twisting and finger-bending if she had to." Rosa had to laugh. "But Eloise couldn't *wait* to get going, and Ivor was glaring at Darrell as if he were a wife-beater, and saying Jamie Sorensen ought to be hanged."

"Oh my God, what an unbelievable mess this is," Joanna mourned. "What about Jamie now?" Was he still sitting there in the devastated bedroom, trying desperately to recover from the blow, or was he giving up under it? A gun—a rope—Pain shot shatteringly under her ribs, she began to sweat. "*Nils*," she heard herself saying.

"Hannah and I both went back to him," Rosa said. "We told him she'd left the island for good, and he might as well go home. He said, 'What about this mess?' and Hannah said she'd clean it up."

"Jamie was legally renting it, so Linnie and I should clean it," Joanna said automatically.

"Where is he now?" Nils asked.

"I told him I was going home before it got dark and he'd better come along pretty soon or there'd be a posse out after him. He wouldn't be left in peace until he got back onto

Bennett's. Then nobody'd speak to him if that's what he wanted. I hope that was all right to say."

"That's all right, it's fine," Nils assured her.

"Can I have some more tea? I'm as dry as if I've been running for miles." Linnie jumped up to refill the cup.

"Rosa, I can't tell you how much we appreciate this," Joanna said. The cramp was ebbing away now; not for good, she knew.

"For Jamie, any time," Rosa said. "It's a good thing I never laid eyes on her today. I might not have twisted a wrist or bent back a little finger, but I know some words that could have cut her up in little strips and hung her out to dry."

There was a tentative knock at the sun parlor door, and Linnie went to open it. Sam said in a subdued voice, "Dad said to tell you Jamie just came into the harbor."

"Thanks, Sam," she said with remarkable nonchalance. She closed the door and came back almost dancing. "Who's going down there?"

"Nobody," said Nils. "He's home and that's enough for now."

"But he needs to know—"

"He knows. He's got to have time alone to lick his wounds."

Rosa got up. "Thanks for the tea. I'll go home now." She too needed to have time alone. When she had said so painfully, I *know*, it was the truth. "Once I thought," she said now, "that Jamie could never make a mistake like this one. Now I know better, and it makes a difference. I can't tell you how, but it does." She sounded exhausted and wondering; as if she were talking to herself on the edge of sleep.

The evening was gotten through somehow. The awareness of Jamie's unseen presence on the island filled the house as fog filled the windows and dripped unceasingly off the lilacs. But what if in the morning the sense of his presence was no longer there? Like the realization that the breathing in the next room has stopped? No Bennett or Sorensen had ever killed himself, as far as she knew; but there was always the first time, and it happened all the time these days, as if some saving virtue had gone out of life.

She didn't want to speak this out loud to Nils; merely to put it into words would be terrible, and then he would tell her he trusted Jamie in spite of the cynical, cutting things he had said in his disgust and disappointment, and make her feel guilty for being afraid. He could not believe that someone not about to die anyway would be willing to leave this life of seas, skies, boats, and island for any other reason, no matter how brutally circumstances had beaten him face down into the mud.

He slept because Jamie was back in the fishhouse loft; the worst had happened to Jamie, so there was nothing else possible now for him but to get over it. But Joanna lay awake aching to get up, all her muscles straining for it while she tried to keep still. She wanted to be near Jamie when the awful hours began, after midnight; the worst hours in the day.

At midnight I'll get up, she promised herself, and go down to the fishhouse. I can wait downstairs until it's daylight. If he's been able to sleep, he'll never know I was there.

It was something after eleven then. Making her plans gave her an almost joyous escape. She would take a blanket with her, and there was that old rocking chair she could settle into; they used to make jokes about Grampa Sorensen's ghost tramping up and down in a rage because a rocking chair in a fishhouse encouraged idleness.

Well, if he visits me tonight, we can have a nice chat about the younger generation gustaleering through life, she thought . . . She became aware of very slight sounds downstairs, none that Rory would make if he got up to stretch and shake himself. She hadn't heard the stairs creak, so Linnie hadn't gone down. She slid out of bed and went to the head of the back stairs. The sounds became clearer; surreptitious clinkings, the cautious closing of the refrigerator door; the teakettle boiling. There was a light, which she knew came from a flashlight standing upended on the counter and directing its beam at the ceiling. She sat down on the top step and leaned her head against the wall and shut her eyes. It was like the time the dragger had signaled them that Jamie was safe in Brigport Harbor. When she smelled coffee, she went back to bed, snuggled up to Nils's back and fell asleep as if jumping off a cliff.

29

She hoped that, according to some law as inexorable as that of the Medes and the Persians which Elsie Dinsmore's insufferable papa was always invoking, things had to get better for Jamie instead of worse. He returned to his room at the house; he ate his meals with them, he hauled his traps, he bagged up, he went to bed at night. He didn't go to play pool or up to Ralph's for the music; he refused to take over the herring operation. He had a bluish and sunken look about his eyes, which meant he wasn't sleeping much, and he ate as if it were only to keep the machine going.

Ivor Riddell was living in one of the old camps, but had plans for rebuilding the cottage; he told this openly at Brigport. He had also named Jamie as the arsonist, and now Nils and Joanna waited for the first signs of legal action. Every mail day was unpleasantly suspenseful.

Bruce came over to see how Jamie was doing, but Jamie wouldn't talk. He kept on stuffing bait bags like an automatic device, and Bruce went up to the house and found Joanna working in her garden. "Nobody believes it," he said. "The only ones who say they do are Whit and Tom. Whit shakes his head and says, 'That's a good boy gone wrong,' and then cackles. He did it, the old—well, everybody knows it. Ivor'll never dare take this to court. But if he does, any smart lawyer could make her admit she wanted to make five hundred bucks and get rid of Jamie in one crack."

"Thanks, Bruce," Joanna said. "I almost wish he would take it to court so we could finish it off now."

"I don't know what she's got—well, yes I do," he admitted with a grin. "She's got a shifty way of looking sidewise at you that makes my hackles rise. Hannah says what it means is, 'Will you come into my parlor? said the spider to the fly.' "

"I think Hannah's right."

The move came at last, not in the form of a legal envelope or a man with a warrant.

Jamie got a mild infection in one finger from a lobster pinch, and was trying to keep his hand dry. For several days he took Linnie with him to haul. She had to swear to keep her mouth shut, and was doing it quite well, until the time came when it was clearly impossible and even Jamie knew it.

He might have been moving through his days in a bad dream, but when his hauling gear fetched up a wire trap, he was not dreaming; he knew whose number the trap carried as well as if the trap bore the man's name instead. Pirate Island lay off to the northeast and *Victrix* loomed across the blue-green chop like a yacht. Linnie was still keeping quiet at this point, and didn't ask him what the matter was. He took his knife and cut off the warp just below the toggle, dropped his buoy into the cockpit, and shoved the trap overboard again. He sped *Valkyrie* on to his next buoy; again the trap was an alien, again he cut off his buoy and toggle. He had hauled six like this, and was reaching for the seventh when they saw *Victrix* hurtling toward them.

"What if they've all been switched?" Linnie cried.

"I'm guessing they haven't," he said, "and Ivor's a little late. He's miscalculated, or else the warden was late at the rendezvous." He gaffed another buoy; Ivor's trap again. It was dropped overboard and sunk. The next one was Jamie's own.

"Hold that trap right there!" the warden shouted as *Victrix* came smashing across the chop, Ivor grinning fiercely in his beard. The young warden was objective and businesslike. He checked the number of the trap with Jamie's license. He leaned over and looked at the seven wet green and white buoys on the platform. "Would you mind explaining those?"

"Somebody got to my gear before I did," Jamie said. "I found these floating." He nodded pleasantly at Ivor. "I'm going to hire me a skin diver to go down and locate those traps of mine. Cost too much to lose, and they're likely full of lobsters too. What do you have down here, Ivor, wood or wire?"

"Wire," said Ivor dismally.

"Ayuh? I've been thinking of changing over. Gradually. It doesn't pay to jump at anything."

The warden was not satisfied, but at least he had a legal position to back him up. The buoys in the boat were Jamie's own, the trap on the washboard was his. "You have any objections to my underrunning the rest of your string?"

Linnie felt as if someone were stopping off her breath. Jamie waved his hand toward the next buoy and said, "Be my guest."

"Oh, the hell with it!" Ivor said violently. "Come on, let's get out of here. I'll get you in court, Sorensen."

"Not over gear you won't. If he's lost traps, you'd better underrun some Brigport strings," he said to the warden. "Bennett's Islanders have never tried to fish around Pirate."

The warden nodded sternly, then allowed himself a quick glance at Linnie, who smiled at him. "You're new in this territory, aren't you?" she asked.

"Yes, ma'am."

Ivor gunned the engine. Over it Linnie said, "When you come into Bennett's to check my uncle's car, maybe I'll see you again." The warden's reply was drowned out in *Victrix*'s departing roar, but he waved.

At the afternoon coffee session in the sun parlor, Jamie may not have been talkative but he was not withdrawn. "He knew there were only the seven traps. Loaded with lobsters they were too. I hated like hell to cut them off. And mine are down there that *he* cut off."

"Will you get a skin diver?" Linnie asked.

"There's a feller over in Pruitt's Harbor you can hire," said Hugo. "He and his brother have a salvage business."

"Forget all that for now." Owen slapped a hard palm on the table and made the coffee mugs jump. "What are we going to do about it? How about Paddy's hurricane wiping this bastard out completely, huh?"

Philip looked at him and shook his head. Nils said, "Owen, you're like the war horse in *Job*, who saith among the trumpets Ha, ha, and smelleth the battle afar off."

"Yes, stop pawing my good linoleum, you're scratching it," said Joanna.

"Have your fun, everybody. But what do we *do?*"

"Ask Jamie," said Nils. They all looked at him, and he said, "Nothing." The slight animation that had carried him until now had gone. "He won't try that with my gear again, and the Robeys will be giving him a hard time, so—" he shrugged. "That's the end of it."

He pushed away from the table and went upstairs, leaving the rest in an anticlimactic silence. When they heard his door shut, Joanna murmured, "Something comes over him in waves."

"I know," Owen said heavily. "Well, I've got to take my boat around to the cove." He left, and the others didn't stay much longer. There was nothing more to say. It was Jamie's business.

But if Jamie was willing to let it go because it was insignificant beside the loss of Eloise, which must have been as agonizing as the loss of his sight or his hands, Joanna was not willing. She felt a personal enmity toward Ivor, as if he had attacked her. And she was bedeviled by something; she knew it could be imagination, wishful thinking, or a tendency to believe almost anything when her emotions were involved, but the questions returned again and again, and when they came in her hours of clearest thinking and coolest reasoning, she paid attention to them. Surely by now Ivor Riddell must be bothered by some questions of his own, even if in his outrage he didn't want to give up the whipping boy because he had to work it out on *somebody*.

But he was, supposedly, a hard-headed businessman. Granted, he had a soft spot for the baby sitter, and she'd probably choked out her story in reluctant little bits and pieces, weeping in the right places, and then later rushing to him for refuge from a brutal husband and a vindictive lover. But by now he should be able to balance her story against Jamie's reputation and his lack of motive, and begin to wonder if she hadn't simply seen that reward money as an escape from a devoted and boring lover.

By God, he's *going* to wonder about it if I have to ram it down his throat! she thought viciously. There was no way for her to get down to Pirate Island by herself to face him, and she couldn't tell Nils what she was thinking; she didn't want her fire banked. But Ivor had a wife, and he might be approached through her. Bronwen knew her; the two clans knew each other well enough so that the grandfathers had once hoped to make a match between Ivor and Bron's sister.

There was no way to get Bron by telephone from here, with the only instrument in Mark's store. Writing was a waste of time, if it turned out that Bron was hitchhiking through Europe or backpacking in Alaska.

"I think I'll go in on the boat tomorrow," she said at supper one night. "I want to get some paint and some curtain material so I can do over the spare room before Ellen comes. I've been thinking about it." It wasn't altogether a lie, as she had thought of it in passing during the winter and spring, and then it had been forgotten entirely.

"Do you have any objections?" she asked Nils, half-expecting him to say, *What's really on your mind?*

"None at all, as long as you plan to come back," he said innocently.

"Then everybody make a list of anything they want me to get—Linnie, you want to go with me?" She hoped she sounded hospitable instead of as guilty as she felt.

"Nope! I'm right here till school starts again, making all that money for my Swedish trip next summer with Jamie."

Remote as usual these days, Jamie didn't even hear that. Linnie looked both sad and resigned. Then Joanna asked her if she had any suggestions for a new color scheme, and she brightened up and said she'd go up to the room and think about it.

The wind was east the next day, bright, salty and cold. *Clarice Hall* took it on the side all the way in. There was no one else from Bennett's, and only a few from Brigport. Joanna wore slacks and her loden coat, and got herself comfortably wedged and braced against the uneasy motion. She had a short but refreshing nap; she'd been awake since long before daylight, planning what to say when she saw Bronwen. She was fully aware that she might not see Bron, but she was going to work hard at it, and hoped that it was too early in the season for every hotel and motel to be full of tourists.

Once she found a room, she would call the island and leave a number with Mark, but she was excited about being alone, about having the freedom to act, and now she didn't feel guilty. She would have, if she hadn't chosen to follow up her intuition.

Going by signs and portents, the beginning of this adventure was full of promises. She got the last vacancy at the bright new motel that overlooked the public landing. She dropped off her loden coat on the way to the telephone and dialed Ferris Jenkins in Fremont, and Bron answered.

"I can't believe it," said Joanna. "Is that really you, Bron? Are you just on the way to Greece or Colorado or something?"

"I'm just on my way to the bathroom. Who *is* this?"

"Joanna Sorensen. All the way across the bay I've been prepared for not reaching you. Can you have lunch with me? Or supper tonight? Or meet me sometime in between?"

"How about sometime in between?" Bron asked at once. "This afternoon? I'm alone and I will be till late afternoon. If you come up by taxi, I'll drive you back to wherever you're staying."

"Bless you," Joanna said. "I'll be there as soon as I get myself all shipshape."

"And Bristol fashion," said Bron. "There's something mysterious about this, I can hardly wait. I'll go out in the kitchen and madly hurl stuff together."

"Don't fuss. A good cup of coffee will be fine."

"Listen, my new summer job is cook on a windjammer. A cake for two is a mere snap of the fingers."

It turned out that Charley hadn't left her a note after Joanna's earlier call. "Of course I'd have written you!" Bron sputtered. "Honestly, I don't know how that girl lived to grow up, let alone become a wife and mother."

"Well, it wasn't so important then," Joanna said. "But this is."

Bron knew nothing about Jamie and Eloise; she'd been out on the windjammer since the first of June. Charley had heard from Angie Riddell about the cottage, but only that it was believed to be arson. "Somebody trying to keep Ivor away from Pirate Island, that was all she said," Bron said. "Jamie wasn't mentioned—maybe Ivor hadn't given her any names. But, my God, *Jamie*." Bron was appalled. "That little—I can't say bitch because I love dogs—poor Jamie! And poor Darrell too. What a pair of lambs led to the slaughter!"

"You're pretty decent to be sorry for Jamie after the way he treated you," Joanna said.

"What do you mean?"

"Dropping you when things got tough for him."

Bron was horrified. "Oh, Mrs. Sorensen, I dropped *him!* Have you been blaming him all this time? Look, when I found out what was going on, I didn't want to be responsible for a trap war, and it really hit me in the gut when they tried to sink his boat. So I walked out, and missed my one and only chance to be Helen of Troy." She made a long face. "I had

a good time with Jamie, but it was time for it to end, while
it was still good. And I don't mean the good time was the
going-to-bed part, though that was super," she said candidly.
"Nothing kinky about Jamie, and that's a relief after some
of these characters I've met up with."

"I suppose that's something to be grateful for," said Joanna.
They both laughed.

"But he's fabulous company aboard the boat, or just talking, once you can get him started. Those nights we walked
all over Brigport and looked at the stars, and when we stayed
out all night in the moonlight aboard *Valkyrie* after the party.
It's started me off with some good memories, like money in
the bank for when I'm old."

"I hope Jamie feels the same," said Joanna. "I hope Eloise
hasn't wiped them all out . . . You know, I thought it could
be love even when he said love had nothing to do with it,
and I was ashamed of the way he dropped you and then
went for Eloise, another man's wife."

"She went for him, you mean. I've seen her in action. Of
course right then she was being impartial, but she acted as if
she could have eaten them all up."

"He didn't have to be so gullible," his mother said. "He
could have worked a little harder to resist temptation. He
couldn't really have believed in his heart that Darrell was such
a monster. Now he'll have to get over it somehow. If he
loved her, we're all sorry for his suffering, but that's something you have to do alone."

"You sound experienced."

"You can't get to my age without some experience. When
I was Jamie's age I was a widow with a child. My husband
had drowned right in his own harbor one fine summer night,
and he never knew he would be a father. Then there was a
long time during the war when I was sure Nils would never
come home alive, and I'd be a widow again, with two children. But here I am, and one of the children is having to travel
alone through something pretty awful."

"I wish there was something I could do," Bron said worriedly. "But betrayal like that from somebody you've adored is almost worse than if they'd suddenly up and died." She blushed to the eyes. "Excuse me."

"It was over thirty years ago, Bron," Joanna told her. "What you can help with is a little information. I don't want you to stick your neck out or anything like that," she added quickly. "But I'm looking for something—*anything*—I can use to stop this harassment from Ivor. Evidently he knows he hasn't got much to go to court on, but he's going to be nasty, and he has a real talent for it. A couple of my brothers were all for settling things the way they used to do when everybody didn't yell for the sheriff or the warden."

"Those were some of Gramp's good old days," said Bron. "No fuzz."

"Well, you know Ivor's background pretty well. So what about Eloise? Do you know anything about *her*, besides what was written in the paper when she was a candidate for Sea Goddess?"

Bron stared into her palms, latticed her fingers, made a church roof and then the steeple. "Indirectly," she said, peering into the arch.

"Don't say anything if you don't want to. But I keep wondering why a man of Ivor's age—a businessman—would listen to such a crackpot story without going any further, pay her the reward, and start trying to make life hell for Jamie, who's already been knocked down."

"How about some more warm coffee cake?" asked Bron. She jumped up and went to the dresser.

"Oh, forget it, Bron," Joanna said impulsively. "I don't have any right to haul you into this. I'm darn sure Jamie'd never thank me for it. He wouldn't speak to me for a year if he knew. So I'll have another cup of coffee with you and go along."

"It's not that." Bron brought fresh cake back to the table. She was still solemn but not disagreeably so. "I do know something about the time when she was their sitter. But I'd never have mentioned it because it's the past, and she was just a kid then, and you always hope somebody knows better by now. And it wasn't anything *criminal*. But after what she's done to Jamie—" She stopped and poured coffee into their cups, very carefully. "My sister told me this. Eloise was only about fourteen, but she was so flirtatious, making eyes at Ivor and showing off to him, and he was enjoying it so much, that the two of them began getting under Angie's skin. One night when he took two hours to drive her home, Angie decided to get another sitter. So her whole time with them was under a year. Just a few months actually."

"But whenever he mentions her it's as if she's some youngster they've watched grow up," said Joanna. "A favorite niece, maybe."

"Some niece," Bron said sardonically. "He always stopped off in the harbor on his way to or from Pirate, and almost always she just *happened* to be at the shore. She could have heard from him by radio, Darrell has one in the house. I didn't think that then, but I'm beginning to realize I'm pretty dense sometimes. If she wasn't at the shore, he'd disappear on the island somewhere. I thought he was in the store or calling on somebody up on the island. I never gave it another thought then, but if it was when Darrell was out to haul—well, you know where his house is."

"No close neighbors to keep tab," said Joanna.

"And one time," Bron went on, "she came up to my place and hung around babbling on and on about this married man with money who was so crazy about her, and with him she could travel, and have a big house on the mainland, and so forth and so on. So I asked her why she'd settled for Darrell, a girl with all her opportunities, and she said very grandly that she'd told this rich lover not to come near her until he was free."

" 'It's pretty rough on Darrell, isn't it?' I asked her. 'Having to be a last resort?' And she managed to laugh and look tragic at the same time, and said she knew this other life was all fantasy, it could never happen because *he'd* never desert his children, and *she* wouldn't want him to, blah blah, but Dar-

rell was sweet and good and one had to live life day by day."
Bron laughed. "It sounded deep and poetic and confusing, and
you could see she was pretty proud of herself. She said it was
just one of those might-have-been-things, didn't I ever have
one? I said, 'Yup, with a little luck I might have been Raquel
Welch.' " She crossed her eyes, and they both laughed.

Joanna said, "Then if he's kept something going with her
—I'm dirty-minded, maybe—he'd have a good reason to hate
Jamie, I suppose. Not a sensible reason, but for him a good
one."

"Sure. Jamie's known her fair body! I don't suppose he
considered poor Darrell much competition, but Jamie's something else. Ivor could be eaten alive with jealousy about this
seductive kid he can't have. I sound as if I read too many
books or watch too many soap operas, don't I?"

"But it's not far-fetched," Joanna said. "There could be
more truth than poetry to her story about the rich married
man. She might even have snapped up Darrell to be near Ivor.
After this insane story about Jamie being a firebug I'm ready
to believe some people would do anything. Ivor might even
believe Jamie burnt down the place because Jamie was jealous
of *him*."

They were both quiet and depressed. Joanna reflected that
Nils was right, as usual, when he said it should be left alone.
She wandered into a strangling kelpy tangle, guided by intui-
tion and not the impartial, lucid reasoning of the compass that
Nils carried always.

"Thanks for a good mug-up and for listening, Bron," she
said finally. "Also for all you've told me. If I'd ever dreamed
when I was eight I'd be having cake in Ferris Jenkins's house
I'd have blown up."

"I should've told him to drop home for an hour, I had a
big surprise for him," Bron said mischievously. "But maybe
you should be allowed to keep your illusions."

30

*S*he went shopping that afternoon and found what she wanted without any difficulties. At suppertime she called Dave's number in Port George, and Dave answered, sounding strong and well. He wanted her to come down, he himself would drive up to get her, but she told him she'd be no fit company; she'd had a long day and wanted only to go to bed.

"You aren't letting this bullshit about Jamie get you down, are you?" he asked. "Because neither that girl nor Riddell are worth the powder to blow 'em up State Street. Alice hears stuff, you know. The Paisleys are decent and they were fit to be tied the way their girl was carrying on. Looks as if she up and snatched the Robey boy because she had to go somewhere away from home, and couldn't afford to get any distance on her own. And Riddell's a real whoremaster, got women stashed away all over the place."

"Listen, Dave," she said. "I know they're no good, but Jamie's the one who's suffering. If anything could get me down, it's that. But he'll get over it." By making a great effort she sounded almost callously optimistic, and Dave praised her for it. She decided to end the talk on an upward stroke, so she didn't mention Phoebe and Freddy, but sent her love to Alice.

She tried to watch television, and then to read, but gave up finally and was lying in the dark room watching the stars over the harbor and listening to the alien sounds when the telephone rang.

"Were you asleep?" Bron asked apologetically.

"No—just far, far away in my mind."

"Well, I've been to Charley's, and I found out something." Her voice was dulled. "It shoots down our theory. Maybe the rich-married-man yarn *was* a fantasy, built up on those old baby-sitting days when the man was fooling around. His wife's started divorce proceedings, and there's another woman, but it's *not* the bonny one. The wife told Charley the cottage is to be a honeymoon cottage—it was never intended for her and the kids!"

"Then maybe he believed the crackpot story simply because he's a crackpot," Joanna said despondently, "and that's pretty hard to cure."

"*If* he believes it. There could be an element of jealousy—after all, You-know-who got this young stuff *he* wasn't supposed to touch, though if you ask me he managed quite a bit of it. Touching, I mean. He could still have a yen for it even with this other woman in the picture, whoever she is. As for Little Miss Muffet, if she had a crush on him once and he'd responded, he probably looked pretty exciting to her when he showed up out there, and she was stuck with innocent Little Boy Blue."

Joanna had to laugh. "Bron, I love your names. You do me good. But you know what? I'm going home and try to forget all about it. I'll consider that You-know-who stumbled into a hornet's nest, but it didn't kill him, and it won't."

"Oh—there's one more thing!" Bron's voice lifted. "The wife says she knows he hasn't found out anything definite yet about the fire, because he's never paid out any reward money. He told around that somebody swore to a wild yarn and he gave them a check, then stopped payment on it, and he's no longer offering any reward. And as far as the wife's concerned, she thinks it must be the locals who want to keep him out. *And*," Bron said with dramatic emphasis, "Little Miss Muffet's gone back to her husband, which makes me positive she never got the money. If she's gone back to Little Boy Blue, she must be some desperate."

"Well, seeing as I can't put her over my knee, I'm glad if she *is* desperate," said Joanna. "Well, Bron, thanks for all this."

"I wish there was some way you could use it."

"I do too, but it would only be for my own satisfaction. He's got to get over this by himself, and nothing will make any difference in that. Have a good summer at sea, Bron, and thank you again. It was good seeing you."

"It was good seeing *you*. Can you tell him you met me on the street and I sent my best? Or don't you think he'd give a damn?"

"I think he'd give a couple of damns." They both laughed. It was a good way to end.

The day seemed to have been a week long since her waking in the dark this morning. The curious thing was her increasing assurance that questions had been answered. She forced herself to leave it as it was, not to dissect or analyze, and finally got to sleep and slept well in spite of the foreign sounds. They woke her early, though, and she ate her breakfast at sun-up in The Crow's Nest, with travelers and early fishermen. Her assurance was a solid fact this morning; she had awakened knowing it existed as the sun existed out there, a red globe through the morning fog. There was some way in which she could use the facts Bron had given her. She didn't see the way yet, but it would open before her.

Ordinarily she'd have waited to go out on the boat the next day; she could have found something to do in Limerock, gone to the museum, the library, done some advance birthday shopping, seen a movie that night. But whatever she felt had to be used now, or never.

She went back to the motel and called the airfield, and was told she could go out to Brigport as soon as the fog lifted; she was to call back at ten . . . She had three hours to use up, and to keep from planning. The instant you began that, you diminished the power surge and the certainty that you were meant to act *now*.

She concentrated on family birthdays, and a selection of new paperbacks. By then the wind had come around to the northwest, and burnished the world.

She was the only passenger out to Brigport on this trip, and no one was waiting at the remote airstrip to fly back to the main. She hid her suitcase and parcels in a thick clump of bay at the edge of the once-pasture, and kept only her shoulder bag with her.

It was nearly noon, and she met no one on the hard-beaten dirt road between the spruces. Sometimes she passed a house deep in its old apple trees and early flowering shrubs, but she could have been in some remote country setting a hundred miles inland. The nearer she got to the harbor, the more houses there were, and sometimes a woman waved from the garden or the clotheslines, but all the men would be out. Then she came to the turn-off that led down to Popple-rocks Cove, where Darrell Robey had set up housekeeping in a little house that had been a Robey place since Joanna's earliest memories. The family had once owned most of the land on this southeastern shore of Brigport.

The front yard of Darrell's house slanted to the pink granite terraces of the cove and the blue water shifting and sparkling under the wind. Nobody came to Joanna's knock. She walked around to the back, and found a tiny lawn walled in securely by spruce and alder. Eloise lay in a deck chair, her face half-hidden by large dark glasses. She wore a pink bikini, and her dark hair was pulled up tightly to the top of her head. She looked elegantly naked and lifeless, arranged there like a mannequin, the dark glasses turned blindly toward Joanna. Was she asleep or not? Joanna stood motionless until the girl could stand it no longer, and had to twitch a slender bare foot, then a hand. She went through a pantomime of waking up.

"Hello, Eloise," Joanna said pleasantly. She went forward and sat down on the opposite chair.

"Have a seat," the girl said with languid malice. She yawned and tapped her long fingers across her mouth.

"Thanks," said Joanna. "Well, I'm surprised to see you back with your beastly husband, once you'd gotten free of him, and with money to spend, too."

"So what else did Baby Bear tell Mama and Papa Bear when he toddled home?"

"If you mean Jamie, he's never said anything except that you were a battered wife. It's what other people want to tell. They all seem to have loads of good stuff all at once."

The girl was stiffening. Her hand went up to the glasses and away again, to fiddle with the burst of curls on top of her head. "I don't know why you think I'd be interested. I don't know why you made a special trip to trespass on my property."

"Why did *you* make up such a story about Jamie? For the money? But you didn't get it, did you? That's what I hear. Ivor didn't believe you, and besides, he needs every cent toward rebuilding the cottage for him and this woman he's going to marry."

"That's all you know about it!"

Eloise came up out of the deck chair. She was blushing phenomenally all up her long brown legs. She snatched off her sunglasses like someone grabbing at a weapon. "She's nothing to him!"

"You and he go way back, don't you?" Joanna asked pleasantly. "When you were still just a kid you must have dreamed a lot about him and you together. Did you rush into marriage with Darrell because Ivor took up with this woman, or did he take up with her because you married Darrell?"

Eloise tried to interrupt, glaring through tears, but Joanna wouldn't let her.

"Whichever way it was, it must have been hard on you to see him coming and going all the time, and that handsome cottage going up down there for *her*. Then when he held back the money—that must have been awful, Eloise!"

"He didn't hold back on the money because he needs it!" Eloise cried. "He's rich! Five hundred is nothing to him! He held back because he was afraid I'd take off for somewhere

and he'd never see me again! It's *me* he loves—there isn't any
other woman, not really. She's just to fool Angie, and she's
the same kind of stupid jerk as Jamie and Darrell."

"You mean you and Ivor had it all figured out?" Joanna
sounded awe-stricken.

"Of course we did! I met Darrell through his cousin, and
it just seemed *meant.* I could be out here close to Ivor and
nobody could make a stink about it." Her mouth twisted
turning the narrow delicate face ugly. "I didn't know about
his damn cottage then. I wanted to go to Hawaii as soon as
we got rid of Angie and Darrell, then have a nice new house
in Fremont, all decks—" Unconsciously she preened as she
must have been preening for years whenever she thought of
being Mrs. Ivor Riddell.

"I'd have a Porsche," she said dreamily. Then her dream
cracked. "I never had the slightest idea that he'd want to go
lobstering himself, and us live all summer on that *rock*, and
all those birds I'd like to clean out with poison and machine
guns—" Her mouth went square and she cried, "Oh, what's
the *use?* What's the shitting *use?*"

"I suppose when you got tired of Darrell, and you were
mad with Ivor about the cottage, Jamie came in handy to slap
them both."

"*That* creep. I gave him that yarn on the way back from
Stonehaven and he swallowed it whole. Kept trying to stick
up for Darrell, but I knew his mouth was watering . . . I wasn't
running away—not from Ivor—but I was some sick of being
Darrell's little wifie on Brigport. Yuck! He was too tender
to fight, so he'd drink instead. I was about half crazy, what
with that and Ivor's goofy romantic ideas about us being
alone with the sea." She dragged it out in a hollow, artificial
voice. "I used to see Jamie with Bron, and he looked good.
Well, anybody would, compared to that mushy kid I married.
And I found out just how good he was. Solid rock! When he's
devoted, he's devoted. Ivor had a shit hemorrhage about Jamie,
but I was having fits about the cottage, so I thought, Good
enough for him. And if he got desperate enough about Jamie

and me making out, maybe I could force him to give up the cottage. I mean, if anything happened to it, he wouldn't likely be building it again, would he? Especially if he wanted me, too?"

Joanna could hardly believe what she was hearing. She said softly, "No, I wouldn't believe that. Not if he was really crazy about you... So you did it. That was pretty smart, and courageous too. You're one of those people who don't wait for things to happen, they *make* things happen."

"I made plenty happen," she said complacently. "I may not have made Sea Goddess, but I've done a hell of a lot more for myself."

"Yes, you have," Joanna agreed.

"Of course I couldn't tell if the fire took or not. I had these oily rags and a candle in a plastic bag in my tote bag, but I couldn't wait around to see how things went. When Ivor came up here feather-white and said all that was left was the chimney, I was so glad I almost puked. He thought it was shock." She smiled with something too languorous to be triumph. "*Then* he told me he was going to rebuild— for *us*, he kept saying. Then I really wanted to upchuck. After all my plans, and the way I had to work it, putting up with Darrell pawing me over, taking up with Baby Bear, worrying about a divorce, then getting down there to Pirate Island, being away from Jamie long enough to do what I had to do, and scared I'd be caught at it—well, anyway, it was like the end of the world when he said he'd rebuild. So I teased him for the reward, even though he said I'd have plenty more when we got together. With five hundred I could split, and he could whistle for me. And I wouldn't come back till he promised in writing everything I wanted."

She stretched, and smiled almost affectionately at Joanna.

"But he didn't keep his promise on the money, so how can you expect him to keep any other promises?" Joanna tried to sound maternally concerned.

"I *told* you!" she said crossly. "He held back the money so I couldn't go away from him. He'd do anything rather than lose me. He's had me since I was fifteen and he still won't trust his luck. And he's right not to. Because nobody can tell which way *this* cat's going to jump. You see?" she asked lazily.

"Yes." Joanna brought out the small notebook in which she'd carried her shopping list, and unclipped the pen from the cover. "Excuse me a minute, will you? I've been in Limerock, and there was a message I was supposed to carry home, and I forgot to write it down."

On June 5th, she printed in tidy block letters, *I set the fire that burned down Ivor Riddell's cottage on Pirate Island. Jamie Sorensen didn't know anything about it.*

"How is old Jamie anyway?" Eloise asked graciously. "He's a good kid, really. Just not my type." Something to be thankful for, Joanna thought.

"Would you mind giving me your autograph?" she asked.

"What?" Eloise half-laughed, then sat up belligerently. "What are you talking about?"

"Would you just sign this?" She turned the notebook toward the girl, keeping a tight hold. "I will not!" she cried shrilly. "And you just get the hell out of here before I—"

"Before you call the police? How would you like to have Angie Riddell find out her husband was having an affair with the ex-baby sitter, and the other woman was just a blind, like Darrell? Don't you think she'd call off that divorce in one big hurry? Or, if she ever did give in, she could make him pay plenty for you? Where's your Porsche and your new house in Fremont and your warm winters then? He wouldn't even be able to afford another cottage." She said it quietly without obvious brutality. The girl sat staring at her, licking her lips, greed and terror in combat.

"If I sign it, what are you going to do with it?"

"Show it to Jamie, and probably to Ivor so he'll mind his own business from now on. Then I'll lock it up in a safe place."

"He'll never believe it!"

"Whether he believes it or not, he won't want Angie to know about you, will he?"

Pallor under her tan gave her a jaundiced look. The whites of her eyes were suffused with pink. She said just above a whisper, "You're absolutely gross. You're rotten."

Silently Joanna handed her the pen. She put the open notebook on the table between them, keeping her hand down flat and hard on the other pages. Eloise wrote her name with enough pressure to dig into the paper, ended with a defiant flourish.

"Thank you," Joanna said politely. She wasted no time putting the notebook away, and stood up. "You've got a couple of choices, Eloise. You can either put up with Darrell for as long as he'll put up with you, or you can convince Ivor you did it out of love, and you're sorry, and you'd be happy to live anywhere with him in a cottage. One thing, nobody ever tries to live on Pirate in the winter, so you might get a couple of weeks in Florida after all."

She turned away toward the road. There was a rush of motion behind her and the door slammed and locked. She felt neither elation nor hatred; she was almost light-headed from the combat, and she pitied the girl locked in the house behind her. It wasn't in her nature to gladly trap or corner anything.

But dear God, she thought, the destruction! Beginning with Eloise herself, right down to those two children who were so happy to be with their father, and who now faced the death of their innocence where he was concerned.

The wind poured through the trees, cold and reviving. How long since it had all smelled this good? She could hardly wait to get home.

She had just started along the main road as an old jeep trundled by. It backed up and stopped. Young Lad MacKenzie called, "Want a lift?"

"I sure do." She climbed in beside him. "You can take me to the airstrip to pick up my loot. How's the seining going?"

"Stavin'! We stopped off twenty thousand bushels the other night. Tell Jamie, will you? He'd like to know we're doing good, he started us off. But we never see him anymore." He chopped off the last word and glared through the windshield. "I suppose he's real drove up with seining himself. I mean he—well—"

She rescued him. "He's been pretty depressed, but he'll work out of it. Have you seen Eloise since she came back?"

"Eloise?" His voice almost went into a squeak. "She's *here?* Back with *Darrell?*"

"She certainly is."

"Hey, that poor slob would put up with anything, wouldn't he? I don't think anybody's seen her, he must have snuck her home in the middle of the night sometime. She's probably scared to show her nose outside the door, for fear Jamie'll show up and bust it. *I* would, by God." He drove recklessly toward a ditch to give room to an elderly couple with a large dog, and called greetings to them. "Summer people," he explained to Joanna.

They made the turn out of the woods onto the rough slope to the store and the wharves, and he swung the jeep around at the end of a line of four vehicles. "How are you getting home?"

"I'll call the store down there and see who's around."

"I'd take you, but it'd be an awful wet trip in that boat of mine, the way the wind is."

"Thanks anyway, Laddie, for the ride and the conversation."

31

There were a few women around the store, and she received two invitations for a meal and a place to wait if nobody could come and get her right away. But when Mark answered he said, "Your man must have the second sight. He decided to stay in today."

"Is he all right?"

"Don't come through the phone at me, darlin mine. He's fine. Just letting 'em set over a day, that's all ... Looks from here as if he's putting a new corner post on the fishhouse and Jamie's helping him. I'll give him a holler."

She went out on the end of the Fowler dock to wait. The harbor was almost deserted except for the skiffs on the moorings, seine dories, and a big carrier lying off Marriott's Island. Randy Fowler was out on his lobster car dipping lobsters to pack in crates. She wondered if Bron's windjammer would ever lie over here, and if Bron would think of those February sunsets over Powderhorn Hill, and the way the stars looked from the cemetery wall. Or, in summer, would it all have become a dream?

Joanna S. was coming up the Gut.

"Glad to see you back," Nils said with his customary restraint.

"I got everything done, and I couldn't wait until tomorrow." She almost couldn't wait until they were out of the harbor, but she accomplished it. "I got you some good reading,

and some extra special good reading you don't find in books."
She took the notebook from her bag, and when they cleared
the Gut she handed it to him.

"How the hell did you get this?" He was no longer restrained.

"I went to see her and I twitted her about Ivor's woman,
that Bron told me about. And she came out with the whole
thing, about her and Ivor and why she hated the cottage. I'll
give you the details when I don't have to talk over the engine."

He swung the wheel hard over, and the boat began a sharp
swing around Tenpound. "He's down there. We're going to
show it to him."

She was taken aback. "I hadn't even got that far! I just
thought we'd have it if Ivor keeps acting up, and then we
could use it on him."

"Did you intend to tell Jamie about her and Riddell?" he
asked severely.

"I thought it would kill her off forever as far as he was
concerned. It would be better for him to hate her than go on
as he is."

"How do you know what he's already thinking about her?
He won't love us any more for telling him the whole story.
If she ever makes it with Riddell, let Jamie think she worked
it the same way she worked it with him. Let him go on believing she's weak and foolish and greedy, but Jo, for God's
sake, can't you *see* what knowing about this scheme of theirs
would do to him?"

She couldn't think of any answer. She sat down on the
washboard, finally out of energy, and the familiar old depression was rushing in to fill the vacuum. She'd been too high
for the last twenty-four hours, and right now it didn't seem
worth it. She stared down at the platform.

Nils reached out and put his hand on the side of her face,
gently forcing her to look up. "You did fine, *älskling*. We
can wind Riddell up like an eight-day clock."

The endearment put foolish tears in her eyes. She was

humiliated and a little angry with Nils for it, but there he was, safe and solid at the wheel, and he was hers. She got up and stood beside him.

Victrix was on her mooring, and Ivor was hauling from his small fiberglass boat. He waved and smiled when he saw them, and came to meet them. Nils cut down the engine so they made slow headway among the red-and-green buoys.

"Don't let him take that notebook into his own hands," Joanna warned him. "He could destroy it, and I worked hard to get it."

"Don't worry."

"Hi there!" Ivor came up alongside, not at all self-conscious. "Well, they haven't cleaned me out yet, you see! They must be feeling their years, or else they think I've got a couple of sharpshooters stashed away on shore." He laughed merrily. "I'm getting ready to rebuild. Your boy's cost me plenty, but I don't hold that against him. After all, I can afford to buy and sell him a dozen times."

"You've already tried that once," Nils said amiably, "but I understand you changed your mind about paying out the cash."

Ivor's jollity went. "What's that supposed to mean?" he asked aggressively.

Nils read him the statement, and then showed it to him, with Eloise's signature. His ruddy color went, leaving him with the strange pallor he'd had on the day he came to Bennett's about his burned cottage. His mouth worked silently before the words jolted out.

"It's a fake! You'd do anything to clear that crazy kid of yours!"

"Do you want to go to court about it?" Nils inquired. "It'll liven up the *Patriot*. While you're talking about fakes, how about the fake other woman and the fake husband?"

"And can't you see Eloise on the stand?" Joanna asked with venomous relish. "Weeping her heart out about the married man who seduced her when she was a fifteen-year-old baby sitter."

Ivor sat down on the engine box as if he couldn't stand up any longer. "What do you want?" he asked in a dead voice.

'An end to harassing Jamie, that's all," Nils said. "And you'll start by telling everybody that you were wrong about the fire. You don't have to name the girl as long as you clear our son. You could even say you're sure now it was an accident. Spontaneous combustion." Nils smiled. "That happens all the time. And we have the statement in case either you or your girl kick up again." Joanna would never have believed him capable of his finishing sentence. "We wish you a long and merry life with her."

"*Jesus God.*" Ivor was too winded to shout it. "That damned little slut, I wouldn't take her now if she was the last girl on earth."

"Well, she is getting a bit old for you," Joanna said. When they left he was still slumped on the engine box.

She had never in her life, except once when she was young, been so glad to turn her back on a man and hope it was the last of him as far as she was concerned. His wife wouldn't be so lucky, and the children were his victims as much as the flirtatious fifteen-year-old sitter had been. In time she might be able to hear his name without these qualms of loathing, but right now she doubted it.

Home lay ahead. It would have been lovely even in a brawling no'th-easter, and she saw it with an almost religious rejoicing. "You know what I'm remembering all at once?" she asked Nils. "That poor cheated little boy who was going to have such a great summer down here with his dory. And the little girl too. Ivor promised them everything, knowing he was lying with every breath. And look what he's done to another child, the one that Eloise used to be."

"Don't think about it any more," said Nils. He watched not only the way ahead, but effortlessly saw what lay on every side, buoys, birds, floating logs, distant boats, smoke on the horizon.

"That's what you always say, but I can't help it." She put her arm through his. "I'll have to write and tell Bron everything. I wish there was some way to tip off that woman he's been stringing along."

Nils sighed. "There's no way to save her any grief, Joanna. She took up with a married man, she shouldn't be surprised at anything she gets. Now will you think about something else?"

"Yes," she said. "Summer and strawberries. No, I don't want to think beyond this minute, going home with you and the way the island looks up there in this light. It's like the Lovely Dark Island that Rosa sings about. And is Rosa getting over her fondness for charm bracelets? Maybe." He gave her a sidewise look and she said, "I will be quiet for the rest of the way."

She wondered how long it would be before she was convinced that Bron had told the truth about herself and Jamie, and was not merely wearing a good, gallant face. *In every kiss sealed fast/ To feel the first kiss and forebode the last.* It didn't have to mean Jamie; there could have been someone else before him. Whoever it was that had made her so wisely aware, she was doing all right. So would Jamie do, when the memories could no longer shake him like a rag doll in a dog's teeth. He and Bron were children still, resilient in spite of their woes; they had *time*.

It's the punches you take at fifty that kill, Owen said.

She slid her hand down Nils's arm and into his pocket, and their fingers moved into the familiar lock. With the old arrogant determination to meet everything head on and conquer it, *demolish* it, she thought, There'll be no last kiss for us until we're a hundred and fifty or so.

They were still holding hands when they rounded Eastern Harbor Point and crossed the glittering tide-rip into the harbor, and saw their fair-haired son and daughter on the wharf waiting for them.